SHIELD AND GUARDED SHADOW

ENERGY OF MAGIC
BOOK SEVEN

J.E. NEAL

Copyright © 2023 by J.E. Neal

All rights reserved.

No part of this book may be reproduced in any form or by any electronic or mechanical means, including information storage and retrieval systems, without written permission from the author, except for the use of brief quotations in a book review.

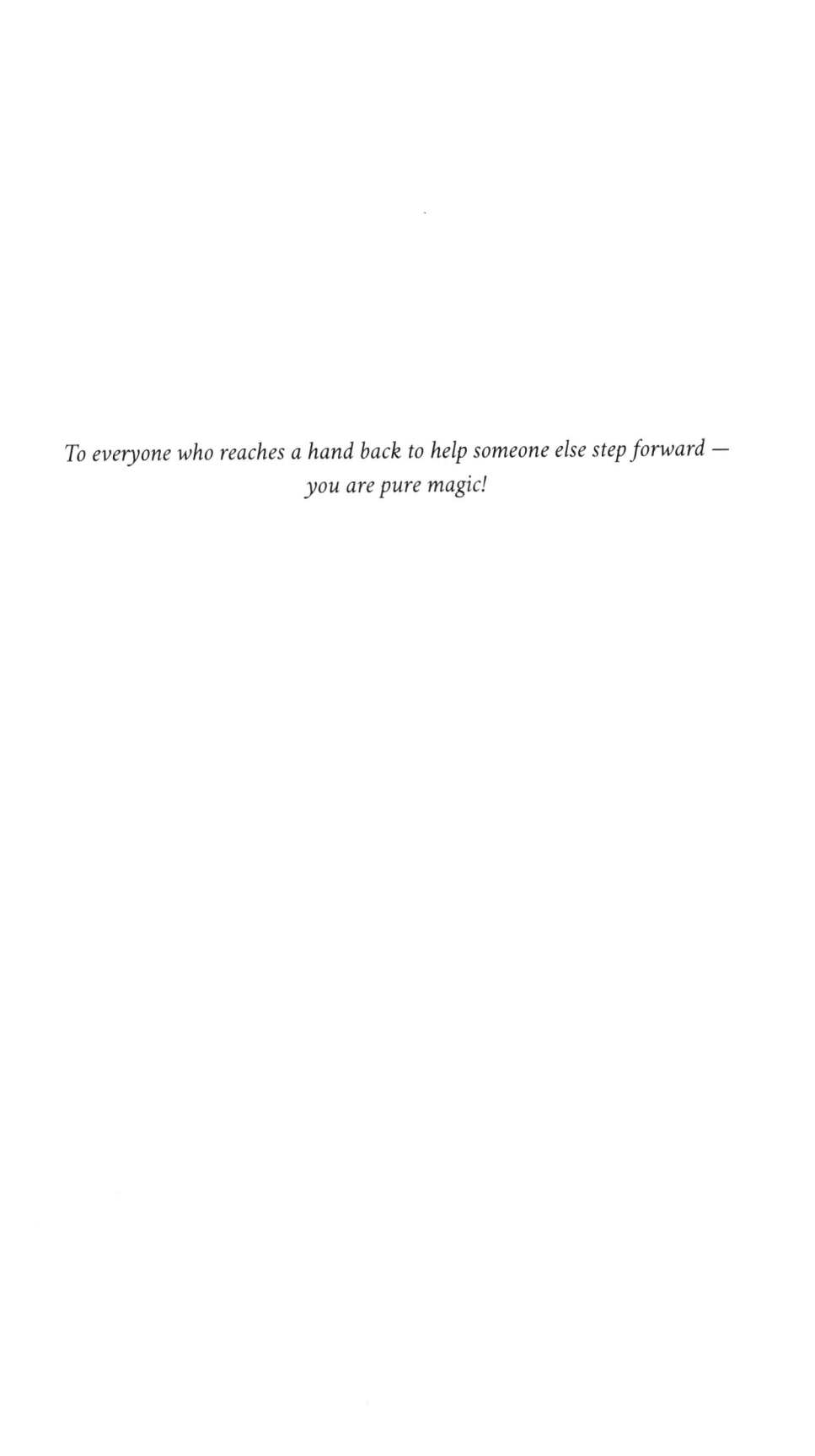

*To everyone who reaches a hand back to help someone else step forward —
you are pure magic!*

CONTENTS

1. Tipsy — 1
2. The Proof Is In the Dip — 5
3. Not Daddy's Little Girl — 17
4. Impetuous Desires — 23
5. Intrusions — 31
6. Confessions and Regrets — 39
7. Moving On — 47
8. Fourteen Days — 55
9. With Her, For Her — 61
10. Highway Bribery — 71
11. Welcome to Haydenshire Farm — 81
12. His Baby — 91
13. Where You Are Going — 97
14. Un-'Will'ing Confessions — 101
15. Claimed — 109
16. Terrors of the Night — 117
17. Sun Rise, Son Set — 119
18. Oh, What a Beautiful Morning — 123
19. The Ace of Hearts — 127
20. An Angel in Action — 135
21. Lost and Abandoned — 143
22. Christmas Eve — 149
23. Collisions — 155
24. Not Quite Christmas Dinner — 161
25. Echoes of Home — 177
26. Perfection — 189
27. Words — 199
28. Storms — 203
29. Apologies — 211
30. Not So Merry Christmas — 215
31. Presents — 223
32. Mile High — 239
33. What Needs To Be Said — 249
34. Don't Count Your Cards — 257
35. The Many Moods of a Woman in Love — 265

36. Let's Have a Ball	273
37. Requisition	287
38. Vitrio	295
39. War	301
40. The Man	307
41. A Demon's Challenge	315
42. Contentment	329
43. The Taming	337
44. The List	345
About the Author	353
Also by J.E. Neal	355

CHAPTER 1
TIPSY
DAN VINDICO

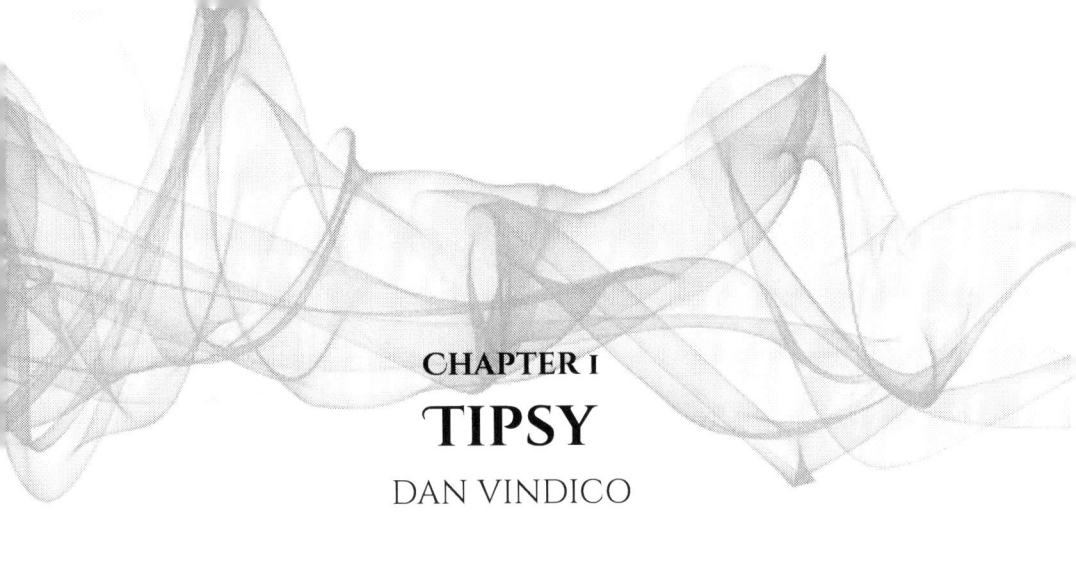

Fionna whimpered as Dan cradled her to his chest. Sunlight poured into the room. "You know, when my mom kept telling me to get curtains, I don't think she meant so that my girlfriend, who has a little bit of a headache from having a bit too much wine the night before, wouldn't be in pain. But I still really wish I'd listened." He attempted to shield Fionna from the sunlight with his body. She buried her face against his chest. "I'm sorry, baby. Do you want me to stay here with you or go fix you some hangover food?"

She smiled against him as he rubbed her back and brushed kisses in her hair.

"I'm all right, just a little dizzy."

"Let me up for just a second. I put some aspirin and water on your bedside table last night. I'll get them for you."

"Okay, I so do not deserve you." She rolled off him and helped herself to the meds and water before tucking herself back into his embrace. "I'm really not hungover."

Dan laughed outright. "Is this the same way you really weren't tipsy last night?"

"No, I was tipsy last night," she admitted. "I was sort of hoping that if you thought I wasn't really tipsy you'd bring me back here and take advantage of me."

Dan kissed her forehead. He was surprised she did seem to be recovering quickly.

"If I'm going to take advantage of you, I'd prefer for you to remember it the next morning."

She gave him a deliciously naughty grin as she giggled. "I always remember it, trust me." She waggled her eyebrows. "Let's just stay in bed naked all day."

Dan growled as he rolled her until she was under him. "And do what, baby doll?" Just discussing sex with her drove him wild. That was more fulfilling than anything he'd done with any other woman in the last decade.

"Dirty, dirty things."

"Oh, honey, if you want to be a bad girl for me, I'll show you just how dirty we can play." His mind was full of her, and his voice was low and thrumming. Her breath caught deliciously. "But, I think we better play host and hostess for Fitz for a little while and then take him to the airport. And I'm pretty sure your dad doesn't want to think about the things I'm going to do to you when I get you back home tonight."

Fionna wrinkled her nose with a dejected pout. "Sort of forgot I'm introducing you to my parents tonight and that Fitz is downstairs. Maybe I'm more hungover than I thought."

"Don't worry, I'll get you feeling better, and then we can hang with Fitzroy until he flies out. I will be a perfect gentleman at your parents' house tonight, but then,"—he slid his hand from her cheek, down her side, until he landed on her backside and squeezed—"when we get back from your parents' house, trust me, I won't be a perfect gentleman."

She trembled and her eyes flashed excitedly. A low moan sizzled over her entire body. She tensed beside him.

"I don't want to wait. I want it now. I want to feel you inside of me. I want you to make me take it hard and rough."

Dan tried to remember why he shouldn't take her up on her tantalizing offer. She reached her hand down and stroked him through his boxers. His eyes rolled back in his head as she tended to his morning wood.

An extremely frustrating reminder of why they couldn't continue came in the way of Fitzroy calling up the stairs. "Hey, Chloe and Garrett are here with a ton of food. This'll get her up."

Dan clenched his jaw shut so tightly it throbbed and reminded himself that if she ate a big breakfast she would feel normal again.

"I'll make it worth your wait, baby doll," he promised as ardent frustration set in her eyes.

"Fine." She crawled out of bed and took a moment to steady herself. She moved gingerly to her bags and pulled out some sweats to wear. "Would you mind if we stayed at my house just until Christmas? Then I'll move."

Dan stood and wrapped his arms around her.

"We'll do whatever you want, whenever you want to do it."

"Thank you." They paused there, in what would become their bedroom, and took that moment for themselves. He held her to him and swayed her softly, until she began brushing kisses along his collarbone. "I love you," she whispered

"Me too."

She pulled on sweatpants with Arlington written down the right leg and Angel written in an arc over her backside. Dan swallowed hard as he found himself unable to stop thinking about what she'd said she wanted and how much he enjoyed the hellcat side of his Angel.

"I can still redo your house, right?"

Dan shook himself from his erotic fantasies. "Of course, whatever you want."

"But this is your house. You must like it like this. I don't want to come in and change it." She sank back down on the bed dejectedly.

"Fi, baby, I don't like it this way. I've never done anything to it. I never wanted to have anything more than a place to sleep when I was too tired to work anymore until I met you. I want to be anywhere you are. To me, *you* are home. The only reason I want you to move in over here is because I'm being selfish. I want you close to me when I'm at work and you're at home. I think this house is safer than yours."

He sighed and continued, "Actually, I *know* this house is safer than yours. When I think about members of the Interfeci being at your house the other night, it makes me physically ill. But I want you to turn this into anything that will make you happy and content. I want you to make it a home for us because right now it's just a house."

She blinked back tears as she nodded her understanding. She gave him his smile through the emotion flowing from her eyes.

"Okay." She tucked her head on his shoulder as he cradled her close. Suddenly a loud banging sounded on the bedroom door.

"Would you put your clothes on? I'm hungry!" Chloe demanded.

"I'm coming," Fionna called.

"Not fair," Chloe sassed as she and Fionna both cracked up.

"I'm gonna have to get used to her, but for you, anything." Dan tousled Fionna's hair as she continued to laugh.

They made their way down the stairs. She studied each room they passed.

"After we eat, would you two help me do something?" Dan asked Garrett and Fitzroy.

They both nodded readily.

"All of this,"—he gestured to the desk and dozens of boxes of copied evidence files—"needs to go upstairs in whichever room Fi wants it in."

Fionna's entire being lit as she wrapped her arms around his waist, and he hugged her tightly.

"You do know that you're technically not supposed to have any of this here, right?" Garrett reminded him.

Fionna laughed. "Let's just take it one step at a time."

CHAPTER 2
THE PROOF IS IN THE DIP

"Maylea." Fionna's stepmother pulled her in for an all-encompassing embrace.

Dan reminded himself that her parents only referred to her as Maylea, her childhood nickname given to her by her mother.

"Hi, Mama. I missed you."

"Me too, but you're working in the bakery this week, no?"

"Of course I am. Emily and Sasha are coming too." Fionna glanced at Dan and beamed. "Mama, this is my boyfriend, Dan."

Dan extended his hand, but Mrs. Styler batted it away. "Dan," she hugged him as well, startling him momentarily. "You were right, Maylea, he is a dreamboat." They laughed as Dan shook his head.

Mrs. Styler welcomed them into the house and insisted that Dan call her Gretta.

Dan glanced around. It was a small ranch in an older part of town. There wasn't much to it. The entire home would fit on half of one floor of the mansion where Dan had been raised.

The Stylers' bakery was only a few miles away, and though it was successful, it clearly hadn't made her parents a fortune. Their home was warm and somewhat cluttered with furniture, books, and knickknacks. It was so much more comfortable than the Vindicos' manor home, but the interrogating glare Fionna's father was giving Dan dampened the cozy appeal.

"Maylea, finally. I'd forgotten what you looked like," her father pouted as Dan and Fionna made their way into the cramped house.

Dan studied her father. He'd lived in Texas most of his life but had been born in Reynosa. He'd met Fionna's mother when he was in the Gifted Navy for a few brief years. His accent was unlike any other Dan had ever heard, an eclectic mix of American English, with a heavy Spanish influence and notes of Hawaiian.

"I saw you at the beginning of the week." Fionna sighed as her father hugged her. Dan heard her whisper, "Be nice." He forced a smile and shook Mr. Styler's hand. "This is my boyfriend, Dan."

"It's an honor to meet you, sir." Dan tried not to let his nerves resonate in his voice. Fionna's father narrowed his eyes until she shot him a warning glare. Her mother shook her head and sighed.

"We're thrilled to meet you as well. We're so pleased you're here for dinner, and *Mele Kalikimaka*."

Dan racked his brain. He knew what that meant, but he seemed unable to access any of the information formerly held in his mind.

"Merry Christmas," Fionna whispered.

"Oh, right, uh, to you as well." Dan ordered himself to get it together.

"Here, why don't we go enjoy the tree? Your padre made you some onion dip and your taro chips," Gretta offered kindly. Fionna looked thrilled with the appetizers. "Dan, what can I get you to drink?"

"Whatever Fi's having is fine."

Gretta chuckled. "Well, I doubt Maylea is having one, but it might come in handy, so how about a beer?"

"Thank you." Dan's shield tensed as if it sensed an incoming assailant. They followed her parents into the living room and helped themselves to the appetizers.

"You're still running Iodex here in the States, yes?" Mr. Styler demanded, with the first words he'd actually spoken directly to Dan.

He happened to have asked the question just as Dan had bitten into a large taro chip covered in dip. He choked down the bite as he nodded.

"Yes, sir." Dan wiped his mouth with his napkin quickly. "I've been Chief of Iodex and head of the Elite Squadron for about nine years now."

He tried to soften his tone and reminded himself that this wasn't a job interview. *It's so much more important* pulsed through his mind, doing nothing to calm his nerves. "These are delicious. I certainly see where Fionna learned to cook so well." He reached and took Fionna's hand. Her father's eyes narrowed again, and Dan started to pull away. Fionna strengthened her grasp and raised her left eyebrow to her father in challenge.

Gretta patted her husband's leg consolingly and offered Dan a sympathetic expression. "Maylea, you look beautiful this evening. Love suits you well."

Fionna beamed at Dan, who squeezed her hand and fought the urge to kiss her overly pink cheek.

"Of course she looks beautiful," her father argued. "She's a beautiful girl. You tell her this, I hope." Fionna's father turned his glare back to Dan.

"Of course," Dan huffed. He was already weary of his opposition. "She's stunning, inside and out."

Fionna's mother smiled at him again as she nodded her agreement. Fionna's father was still staring at Dan. He racked his brain for something else to say. The beer and appetizers began to swirl in his stomach.

He said the first thing that popped into his head. "I actually think she's probably most adorable when she first wakes"—he halted abruptly as Fionna's eyes goggled, and she shook her head violently—"...uh, smiles."

Fionna's head fell into her hand in defeat. Deafening silence flooded the room as Fionna's father's glare turned livid.

"Maylea, tell us all about Sydney," Gretta pled as she kept a firm grip on her husband's arm. Fionna was still staring at Dan like he might've lost his mind, which he was beginning to think he most certainly had.

"Oh." Fionna appeared to try to recall their vacation just a few weeks before. "It was amazing, actually. I gave Dan a surfing lesson, and we went to the Premier's castle, which was kind of crazy." She laughed, and Gretta immediately joined in.

"Had you ever surfed before, Dan?" Gretta asked as Mr. Styler kept his scowl leveled on Dan.

"No, ma'am, but Fi's amazing. It was really something to see."

"Yes, well, my little girl has been surfing all her life. I think she's happier with the fish than with the boys."

Dan tried to hide his chuckle as Gretta and Fionna turned on Mr. Styler.

"Daddy, stop it!"

"Ella es veintinueve no cinco. Se amable!" Gretta ordered fiercely. Dan didn't let on that he spoke a fair amount of Spanish and was well aware that Fionna's father had just been informed that his little girl was twenty-nine, not five, and then was commanded to be nice.

"How's Nana?" Fionna asked. Dan squeezed her hand again after seeing the worry color her eyes.

Mrs. Styler gazed at Dan and Fionna lovingly. "She has good days and bad days."

Dan tensed as he felt Fionna draw from him. In his relative ineptitude with relationships with Gifted women, he hadn't quite mastered the ability to supply Fionna with his energy without his face displaying the heavenly feeling that came when their energies combined. It seemed a distinctly intimate thing to do in front of her father. Dan felt like her dad had just walked in on him stripping her down and taking her to bed.

He tried to draw measured breaths as he supplied Fionna with the peace and strength that she needed, without letting his face go slack-jawed as his eyes rolled back in his head.

"She's looking forward to our visit. She wishes you could come."

"I know. I wish I could go too. I have to be at the exhibition. It's the most important day of the season, and that's even more important now." She glanced nervously at Dan.

Realization added to Dan's stress. He shook his head and started to vow that just because he was an owner didn't not mean she had to perform, but her father interrupted his thoughts.

"That's all the Angels do, Maylea. They party. You should settle down. Come work at the bakery. Find someone who wants to marry you. Have children."

Dan noted the test. He fought not to roll his eyes. Did he look like a coward? He wasn't running away from a commitment, not anymore.

"Daddy, you know I love challenging for the Angels. I plan on playing even after I get married, if I ever get married," Fionna informed her father.

Dan felt truly sorry for her. He knew the pressure of having your parents think that their plan for your life was so much better than your own.

"Why don't we eat? I'll go get everything ready." Gretta stood and herded everyone toward the kitchen. Fionna's father caught her hand and halted her progress.

"I'll be right there," she assured Gretta. Everything about her broadcasted a distress signal. Her eyes begged Dan to rescue her, but he had no idea how to save her from her father. He offered her a consoling look and moved slowly in hopes of catching some of the conversation and not leaving her alone.

"What?" she sniped.

"This boy is no good for you. He takes what he wants, and then he leaves."

"Daddy, stop it. That isn't true."

Dan's heart sank rapidly toward his feet.

"I know what boys think, especially boys like Vindico. I used to be a boy like that. You're not smart enough to see. You never think, Maylea."

Fury flashed in Dan's eyes. How dare he? Her father *was* an asshole, just like he'd suspected. Who the hell would take a little girl away from her home and her grandmother after her mother had just drowned? And who the fuck did he think he was telling his daughter that she wasn't intelligent? Dan's fists clenched in abject fury.

"You settled down twice," Fionna defied.

"You settled me down, Maylea. You're my little girl. I don't want you to get hurt."

"Daddy," Fionna sighed, "he won't hurt me. I trust him, and he loves me."

"He says he loves you until he gets what he wants. You believe his lies because you don't think."

Dan seethed, but then he began to understand how Fionna had gotten her nickname *wildflower*. In a fit of rebellion, she narrowed her eyes in on her father and sneered, "If that were true, he would've already left, trust me."

Every muscle in Dan's body clenched. By this point, he'd made his way into the kitchen. Fionna's mother cringed. Dan assumed she'd also heard Fionna's declaration. She pulled something that smelled delicious from the oven and shook her head.

"Give him a little time. She's his precious little girl. He's had to protect her from so many things, even if the way he went about it was entirely wrong. He thought he was doing right. She hasn't had an easy life. He can't stand to think that something else might hurt her."

"I know, and I won't."

"I know," Gretta agreed. "I saw how you looked at her, and your energies, they seem to mesh. Not everyone's does that. You both seem better together than apart. That's how I know. Samuel will come around."

Fionna was blinking back tears as she stomped into the kitchen.

"You know..." Her mother wiped away Fionna's tears with a worn dishrag and hugged her. Dan noted that Fionna relaxed instantly in Gretta's embrace. "Love doesn't often come without cost, and sometimes the pain is for the ones who might be feeling just a little bit replaced." She rubbed Fionna's back. Fionna was still wiping away silent, angry tears. "But there's room in your heart for everyone, Maylea. You just have to remind everyone in there that there's always room for more."

"I know."

Her mother released her, and Dan stood ready to wrap her up in his arms as she fell against his chest. He kissed the top of her head soothingly. "I'm sorry, baby. This is my fault." Her father's obvious prejudice against women and their intellect was not his fault, but the lecture certainly had been.

"No, it's not."

"You know, I think we'll have the pani popo with dinner. I'll just heat it up. Why don't you take Dan to see your old room? I'll call you when it's ready."

They both understood that they were to find somewhere else to be, so that Gretta could give Fionna's father a few thoughts on what he was doing to his daughter.

Fionna didn't look terribly excited about showing Dan the room that had raised her, but she took his hand and led him out of the kitchen and down a narrow hallway.

"Oh wait, wait, wait." Dan halted her progress down the cheery yellow hallway with old parquet floors. "Very nice." He chuckled as he took in a large, framed picture of Fionna, no more than three years old, with her hair fixed in tiny pigtails, lying on her stomach, buck naked on a surf board. She was propped up on her elbows, preening for the camera on the beach. "Aww, you had a cute tush even then."

She blushed violently and began giggling. "My room is down here." She tugged on his hands.

"Uh-huh, in a minute." Dan began going over all of the framed photographs of Fionna that hung in the hallway.

"You do *not* want to see all of these."

"Oh, I definitely do." Dan laughed as he pointed out one of a preteen Fionna Styler in a baby doll dress she didn't quite fill the top on yet. Half of her head was her side-swiped bangs. Her broad grin showed off the braces on her teeth.

There was a collage photo frame of Fionna as a toddler. In all of the numerous poses, she was hoisting her skirt over her head.

Dan laughed hysterically. "Can I get a picture the next time you do this for me?"

Fionna glared, but she couldn't quite contain her laughter. "It was obviously a phase."

"Mmm, I really think you should consider going through that phase again, although I would prefer you skip the Little Mermaid panties."

She smacked his chest as he laughed. Farther down the hall were shots of Fionna in high school.

He studied a dozen photos of her in intricate hula outfits complete with Ti leaves and tropical flowers.

"Who's the punk?" Dan pointed to a picture of a relatively young Fionna being escorted to what appeared to be a high school dance. She was wearing a blush-colored gown that looked like it had consumed her. Her hair was piled high on her head. The top of the dress was fitted, and Dan noted that she hadn't developed near the cleavage she currently sported.

"I'm not telling you." Her face was glowing crimson. The heat of her embarrassment was palpable in her rhythms.

"Come on," Dan urged, "and please tell me you were older than this when you…" He felt sick momentarily.

Fionna shook her head. "I don't know who's worse, you or Daddy. We didn't move up here until I started at the academy. Daddy wanted me to go to Venton, so that was taken in Texas. And…that's my cousin."

Dan cracked up as they moved closer to the room at the end of the hall. There were several extremely impressive shots of Fionna surfing that had her beaming as Dan studied them. There was one of her crouched low on a custom board with a massive wave curved over her head. The fierce determination in her eyes spoke volumes. "That was from a youth surfing competition in Oahu." But she stopped talking abruptly. A slight blush colored her features.

"That you won." He knew the end of the story and that she felt she was bragging.

She gave a hesitant nod.

"Because you're an incredible surfer and an incredible woman."

Beside the ones of her with her beloved board was a large canvas of Fionna as a young girl, hugging a woman who was most certainly her mother.

Tears pricked her eyes again, and Dan hugged her tightly to him. You couldn't lose someone who meant the world to you and be expected to just get over it.

"You look just like her, baby. You're both beautiful."

"Thank you." Fionna shuddered and let Dan wipe away her tears as he kissed her forehead. The walls outside her bedroom door held pictures of her from Venton. There were several of her graduation photos along with her challenging for the Venton Vixens. There were pictures of her and Chloe and Garrett from all six years. They were laughing and hugging in all of them. Dan hated himself for wishing Garrett out of her life. She'd already lost enough.

"Would you just come on so I can complete my mortification?"

Dan grinned. "You were adorable, and you still are."

She rolled her eyes as she opened the door to her childhood bedroom. It was like taking a step back in time. Her parents hadn't changed a single thing since she moved out. A large, purple Auxiliary Order banner hung over the bed. It was situated in the middle of the room with a white eyelet comforter. Numerous Arlington Angel posters hung on the walls, all taken before Fionna made the team. There was a full-length poster of a drummer. Dan couldn't recall his name or the band he'd been in, but there were lipstick smears all over the face of the poster.

"Do I have him to thank for your incredible kissing abilities?"

Fionna laughed. Her face was now glowing purple. "That's how I blotted my lipstick."

"Uh-huh," Dan goaded, "right." Small, framed photos of Fionna and her friends in Hawaii and at academy functions were on the desk and bookshelves.

"Is this Malani?" Dan picked up one of the many snapshots of Fionna on a stunning beach. She'd told him all about her best friend in Kauai. Whenever Fionna spoke of Malani, her energy trilled with love and happiness. In the photo, her head was thrown back in laughter, and her right arm was around a Hawaiian girl of about the same age.

Fionna grinned and nodded. "I miss her so much. I used to get in trouble for calling her all the time after we moved. It made Daddy so mad."

Dan tried not to let that information further infuriate him since he still had to make it through a meal with Samuel Styler.

There was a photo in a white frame of Fionna in a skimpy bikini, being carried on the beach by a rather well-built Hawaiian guy. He looked quite pleased to have her caught up in his arms.

Dan cocked his jaw to the side as he huffed, "I take it that's not your cousin."

"Are you jealous, Chief Vindico?" She tried to flirt but the evening's emotions had exhausted her.

"Maybe."

"Well, don't be." Pain replaced her earlier self-consciousness. "You don't have anything to worry about. He was a summer fling, when I spent the summer between my freshman and sophomore years with my grandparents." Her graceful neck contracted as she swallowed down regret. "He never even called after I came back to DC. I don't know why it's even still up in here."

Dan had three sisters. He knew perfectly well why this picture had remained on her desk, despite the fact that it was a relationship that had lasted the length of one summer. It wasn't that she loved the guy or wanted him again. It was the memory of what he'd taken from her that she couldn't have back.

"Then he was an idiot." Dan elicited a small smile. He set the picture down, not wanting to linger on that too long. Fionna looked uncomfortable as she ran her hand along the footboard. There was an ancient rack-mount stereo system, the kind Dan hadn't seen in decades.

"Daddy never gets rid of anything. That was his old stereo. It's easy to cast. That's why I had it."

Dan cradled Fionna and swayed her. "Are you okay, sweetheart?" He wondered if the walk down memory lane coupled with her father's insistence that Dan was going to break her heart had been more than she could take on top of hearing that her grandmother wasn't doing well.

His eyes continued to scan the room. There was a picture of Fionna, Malani, and another girl Dan didn't know, at a luau in front of a beach fire. Their arms were up over their heads. The sway of the grass skirts they were wearing made them appear to move in the photo. Fionna was wearing a traditional hula top and had on a floral crown. The authenticity of her was stunning. Her father should never have taken her from her home. What was he thinking?

She shrugged against him. "I don't know." Dan brought his attention back to her in the present.

"Do you want to go home?" He prayed she wouldn't. He wanted to prove to her father that he adored her. He wanted to show Sam Styler how Fionna should have been taken care of her entire life. But he also wanted to be Fionna's escape. If she needed to go, he'd take her. He was her Shield.

"No, let's just go eat and hope Mama got through to him."

"I will prove myself to him, and I'll prove myself to you. Even if it takes me years, I'll do it."

She looked momentarily shocked by his vow. "You've already proven yourself to me. That's all that matters."

CHAPTER 3
NOT DADDY'S LITTLE GIRL

Things went relatively well until Mr. Styler asked Fionna if she'd gotten her gas leak fixed.

"Dan had a friend of his dad's do it. It works great now."

"I'll come by tomorrow and check it myself."

"Daddy, it's fine." Fionna viciously stabbed a piece of the most delicious pork Dan had ever tasted with her fork. Mr. Styler gave an audible humph.

"Where would you say you see yourself in ten years?" Samuel turned his disdain back to Dan. Fionna rolled her eyes and glared at her father.

Dan considered. He'd grown up next door to Amelia's parents. They'd known him since he was a toddler, and he'd certainly never gotten to the parental-meeting portion of a relationship with any of his hook-ups over the past ten years.

Dan assumed this was probably a standard fatherly question. He'd heard his own father pose it to both Kara and Meredith's husbands before they were married.

"I'm not sure, sir, in terms of my career, so I would say the only thing I know for certain is that I want to be with Fionna." Dan kept his eyes locked on Mr. Styler who couldn't quite hide his shock. Not to be beaten, he upped the ante.

"And what about children?"

"Daddy, stop it. I know what you're doing," Fionna demanded. She didn't have to worry. Dan knew her father was trying to scare him off, and he wasn't playing along.

"I certainly don't know what the future holds. Children aren't something I'm looking for anytime in the next several years, but maybe down the road. I have two godsons. They live in Paris. I don't get to see them often, but they're great. I'd like to have a family someday, as long as I'm doing that with Fi."

Fionna shot her father a smirk as she continued to eat her dinner.

"And do you have any intention of making any kind of permanent commitment to my little girl before you decide that you might want children?"

Before Dan could make a rebuttal, Fionna's eyes narrowed. "I'm moving in with Dan after Christmas."

Dan coughed as he took a sip of his water. He had no idea what the reaction to that might be.

"What?" Mr. Styler screeched. "May-le-a!" Mr. Styler drew her nickname out several syllables longer than it normally was.

"Samuel," Mrs. Styler soothed, "please eat. We'll discuss this later."

Silence loomed over the table like blackening storm clouds. Mr. Styler kept a steady glower headed Dan's way. Dan tried to think of something to say. It seemed Fionna both loved and hated her father in equal measure.

He drew out her rebellious side like nothing Dan had ever seen. Her indignation was visible in her features, and every time her father scowled at Dan, she huffed audibly. As the delicious food was consumed, Dan sat anxiously awaiting an opportunity to plead his case to Fionna's parents.

"Maylea, why don't you and Dan go in the living room, and your father and I'll bring in dessert and coffee?" Gretta suggested.

"I can help," Fionna offered her mother. She let her father know precisely where her loyalties lay.

"No, sweetheart, why don't you and Dan go have a seat? Enjoy each other's company."

"Yes, ma'am." Fionna shot one last dagger toward her father from her eyes.

"Dinner was delicious. Can I help you clear the table?" Dan may have been out of practice, but he was raised right.

"Thank you, but we'll get it. Maylea loves the Christmas tree. It's her favorite. Go sit with her. She would like that."

Fionna smiled and nodded her agreement. Dan took her hand as she led him back into the living room. He sank onto the worn, plaid sofa. He was shocked when Fionna curled up in her customary ball in his lap. Her father would most definitely not like her in that position, but Dan wrapped his arms around her and let her bury her face in his neck. Her father could get over it.

"Samuel, when will you learn that you cannot keep her from doing what is in her heart?" Gretta's frustration was audible since they were only one room away. "There is nothing wrong with her taking a chance on love. You are doing nothing but pushing her away again. She loves him. I can feel that. And he loves her as much as he is able right now. It will continue to grow." Gretta stated this information as if she'd known Dan his entire life.

"Yeah, I know. She's kind of incredible," Fionna whispered with a sigh.

"Why must she always think with her heart and never her head? This is why she keeps getting hurt. She never listens," her father fired back angrily.

"Because that is what makes her *Maylea*. That is why he loves her, and she will never be anything but who she was made to be. She is happier now than she has been since you insisted we move her up here. She has been miserable for years, and I'm sorry, but that was entirely your doing. I have a good feeling about this. Now, make some of Maylea's coffee, and try to get her to forgive you before he takes her home."

"Fat chance," Fionna huffed.

"Come on, honey. He's misguided, but he does love you. And let's be real, my reputation certainly precedes me."

Before Fionna could combat Dan's reasoning, her parents returned. Her mother grinned at Dan with Fionna cradled in his lap.

Her father, however, appeared to bite holes in his tongue. Fionna threw her father defiant glares and refused to move.

"Come on, Fi," Dan whispered in her ear. Without thinking, he patted and squeezed her backside as he helped her scoot off his lap to sit beside him.

Rage burned in Mr. Styler's eyes. Gretta all but slapped her hand over his mouth. It took several long moments for him to calm. Dan refused to apologize, and the standoff between them caused the rhythms in the air to tense. Dan's shield continued to try to cover Fionna without being summoned.

Finally, Gretta pried the tray of pecan and cinnamon donuts out of Mr. Styler's hands and offered them to Dan.

"Maylea, I just love you," her father huffed.

"If you love me, stop trying to change me. I'm not a little girl anymore."

A deep and distant pain etched her father's features.

"You are just as stubborn as your Tutu, lunatic woman."

"Samuel," Gretta spat.

"Stop it, Daddy, or we're leaving."

"You are always my little girl, Maylea. No matter how old you think you are," he ignored her protests completely.

Fionna rolled her eyes and took a pointed sip of the coffee Gretta offered her.

"If you're certain about this,"—he gestured to Dan as if he were an inanimate object—"do you plan on selling your home?"

"I don't know. I thought about renting it out. It's close to the arena. No one can know where I move. It's to keep me safe, so we won't be doing anything with my house immediately."

"You can always move back in here."

Dan understood that her father wanted her to have an out if she should move in with Dan and decide she didn't want to stay.

"You know you can *always* come back home," he repeated.

Fionna made no effort to hide her eye roll. "I am never coming back here."

Already at the end of his rope, Dan stepped in. "Mr. Styler, sir, I know that you're concerned about Fionna being in a relationship with me."

"Dan," Fionna interrupted, but Dan shook his head and took her right hand tenderly in his own.

"I promise you that I have not lived with another woman since I lived with my fiancée ten years ago before she was killed. I will take care of Fionna. I'm not going to walk away and break her heart or mine. I'm just asking for a chance. I adore her. She is everything to me. And I would never treat her with anything but the utmost respect and dignity. I really do love her." His heart stuttered from saying the word, and he hoped that telling her father would cement it in Fionna's heart, because he still didn't think he could actually say it to her.

Tears leaked down Fionna's beautiful face as she gazed at Dan.

"Well, Samuel, do you have anything to say?" Gretta urged.

"Yes, well," Mr. Styler huffed, "he better."

CHAPTER 4
IMPETUOUS DESIRES

Dan helped Fionna with her coat and thanked the Stylers again for dinner. Gretta hugged him goodbye, and Mr. Styler did offer his hand which Dan accepted gratefully.

After seating Fionna in the Expedition, Dan rushed to the driver's side, turned on the car, and forced warm air from the heater with a cast.

"So, other than my becoming a complete idiot and announcing to your father that I think you're adorable when you first wake up, all in all, not a horrible evening."

Fionna shook her head and rolled her eyes. "I'm sorry. He has hated everyone I've ever dated. It's not just you."

"Well,"—Dan winked at her—"your dad and I have something in common then, because I also find myself hating everyone you've ever dated, only I would add *before me*."

She giggled. "It was still a horrible evening."

He wasn't accustomed to her lack of optimism. It bothered him.

"I got to see you naked, so for me it was a fantastic evening." A warm smile finally broke through her dejected anger. She cracked up.

"You know, if you want to pose like that on the beach for me now, I could take the pictures, just so you could have a then and now comparison." Dan reveled in her hysterical laughter.

"Chief Vindico, that is the second time you've offered to take naked photographs of me. I'm starting to think you have a deep, dark fantasy about having pictures of me without clothes on."

Dan laughed. "Honey, that fantasy isn't deep or dark. It's pretty much an affliction of heterosexual males. You're gorgeous in clothes. You're drop dead stunning naked, and you know, since I haven't convinced you to forgo clothing altogether, pictures are my only outlet when you're dressed."

"Sorry, babe, but I love clothes way, way, way too much to stop wearing them. Plus, I love the way you take them off me." The flirtatious challenge tugged at his zipper line. Dan gave her the growl she was clearly after. His heart picked up pace.

"When I get you home, I might have to see what I can do about that. I'll see if I can't show off my skills."

A few minutes later, Dan pulled in to her driveway with his mind full of the things he wanted to do to her. Suddenly, Fionna leapt. She crawled over the center console, straddled her legs across Dan's lap, and hoisted her cleavage in his face.

The wild look in her eye had Dan reeling as he pulled her face to his and kissed her heatedly. He moved his hands down her back and then to her backside. He began guiding her hips in rhythmic circles over his burgeoning erection.

"You feel that, honey? You make me so damn hard. I ache for you."

Loud, hungry moans began to sear from her chest. Unable to think with the head above his belt line, Dan popped the snap on her jeans and had the zipper down in under a second. His eyes goggled as he took her in, illuminated by the streetlight at the end of her driveway.

"You are a naughty girl, aren't you, baby doll? All for me." He pulled her jeans down. There was nothing underneath them. He knew he'd said the very thing she so desperately wanted to hear, and she went wild. "Now what am I gonna do with you?" Dan growled as he traced his fingers tenderly over her mound.

Her eyes flashed as her energy spiked in hard jagged arcs. She was spun so tightly she was frantic in her need.

"Something my father would hate," she commanded as rebellion flooded her energy. He'd never seen her so wild and impetuous. Dan had spent the last decade doing things to women their fathers would most certainly hate, so he considered himself an expert on her request.

Fionna leaned in and devoured his mouth again. He nipped her bottom lip and listened to her gasp as her mouth fell open for him. She pulled his tongue inside and sucked hard until he jerked away.

"Oh, baby, I have something I'm gonna make you suck." He let his voice take on the commanding tone he knew she craved. "I'm gonna make you suck it, and then I'm gonna make you take it all, just the way I want you to. And if you don't, I'm gonna spank that sexy ass because it's all mine."

"Yes," she panted and trembled from the effort of fighting what he planned on being the first of many orgasms of the evening.

"Now, go inside the house, and I want you to put on something I can fuck you hard in. You know what I like. Then I want you to wait for me like a good girl." Another gasping moan lit through her as she writhed over him. Her head fell back in the erotic dance, and he grasped her breasts. She shuddered as his fingers sought her nipples. He squeezed them between his thumbs and index fingers and spun them until she trembled against him. "All mine."

She pulled the handle on the door and stepped out. She hoisted her jeans back up.

"Don't make me wait long. I *will* start without you."

A desperate groan echoed from him as he envisioned that. "I'd love to see that, so go right ahead, baby."

Her eyes lit, and she turned away from him and sauntered up her walkway. He stared unabashedly at her ass, bare under the tight jeans she was wearing, until he couldn't see her anymore.

Panting and forcing himself to calm lest he lose it all before he'd even begun, he reached and yanked the wires from the camera inside the car that he'd completely forgotten about until that moment.

He sent several pulses back through the camera, effectively erasing the digital copy of what went on in Senate owned vehicles. He reminded himself that he was the guy who ordered them to be checked if he was concerned about the activities of his officers, and that no one checked them except on his orders. He turned his attention back to Fionna and what she needed from him.

He had to force himself not to sprint up the walkway. He jerked open the front door, halted, and remembered to turn the locks before he raced up the stairs.

His heart thundered out his applause as he took in Fionna posed on her bed, lying on her stomach, and propped up on her elbows. Her knees were bent, with her feet crossed, showing off the highest black lace stiletto heels Dan had ever seen. She was wearing nothing else.

Her eyes were dark and ravenous. She shot him looks that said not only to *come hither* but to take whatever he wanted.

Removing everything he was wearing in a second flat, he moved to her.

"You are sexy as sin, honey." He moved his groin in front of her face. She licked her lips and kept her eyes locked on his. He'd never seen anything hotter. She didn't move. She wanted to be commanded.

Desperate need leaked from his head. "Clean that up," he ordered.

She moaned as she spun her tongue over his head and gave a hungry suck. She opened her mouth to let him see what she'd consumed.

A low wounded growl tore from his lungs. "My good girl loves the way I taste, don't you, baby? Now suck me. Show me how much you like it."

A breathy moan panted from her as she dragged her tongue up his length. She cupped his sac as he shuddered from the exquisite sensation. She spun her tongue over his head again. "That's it. Good girl—now take me deep." She drew him in. He wrapped her hair around his right fist and guided her.

He watched her intently as she sucked, and licked, and pulled the erotic energy from him in lust-driven, rebellious passion.

"Such a good girl, now more," he ordered as she pulled him deeper. He was unable to stop the guttural groans that echoed from him. It just felt too damn good.

He pulled away as she pouted. He stalked quickly to the other side of the bed. She watched his every move. His heart stormed against his rib cage as she waited for his next command.

"Spread your legs, and shake that sexy ass for me, right now. Show me how wet you are. I want you dripping for me."

"Oh yes," panted from her. She was on fire. She did as she was told. She held her legs wide, backed up on her knees, and arched her back low, shaking her ass for him. Dan's body seized from the provocative sight.

He leaned and licked up her slit. He sucked the nectar as it poured from her. He groaned against her, before gently dragging his teeth over her swollen lips. She shook from the sensations he was bringing her.

"You're so wet, baby. I could make you take it now. You've been thinking about me, haven't you? Such a good girl. You've been thinking about me filling up that greedy little hole all day, haven't you?"

"Give it to me. I need it." She threw her head to the side, staring him down and daring him to own her.

"I'll give it to you when I'm damn good and ready."

Her entire body shook in need as he slapped her ass. He leaned again and sucked the top of her thigh where it met her backside, right beside her lips. He left a mark of ownership on her left leg and then a matching one on her right. "You are mine."

Her moans were unending. He'd never heard her so loud or so desperate.

Unable to draw it out any longer, he traced his fingers down the center of her backside and then spread her apart with one hand and dipped his two fingers from the other hand deep inside her.

She pulsed as her muscles clenched tightly around his fingers.

"So nice and wet, baby. My God, you are perfect." Blood laced with need seared through his veins as he throbbed against her backside.

She spilled out in his hand, and he immediately summoned the erotic energy and sealed her off. He poured soothing energy into her, pleased that she'd let him perform the cast this time.

"You ready for it? It's so empty it aches, doesn't it, baby doll? Ready for me to make it better?"

She panted and pitched as please echoed from her in a low, throaty plea.

He leaned and thrust hard. He drove himself between her lips as her body closed around him, drowning him in the depths of her perfection. He grasped her hips and kept her up on her knees. He watched himself enter her and pull back. He pushed harder with each thrust. "Put your head down for me, arch your hips up, and push that sweet ass against me."

She trembled and pushed her backside into him as he pounded into her hard and unrelenting. She screamed out his name as another orgasm claimed her.

"Good girl. Now I want more. I want them all." His name fell from her lips repeatedly in abject elation. "Feels better, doesn't it, baby doll? You need to come for me again, don't you? Say please."

She cried out for another release. Her body contracted tightly around him. "Not yet, baby. Be a good girl and let it build for me." She whimpered and writhed from the effort. "I just make it feel too good, don't I?"

"Please, please," she pled.

He pounded into her with force. "My good girl takes it so hard. All right, baby, come," he commanded. She immediately complied. "Such a good girl—comes when I tell her to."

Her body surged and shuddered. She convulsed against his throbbing length. He felt it build as he formed her around him like she was made for him alone.

He continued to pound into her just like she liked it, until his climax gathered fiercely in his groin. Everything pulled taut. His muscles vibrated in ecstasy. She arched her feet and pressed the tips of the heels against the back of his thighs. The slight pain was unadulterated pleasure.

Their energy spun in tantric twists all around them. It filled him and made him whole again. His vision clouded. He couldn't stop it. He buried himself inside of her. His heart beat wildly as he gasped for breath. He forced her flat on her stomach under him as, "You take it all," poured from his mouth and his muscles seized.

She screamed out his name as his energy and everything that he was ripped through his resolve, and he filled her full.

He pulled out after the first desperate throb. "All mine," he growled as the next spurt of cum landed on her ass.

"Oh god, yes," she groaned in ecstasy. He shuddered as he milked more out over her.

His legs were weak, his breaths haggard. He fell back to the bed and pulled her onto his chest as he tried to regain the ability to breathe and to form coherent sentences. As his brain reengaged, he soothed, "Wait one second." He tried to catch his breath as he rushed to her bathroom and got a washcloth to clean her up.

She kicked off the heels with an extremely satisfied smile on her face while he wiped off his claim of ownership.

"Hottest sex I ever, ever, ever, ever had," were the first words out of her mouth when she stopped trembling from her climaxes.

Covered in sweat, Dan chuckled. "I aim to please."

She gave him an extremely contented grin.

"Sometimes, I'm really afraid I'm going to wake up and this will all have been some kind of fantastic dream," she admitted in a heartfelt whisper.

"Sweetheart, I've been living a nightmare for a long, long time, and you are truly the woman of my dreams. If this is a dream, I don't ever want to wake up, but I'm not finished with you."

Her eyes flashed both in surprise and concern. He stood and lifted her into his arms. He glided to her bathtub, ran the water, and climbed in behind her. He washed away the remnants of everything he'd done.

"You're tender, aren't you?" he soothed as he gently touched her again. She nodded and then melted in his arms as he moved his slick hands up her body to massage her neck and shoulders and then back down. He sent soothing pulses of his energy through her mound.

When he finished his work, he stepped out of the tub, heated a towel with his hands, and dried her thoroughly.

"Come here to me." He took her hand and led her back to bed. Slowly, he lay on his side and cradled her back to his chest. "I need you again. I'll never get enough." Every touch was slow and gentle this time. He moved his hands over her body in soft, tranquil caresses. She was still swollen and wet from her many climaxes. She gave a quiet moan as he cupped her again. "So tender and full for me, so damn sweet. We're gonna take it nice and slow this time, but I need you again. I'll be gentle, baby, but I need you to be a good girl for me and take some more."

"Yes," she whispered in the darkness as he traced her swollen inner lips. He opened her and entered her slowly and then rhythmically claimed her again. This time he filled her full of every ounce of him.

CHAPTER 5
INTRUSIONS

Dan gasped as Fionna shook him. "Someone is here," she whispered frantically. "They're here. I can feel them!" She shook in her terror.

His heart thundered and choked his lungs as he heard glass shatter.

Dan kept her behind his body as he reached and pulled his Colt from the jacket lying on the bench in Fionna's room. He heard stumbling footsteps in the entryway.

He did know. All of Governor Haydenshire's assurances that Wretchkinsides didn't know Dan had fallen in love were dead wrong. Dan's mind reeled as he chambered the pistol.

Silent tears leaked down Fionna's face. Her body shook in her terror. Dan eased out of bed and pulled on his jeans quickly.

"Put some clothes on for me, baby, and then I want you to stay right beside me." He forced himself to remain calm by sheer strength of will. Fionna threw on sweats and a T-shirt and clung to Dan as he padded to the bedroom door.

He listened intently. Only one set of feet moved below him. Wretchkinsides always sent two men. There had to be another somewhere.

Dan guided Fionna to the window. He scanned what portion of her front yard he could see. The streetlights were still glowing.

Something wasn't right. Wretchkinsides's hitmen were highly trained. Why had they left the lights on unless they didn't intend on leaving any witnesses? Bile flooded Dan's throat. How could he have done this to her? He had to save her and then he had to leave her.

"Listen to me. When I open the door and step out, immediately lock it back and slide that trunk in front of it. Call Garrett. He's at Chloe's. He can be here in just a second. Then I want you to stay in that corner down on the ground until I come back and get you. I'll cast the door when I leave, so no matter what, don't try to leave this room." He pointed to the back corner of her closet. If he died, his cast would die with him. He had to keep her safe until Garrett could get her out.

"No! What if they hurt you? I need to help you."

The thought of that robbed him of breath.

"I will be fine. I have taken on more than two of his guys before, but I can only take care of this if I know you're safe." He kept his single-minded focus on the intruder to keep from breaking down in front of her. He couldn't do this. If he got her out of this alive, he had to walk away.

With tears staining her face and her body trembling, Fionna slid silently across the floor and pulled her cell phone off the bedside table. She touched Garrett's name on the screen.

Dan heard the intruder move into the kitchen as he eased the door open.

"Dan, please," she whispered in the darkness. "Please be careful. I love you."

His heart shattered. Dan set his shield over himself to give her peace. He slipped into the darkened hallway and threw another shield over the door. He led with his gun and slid silently along the wall.

I have to leave her. He'll never leave her alone, not as long as she's with me. Tears stung his eyes. He blinked them away and continued his slow trek toward his fate.

He'll kill her too, all because of me. Dan swallowed back vomit as it singed his throat. He reached the stairs and listened again. They were moving in the kitchen, looking for something. Still only one set of moving feet. He heard drawers bang open—*a knife.* The thought had Dan reeling.

Pravus ran guns for Wretchkinsides and could've gotten any weapon he wanted. If they were looking for a knife... Terror gripped his chest and tore his breath from his lungs. My god. How could he have done this?

In two quick steps, he slid to the other side of the hallway, the wall that bordered the kitchen. He bent his elbows and raised the pistol up near his face. If he could get the guy in the kitchen with one shot, he could find the guy outside without giving too much warning that he was coming for him.

His blood ran in icy shards through his veins. His heart ached. His focus was the only thing he clung to so he could keep from losing his mind. He heard a car he prayed was Garrett's screech onto the street. The intruder didn't seem to notice.

If he kills me, Garrett will get her out. Dan let the thought soothe him. But Garrett didn't come in. What was taking him so long?

The front door was standing open. They'd shattered the pane of glass beside the lock and unbolted it. Dan eased into the hallway.

Lackey move. It isn't Adderand or Malicai. Pendergrath's son, Clarence, crossed his mind. You had to perform a hit to move up the ranks of the Interfeci.

Dan saw Garrett's personal .45 before he saw Garrett ease in through the open door. But Garrett's boot squeaked on the hardwood. Before the intruder could fire, Dan leapt.

He clobbered the man and brought him to the ground without a sound. He still had to get the guy outside. With the intruder on the ground, Dan stood. He slammed his foot into his back. He heard several ribs crack.

The man groaned.

"I cleared outside. There's no one else. Rainer and Logan are on the way, and the squad cars are here. I told them not to make a sound." Garrett hit the lights and kept his gun on the intruder's back as Dan kept his on his head.

"I will kill you. You will not hurt her!" Dan was shaking in his fury. His voice trembled as he fought back terror and weakness.

"Dan, it's not them. That's Kent." Garrett pulled Dan away.

"What?" Dan couldn't understand what Garrett was telling him. He was too terrified and furious to allow the odd sense of relief to set in.

Garrett hoisted Eric Kent off Fionna's kitchen floor and shoved him into one of the chairs. "What the hell, Eric? You're going to jail. I hope you know that."

As Dan allowed breath to fill his lungs, he smelled the heavy odor of liquor.

"Did you bathe in whiskey, fucker?" Garrett spat furiously. Eric's head jerked forward as he tried to focus. In a shocking move, he managed to grab the knife he'd held and lunged forward.

Unmitigated fury burned through Dan. He worked on instinct alone. He spun Eric and wrapped his massive arms around him. He held Eric's hand with the knife to his own throat. Eric jerked and tried to squirm away.

"Go ahead and dance, motherfucker. Slice your own throat. See if I give a damn."

"I need Fionna," Eric pled almost incoherently.

"No, you need a shrink." Garrett handed Dan some cuffs. Dan threw the knife back on the counter and cuffed Eric before shoving him back in the chair.

As his brain began receiving oxygen again, Dan tried to make sense of what had happened. He couldn't make his mind understand the images.

"I thought..." he stuttered.

"I know," Garrett soothed, "but it isn't them, and what would've happened if you hadn't been here? He's fucked up, and she would've been all alone. She needs you. Don't freak out now. No one knows."

"She wants *me*!" Eric shouted in his stupor. He fell forward in an effort to stand.

Garrett swung. Eric's head lobbed harshly to the side under the power of Garrett's fist. "You stay the hell away from her and right where Dan put you."

Eric's eyes were malevolent and insane.

"Here, I've got him. I'll take him out. Go get her. She's a disaster." Garrett gestured up the stairs. Dan still couldn't will his heart to beat in rhythm as he tried to think of what to say to Fionna. How could he make this right?

Hope, blasted, infuriating hope formed in his mind. Maybe, just maybe, Fionna really was better off with him than without him.

He tried to normalize his thoughts and his emotions as he pulled his shield from the door and knocked. "Fi, baby, it's me. Garrett's got him. Let me in. It's okay." Dan tried to force his hands to stop shaking.

He heard the chest slide hesitantly along the floor and then watched the door open. He caught Fionna as she fell into him, sobbing uncontrollably.

"Shh, baby, shh. It's okay. I've got you." Her nails dug into his chest as she clung to him in her panic. "I'm right here." Her energy was terror-ridden and frantic, but it soothed slightly when he spoke.

She was crying far too hard to breathe. Dan willed her to calm. "It's okay. Garrett's got him. It was Eric Kent, but he's going to jail. I will not let anything happen to you," he vowed, so much more for himself than for her. She trembled violently, hardly able to hold herself up.

"Come here, sweetheart." Dan lifted her in his arms. He debated for a moment, but he knew seeing Eric drunk off his ass and violent inside her home wasn't going to do anything to soothe her, so he moved into her bedroom and seated himself on her bed. She curled up into a tight ball and let him cradle and rock her.

Numerous flashing blue lights sprang to life in Fionna's driveway. Garrett tapped on the already-open door a minute later. He gave Dan a sorrowful look as he took in Fionna sobbing on his bare chest.

"Can I come in?"

Dan nodded. He was still rocking her back and forth as he attempted to wipe away the steady cascade of tears.

"Hey baby, he's got you. You're all right." Garrett caressed Fionna's long, chestnut locks, wet from her tears. Fionna tensed and buried her face farther in Dan's embrace. Garrett understood.

With a smirk, he raised his eyebrows. "See, it isn't me she wants, but I signed the warrants, and I'm going to tell the press that just pulled up that I was here with her."

Having experienced far too many emotions already at barely four in the morning, Dan nodded his agreement. He drew a deep breath.

"Take him on to Felsink. He can sober up there, and I'm certain his father will have quite a bit to say about this. I was phoned, but sent Iodex out here. I'm not here. I wouldn't normally come out for a B and E." Dan felt his brain try to function at full force again.

"You got it." Garrett seemed pleased by Dan's decision.

"Thank you," Fionna shuddered, barely able to formulate the two words.

"I'll be back in a few minutes." Garrett shut the door on his way out.

"I…was… so…scared," she stuttered and effectively broke Dan's heart.

"I know, baby, but you're all right. I'm right here. I'm not going anywhere." The words he spoke soothed his own heart.

"I…wasn't…scared for…me."

Dan swallowed down his own emotions. He didn't deserve a love like this. They heard the press swarm outside her bedroom window.

"Was Miss Styler injured? Will she be able to challenge? Will Mr. Kent continue his bid for governor? Where is Miss Styler now?" The questions were endless.

"Get him out of here!" Garrett bellowed.

"Were you the arresting officer?"

"Yes, ma'am, I was," Garrett huffed as Dan and Fionna listened from their hiding place.

"Miss Styler filed a restraining order against Eric Kent, is that correct, Officer Haydenshire?" another reporter called.

"Yes, she did, and all of that will be taken into consideration when he goes before the governors."

"Did Miss Styler confront her attacker?" was the next question.

Dan was sick from the thought alone.

"No, I was here with her."

An audible buzz arose in the crowd.

"When will Miss Styler be available for comment?"

"Miss Styler is understandably upset, and I don't know that she'll ever be available for comment on the incident, nor do I believe you deserve one," Garrett defied. Dan's face pulled into a smile. "Why don't we leave Miss Styler in peace and allow her time to get her bearings after this harrowing ordeal?"

"Was she injured?" The next question rang loudly from someone very near Fionna's bedroom window.

"Miss Styler was not injured in any way."

"Will you be staying the rest of the night with Miss Styler?"

Dan could almost see the look Garrett was most certainly giving the reporter.

"Next question," Garrett demanded. Keeping everyone guessing did seem to be the way to keep Fionna safe. Dan had to allow that.

"What will be the next steps for Eric Kent in his run for governor?"

"I couldn't answer that, but I will say Mr. Kent was highly intoxicated. He forcibly broke into Miss Styler's home, and that is not the kind of man I want seated on our governing board. Do you?"

Dan was extremely impressed.

"Was he given a breathalyzer test when you made the arrest?"

"My first course of action was to make certain that he was removed from Miss Styler's home and to ensure her safety. He'll be given a test in the squad car on the way to the Senate, but I certainly don't have those results yet."

Fionna's cell phone rang. Dan leaned and handed it to her.

"Hey." She shuddered as she answered Chloe's call. "I'm okay." Her voice was weak and broken. "Yes, in his lap," she informed Chloe. Dan smiled again. "You can come over, but I'm not getting out of his lap any time soon." Dan cradled her closer. That was perfectly fine with him. "I'm just completely freaked out." She paused. "I love you too." Fionna ended the call.

"Iodex is moving in. I'm telling you now to leave by order of the Crown Governor. She'll be at the trial. Maybe you can interview her then," Garrett baited the press.

He knocked again before entering Fionna's bedroom several minutes later. She gave him the most pitiful look either Garrett or Dan had ever seen. It physically affected both of them as tears welled from her eyes.

"Thank you." She crawled out of Dan's lap and fell into Garrett's arms.

"You're welcome, baby." Garrett hugged her fiercely. She let him sway her back and forth for several long minutes.

"You always take such good care of me. I don't deserve either of you." She hugged him tighter.

"We'll always take care of you," Garrett promised. "And you take good care of everyone, us included. Never forget that." He kissed the top of her head.

She turned back to Dan, still wearing a sorrowful expression.

"Will you help me take down the tree and then put it back up at your house?" she asked in a tone that Dan couldn't have denied if he wanted to.

"Of course." He wondered what she was planning.

She turned back to Garrett. "Will you and Logan and Rainer come over and help me move tomorrow?"

Garrett gave Dan a grin as he nodded. "Nowhere else any of us would be. I'll even grab a few more of my brothers. If all the Haydenshires are involved, it won't take long."

A second later, she crawled back into Dan's lap and resumed her previous ball form. Garrett and Dan both grinned at her adoringly.

"I still don't know how she gets all that leg up into a ball like that, but she'll stay like that for a while," Garrett explained.

Fionna giggled while keeping herself in her cocoon. Dan kissed the top of her head, as that was the only thing he had access to at the moment. "She can stay like this as long as she likes. I'll be right here."

Garrett gave Dan an extremely impressed smile. "Had a feeling."

"Thank you. Seriously, thank you for everything. I'm sorry I've been such an ass."

Garrett chuckled. "Anytime, and you're always an ass, but so am I. That's why we work so well together. I'm gonna head back to Chloe's. We'll bring coffee early. Do you want me to help you tape that window before I go?"

"I'll take care of it," Dan assured. "I want to pull his prints off of it first."

Garrett nodded and kissed the top of Fionna's head before he disappeared down the stairs.

CHAPTER 6
CONFESSIONS AND REGRETS

"I'm not going back to sleep," Fionna declared.

"I'm pretty sure you mean *we're* not going back to sleep."

"I'm going to pack, and we're moving tomorrow."

"I won't argue with that, but I really don't want you to move in with me just because you're scared. I will keep you safe. I don't want you to run away from something you love so much." Dan gestured to her house in general.

She shook her head. "I've been scared for a long time," she admitted in a choked whisper. "I screwed up. I've been screwing up for a long while, actually." Dan, of all people, knew when a confession was weighing on someone. She needed to get whatever she was trying to tell him off her chest, and he wanted to help her heal from every wound. "I went through a bad-boy phase... I guess... because...." She shuddered against him. "If I tell you all of this, can we never talk about it again after tonight?"

"Sure."

"Until I met you, I didn't think any guys like you existed."

That wasn't what he'd expected. His brow furrowed, but he didn't want to say too much. He was afraid she might stop talking.

"What do you mean?"

Fionna buried her face against him, and Dan leaned in to hear her.

"Again, not a sex maniac," she insisted. He chuckled as he recalled that her original declaration that she was not a sex addict was accompanied by her explanation that she preferred to sleep naked. As he found every single thing about her absolutely intoxicating, he wasn't too concerned about this confession either.

"Got it." He brushed another kiss in her hair.

"I guess I really like that *take-charge* kind of deal in bed, so I went out with bad boys because they were better in bed. They were more aggressive or whatever." She didn't seem to like the way that sounded when she said it out loud. Dan had a feeling he knew where this was going.

"So, I've been scared for a long time, because there are several guys out there who know where I live. Only they aren't just aggressive in bed. They're just aggressive, jerky guys all the time."

Dan felt relief begin to form in her energy as she made her confession.

"That's another reason I wanted to stay here all the time once we started dating. I finally felt safe here again, and I do love my house." She sounded thoroughly disgusted with herself. With a deep breath, she shrugged. "I guess I thought I couldn't have it both ways until I met you. How do you do that? How are you such a nice, sweet guy all the time, but then you know exactly how I want you to be in bed, bad boy and all? You aren't supposed to exist."

Although he did understand what she was asking him, Dan was at a complete loss as to how to respond.

"Tell me, please. I want to know. I want to understand. Believe me, I've picked some real doozies the last few years."

She made his heart ache. "I don't really know, sweetheart." Dan tried to formulate his answer. "I guess a lot of morons don't seem to know the difference between being dominant and being a domineering, controlling prick who women should stay the hell away from." He didn't want to add to her self-imposed guilt as he let her see a rather deep part of his psyche.

As the thoughts of what might've happened if he hadn't been there mixed with his desperate need to protect her and her plea that they never discuss this again, Dan decided to go ahead and lay it out for her. As much as it pained him to scare her, he knew he was going to, because it was to keep her safe.

"You don't need to control every aspect of her life to drive her wild and give her what she wants in bed." Men who thought that way generally pissed him off.

"Oh well, see, the way it was explained to me was that it would be my pleasure to pleasure him," she spat indignantly.

"Guy Garrett beat the shit out of?" Fury burned through him all over again.

"Yep."

"Gonna have to give Haydenshire a raise." Dan squeezed her to him and decided to get on with it. He wanted to give her a fresh start, and that meant giving her a new place to call home.

"Listen, I know there are just as many women who get off on the super kinky stuff as there are men, and if that's what you both want, then have at it. But that wasn't what you wanted, and then he tried to lock you in a room. That, right there, is where we have a big problem. No means no. I don't care how much pleasure he's planning on allowing you." He tried to quell his disgust, but she felt it work through his rhythms.

"It just better as hell not be what he wants and what he can talk her into. Far too often, I've seen guys into that kind of shit who don't like to be told no, and girls have some crazy idea that he's a guy out of a novel that she can magically change." Dan didn't really want to recall what he was telling her.

She nodded and stared up at him with those enchanting eyes, both intrigued and frightened. "Yeah, he was way more kinky-crazy than what I was looking for. I just kind of wanted to do something different, you know?"

She needed to be told that it was perfectly normal and healthy to want a little adventure in the bedroom, but that it had to be with the right guy.

"I know, honey, and believe me, I get everything you're saying. I'll kink it up as much as you want, but I'm not going to hurt you. I will never put you in a situation where you could even be hurt accidentally. I don't care how much it turns some women on, because

I've been called out to more cases of that kind of thing gone very, very wrong than I care to remember."

"Really?" She looked appalled as he nodded morosely.

"There are the humorous ones too. You know, the guy's cheating on his wife, so she tells him she wants to go wild. Then she strips him down and handcuffs him to the bed. Then she tells him to call his mistress and leaves with the keys.

"There are the stupid ones where the woman they hardly know cuffs them somewhere and robs them blind or vice versa. So baby, if you want to have a wild night where I cuff you to the bed and have my way with you, or you tie me up and make me do your bidding, then I'm game. But I'll say this, you sure as hell better trust the person doing the cuffing because you're giving up your options. You need to know that he wants you to have what *you* want, not what he wants, and both people need to know what the hell they're doing before you break out whips, gags, crops, collars, and paddles. Because the good ones only end up in courtrooms or in jail, the bad ones end up in the hospital, the worst I've seen ended up in a morgue." He was sick as he recalled that night several years ago just after he'd been named Chief of Iodex.

"Oh, my gosh."

"Some guys get going, and they don't know when to quit."

"I'm sorry. Your job is really hard."

Dan shook his head. "I kind of like to think about the justice portion of my job. The guy who killed her to get his jollies is rotting away in Coriolis, so he'll never hurt anyone else."

"You mean, he meant to kill her?"

"No." Dan shook his head. "Don't get me wrong, he was a sicko and high as a kite, but he was enjoying himself. Right up until the end, he thought she was too. Typically, people who enjoy that kind of kink know never to drink or to use before they engage. They do have very strict rules, but he was fucked up. They met online, and he told her he was a fully trained Dom looking for a sub." Dan shook his head. "He wasn't by a long shot. His lawyers dragged out the contract he'd had her sign, but it took my guys almost thirty minutes to get all of the chains off her. The contract didn't get him very far."

"Stop." She looked physically ill. "I don't want to know."

"I'm sorry, baby. I didn't mean to tell you that." Their harrowing night, coupled with the fact that he seemed to lose all of his filters when it came to her, had gotten to him.

"Okay, I'm going to go back to your very impressive answer about how you're the perfect guy for me and forget the rest of that for now."

"One more thing." Dan wasn't going to walk away from this conversation until he was certain she knew that he did understand where she was coming from. "I know that being a woman, that being you, is hard. You have a lot of roles to play, sweetheart. Your parents have a version of you that they want. You have to play famed Arlington Angels Receiver, America's sweetheart, and all that goes with that for the fans and for the team. My girlfriend, what you think my parents expect, be a friend to Chloe, and Garrett, and Emily… the list goes on and on. And every step holds the potential for shame because people seem to have no issue demanding that a woman be who they want her to be, and they give no shits if it's who she wants to be.

"I completely understand that sometimes it's nice just not to think, just to be, and to let someone else make you feel incredible. I want to be the guy you give that kind of power and control to, but I want you to understand that I know what you're entrusting me with. I know what that could cost you. I would never, ever take that for granted, and I would never make you feel ashamed for what you want."

"Wow." She swallowed harshly as she took in his vow. "Thank you for saying that. I don't deserve you."

"That's most certainly not true." She was the angel who had pulled him straight out of hell. The only one who could damn his demons back to the abyss that had been his life and baptize him anew. It was him who didn't deserve her.

"I've never done the handcuff or blindfold thing." She blushed violently.

Dan nodded his understanding. "And you never have to, baby doll. But, if you want to, I don't think that's something you should be ashamed of as long as it's what you want and what I want. As long as we trust each other enough to know it's just for fun, then it's fine."

He felt no remorse in making his next statement, because he knew it wasn't what she wanted either. "If you want to be spanked with anything more than a wooden spoon through a pair of jeans, or on your bare sexy ass with my hands, when the moment calls for that, then I'm probably not the guy for you. If you're looking for riding crops or whips, you'll have to find someone else."

She grinned and brushed a sweet kiss on his cheek before she settled back down in his protective embrace. "You *are* the guy for me. You know that."

He knew who he was, and the wonderful feeling that settled on him as he explained all of this to her was that he knew who she was as well.

Dan grinned but continued his speech. "There are things that add to the arousal and the physical excitement of it all. From the very first moment I undressed you, I tried to learn what would make you get the most out of the experience. My girl happens to enjoy that little walk on the wild side where I leave a hickey here and there that no one else can see.

"She likes a few other things I say and do that other women might not like. If that's what you want—and just so you know, I think it's sexy as hell—then that's what I'm going to do. Our kinks line up perfectly. But this is a relationship, sweetheart, and our sex life is only one part of this relationship. I want to do anything that drives you wild, but it should add to the experience for both of us, not just one of us. That sound okay to you?"

A genuine smile washed away the guilt and fear that had permeated her being. "I have everything I've ever wanted, and he's holding me in my ball right now."

Certain she was the most precious thing he'd ever seen, Dan squeezed her tightly. "If you'll let me unfold you, then I'll help you start packing, but if you want to stay balled up in my lap then I'll hold you as long as you want."

She sighed. "Do you think I'm wild now too?" Tears pricked her eyes once again. He recalled her telling him in Sydney that her father thought she was a wild child.

"No, baby. I think you're a woman with her very own special

cocktail of being the sweetest, kindest, most wonderful woman I've ever met, and then there are those parts of you that like to be just a little bit wild. I think you like to think of yourself as a bad girl occasionally, and believe me, I appreciate all of the many, many sides of you. I plan to cater to each and every one of them as long as it's what you want and what you need at that moment.

"Part of being in a relationship is knowing when you want to be sucked, spanked, and bitten, when you want it rough, when you want me to indulge in just a few of our mutual kinks. And when you want a slow, sensuous, romantic session where I stare into your eyes instead of staring at your ass,"—he felt her blush against him—"sometimes we want those all in the same night." He tried to gently bring up the ecstasy they'd experienced just a few hours before. It seemed like days had gone by since he'd cradled her in bed and had taken her the second time.

"I told you, honey, you're the girl of my dreams. I didn't think you existed," he quoted her line for him. "The kind of beautiful, sweet, brilliant woman I want in my bedroom taking care of me when I'm sick and the hot, sexy, seductress I want in my bed when I'm not." His love for her surged rapidly through him. The look in her eyes said she felt it too. "You know, the girl I can't wait to take home to meet my parents, and if I do everything right, the woman who might just suck me off on the way."

She giggled delightedly. "I might do something like that."

"My dream girl."

"Eric's not the only scary, controlling guy I went out with. Sometimes, I don't feel safe here when I'm all alone." Her voice was filled with regret.

"I know, but listen to me. What Eric did tonight is not your fault. You didn't even kiss him after going out with him once. He's a prick who refuses to take no for an answer. It isn't your job to make him not that way. The same way it isn't your job to make any other man be a human instead of an animal. None of it is your fault."

Dan recalled the last time she'd been at home alone. He suddenly understood why she'd gotten Chloe, Emily, and the twins to stay all day. Why she'd wanted Fitz to stay there—and he understood why Garrett stayed over so often.

Garrett had known she was scared, but he wouldn't call her on it because, when it came right down to it, Garrett Haydenshire was an outstanding human being and a hell of a friend. He'd saved Dan's life more times than he could count.

Garrett had done nothing but take care of the woman Dan found himself incurably in love with, and Dan had done nothing but treat him like an interfering annoyance. Deep regret settled on him as well.

"Believe me, honey, I've dated several doozies myself." He shuddered from the thought. "But I generally went to their houses. So, how about if we make my house our home, and we start over. Because this,"—he gestured his head to her—"this is what I want, and nothing else. We deserve a fresh start." The statement was so foreign to him. For the past ten years, he'd been certain he deserved nothing good at all.

"I was so stupid."

"Hey, stop. You're certainly not the first woman who's liked a bad boy, and if you didn't like bad boys, I'm pretty sure you never would have brought me home that fateful night a few weeks ago."

CHAPTER 7
MOVING ON

She unwound herself and drew a haggard breath.

"Where shall we start?" Dan wanted to help her do anything in the world.

"I still have a bunch of boxes in the garage from when I moved in here. Are we going to rent a truck?"

"I can if we need to but no movers. Part of no one knowing where my house is means I do most things myself or I get my dad to help me."

Fionna nodded and gave him his smile. "It will be really nice to feel safe at home again."

Dan wrapped her up in his arms. "I always want you to feel safe, and I will do everything in my power to keep you that way."

Though it was barely five in the morning, Fionna turned on all of the lights in the house and turned music on the speaker system as they began boxing up her life.

Dan dragged duct tape over the shattered glass window to keep the freezing cold air out of the house.

. . .

At six thirty, Garrett and Chloe showed up with breakfast and coffee. By seven, Rainer, Emily, Logan, Adeline, Connor, Levi, and Will were loading furniture and boxes into their cars.

"I think we better tell our parents we're doing this today," Dan pointed out as he passed Fionna on the steps.

"I guess we have to."

In another hour's time, the Stylers were being haphazardly introduced to the Vindicos. Both sets of parents were somewhat bewildered. Gretta managed to keep her husband in line though he made several snide remarks to Fionna about moving in with Dan before they were married.

Dan's sister Kara and her husband, Zach, arrived to help. "I told Mom this was one step closer to you getting married in order to keep her from coming over and lecturing you on this being inappropriate and disgraceful." Kara rolled her eyes. Dan thanked her, but he couldn't have cared less what his mother thought.

Kara was told repeatedly by her husband, her brother, and her father not to lift anything. "I'm putting dishes into a box. The baby will be perfectly fine. I do unload the dishwasher at home."

Fionna and Emily gave her sympathetic looks.

In her uncanny ability to pretend that anything she didn't approve of simply didn't exist, Mrs. Vindico brought numerous window treatment and decor catalogs that she was eager to show Fionna once they'd unloaded everything at Dan's.

"Although I do understand that your home is not safe, dear, I strongly suggest that you and Daniel stay in separate rooms until you're married. That's how we do things in our family, but I am looking forward to helping you with Daniel's house."

"I'm just going to go ahead and tell you how sorry I am," Dan said when he got Fionna alone for a split second in her guest bedroom while unloading a closet.

She chuckled. "It's oddly sweet, but I still don't like curtains or blue carpet."

"Add those to the very lengthy list of things I adore about you." He glanced around the room and saw how much they had left.

Fionna's face fell. "I don't want to hurt her feelings."

"There are many ways to deal with my mother. If you want to take the approach Kara has used for the last twenty-nine years or so, you just nod, smile, tell her what she wants to hear, and agree with whatever it is she's decided, and then do whatever the hell you want to do once she finally shuts up. I prefer to argue with her because she drives me insane." Dan effectively cracked her up.

He headed to the corner of the room and began loading Fionna's sewing machine into its box.

"Please be careful with that. My, uh," she paused and swallowed down raw emotion. The day was getting to her.

"Your mom gave it to you. I know, baby. I'll be careful. I promise." Dan held her eyes with his own. Desperation to just pick her up and take her away from everything pulsed in his shield.

Wretchkinsides, Eric, her father, and his mother...she didn't deserve any of this. He wanted to take it all away.

"It doesn't work anymore." Her voice was weak and forlorn. Dan eased the sewing machine back into its table and moved to her.

"Does it still remind you of her?"

She managed a nod. The tremble of her chin shook his heart.

"She taught you to sew, right?" He wrapped her up in his arms and felt her nod against him. "She and Tutu," she choked.

"And when you look at it, you remember the lessons and the time you spent with her?"

Fionna nodded again as she blinked back tears.

"Then it works perfectly."

"I love you." She broke down in his arms. His shield orbed around her.

"Me too, baby. And I know you're scared, but I'm right here."

Kara halted Mrs. Vindico in the hallway while Dan dried Fionna's tears by engaging her in several intense kisses.

Kara cleared her throat and then gave Dan a wry grin.

"Having fun?"

"I was until we were so rudely interrupted." He tousled his sister's hair as she laughed. He ignored his mother pursing her lips in aggravation.

"What else can we do?" Kara asked.

"I think most of the kitchen and dining room are done. Garrett and Chloe are loading up the stuff in my entertainment center. I think I do want to take that big chair in my living room, but we're going to use Dan's sofa and love seat, but I do want all of the pillows I made that are on the couch. So, the guest bedrooms, bathrooms, and my room."

"Yes, well, perhaps you two should make better use of your time. I know you'll want to get some things arranged at Dan's before we go over the catalogs I brought for you," Mrs. Vindico chirped.

Kara and Dan shuddered simultaneously. "First of all, Mother, it's *ours* not Dan's, and Fi can decorate it anyway she wants. She doesn't need any help. She did all of this"—he gestured around Fionna's current home with its bright accents and meaningful pieces that he loved—"all on her own." He was already thoroughly annoyed with his mother, and he'd only been with her for the grand total of an hour.

"Yes, well, such as it is." Mrs. Vindico glanced around the home she very obviously did not approve of. Dan bit back fury.

"Uh, Meredith's bringing a big dinner over to your place for everyone," Kara, ever the peacemaker, announced. She seemed to have just remembered that she was supposed to tell Dan this.

"Really?"

"Yeah, we're really, really happy for you. We want to help."

"Thanks," he choked. The emotion of everything that had happened to him in the past month settled in his throat.

Kara nodded, and in a moment of what seemed to be overwhelming adoration for her big brother, she scooted Fionna out of the way and threw her arms around Dan. She squeezed him tight.

Fionna beamed at them.

"Besides, I need you to chill out and settle down because I'm having a baby, and you're my only sane sibling," Kara reminded him as Fionna and Dan watched the extent of her pregnancy hormones come on full tilt. She smiled adoringly at Dan and then promptly began to sob.

Dan shook his head, but he embraced his little sister and let her cry against his chest. Fionna looked at him like she couldn't possibly love anyone more.

"Meredith's not nuts, just Tim," Dan teased as Kara began to laugh at herself for crying.

"I know, but they come as a package. Oh, yeah, I'm supposed to tell you that Tim may not be able to come because he thinks his immunizations must've run out. He's decided that he contracted Rubella, and therefore he can't be around me because it might hurt the baby," Kara explained just before she cracked up.

"What?" Dan's brother-in-law and his insistence that he couldn't work, because of his illness of the day, drove Dan insane.

Kara was still giggling. "It's a few pimples on his ass. Meredith told me." She managed to get out the explanation before she began crying again from her own laughter.

Fionna and Dan laughed hysterically at the story and Kara's reaction.

Suddenly, Fionna stopped laughing. Her eyes goggled. "Dan, where's your mom?"

Kara, Dan, and Fionna all took off toward the master bedroom in a heated sprint. It was very clear to Dan that his little sister had a drawer similar to Fionna's, and she completely understood why it was imperative that Mrs. Vindico not get into Fionna's bedside table.

Dan rushed into the room with Fionna and Kara right behind him. "Mom!"

Mrs. Vindico was in Fionna's closet gathering clothes on their hangers. She was laying them gingerly on Fionna's bed.

"Dan, my lingerie is in there," Fionna hissed through clenched teeth as she gestured to a massive antique French armoire in the back of the closet.

Dan took guard in front of the bedside table. He crossed his massive arms over his chest, determined to protect the delicate intricate pieces of the woman he adored from his mother's bulldozer approach to life.

"Mom," he barked, "let Fionna pack her own clothes!"

"Daniel, we have things to get done. Now, clearly, after what happened last night, this isn't a safe place for our sweet Fionna to stay. Your father and Governor Haydenshire's boys are loading up the last of the furniture. Emily, Adeline, and Fionna's dear mother, who must be who she gets her beautiful complexion from, are finishing up the kitchen, so I'll just get this room done quickly. Then we can go and get your home all squared away." She looked extremely proud of her plan.

Dan refused to move away from Fionna's bedside table drawer which contained a vast collection of sex toys and an endless supply of well-worn erotic novels.

He decided to command from his current post. "We'll get everything taken care of. It doesn't all have to be done today, but Fionna and I will take care of her bedroom, as it is hers, and she doesn't want it intruded upon."

Mrs. Vindico rolled her eyes and gave Dan the look she reserved for him when he'd done anything that didn't meet her ridiculous expectations.

"All women have more shoes than we let our husbands know we have, and a long silk dressing robe that we don't want anyone but our husband to know about. I certainly don't have any problem packing up Fionna's. She is a sweet, kind, wonderful girl. There is absolutely nothing in here that she wouldn't want me to see."

Fionna whimpered and shot Dan pleading looks.

Kara stepped in. She pulled her mother from Fionna's closet. "Mom, why don't you and I go get the guest bedrooms all packed up? We'll just let Dan and Fionna finish in here."

Ignoring Kara, Mrs. Vindico continued piling Fionna's clothing on the bed. She happened to grab the tight, leather miniskirt that Fionna had worn the night Dan had come home with her. She furrowed her brow, but then crafted her own story. "I bet that was part of a cute Halloween costume. Did you wear it with colorful tights?"

Fionna dropped her head into her hands.

"Mom!" Dan and Kara both shouted.

At that moment, Governor Vindico came to his children's rescue. He took in Dan standing rigidly, arms crossed, in front of Fionna's bedside table, the pile of clothing on the bed, Kara's wide-eyed horror as she stood in front of the armoire in the closet, and Fionna's face in her hands.

With a sigh, he rubbed his temples. "Marion, dear, the car is full.

Would you ride with me over to Dan's. We'll unload the boxes in his garage and then come back for another load. I could really use your help."

"I suppose, but everyone needs to pick up the pace. They need to get squared away before Daniel has to go back to work tomorrow."

"We'll get everything done. Dan will take care of Fionna, and she will take care of him." Governor Vindico guided his wife out of Fionna's closet and then out of her room.

"Thank you," Dan sighed.

"I'd get this room done quickly, son."

"I really, really love your dad," Fionna gushed. Kara looked almost as relieved as Fionna. But suddenly Dan found himself being glared at by Fionna. Kara's eyes lit in delight as she watched.

"Uh, Chief Vindico, how exactly did you know which drawer I didn't want your mother finding?"

CHAPTER 8
FOURTEEN DAYS

Fionna was trying hard to look threatening but was failing miserably.

Kara cracked up. "Oh, this is so fun. Please don't make me leave." She and Fionna shared conspiratorial laughter.

"You don't have to leave. You have to hold him down while I tickle him."

His little sister and his girlfriend teaming up to attack him had Dan laughing. "Bring it on, baby doll."

"Well, let's have it, darling." Fionna cocked her jaw to the side and put her hands on her hips. She gestured her head toward the drawer in question.

Dan tried to think of a way out, but he was quite certain he was had. "I don't guess you'd buy that it was an incredibly good guess?"

"Not a chance."

Kara's entire face lit as she moved beside Fionna in a show of staunch solidarity. "Here, watch me work. This is so much more effective than tickling."

With a genuine laugh, Dan seriously doubted that his little sister had anything up her sleeve.

"Hey Fionna," Kara drawled.

"Yeah, Kara?"

"You know that stuff that my incredibly nosy brother found of yours that everyone has, but no one talks about, and that your boyfriend should never go looking for?"

Fionna gave Dan a goading glare. "Yes, I do know that stuff."

"Well, I was just wondering if you thought it was okay for me to use mine while I'm pregnant. Because sometimes Zach and I…"

Dan shuddered in horror. "Stop. For the love of God, stop now!"

"No, no, go on." Fionna giggled hysterically.

"See, Zach does this thing…" Kara baited as Dan gagged reflexively.

"Okay, okay, I was a jerk. The first night I stayed over here, I poked around a little while you were in the bathroom. I'm really sorry. I don't care. I think it's really hot. Just please don't make me listen to anything else about my sister's sex life."

Fionna and Kara gave each other high fives and laughed. Dan was quite certain his face was the color of an overripe tomato.

"Now, make him pack them," Kara ordered. Fionna shot Dan another irritated glare.

Kara shook her head at him. "I'm going to go check on Zach and let her yell at you. Call me if you need me," Kara urged Fionna.

"I'll take care of him. Don't worry."

"I'm sorry. I shouldn't have done that. I was desperate to find out everything I could about you, and I wanted to know what kinds of things you might like. I wanted to make you happy. It was a horrible invasion of privacy."

Fionna crossed her arms over her chest and kept her eyes narrowed. Her face was still glowing crimson.

Since his mother was no longer in the room and wouldn't decide at any given moment to stalk to the bedside table and unload it, Dan moved to Fionna. "I'm really sorry. Please don't be embarrassed. It's incredibly hot. I would love to get in on that someday." He took a chance and wrapped his arms around her. She bristled and debated.

"I'm so embarrassed." After a moment of resistance, she buried her face in his chest. "Oh, my gosh! Your mom. There is so, so, so, much more in there than a long silk robe. I don't think I even own a long silk robe."

Her energy spun tight pulses in her humiliation. "Honey, you have nothing to be embarrassed about. I love that you love lingerie. Obviously, I love seeing you in stuff like that, but it means a lot to me that you want there to be more to it than just the act itself. It's incredibly refreshing actually. And the stuff in there..." He gestured to the bedside table drawer and paused. He wasn't certain how to explain it to her. "Do you remember this morning when you asked me if I thought you were wild the way your dad thinks you are?"

Fionna nodded against him.

"I think that all of that, and all of the lingerie, they all make up this incredible cocktail of you—the sweet, smart, amazing woman that I'm head over heels for. The woman I can't wait to move into my house. You may not have known much about me before we got together, but believe me, you've changed me completely and all for the better. And," —he pulled away just enough to kiss her forehead—"I think you should definitely keep all of the same stuff in the bedside table in our room, at our house. You know, the one you threw all of the condoms out of when you went through my stuff." He finally broke through her abashed state and made her laugh.

A minute later, she pulled away and moved to sit on her bed beside the piles of clothes. She looked overwrought.

"What's wrong, baby?" Dan seated himself beside her.

"Nothing, but maybe that's what's wrong."

"Fi?" He'd gleaned nothing from her cryptic reply.

She drew a deep breath and turned to study him. "We've been going out less than a month. Now, I'm moving into your house. Doesn't that scare you even a little? What if we're only doing this because I was an idiot, and my house really isn't safe anymore? I'm just dumping my stupid mistakes in your lap."

Dan lifted her face tenderly into his hands and gazed down at the most amazing women he'd ever come in contact with. "Fourteen days." She furrowed her brow. "Fourteen days is how long we've been dating. And in the past fourteen days, you've made me feel things I swore I'd never feel again. You've made me believe that maybe life really is worth living, because for ten damn years, I never believed that.

"You made me understand that I *could* have it both ways. See, I was damned and determined never to fall in love again because that meant I had to stop loving Amelia and I couldn't. I can't. I never thought there was a woman in the world who would understand that, who would allow it and accept it. But you,"—he shook his head in disbelief—"you did so much more than accepting it. You welcomed it because you are the most astounding thing that has ever happened to me. So, for fourteen days, I've lived. I've done more than breathe in hatred and exhale vengeance when I drew breath, and I've seen the world through your eyes, instead of through a red haze of anger and volatility.

"I've slept for the first time in years. You have healed me and filled me in ways I thought I'd never be filled again. So, yeah, I'm scared. Scared I won't be enough for you because, my God, you deserve so much more than me."

She shook her head vehemently, but he continued. "But what absolutely terrifies me is thinking about waking up and you not being in my arms, or coming back to the house I've occupied for the last few years, and it not being my home because you aren't there. I've done a whole lot of incredibly stupid things in my life, but I will do anything in my power to be everything you need and you want me to be. I cannot lose you. That would end me. I couldn't go on. I know this is fast and it's been kind of a crazy ride, baby doll, but I've experienced enough of the absolute worst possible things this world has to offer to know when I just happened to somehow, by some incredible miracle, get the absolute best thing there is out there."

"Dan," she choked and shook her head, but he continued.

"If you don't want to move in with me, then I'll have them unload the trucks. But please, I'm begging you, let me move in here, because I can't survive without you. I can't. I'm just not that strong," he choked.

Fionna wrapped her arms around him as he cradled her to him. "I just love you so much sometimes it scares me, because I can't live without you either, not anymore. I just can't, and I know I'm not supposed to. We're not supposed to exist without each other. It's just a lot."

"I'm not going anywhere. I will always be right here."

She nodded against him and began shuddering with her sobs.

"Baby, please don't cry." Her tears pierced him like dagger tips. He rubbed her back and tried to brush away the emotion.

Her exhaustion from their horrific night, his mother penetrating her safe-hold, her discovery that he'd found out a little more than she was quite ready to share, and then giving up her home had been more than she could withstand. Dan held her close and felt guilt over his part swirl relentlessly in his shield.

Garrett knocked on the open door. Emily followed him into the room. He caught Dan's eye and gave him a sympathetic headshake. "Happy tears, angry tears, exhausted tears? Geez, girls cry about everything."

Fionna turned from Dan and let Garrett embrace her.

"I'm gonna go with angry and exhausted." Defeat settled on Dan.

"No, it's just…it's kind of been a lot lately," Fionna explained into Garrett's chest.

"Yeah, well, take it from me, you two need each other. I've never seen either of you so happy," Garrett scoffed. "You know, I gave him hell thinking he was gonna be the one to freak. Maybe I should have been yelling at you." He kissed the top of her head and swayed her back and forth. His voice was kind and gentle.

"You would never yell at me," she reminded him.

"True."

"It was just a little freak-out. I have them occasionally." She squeezed him tighter.

"I'm pretty certain this one was my fault," Dan admitted.

Emily cringed. "Kara said Mrs. Vindico was trying to pack up your room." She bit her lip before continuing. "I'll help you finish. If we hurry, we can get everything done before she gets back."

"Baby, is there anything in there that might break or that's hanging up?" Dan gestured to the armoire.

Fionna shook her head. "It's a bunch of drawers, so everything is folded."

"Why don't Garrett and I just carry it out like it is? We can put it in our closet at the house. It'll never have to be packed or unpacked."

Relief eased over Fionna's features as she nodded. "Thank you."

Garrett chuckled and kissed the top of her head again. "Satin and lace can't possibly weigh that much."

"Shut up." Fionna pretended to push him back. He feigned injury. Dan shook his head.

Quickly figuring that having a few minutes alone with Emily might help, Dan tried not to lament the fact that he alone hadn't been able to soothe her.

"Come on, Haydenshire. Lift with your legs."

Garrett laughed as he and Dan lifted the large, heavy piece of furniture and maneuvered it carefully out of Fionna's closet and down the stairs.

CHAPTER 9
WITH HER, FOR HER

Dan climbed back up the stairs without consciously deciding to eavesdrop. He halted outside the door when he heard the words, "He really does love you. I can tell. He's crazy about you." Emily was vehement as if Fionna didn't believe that herself.

"I know. I can't believe how lucky I am. I just kind of freaked. Do you think I'm crazy moving in with him? It's been two weeks, even if I kind of knew beforehand."

Silence loomed. Dan's pulse churned and then sped rapidly. He prayed Emily would tell her that it wasn't crazy, that she should move in with him. He didn't understand how she'd known before, but he didn't care.

"You know, I think everyone thought I was just a sassy kid when I said I was going to marry Rainer when I was four, but I was serious. I still think people are just waiting on us to fall apart because you can't possibly love the same guy your entire life. But just because everyone else doesn't do it the way I did it, or the way you and Dan are doing it, doesn't make their way right and our way wrong." Dan was deeply impressed. He just needed Fionna to hear what her friend was saying. "I don't know about you, but I kind of think my love story is the best."

Fionna laughed at Emily's teasing words, but Dan knew she did believe that.

"Other people moving in together after two weeks might make me concerned, but something about the two of you when you're together is right. I can feel it, and I know you can feel it too."

"I can, but I'm really mad at him. I don't know how to feel about that. If he weren't so sweet, and so freaking good-looking, and so damn good in bed, I'd be really pissed that he found my vibes. I am pissed, but being mad at him makes *me* hurt. I knew he'd done something. He felt guilty that morning when I walked him out."

Fionna's words rocked through Dan. He'd had no idea that morning how incredibly powerful she was.

"You can be mad at him and still be in love with him. That will happen throughout your life. I've been furious with Rainer more times than I can count. That doesn't mean I've ever loved him any less. But, I'll tell you this, being with guys who are really strong Ioses Predilects can take some getting used to. It's in their very being to find out everything they can, especially about people they care about. I'm sure that's why he decided to snoop. He probably really didn't mean to hurt your feelings or to be nosy. Everything they do is to protect the people they love. Sometimes their shields take over their brains. And now he's become your Shield, so he's always going to be intense when it comes to you. Surely you remember how Rainer acted about the topless beach. They can't always see through their shields."

"Ugh," Fionna huffed. Dan allowed himself to breathe again when he caught the note of teasing in her tone. "You're my friend. You have to take my side."

"Oh, right, sorry." Emily giggled. "Boys are just nosy, and annoying, and stupid."

"I know, right?"

Dan listened to them both crack up.

"You could torture him. Use them in front of him but don't let him join in."

Dan almost choked over Emily's strategizing.

"Oh, honey, if you think that's torture, I still have so much to teach you." They began laughing again. Fionna stopped abruptly. "But he's a boy, and I don't know how to live with a boy. I've never lived with a boy. Boys are gross!"

Dan had to forcibly quell his laughter.

"You teach me all the stuff to do to torture Rainer, and I'll teach you all about living with boys because I've never *not* lived with boys. So many boys!"

"I'm listening," Fionna commanded.

"Does he leave the toilet seat up?"

"Never," Fionna replied. Dan huffed silently. He grew up with sisters, and he was a gentleman.

"Oh, you have no idea how good you have it. Rainer always lowers it, but I have nine brothers, remember?"

Fionna giggled. "Yes, but two of them are still in diapers."

"That is true."

"I'm serious. I don't know how to do this. What if I need to wear that pink pimple stuff on my face to bed? What if I throw up or really stink up the bathroom? What if I get something on his sheets when I'm on my period, or I drool in my sleep, or what if I want to play with *those*?"

Dan assumed she'd gestured to the bedside table drawer.

"He's never seen me in curlers or when I wear that green mask to clean out my pores. What about when I put smashed up avocado and egg on my hair with a shower cap for like an hour? How am I supposed to wax my lip? What if I want to go to Sephora and spend a ridiculous amount of money and come home and use everything I bought? Oh, my gosh. I'm gonna completely freak him out. He's gonna kick me out for being a weirdo." Fionna sounded truly devastated.

Dan's heart sank as he awaited Emily's reply.

"Deep breath. He is not going to kick you out. He loves you, and the best part about living together is that you get to see that he's going to love you even with wax on your lip and avocado in your hair," Emily assured her. "And, very conveniently, Iodex officers usually have to work late a few times a month, so you could do all of that then."

"Do you shave every day because you know Rainer's going to be in bed with you every night?"

"No, I don't shave every day, and we don't have sex every night. Rainer's fine with both. And you know what else? Sometimes we have sex, and I haven't shaved that day, and he's still fine. He still loves me. He doesn't care."

Fionna whimpered, "Yeah, but you know he's always going to love you. He always *has* loved you."

"Are you going to get mad and leave if he jacks off in the shower?"

Dan was stunned. Heat gathered in his face. He was shocked by Emily's frankness.

"Of course not, he's a guy."

"Ah," Emily tried to make Fionna understand. "Are you going to leave him if he gets a stomach virus?"

"No, of course not. Poor thing, I would take care of him."

"Uh-huh."

"I know. I just…what if I love him more than he loves me?"

Fionna finally stated the thing that had Dan moving. Simply unable to stand in the hallway and allow her to torture herself anymore, he stalked into the room. He felt doubly guilty that he'd been listening in right after apologizing for snooping. The ladies shared a knowing glance.

"Emily, could I talk to Fionna, please?" Dan wasn't taking no for an answer.

"Of course. She certainly isn't listening to me." Emily pulled the door closed on her way out.

"How much of that did you hear?" Fionna grabbed a pillow and hugged it to her chest. She physically shielded herself from him, and Dan could feel her internal shield set firmly.

The absence robbed him of breath and peace. His entire body ached. His shield tensed and tried to move over his body. He pushed it back.

"Enough to know that I haven't really made you understand how much you mean to me." He'd fight with her for her if he had to, and he was about to show her that. Pain broadcast from Fionna's entire being.

"Fi, baby." Dan eased to the bed. He was careful not to touch her. He'd give her as much space as she needed. "I adore every single thing about you, even the things that you don't like, or that you're just a little bit ashamed of." He gestured to the bedside table and hated that she felt shame at all. "If you want to lock me out of our bathroom, or bedroom or, hell, the whole house, for an entire evening and tell me to leave you the hell alone, then do it. I won't ask questions, just so long as I get you back whenever you're ready to let me back in.

"I will give you as much time and as much space as you need. I just want to know that you're mine and that you want to be mine. I'd like to think that you're comfortable enough with me to tell me you need a little space."

"I don't want space. I love to be with you. I just don't think you're going to want to be with me while I do really embarrassing girl stuff." Her entire body folded in around the pillow with every word she uttered.

"Hey," he hesitantly caressed her shoulder. She seemed to soften as he touched her, so he pulled her in closer. "You are talking to the guy who spent his entire adolescence sharing a bathroom with his three sisters all going through their formative years. There is very little that I haven't seen or that would shock me." He reveled in her slight giggle.

She was quiet for the length of one heartbeat. "What if I get sick?" Determined fire lit in her eyes as she began her test.

"Then I'll take care of you. And I happen to know of several times that Rainer and Logan have cleaned up after Emily and Adeline, and they still adore them."

"What if I bleed all over your sheets?" Desperation to know that he wouldn't come unglued overrode her embarrassment over the subject matter.

Dan never missed a beat. "Then I will make certain you're okay. I'd make you comfortable on the couch, and then I'll wash the sheets. I'll put a different set on the bed, and then I will put you back to bed until you feel better." He never dropped her gaze. "And I also happen to know that before Adeline's surgery, she was waking up in pools of her own blood regularly, and Logan Haydenshire couldn't wait to meet her at the end of that aisle and vow to love her forever."

"What if I don't want to have sex, or I'm tired after practice?"

"Then I'll lie down beside you and hold on to you as tightly as you'll let me. I'll watch you go to sleep, and then I'll thank God that you're there with me."

This elicited a slight smile.

"What if I have to wear pink pimple cream to bed because I have a huge, nasty zit?"

Dan chuckled and shook his head. He was quite certain he was the luckiest man alive. "Then I will think you're adorable and that you freaking out about a pimple I never even noticed is quite cute. Then I'll probably steal some of the stuff whenever I have one."

"What if I get sick?" she asked again. "I mean like pale, fever-y sick, and I don't shave or shower for days, and the only time I get up is to puke?" She pulled away from Dan, horrified for being a human, he supposed.

"I will take care of you, but I guess I'd be shocked." Fire burned in him as well. He would get her to listen if it was the last thing he did. "I didn't know that angels sent straight from heaven to pull me right out of the depths of hell could get sick, but you can be damn certain I'll take care of the one heaven sent me."

She melted. "Thank you," she swooned, and he allowed himself to breathe. "That was so sweet, but…" She continued to equivocate.

"I adore each and every single thing about you. Sick, mad, happy, sad, horny, every emotion you could name, I want them all. I want to be there for every single thing."

Staring into her eyes, he offered her his hand. A moment later he orbed his shield around her. An Ioses Shield held the very essence of their energy. He would never lie to her, but she needed him to prove himself. "I want every single thing." He repeated his vow. His rhythms proved his words.

"Okay." She swallowed hard and seemed to draw on deep determination. "Let's finish packing."

She opened her other closet door and revealed a vast inventory of shoes. She pulled a makeup bag from the depths of the closet and then moved to the bedside table. With a slight shudder, she pulled it open.

While holding her eyes with his own, Dan caught her hand and stopped her from reaching for everything in the drawer. He grabbed the vibrators, lube, feather teasers, and a very intriguing yellow toy duck, and slid them into the bag. Instead of asking, he took an empty box and loaded in the vast inventory of books from the lower drawer. "See? No big deal. Incredibly hot, actually." He winked at her and watched another deep blush travel up her neck and settle in her face.

"Ask me," she commanded.

He laughed. "Just curious about the duck," he admitted. "The beak?"

"Sometimes it's the beak. Sometimes it's the tail. He's my favorite shower buddy."

Dan winked at her. "I'm only a little jealous."

"Maybe you two could team up." She waggled her eyebrows.

He leaned and gave her the shuddering growl she was after. "If you'll let me in the shower with you two, I promise I'll teach the duck several new tricks."

Dan moved to the shoe closet. "Do we have a padded suitcase with a fingerprint lock or something for this?" He lifted the pink suede case that contained all of the seasons of *Sex and the City* into his hands.

Fionna giggled. "No, but I'm thinking that your mother wouldn't believe I was a sweet, kind, wonderful girl if she knew that was my all-time favorite show."

Dan rolled his eyes, shook his head, and pulled Fionna into the shoe closet with him. "My mother has a way that her world works, and as much as I love and respect my dad, he's just gone along with the way my mom likes to think everything should be. He's never challenged her views on anything."

Fionna studied him intently. She seemed eager to learn more about Vindico family dynamics.

"Example," Dan continued. "When Meredith threw Kara a bachelorette party in Nashville, our mother just pretended that it wasn't happening. She refused to hear anything about it at all. That's the way she always was with Lindley. She just wanted to ignore the problems away.

"After Amelia died, when I was a complete disaster, she pretended nothing was wrong. When Governor Lawson brought me home for weeks to clean me up, and there was serious discussion of me going into rehab, she told her friends I was doing volunteer work in the

Congo. My mother's perception of reality is very, very skewed, because she believes the lies she tells.

"I'm serious. Ask Kara. Zach was jumping in the sack with my sister for years before he ever put a ring on her finger, but Mom pretended Kara hadn't had sex before and told her the night before their wedding that she would have to do that occasionally to keep Zach happy after the wedding, but that it wasn't for her to enjoy."

Fionna gave him an incredulous look.

"Do you want me to get Kara back up here?"

"No, I believe you. It just seems like…" She halted abruptly, not certain if she should go on.

"What, honey? Just tell me."

"Like your mom might not be very happy."

"My mother is all about the show. If everything falls into place to make her family look like we've got it all together, like life has somehow magically skipped over us, then she's very happy."

"So, she's never really happy, then?"

Dan let the realization work through him. He'd never looked at it that way. His mother was constantly disappointed because life never worked out just the way she dreamed it should. "No, I guess she's not."

They began gingerly loading shoes into the boxes Dan had brought into the room.

"So, your mom's basic opinion of sex would be…?"

Dan scowled. He tried never to think about his mother and sex at the same moment, but Fionna deserved to know after his mother's diatribe on how she was certain that Fionna was a kind, sweet girl.

"That women don't like it and give in only occasionally to keep a guy around. It's improper and should certainly only be done in the confines of marriage. Its main purpose is procreation."

Fionna wrinkled her nose adorably. "Maybe your dad's doing it wrong."

Dan shuddered. "Do not *ever* want to think about that."

By nine o'clock that evening, all of the furniture had been placed and the tree had been resurrected in Dan's living room. Some of the boxes had been unpacked, but there were several dozen left to be sorted through. Fionna was thoroughly exhausted, and Dan had thanked everyone profusely for their help just prior to telling them to go on home and get some rest.

He was fairly certain everyone knew he was politely kicking them out so he could take care of Fionna. His mother was the only one who seemed to mind.

In all of her rabid enthusiasm, she'd left the stacks and stacks of catalogs that Fionna hadn't had time to go through with sticky notes marking the items she thought would be best in the house.

Dan heated a mug of water with his hand. He dipped a loosely folded teabag from Fionna's grandparents' farm in the mug. He joined her on the couch and supplied her with the tea.

"I'm so tired," she whimpered as she took restorative sips.

"I know, sweetheart. I'm taking you to bed as soon as you finish that tea."

Fionna's weary eyes fell to the stacks of catalogs on the table. She shook her head with a slight sigh.

"I swear I will try to limit your exposure to her."

"She's really sweet. Kind of. She's just a little…insistent."

Dan knew *insistent* was the nicest thing Fionna could come up with at the moment, not that he blamed her at all.

A deep yawn overtook her as she continued to nurse the tea. Her blinks grew heavier the longer they sat in the calm serenity of the lights of the Christmas tree. After the emotional chaos of nighttime intruders and the onslaught of family and friends throughout their endless day, she was out of emotional bandwidth.

Dan relieved her of the mug. "Come on, baby." He helped her up. Then he stood and lifted her into his arms. He carried her up the stairs. It was the first time he'd ever felt at home inside the house he'd lived in for the past nine years.

Fionna pulled her clothes off and fell into bed. Dan brushed his teeth and leaned in to whisper a kiss across her cheek.

She was already sleeping. He covered her up tenderly and moved in beside her, thanking God she was there and holding her close, just as he'd promised.

CHAPTER 10
HIGHWAY BRIBERY

The next morning, Fionna insisted that Dan go into work because Emily was picking her up for their day at the Stylers' bakery. She'd decided they could start unpacking that evening.

Dan leapt off the treadmill. He was covered in sweat and smiling at the information displayed on the screen.

He'd spent the hour before pounding out his frustrations into the heavy bag. Wretchkinsides, Eric Kent, the monumental task of ending the Interfeci before he could really have Fionna, and the heated desire that came from having her voluptuous curves tucked up in his arms while she slept, reverberated with every hardened blow he made.

Every lush contour of her body drove him harder. He wanted the world to know to whom she belonged. She'd complained about her weight that morning. He was certain she was absolute perfection.

He stepped into the shower with thoughts of her thick hips swaying over him and of her ample cleavage dancing before his eyes.

The shower water did little to wash away his hunger, but it chiseled away the sweat he'd drowned himself in.

He heard his cell chirp as he shut off the powerful stream. After drying off, he read, *Em's here. We're heading out. Emily's leaving the bakery at lunch to go help her mom. I'll get Garrett to bring me home when I've finished working.*

He glared at the screen as if the phone had mortally wounded him. Resisting the jealously had proved futile. He tried to shift it from Garrett to the things that Garrett was able to do both with and for her that he couldn't do.

He replied to her text and then sank into his desk chair, still trying to avoid looking at the paperwork on Eric Kent he was going to have to go over. He'd been taken to Felsink early Sunday morning.

Everyone arrived for the Monday morning meeting.

Before Dan could dive in, Missy Rifken, who served as the head coordinator for Iodex, poked her head in Dan's office. "Dan, Thomas Kent is here. He's demanding to see you. I've told him repeatedly you're in a meeting and that he'd have to wait. But he isn't taking no for an answer."

"Guess I know where Eric gets it from," Dan huffed. "Tell him he can either wait patiently or wait in a cell."

Missy nodded her agreement and backed out of Dan's office. "All right, let's actually accomplish something. I'm sending a Non-Elite, undercover, partnered team back to The Tantra for the next few days. I want every Interfeci phone we can get a signal on cloned. Currently, we have enough evidence to put Adderand away for life. Fitz is holding the gun he used in two homicides in Lyon a month ago. We've got his prints and traces of his and the victim's blood on a shirt he tossed. I just need the shit-sack himself. He's taken Cascavel's place, but I don't intend for him to hold the title for long."

He ignored the concerned glances he was receiving from most of his Elite team. Having cell phones cloned wasn't exactly legal, and the information they obtained wouldn't be admissible in court. Dan had decided that whatever they found out probably wouldn't be what they arrested them for so it wouldn't matter. He was tired of playing by the rules.

"I want this over with and Wretchkinsides ended. I have things I want to do, and I can't do them until I know he's in the ground somewhere." As Coriolis prison was far beneath the earth's surface, Dan didn't particularly care if his team thought that was what he meant. "After New Year's, when we all get back, we're going to focus on taking them down. This has gone on long enough."

Before his hand-selected, highly skilled team could attempt to talk him out of his renewed obsession, Dan ended the meeting. "All right, Officer Haydenshire, let's go talk to Papa Kent."

Garrett chuckled. "You got it, boss." He brushed off Logan and Rainer's concerned glances and mouthed the word, "Later."

Dan and Garrett exited the office after handing out assignments for the week.

"These things you have planned after we end Wretchkinsides—do they happen to involve a big, fat diamond ring?" His expression was a mix of concern, curiosity, and bewilderment.

"Is that a problem?"

"No, I just never thought I'd hear that from you. Does she want to get married too?"

"We haven't discussed it yet. I'm sure as hell not ready to do it any time soon, but having the option would be nice. I don't have that until he's gone. Didn't you tell me that's what kind of man Fionna deserves?"

Garrett nodded. "All right, what's your plan for Mr. Kent, here?" They approached the room where Thomas Kent was being held. "You know we're about to get bribed."

"I know, and my plan is to give him enough rope to hang himself and then make him sorry he raised such a low-life prick and that he was born with ears."

"That's one way, I guess. It's been a long time since I heard an official Dan Vindico dressing down, but I think you better let me handle this one since everyone thinks I was there."

"Fine, but don't take any of his crap." Dan flung the door open and leveled a derisive glare at Kent as he stalked into the room.

"I do not like to be kept waiting, Chief Vindico. I have important things that demand my attention today," was Kent's scornful greeting as he paced in the room.

Garrett's eyes goggled in shock as Dan bared his teeth in rage. "If I were you, I'd sit down and shut the fuck up before I do several other things you're not going to like." Dan leaned across the table on his fists and stared down Thomas Kent.

Kent sank into one of the chairs in the conference room.

Garrett moved his enraged scowl within inches of Kent's face. "Let me tell you a few things I don't like, Thomas. I do not like to be awakened in the middle of the night because some shit-faced moron is breaking into my girlfriend's home, terrifying her. I do not like men who can't seem to figure out that 'no, I will not go on another date with you, and by the way, here's a restraining order to prove my point,' means leave her the hell alone. I do not like having to leave my girlfriend terrified and crying, locked in a room, while I stalk around her home with a pistol because some idiot can't take no for an answer." He raged in fury. Dan was impressed. "I do not like having to call my officers out of bed in the middle of the night for backup. I do not like men who try to buy their way out of their problems, and I sure as hell don't like your son. So, I'm not certain why you're here today, but I suggest you make it quick, because you'll find I have a very, very short fuse when it comes to Fionna," he snarled.

"Couldn't have said that better myself," Dan added. As Garrett had taken the very words Dan would've used, the statement was the truth.

"Fine, I can see that neither of you are to be taken lightly," Kent huffed. Dan drew himself up to full height. His muscles clenched of their own accord.

"You could say that." Garrett shook his head in disgust.

Kent reached into his jacket pocket. Garrett and Dan both immediately slipped their hands to the pistols on their holsters. They pulled on instinct.

A simultaneous breath of relief exited their lungs when Kent slipped a checkbook from his pocket and flipped it open. "Eric told me you both have some kind of odd relationship with Ms. Styler, so there must be something for Christmas that would delight her—a new car, a Rolex, tennis bracelet, hell, a new house. Just name your price for making this all go away."

"I'm not sure what Eric might've told you, but I have nothing going on with Fionna beyond her being a friend of mine," Dan corrected.

"Yes, well, Eric never liked competition."

Dan had certainly experienced his fair share of attempted bribery for shortening a sentence or hiding an arrest, but never anything so overt. "You are aware that you just attempted to bribe the Chief of Iodex and the top ranking Elite officer?"

Kent rolled his eyes. "Don't be juvenile, gentlemen. The world runs on cash, and the one with the biggest bank account wins. Name your price."

Ire shot rapidly through Dan's veins. He leaned back across the marble table and dared Thomas Kent to drop his gaze. "You're under arrest for attempting to bribe officers of the American Gifted Realm." Dan kept his voice low but toxic.

Garrett moved to Kent, hoisted him from his seat, and slapped cuffs on him.

"You know you're only keeping Eric in prison because he happens to have a crush on your plaything. He'll get over it. He'll move on. Just let him out."

"Let me tell you why I am keeping your son in Felsink Prison, and why he'll stay there for a very, very long time," Dan threatened furiously. He threw Eric's file down on the marble table. The *thwack* of the folder as it hit the marble startled Kent.

"I don't give a damn who your son has a crush on. He is a prick, and as far as I'm concerned, an abusive asshole with some extremely concerning sexually deviant behaviors. Your son showed up repeatedly at Fionna Styler's home, uninvited, and continued to do so after being asked to stop. He was presented with a restraining order."

"That *he* forced her to sign," Kent motioned his head toward Garrett. Dan's eyes flashed furiously as Garrett shook his head.

"Shut the fuck up, and listen to me. You're in so deep right now you need a backhoe just to dig your way to the surface. Officer Haydenshire does not force his girlfriend, or any woman for that matter, to do anything they do not want to do, but I am definitely beginning to understand how it is that Eric became such a chauvinistic moron. I guess the apple doesn't fall too far from the proverbial tree, now does it, Thomas? Not only did Eric choose to ignore the restraining order, he proceeded to take himself down to Angels Arena, where he threatened Ms. Styler and the team.

"We locked him up. The Crown Governor told you that if he screwed up again he was going to jail. Guess what? Governor Haydenshire always follows through on his threats and so do I.

"He shattered a window in Miss Styler's home with his bare hands, and yes, I have fingerprints to prove that. He gained himself access to the deadbolt, which is also covered in his prints. His blood alcohol content when Officer Haydenshire arrested him was over four times the legal limit. He was belligerent when approached. I also have his prints all over Ms. Styler's kitchen. He then lunged at Officer Haydenshire with a knife!

"Eric has a problem, and I think it's high time you stop buying his way out. You need to deal with the problem, but as it stands right now, he'll serve several years for driving drunk, ten for breaking and entering with the intent to harm, and we'll add another five for resisting arrest and battering an officer. It will be another three to five because he's a menace to society. So, the next time you see your son, when he's brought into the courtroom in enhanced cuffs and shackles, you just think about what your checkbook has gained you because our integrity and the safety of Officer Haydenshire's girlfriend do not have a price tag."

Dan scooped the file up off the table. "Take the cuffs off. If he tries anything else stupid, he can share a cell with his kid." He stalked from the room and slammed the door behind him.

Garrett escorted Kent out and then located Dan who'd returned to his office.

"What'd he say?" Dan was still furious.

"That his lawyers would be calling you, and that we'd left Eric no options because we deleted Fi's number from his phone."

"Unbelievable."

"You can't save 'em all. At least Eric's not going to be a problem for quite a while."

Dan nodded. "Hey, let me take you out to lunch." The need to make amends for all of Garrett's help settled with a hearty dose of guilt in Dan's gut.

Garrett looked surprised but gave Dan his signature smirk. "Love to, but can't. I'm taking Logan and Rainer to Sam's to pick up Logan's new truck. You wanna come along? We're gonna grab something on the way back. You know Rainer and Logan will be all over the truck, and one doesn't travel without the other, ever."

Dan chuckled. "Sure, if Logan and Rainer won't mind. I need to talk to Sam about something anyway."

"Are you shitting me? They should be honored. They're definitely not cool enough to get to hang out with us." Garrett and Dan laughed at all that had changed in the last decade and all that hadn't.

Fionna texted again as Dan climbed into Garrett's Highlander. He was still shocked at how much he liked hearing from her throughout the day. It gave him peace, and he liked the way his heart picked up pace when he saw her name.

Mrs. Haydenshire invited us to dinner at the farmhouse. Lucas is coming into town for Christmas. I think she needs some help. I'll just go home with Emily.

"So, your father-in-law's arriving today, Haydenshire?" Dan quipped as he replied that he was more than happy to come over and help out.

"Please don't remind me." Logan rolled his eyes. "Adeline's a disaster. Mom's a disaster. They're driving me crazy."

"Mom's afraid he's going to show up with a full-blown staff that's going to ruin Christmas," Garrett explained.

"Could happen." Dan thought back to their time at the castle in Sydney.

"No joke. And you know *Santa* brings presents for Keaton and Henry, and then the rest of us just try to do something for the community or whatever."

"Yeah, I think that's an outstanding idea. I wish my family would do that." Dan had always admired the Haydenshires' willingness to give of themselves, no matter what rank and pay they held in the Realm.

"Well, the Premier's son is apparently arriving with gifts for us all." Garrett, Rainer, and Logan all shuddered uncomfortably. None of them liked elaborate displays of presentation.

"You know,"—Logan shook his head—"although obviously his DNA is part of the most phenomenal woman in the world, so I'm thrilled that he exists, he's really just an idiot who banged a prostitute when he was seventeen years old. I don't see how that warrants everyone freaking out about his arrival or any special treatment."

Rainer laughed. "Geez, tell us what you really think, Lo."

A few hours later, Dan followed Logan and Garrett out to the Iodex parking deck. "Good luck with Daddy Nguyen. We'll all be there to back you up tonight," Dan offered Logan.

The longing to leave work and to get to Fionna continued to both confuse and irritate Dan. He couldn't end Wretchkinsides without actually working, but Fionna was the most intoxicating aphrodisiac Dan had ever experienced. He wanted no reprieve from his enslavement.

Logan was meeting Lucas's plane at six and then driving him back to the farm in his new GMC Sierra Denali Ultimate. Rainer had already left to pick Adeline up from the hospital, and Garrett and Dan were heading to the farm.

"Do you think you're gonna buy it?" Garrett gestured to the car parked beside Dan's bike. Sam had it on the lot when they arrived, and Dan had been salivating over it as soon as his boots hit the gravel.

Sam offered to let him drive it home to see what he thought, and then he'd sweetened the deal by informing Dan that it had already been enhanced. Sam had taken it in from a Ferrari dealership, and it had a few thousand miles. He'd offered Dan a pretty sweet deal.

"I have to see what Fi thinks."

"Oh, I'm sure she'll hate it," Garrett joked as he visibly admired the jet-black Ferrari 599 GTB Fiorano. Dan had never driven anything like it.

The car seemed to read his thoughts, and it topped out well over 300 mph, if he should find himself somewhere he needed to get away from quickly. Had Dan not just spent millions on Angels stock, he probably would have made the purchase that afternoon. Sam had pointed out that he should probably include Fionna in the decision.

. . .

Dan pulled onto the Haydenshires' vast farm and let the peace he always felt whenever he visited ease his weary mood. It occurred to him, as he watched the gates open, that he'd never felt that at his own home growing up.

Fionna and Emily emerged from the kitchen, each carrying one of the twins.

"Wow, Chief Vindico, did you do a little shopping at lunch?" Fionna's curious glance flickered back and forth between Dan and the car.

Dan chuckled as he popped a kiss onto her cheek.

"No kissing. Juck!" Keaton scolded him. He pointed his tiny finger at Dan in consternation. Fionna and Emily both cracked up. Dan joined in the laughter and scrubbed the little guy's head gently.

"He's clearly been talking with your father."

"I think Keaton has a little crush," Emily explained unnecessarily.

"Well, he has excellent taste." Dan winked at Fionna, who was shaking her head. He turned back to the car. "This is just on loan. I went with Garrett to get Logan's new truck, and Sam had it on the lot. I thought I'd see if you liked it."

"Very nice." There it was again, that devious grin with the twinkle in her eye. Visions of laying her back over the hood quickly formed in his mind.

"Exactly how much does a Ferrari cost?" Fionna asked.

She'd continued to insist that Dan wouldn't be buying a car if it weren't for her. Determination to make him money on his Angels stock had set her on an edge that Dan was still trying to talk her back from.

"Sam's about as fair as they come, and the price is more than reasonable."

Emily laughed. "You might as well drop that now. Trust me, it won't get you anywhere."

CHAPTER 11
WELCOME TO HAYDENSHIRE FARM
LOGAN HAYDENSHIRE

Logan held his cell phone as he watched the Premier's plane land on the Senate runway. He'd been given explicit instructions by his mother to text her with the number of servants Lucas was bringing with him when he exited the plane.

He was extremely annoyed that he felt nervous. Logan chastised himself. *If you're nervous, you'll just make Adeline more nervous. Get it together, Haydenshire.*

The plane touched down, and Logan drew a steadying breath. He appreciated the fact that his father had gone home, just as he normally would have, and had left Logan to deal with Lucas.

As he studied the plane, Logan grimaced. He watched Lucas descend, followed by his personal assistant and another man who was carrying several suitcases. He texted his mother immediately.

Lucas did thank the pilots and coolant officers before scanning the field and locating Logan, who offered him a halfhearted wave.

Logan forced himself to walk out to meet Lucas and to try to remember his manners. His father-in-law appeared genuinely thrilled to have arrived.

As Logan hadn't really believed that Lucas would travel with his own staff to his daughter's home, he hadn't really planned on the fact that he now had to squeeze four men and ten suitcases into his brand-new truck.

He extended his hand. "Welcome. How was your flight?" He debated as he made his greetings. Normally, he would offer to carry the luggage of whomever he was meeting at the airport. Stephen and Lillian Haydenshire had raised him, after all, but there were people being paid to do that very thing. Logan wondered if it was rude to offer or rude not to. "My truck's this way." He gestured back toward the parking deck.

Lucas suddenly looked as nervous as Logan felt. "Is Adeline here?"

"No, sorry. Rainer picked her up from work. She'll be at the farmhouse when we get there."

"She doesn't have her own means of transportation?" Lucas didn't seem very impressed with Logan's truck.

"She does now, actually. It's a quad cab, so do you mind riding in the backseat?" he asked Lucas's attendants.

"No, sir, but where shall we put the luggage?" After racking his brain for several minutes, Logan recalled that Lucas's personal assistant's name was Fred.

"It'll have to be in the back. At least it's not raining."

"Yes, sir." He looked none too enthused.

Unhidden bewilderment pursed Lucas's lips as he took the passenger seat beside Logan. "You said Adeline has her own car?"

Logan tried very hard not to laugh at the horrified expression on his father-in-law's face. "She does, sir. She wanted my old Accord. It runs great, and it's really just a couple of years old. That's what I taught her to drive when we started dating, and her mom agreed to let her get her license as long as my parents paid for it," Logan commented as he backed out of the parking space.

"But you plan for Adeline to ride with you in this?"

Unable to halt the Haydenshire smirk that was forming on his face, Logan nodded. "Yeah, of course. She rides in my brothers' trucks and in Em's Hummer all the time. Why wouldn't she ride with me?"

"Your sister drives a Humvee?" Disbelief rang in Lucas's inquisitive tone.

"Not exactly. Rainer bought it for her when she made the Angels.

It's completely decked out, leather, Bose sound system, enhanced engine, enhanced roll cage and airbags, the works. It's probably the nicest H3 out there."

Lucas shifted uncomfortably to take in the scenery.

"That's Georgetown Hospital where Ad works." Logan pointed out the vast hospital as he made his way to the interstate. Lucas smiled and nodded.

"How far is your family's farm from here?"

"A little over a half hour if traffic's not too bad. It's in an unincorporated part of Fairfax County. We own about a hundred and twenty acres." He wasn't certain why, but he felt the need to fill the uncomfortable silence.

"It's quite chilly here."

"Yeah, it gets pretty cold in Virginia in the winter." Logan nudged the pedal a little harder. Relieved to have a distraction, he answered his ringing cell.

"Hey, baby, we're on our way." He was delighted to hear his wife's voice on the other end.

"So, he brought his servant people with him?" Adeline sighed.

"Yep," Logan answered carefully.

"I feel terrible. Your poor mom."

"It'll be fine, sweetheart. Don't worry."

"Hey, guess what? I delivered triplets today without anyone but the nurses, and I performed a cesarean. Those were the last things I had to do before I can see patients without Brad there." Excitement lit her words, and Logan's face pulled into a broad grin.

"I'm so proud of you."

"Thank you. That's what your dad said too!"

Logan owed his parents quite a bit where Adeline was concerned. It always made him grin when she was excited that she'd made them proud.

"How's the truck?" she asked.

"It's great. I can't wait for you to see it. You were right. I like the navy blue."

"Oh no!" Adeline gasped.

"What?"

"Keaton is in a mood tonight, and he just stuck his fist into every single pie your mom baked!"

Logan could hear Emily and his mother scolding Keaton in the background. He glanced at his father-in-law and his serving staff and thought about him being served pie with his little brother's fist print in it. He promptly cracked up.

"Don't laugh," Adeline tried to scold him, but she began giggling as well.

"I'll be there in just a minute." Logan exited into McLean.

"Okay, I love you." It still took his breath away whenever she said it.

"I love you too, so much."

Lucas looked impressed as Logan made the approach up to the house and entered through the lion crest gates.

"Will we be staying here or in your guest facilities?" Lucas studied the barns set off by the rolling hills and the vast, picturesque Haydenshire land as the sun set.

"You'll be staying here. We live in the guest facilities." Logan gestured to the farmhouse and followed the well-worn path toward the warm, glowing light from his mother's kitchen.

As he opened the door, Keaton almost bowled him over. He raced out the door, wearing nothing at all and waving what appeared to be a diaper in the air like a flag.

"Keaton!" Mrs. Haydenshire screeched. "I'm sorry, but I cannot chase him."

"We've got it, Mom!" Garrett, Rainer, Governor Haydenshire, Dan, and Levi all took off after him.

Logan guided Lucas and his staff into the kitchen. Henry had climbed up on the window bench seat and then made his way onto the center of the kitchen table. He'd pulled down his jogging pants and announced to Logan that he had Mickey Mouse on his Pull-Ups and that he was wet.

Adeline's eyes goggled as Mrs. Haydenshire shook her head. "I told Stephen those were not going to work."

Emily and Fionna were frantically trying to make the five pies situated on the island not look like a two-year-old's fist had been in the center of them.

Lily Ana's wails echoed off the stone fireplace. Brooke, Will, Patrick, and Lucy were all trying to soothe her. Connor was trying to catch Henry to change his pants. He and Adeline had him cornered, but Henry was contemplating his own escape.

"Well…welcome to Haydenshire Farm," Logan stated in disbelief as he gestured Lucas and his assistants inside the large, chaotic kitchen.

Mrs. Haydenshire patted her face with a kitchen towel. "Please forgive us. Things get a little crazy around here sometimes."

"Hi, Lucas, just one second!" Adeline expertly caught Henry as he leapt off the kitchen table.

"Here, I'll clean him up." Connor relieved Adeline of Henry. "Seriously, man, no one is ever gonna go out with you if you don't get this potty thing down." He carried Henry up the stairs as Logan and Adeline laughed.

Governor Haydenshire returned carrying a naked, screaming Keaton in his arms. He was followed by all of the men who'd assisted in the takedown. They were all short of breath and red-faced from trying to capture a two-year-old.

"Well, I warned you, Lucas. You might get lost in the shuffle. We have quite a brood," the governor joked as he extended his hand to Lucas.

Lucas looked appalled as he shook the governor's hand with Keaton's backside on full display.

"Here, Mrs. Haydenshire, we'll get him dressed." Fionna stepped in as she grabbed Keaton and carried him upstairs.

"That kid is fast." Vindico took a long sip from the glass of water Mrs. Haydenshire handed him.

"Nothing is faster than a two-year-old without their clothes on except maybe a teenager without their clothes on," Governor Haydenshire joked.

Everyone in the kitchen, save Lucas and his staff, laughed heartily.

Brooke had finally gotten Lily Ana to settle down and was bouncing her to sleep which allowed everyone to hear themselves think.

"Adeline, why don't you introduce everyone, sweetheart," Mrs. Haydenshire soothed.

"Yes, ma'am." Adeline nodded. "Well, you know Logan, Rainer, and Dan. That was Connor who took Henry upstairs, and this is Patrick and his wife, Lucy. This is Levi and his girlfriend, Sarah. Will, his wife, Brooke, and their little girl, Lily Ana." Adeline beamed at Lily Ana, who was sucking a pacifier fervently as she fell asleep. "That was Keaton that Emily and Fionna had, and this is Mrs. Haydenshire."

"I would apologize and tell you that it's not normally quite so chaotic," Mrs. Haydenshire chuckled, "but that wouldn't be entirely true. So, I'll just say how pleased we are to meet you."

"Uh…oh…well, yes…uh, thank you," Lucas managed to stammer. "I'm Lucas Nguyen, Adeline's father, and this is my personal assistant, Fred, and my assistant liaison, Oliver."

"Assistant liaison?" Levi mouthed. Garrett and Dan tried to choke back laughter.

"Thank you so much for having me. I hope we're not intruding." Lucas began glancing around the large home. Something about the size seemed to calm him.

Fionna and Emily returned. Keaton, who was quite taken with Fionna, was batting his eyelashes at her coyly and beaming at her, before nuzzling his head in her chest. As she neared Dan, Keaton turned and narrowed his eyes. His little face screwed up in indignation.

"No kisses. Juck!" He wagged his finger in Dan's face.

"Hey, she's my girlfriend," he teased.

"No, no, no!" Keaton shouted and shook his head back and forth spastically.

"Got a little competition there, man." Garrett slapped Dan on the back.

"Yeah, and he's awfully cute," Fionna teased as Dan feigned heartache.

Lucas looked extremely out of place with everyone who was so comfortable in the farmhouse. "Perhaps my assistants could stay with your staff while we eat."

Mrs. Haydenshire visibly held back hysterical laughter. She bit her lips and shook her head. "Oh, sweetheart," she tsked, "we don't have a staff. They're going to have to eat with us, which we'll love. The more the merrier."

"No staff at all?" Lucas sounded as if such a thing should be outlawed at once.

"Nah, that's why we had so many kids," the governor teased as he relieved Fionna of Keaton. He then proceeded to laugh at his own joke.

Dinner was served, and everyone settled in. "Now, Lucas, I wasn't certain what kinds of things you might like, so I made my pot roasts and potatoes. I know it's one of Adeline's favorites," Mrs. Haydenshire explained.

"They're not only Adeline's favorites, Mom," Patrick said. Everyone nodded their agreement.

"I'm so pleased to try them, Mrs. Haydenshire." Lucas hesitated. "I'm so sorry, ma'am, please forgive my confusion. Do you have a title?"

Logan chuckled as his mother shook her head reassuringly. "Everyone here either calls me Mom, Mrs. Haydenshire, or Honey, depending on if I birthed them, raised them, or married them. Will and Garrett are the only ones I've ever denied whether I gave birth to them or not although Keaton is quickly joining their ranks." She glared at Keaton who was smearing mashed potatoes all over his high chair tray with a great deal of focus.

Will and Garrett feigned shock, and hearty laughter sounded around the table.

"Yeah, Keaton can get his clothes off almost as fast as Garrett's dates," Patrick sneered, and all of the Haydenshire boys, along with Rainer and Vindico, guffawed. Emily and Adeline tried hard not to giggle without much success. Fionna gave Garrett a sweet smile just before she cracked up.

Governor Haydenshire narrowed his eyes at Patrick. Mrs. Haydenshire shook her head vehemently.

With an astonished stare, Lucas seemed to zero in on Adeline

87

whenever he could. The large crowd at the dining room table overwhelmed him. He did catch the governor's attention long enough to announce, "Crown Governor Haydenshire, my father sent me with a cooler full of mud crabs, fresh. We'd heard you like them. We'll need to get those to your chef before they go cactus."

Mrs. Haydenshire scowled. Governor Haydenshire looked faint. "He really shouldn't have gone to all that trouble. And I don't have a chef. I do have a wife who is a tremendous cook. In fact, everything she does is phenomenal. I'm an extremely lucky man."

Lucas nodded rather uncomfortably. He lowered his head and continued to eat.

Logan wondered what Lucas thought his mother had meant when she'd said they had no staff.

"What does that mean?" Mrs. Haydenshire demanded under her breath.

"That he sent a cooler full of the nastiest crabs I've ever eaten, and that they're still alive and have to be cooked that way."

"Stephen!" Mrs. Haydenshire huffed furiously as she gestured to her very swollen midsection.

"I know, I know. I'm sorry."

With an annoyed sigh, Mrs. Haydenshire rose to retrieve the dessert plates and the pies. "I'm sorry about the pies, everyone. My little ones are just a little bit faster than I am these days."

"Nonsense, sweetheart, they'll still taste delicious, won't they, kids?" Governor Haydenshire insisted as he stood to help her. Everyone was quick to agree.

"After dessert, we'll get Fred and Oliver all squared away, and then Logan and Adeline can show you their house, Lucas." Mrs. Haydenshire licked a bit of blackberry pie filling from her thumb as she began cutting.

Lucas managed a nod but stared at her like she'd just committed a felony. Adeline and Mrs. Haydenshire shared a quizzical shrug and began cutting the different pies. Adeline cut Logan a piece of apple pie much larger than all the others she'd cut.

"Seriously, Miss Adeline," Garrett scoffed, "you're gonna give him extra pie and let him hit that?" He chuckled as Governor and Mrs. Haydenshire shot him looks that said for him to can it quickly. Everyone else laughed. Adeline blushed, and Lucas looked quite concerned.

"That does not mean what you think it means." Logan glared at Garrett who cringed as he realized what Lucas thought he'd meant.

"Sorry," Garrett choked.

"This is really good, Mom." Logan tried to steer the conversation away from Garrett's quip.

"Thank you, sweetheart. It was fun to bake again. I didn't realize how much I've missed it since I've been lying on the couch with my little Abigail." Mrs. Haydenshire slid her hand over her protruding stomach.

Fionna grinned at Mrs. Haydenshire. "Emily told me the names you'd picked out. I think they're beautiful. I love what they mean."

"She certainly seems to like them," Mrs. Haydenshire commented somewhat cryptically to anyone who wasn't aware that Governor and Mrs. Haydenshire talked to Abigail through Mrs. Haydenshire's stomach all the time.

Logan was surprised Fionna didn't look confused at all. Her grin widened, and she nodded. Lily Ana began fussing again in her bassinet from the living room just as Brooke was bringing a piece of berry pie to her mouth.

"I'm finished. Can I get her for you?" Fionna asked, though it bordered on begging.

"Please do. Thank you." Brooke smiled at Fionna as she nearly leapt from the table.

Logan studied Dan. He wondered what he was seeing when Fionna returned, carrying Logan's niece wrapped up tenderly in her blanket. Garrett chuckled as he and Logan both noted Dan's pallor.

"If you'll just hold her until I finish, I'll go feed her," Brooke explained.

"I'd love to." Fionna cradled Lily Ana tenderly.

The governor raised his eyebrows at Dan with a goading smirk. He shook his head and tried to hide his shudder.

At that moment, Will and Fionna happened to look up and meet each other's eyes. They both blushed and looked away making Logan extremely curious.

Dan narrowed his eyes but didn't comment. Instead, he draped his arm over the top of Fionna's chair possessively.

After the pies were consumed and Brooke had relieved Fionna of the baby, everyone began clearing the table.

"Logan, why don't you and Adeline show Lucas, Fred, and Oliver to their rooms? Then you can show Lucas the guesthouse."

"Sure thing, Mom." Logan took Adeline's hand, but she shook her head.

"We'll help with the dishes and put the twins to bed first."

"I won't turn that down. I don't know what I'd do without you."

Lucas studied this exchange intently but didn't comment.

Dan joined in and carried a stack of plates to the sink. "You go sit down, Mrs. Haydenshire. We can do this."

"Fionna and I will put the boys to bed, Mom. You go rest," Emily instructed. Logan realized he wasn't the only one who thought his mother looked weary and pale.

"Thank you all. I think I will," Mrs. Haydenshire declared, much to everyone's delight. She moved slowly into the living room, and the governor helped her sink into her chair.

Everyone pitched in, and it didn't take long to have things cleaned up for the night and the twins tucked up in their beds.

"Would you like to see our house? Logan and Rainer gutted it and rebuilt most everything." Adeline nervously folded and unfolded her hands.

"Hey, they had a little help," Garrett reminded her.

"That's true. The whole family helped."

"I'd be honored, love. You really have an extremely talented family, Governor Haydenshire."

Governor Haydenshire chuckled and nodded his agreement. "They'll do, I suppose." Everyone watching him saw the pride that filled his eyes.

CHAPTER 12
HIS BABY

Logan helped Adeline into the new truck. He was thoroughly enjoying her grin and her exuberance for him. Lucas climbed in behind Adeline, and Logan cranked the engine.

"You love it, don't you?" Adeline giggled as Logan waggled his eyebrows at her.

"Well, not as much as I love you." He caught Lucas's eye roll in the rearview mirror.

Rainer and Emily followed behind them in the Hummer and the Porsche.

"It gets a little bumpy in the back field," Logan explained.

"Rainer offered to let me shift on the way home. He said he'd teach me to drive a stick, but I was afraid I would break his Porsche," Adeline explained.

Logan chuckled and rubbed her leg. "I'll teach you to drive a stick if you want, but you might want to start out with a car that's not a dual-clutch."

Adeline nodded her adamant agreement.

"Are you planning on living on the farm for a while, or will you be moving or building again?" It seemed Lucas was bored with the talk of new cars.

"Rainer and Emily are getting married in April, and they really want to buy a place in Alexandria somewhere near the arena. I was thinking since Ad loves the farm so much, we'd stay here. If I'm here, I can provide my dad security. I want to pay Rainer back for fixing up the house, but if she's happy, that's all that matters." He watched the broad grin spread across Adeline's beautiful face.

"I love it here. It's perfect. I never want to move. I love the whole farm. It's so peaceful and beautiful. It's the first place I ever felt safe."

Logan squeezed her hand. Whenever she said something like that, his heart ached with regret. He longed to have done a thousand things differently. He should have asked her out sooner, insisted she move onto the farm, and had her mother arrested long before she was.

He did realize that Adeline was sharing more with her father sitting in the cab of his new truck than she'd shared the entire time they were in Sydney.

"Here we are." Logan pulled into the driveway of the guesthouse. Lucas studied the tiny house by the moonlight and the outdoor lighting on the driveway.

Emily and Rainer had been on the phone with each other on the drive home. Logan rolled his eyes as they ended the call and continued their conversation.

"All I'm saying is if he buys the Ferrari, I should get to drive it because I introduced him to Sam."

Emily laughed at him outright.

"Come on in." Logan unlocked the door. Adeline smiled at Lucas as they entered and turned on the lights.

Adeline beamed. "So, this is it. I mean, obviously, this is the living room and kitchen." The hint of color in her cheeks was becoming more pronounced. "And that's Rainer and Emily's room, and this is mine and Logan's room." She flipped on the light to their bedroom.

Logan thought she was adorable, but confusion was the predominant expression on her father's face. "It's...uh...very nice." No one believed he thought the house was nice. Adeline's face fell in disappointment.

Emotion cinched in Logan's throat as Adeline proceeded to try and prove their home to her father. She was visibly offended and wary. Her rhythms stuttered.

With the few quick steps it took to get back to the living room, she gestured to the old sofa. "We watch movies here, and we eat here." She moved to the ancient table in the kitchenette. "We eat up at the farmhouse a lot, but Emily's a great cook just like Mrs. Haydenshire."

"Adeline, you're a great cook too," Emily insisted.

"Your nachos are phenomenal," Rainer agreed as everyone realized what Adeline was trying so desperately to prove.

With another quick inventory of their home, she abruptly stopped speaking. She wasn't going to point out the activities that went on in her and Logan's bedroom, so there wasn't much else to elaborate on.

Fury seared through Logan's veins. He didn't need Adeline's father marching in and making her feel like their home, the first place she'd ever felt completely comfortable and content, was somehow not good enough.

He narrowed his eyes at Lucas. "She loves this house."

"Right, of course." Lucas seemed to realize that he'd given himself away. "Perhaps you could expand it, or if you and Logan would like to live somewhere else on the farm, maybe the Crown Governor would let you build in one of the pastures. The land is quite expansive. I'd be happy to give you the money."

Logan moved to Adeline as she reached her hand discreetly toward him. "But I don't want to live anywhere else. I really like this house. Logan built it."

Logan studied her energy as she drew from him. Confusion and the pain of rejection swirled in the depths of fear.

"It has everything we need, and it's the first place we ever lived together." Her voice was now barely a whisper.

Uncomfortable silence filled the room as Rainer offered Logan a sympathetic glance. Emily blinked back tears. Logan was certain she could feel Adeline's pain move through the air.

"Mr. Nguyen, why don't Em and I take you back up to the farmhouse? I know that time difference is a bear." Rainer's shield had tensed a moment before he'd come to Adeline's rescue.

"I was hoping to get to spend a little more time with you, Adeline."

"Oh,"—Adeline forced a smile—"I have to work an early shift in the morning. I'm pulling several twelve-hour days, so I can have

Christmas off, but I'll see you when I get home tomorrow night. Emily and I were going to make you dinner here." She now sounded concerned about that plan.

"That would be lovely. I guess I'll bid you good night." Lucas looked bereaved as he moved toward Adeline. She gave him a hesitant hug, and Rainer gestured him out to the garage.

Adeline fell against Logan's chest as Rainer stopped at the door. "Em and I are gonna go grab some milkshakes. We'll bring you some back." He obviously knew Logan would need time to try to repair the damage Lucas had caused.

"Are you okay?" Logan knew perfectly well she wasn't.

"Why doesn't he like it here?"

Logan hadn't realized until he'd allowed Lucas into their home that what he thought really did matter to Adeline.

"I don't know, baby. I guess because you're a princess, so he was probably thinking we had something a little closer to a castle." Logan tried not to let his irritation perforate his tone.

"Don't say that," Adeline fumed. She stepped away from Logan with a visible shudder. "I'm not a princess. I don't want to be a princess. I want to be your wife, and I want to be a medio. I want to live here, and that's all I want, nothing else. Why can't he understand that?"

Logan moved back to her and placed his hands gently on her shoulders. "You are my wife and you are a phenomenal medio, baby. You're quickly becoming the best in your field, and you delivered triplets today and did a C-section. I'm so proud of everything you do. And I love our house too, because when I get off work you're here, and that's all that will ever matter to me. So, if you're happy here and I'm happy here, I don't think it should really matter what Lucas thinks."

Adeline tucked herself back into his embrace and nodded against him, but she was still devastated. "But you worked so hard on this house, and it's so nice. And you did it for me. It's more than I could ever have dreamed of." She gave in to the threatening tears.

"Shh, baby, it's okay. Please don't cry. I love you so much. It kills me to see you hurt."

Adeline immediately tried to stop crying which only served to make Logan feel bad for asking. "That wasn't very nice after all of your hard work. You built the entire house, and you did it for us." She restated the thing that galled her more than anything else.

"I had a lot of help, and he's your dad, remember?"

She gave him a quizzical look. "I know that."

Logan chuckled at the misunderstanding. "So, you know how really nothing Rainer ever does will be quite good enough for my old man because at the end of the day he's the guy crawling into bed with my sister?"

Adeline gave him a slight grin as she nodded.

"I think maybe that's how dads are about their little girls."

"I'm not his little girl, and I don't want to be. I want to know him, and I'd like to see him occasionally, but…" She paused, hesitant to say whatever was on her mind.

"But what?" Logan pushed a strand of her long, jet-black hair behind her ear.

She blushed. "I just want to be your baby. That's the only thing that really matters to me."

"You are always, always my baby, and I will always take care of you." He'd never realized, in all the years they'd dated, in his relentless, dogged drive to protect her from her mother and from the world, that the one thing Adeline would fight for above all else…was him.

CHAPTER 13
WHERE YOU ARE GOING
RAINER LAWSON

Rainer and Emily shared quick concerned glances on the way back to the farmhouse.

"How long did you say you'd lived here on the farm, uh," —Lucas paused—"may I call you Rainer?"

"Of course." Rainer tried to remember what Lucas had called him in Sydney. It seemed an odd question. "I moved out here just after I turned fourteen, a few weeks after my father was killed." He still found those particular words haunting and afflicting. Emily took his hand. He felt her intoxicating cast work through him discreetly.

"And where did you live when your father was the Crown Governor?"

Rainer tried not to be irritated with the line of questioning. Lucas didn't know that every time Rainer drove past his old neighborhood, he ached with fresh pain. "My house wasn't too far from here. It's out in Great Falls just in a regular subdivision. We didn't have any land like this or anything."

"But the president of the Non-Gifted Realm lives in the White House, an expansive mansion with places for visiting dignitaries and the like to stay, does he not?"

"He does, and look where that's gotten them. They now have money so entrenched in their politics they can't accomplish anything to save their own people because all they can do is campaign for more of it. Half of their politicians are puppets for corporations with the most money. My father really believed that it wasn't where you came from, it was where you were going. He always taught me that the Gifted people have been given so much there was no need to lord our powers and our money over the Non-Gifted Realm. Governor Haydenshire and Governor Vindico, and the entire governing board, agree with that."

"Trust me, if you saw where Adeline grew up, you'd realize how lucky we all were to grow up here." Emily stung from the rejection of her beloved farm and of her best friend. Rainer squeezed her hand and shook his head slightly.

Instead of parking in the large barn, he parked near the side of the farmhouse. Lucas followed them onto the porch as Emily opened the always unlocked kitchen door.

"Stephen, what on earth are we going to do with twenty pounds of live crab? I can hardly reach the stove! I do not know how to cook crab that is still living," Mrs. Haydenshire sounded furious.

"I know, honey. I'm not asking you to cook them. It was that ridiculous article *Women of the Realm* ran that said that crab was the Crown Governor's favorite meal, and that we'd gone out for crab on our first date. Not only do I despise crab, but I couldn't have afforded to take you out for seafood if I'd wanted to."

"Uh, hi!" Emily nearly shouted as both of her parents whirled around to see her.

"Well, that was a quick trip. How did you like the guesthouse? Didn't the kids do a great job?" Miss Haydenshire turned her frustration off quickly.

"It's really something. I think I might just retire to my bedroll. Been a bit of a day," Lucas sighed.

"I'm certain it has. Can I get you anything before you head up?" Governor Haydenshire studied Lucas.

"No, Crown Governor. I'll just send Fred down for a spot of brandy if you have any."

Governor Haydenshire moved to the built-in liquor cabinet that stood in the butler's pantry between the kitchen and dining room.

"Here we go." Governor Haydenshire pulled a bottle of brandy from the cabinets and poured Lucas a shot. "Save Fred the trip."

"Thank you, sir." Lucas looked appalled that the Crown Governor of the American Realm had fixed him a drink.

"And please call me Stephen. Being Crown is my job. It isn't who I am."

"Yes, I think I'm beginning to understand that. Well, good night then." Lucas turned to stalk quickly up the stairs.

"What happened?" Governor Haydenshire demanded as soon as he was gone.

"He was kind of a jerk about the guesthouse, and it really hurt Adeline's feelings. She was crying when we left." Emily's tone increased with her acrimony.

Mrs. Haydenshire shook her head as she sank down in the rocking chair in the kitchen and accepted the tea the governor made for her.

Governor Haydenshire poured himself a shot of the same brandy he'd given Lucas. He settled down at the table. "He has got to stop judging Adeline's life by his standards."

Emily grabbed two Dr Peppers from the fridge and handed one to Rainer. "He really upset her. I didn't know she was going to get so worked up about what he thought."

Her father smiled at her and patted her hand. "That's the home Logan built for her, baby girl."

"And that means the whole world to Adeline," Mrs. Haydenshire concluded.

CHAPTER 14
UN-'WILL'ING CONFESSIONS
DAN VINDICO

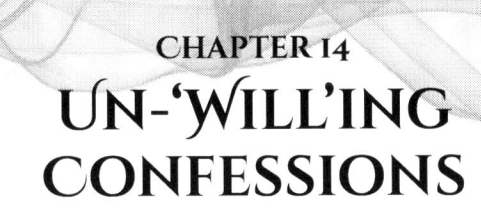

"I don't even want to know what this car cost you nor do I want to think about the sheer amount of money you have spent since we started dating all because of me. You are not allowed to buy me a single Christmas, Valentine, or birthday present for the rest of our lives," Fionna ordered as Dan opened the door to the Ferrari for her and then moved to the driver's side.

He laughed. "That will most definitely not be happening. You hardly let me buy you anything. What do you mean all the money I've spent since we started dating?"

"You just spent millions of dollars on stock in the Angels."

"No," he corrected her as he drove the gravel path off the Haydenshires' farm. The Ferrari drove with ease. It was as if he was on a smooth track. "I invested in the best professional Summation team in the American Realm, which I will most definitely be getting hefty returns on."

"And this car?"

"This car is a sweet, sweet ride and an even sweeter deal. And you were right, I kind of like having heat in the winter." He winked at her. He saw her eye roll from the glint of the streetlamps off the windshield.

They rode in silence back toward their home. Something else was bothering Fionna. Dan could feel it when he held her hand. He just couldn't seem to figure out what it was exactly.

"Do you not like the car?"

"It's a Ferrari, and you're driving it. It's kind of the hottest thing I've ever seen."

He'd fallen in love with the car as soon as Sam had tossed him the keys, so her assessment thrilled him. "Tell me what's wrong then." The scowl that hardened her beautiful face dampened his enjoyment of the car.

"Nothing."

A sudden bolt of memory burned in Dan's mind. Her tone and manner made him tremble. He gripped the steering wheel and fought the haunting memory. *Amelia, what? What the hell is wrong now...?*

"Nothing..."

"Fi, please don't do that. Please."

Her face lost all signs of irritation. She swallowed down what Dan finally figured out was fear.

"I'm sorry. I didn't mean to freak you out by holding the baby." Her devastation was evident in her rhythms. With several measured breaths, Dan came back to the living. He reviewed her explanation in his mind and finally let his body relax.

"That didn't freak me out, sweetheart. You're great with kids. It wouldn't freak me out if you'd like to have a few. I just don't want to do that for a while. As long as you're okay with that, I'm fine."

"I don't want to for a while either, but maybe…someday." Her tone was full of desperate hope.

"'Maybe someday' sounds perfect." He gave her what he hoped was a reassuring smile.

"And you aren't freaking out?"

Dan allowed himself a half second to regulate his heartbeat. After deciding that he was fine, he lifted her hand to his mouth and brushed a tender kiss along her knuckles. "What do you feel in me?" He reminded her of her own phenomenal powers.

"You're…good." She sounded astonished by that fact.

"I told you."

Fionna's energy settled as she sank back into the plush leather seat.

Dan debated, but his curiosity won out over his good sense. "Will you tell me something?"

"Sure." Fionna smiled up at him as a few raindrops splattered against the windshield, making shadowed images across her features. She tucked herself away from the windows.

"Why don't you tell me about how badly I hate Will Haydenshire right now?"

Her eyes goggled, and her face flushed hot before she turned to stare out the window. "Why would you hate Will? You've been the best of friends since you were tiny." Her reply was choked and laced with regret.

Dan was suddenly nauseous. He gripped the steering wheel tighter and tried desperately to think about anything but one of his best friends and Fionna doing what he suspected had happened at some point in the distant past.

"That bad, huh?" Modulating the anger from his voice proved impossible. He wasn't angry with her. He was furious with Will.

"No, not really."

Not certain why he wanted to know, since the concept made him furious, he went on with, "Come on. You and I both know we were with other people before we were together."

"I wasn't *with* him, with him. Please don't ask me this. It was a horrible thing to do, and I still feel so guilty, especially now."

"Don't feel bad. I was just curious. You didn't do anything wrong. You just said you didn't even sleep with him."

She nodded but looked pale and terror-ridden.

Persistent resentment formed rapidly in his shield. He tried to push it away. "So, how far did he get? I won't be mad." *At you* he amended quickly in his head.

"Well..." Fionna looked like she would rather be anywhere else, with anyone else at that moment.

"You don't have to tell me." Dan felt a harrowing sense of loss as Fionna's energy moved away from him and back into her own protective shielding.

"I'll tell you," she sighed, "just please believe me when I say how bad I feel about this now."

Thoroughly confused, Dan nodded his agreement.

"Let me think…uh…I guess he probably got somewhere between second and third base." Her hands trembled. She folded them in her lap and refused to look his direction.

Dan clenched his jaw and kept his glare fixed on the road ahead of him.

Crimson fire burned in her cheeks. "Maybe a little closer to third."

Dan was quite certain he didn't want her to go on. "I wasn't exactly all that into him, so I stopped him about two seconds before Mrs. Haydenshire walked in on us." A mirthless chuckle escaped Dan's lungs. "I keep telling myself she's forgotten about that or maybe praying that she's forgotten. I hope she doesn't still hate me."

Her fear doused some of his gall. "Honey, she has a whole lot of boys. At one point or another, she or the governor walked in on each and every one of them with their hand down someone's pants, trust me." He hoped to bring her a little peace, although his stomach churned combatively when he thought about Will's hands on what he considered to be his and his alone.

"Why'd you let him do that if you weren't that into him?" He recalled that part of her confession.

Fionna's eyes closed in defeat as she let her head fall into her hands. She mumbled something that Dan had no hope of translating.

"Come on, baby. See? I'm not mad." He willed her to believe his lie. The incredulous look she finally granted him told him that she didn't.

She cringed as Dan's brow furrowed. "I did it because I had such a huge crush on you, and I thought maybe he'd tell you. I thought maybe you'd ask me out, but Will's not like that. He would never have told you that. I was trying to get you, and you were going out with Amelia. I am a horrible, horrible person."

Dan shifted the car into park once he'd pulled into the garage, and turned to gaze at Fionna. "I never knew you had a crush on me."

"Obviously, because my plan didn't work," she whimpered.

Dan chuckled and cradled her flushed face in his hands. "Baby, I used to sit in our mixed Creative Writing seminars and stare at your ass while you took notes every single day of my entire sophomore year." He still felt horrendously guilty over that fact, but she needed to hear what he was saying. "I couldn't tell you the mentor's name or one damn thing she said. So, if anyone was a terrible person, it was me."

Fionna shook her head. "You were not a terrible person. You were a horny teenage boy, although I do feel even more guilt now."

"I didn't mean to make you feel worse. I just wanted you to know that I'm honored you liked me and that the feeling was mutual, I guess." He'd always felt so guilty, like he'd cheated on Amelia, whenever he thought about or even dreamed about another girl. "I think I'm just going to go back to being furious with Will."

"You can't be mad at Will. He was just a horny teenage boy too. Do you think Brooke knows?" Guilt broadcast from her entire being.

"No, and I wouldn't bring it up if I were you. She has quite a temper."

Fionna scoffed. "He probably doesn't even remember. Look at who he's married to. She's gorgeous."

"Honey, *you* are gorgeous, and he remembers." Dan bartered his guilt for anger. Incensed fury still took over whenever he thought of his angel in the arms of one of his best friends. He tried to force the images away. "I guess you're right. Will would never have told anyone because I suppose he is kind of a good guy," he allowed begrudgingly.

Fionna laughed at him outright. "It was a long, long time ago."

"Still want to strangle him," Dan huffed. "Come on. Let's go in so I can inhale your perfume instead of Ferrari fumes."

She crawled out of the car and followed Dan into the house. "Want some tea?" Dan helped her out of her black pea coat and kicked off his boots.

"Please." She seated herself on the couch and unbuckled her knee-high boots. Dan returned with tea for her and a beer for himself.

"You're not really mad, are you?"

"I'm not mad at you at all."

"You can't be mad at Will. You've been friends forever."

"Yeah, and I know what a player he used to be before he met Brooke. He's two years older than you. Clearly, he took advantage." Fionna bit her lip to keep from laughing. "You probably had no idea what he had in mind when you agreed to hang out with him." Unable to fight it any longer, with her entire face tensed to halt the outpour, she finally doubled over in hysterical laughter.

"I guess he *was* pretty quick with those hands," she agreed a full minute later, though she was still giggling.

Dan threw his hands out. "See?"

With the past performing rapid-fire assaults on his mind, Dan huffed, "Did he use his, *Oh baby, you don't mind, do you? I just can't keep my hands off you. I want to touch you so bad'* line when he felt you up?"

She continued her hysterical laughter with her face still glowing in heated fever. "You know, I think he did say that." Dan rolled his eyes as Fionna snuggled into his arms. "I really hadn't even thought about it until I saw him tonight."

After drawing a long sip of her tea, she turned her beautiful brown eyes on Dan's. "I was really scheming, and I really do feel terrible about it. It was all to get where I'm sitting right now, and that makes me feel even worse."

Dan set the bottle of beer on the table beside him and wrapped his arms around her. "It was a long time ago, and we were all just teenagers. We all did some things we wish we hadn't."

"I'm sorry."

"Honey, you didn't do anything to me, and trust me, Will isn't sorry."

"Yeah, I know. I just wish I could apologize to the person that I should apologize to." Her whispered regret rocked through his unsteady psyche.

"Fi," Dan's voice shattered. That was too much. He couldn't allow himself to fathom such a thing. He couldn't envision a conversation between Amelia and Fionna. His heart simply couldn't bear it.

"Wanna just never talk about it again?"

"Yeah, that'd be good." He brushed a kiss against her forehead. She gently touched his temple and then moved her caress to his neck. Continuing her journey, she took his right hand, and her cast worked through him.

Defeat plagued him, but he was unable to stop himself. He drew from her and felt his body and his shield calm.

A full minute later, he was able to smile. "Might have to harass Will the next time I see him without his wife," he threatened.

Fionna wrinkled her nose, a sight Dan was growing more addicted to every time he saw it. "Let's not talk to Will, but we could blame him. I'm good with the whole 'he was taking advantage of me in my young and inexperienced state.'"

Dan chuckled but only for a moment. His jaw clenched again before he demanded, "Just how inexperienced were you?"

"Why do you keep asking all of the things I don't want to tell you?"

The air trapped in his lungs escaped in a huff. "Fi, please tell me he wasn't the first guy to ever…?"

She covered her face with her hands and nodded.

"I was a pre-freshman. We'd moved here over the summer, and I didn't know a lot of people. I thought he was cute and polite, and he was your best friend, and I really liked you."

"I'm going to kill him." His eyes landed on the table near the front door where he had all the necessary implements needed for shooting someone.

"Oh, come on, I was sixteen."

"Exactly."

"Didn't you do that before you were sixteen?" She knew perfectly well that she had him cornered.

"I was an asshole. Who do you think taught him the 'I just can't keep my hands off you' line?"

Fionna's adorable giggle did shatter some of his ire.

"Did he hurt you?" Dan demanded as he recalled the first time he'd done that.

"Dan, stop it. No, he didn't hurt me." She rolled her eyes at him. "He was very sweet, very gentle, all the things he was supposed to be."

"Ugh, I do not want to hear about you and Will." Dan shuddered at the recurring images.

"Then stop asking me." She laughed. "I don't really want to tell you, but I always kind of thought he knew he was the first. You know, once he did it, because he backed off really quickly."

Vomit and bile churned in Dan's stomach and singed his throat.

"Yeah, well, you weren't his first, so he probably did. All the more reason he should have stopped."

Fionna shook her head at him. "He did stop as soon as I said stop. His dad yelled at him for a long time."

"Good."

"Would you stop it?"

Dan continued to order away the images his brain had conjured without much success.

"Would you feel better if I let you get to third base?" She seemed to want to put the confessions and adolescent stories away.

CHAPTER 15
CLAIMED

Very intrigued, Dan nodded. "Maybe." With a goading smirk, he cradled her to him, then brushed his thumb over her nipple as he cupped her left breast in his hand. "You know, I just can't keep my hands off them. I want to touch you so bad."

Her breaths came quicker as she gave him a sexy half grin. "It was a pretty good line."

"It's not a line anymore."

A slight, eager moan escaped her. He couldn't fight it. He knew it was ridiculous and chauvinistic, but he wanted to own her, to brand her.

No one else could have her because she was his, and he planned to show her that. He'd make a claim so deep and so intimate she'd never doubt whose bed she belonged in. The stirring, exhilarating waves of her heat rose around him, perfuming the air. She was his.

"If you're sweet, I'll even let you take my bra off," she teased. Her eyes were dark and eager as he traced taunting patterns up her skirt with his index finger.

"Oh, honey, I'm not going to be sweet, but I am going to be very, very thorough." Suddenly only aware of his throbbing erection, the essence of her, those luscious curves, the need ate at him. He ravaged the soft skin of her neck. "I'm gonna take you, baby doll. I'm gonna strip you down. I'm gonna suck you and mark you. I'm going to ruin you, because you're mine. All fucking mine. I'm gonna make you scream out my name, make you take it so deep all you feel is me inside of you, and all you want is sweet relief." The whispered plans swirled heatedly around her neck.

"Yes." Her body began the desperate, needy writhing that drove him wild.

"Are you casted, baby?" He forced himself to make certain of that before he staked his claim. She nodded against him, and he continued to move torturously slowly.

He wanted her to ache for his touch, long for his fullness, to be desperate for him. He continued his devastating moves, swirling his tongue over the hollow of her neck as he edged toward her earlobe.

"Are you wet for me, baby?" As he asked, he found his answer. His fingers had reached their destination under her skirt. "Oh yeah," he groaned as he felt the damp, heated satin that he traced and explored. "Such a good girl." His index finger slid slowly down her slit, and the silky heat continued to develop under her skin.

He pulled her earlobe in his mouth, sucking tenderly and then with intensity. Her breath caught as he slid his teeth over the sweet skin, and she trembled against him.

Reaching, he pulled her sweater over her head and groaned as he took in her breasts, swollen and pert, spilling over the top of the sheer black lace bra.

"These are mine," he declared. Her head fell back, and she panted in anticipation. "All mine, just like those sweet lips and that sexy ass. All for me."

He turned and laid her down on the couch. He lay on his side and dragged his hand from her neck to the top of her skirt. He leaned and stroked his tongue roughly over her right nipple, through the lace that covered it.

She shuddered from the sensation. "Please," she begged as she arched her back and lifted her breasts toward his mouth. Her nipples stood in puckered mounds, raw from the lace of her bra, desperate for relief.

Dan reached and unhooked the bra, in one quick, well-rehearsed move. "That hurts, doesn't it, baby?" Dan gently touched the dark swollen buds as he thought of all the deliciously dirty things he wanted to do. She cried out in a loud, longing moan. "You need me to make it feel better, don't you? But only me, baby."

He leaned and gently moved his tongue over her right nipple in slow, languid vacillations. He huffed hot breath on the sensitive skin.

"When you ache, you ache for me." He drew her left breast deep in his mouth. He sucked fervently as she groaned in ecstasy.

As he sucked, he worked his hands down to her skirt, lifted her up to grant himself better access to her breasts, and pulled the zipper down slowly. He gently lowered her body back to the couch as he eased the skirt away from her.

His tongue set to work again. He laved and licked the skin between her breasts, inhaling deeply of the scent of her as it swirled into his lungs.

He kept his mouth open and soft as he moved back to her neck. His thirsty tongue tasted her dew. He needed more. He sank a gentle love bite into the tendon where her neck met her shoulder and left a deep mark, the shape of his open mouth, on the thin fevered skin. "All mine."

Her entire body shook and trembled as his name moaned from her lips. Still moving with delicate precision, though he longed to rip the slight panties from her and pound into her, Dan began bathing her chest and abdomen with his tongue.

He dragged his teeth over the delicious curve of her right breast, then nipped at the throbbing tips as she cried out for him. He continued his path toward his goal.

As he worked, he undid his belt and trousers. He had them off in a second flat, as she unbuttoned his shirt and began running her hands over his chest and abs. He caught her hand and wrapped it forcefully around his cock, making her gasp.

"You feel how hard you make me, my sweet naughty girl?" Forgoing his need to drink her for a moment, wanting her wetter before he began his feast, he crowded over her and began thrusting against her. He mimicked his movements when he slipped inside of her and forced the satin panties to move over her mound.

"When I see you naked and dripping for me, when you moan for me, make all of those sweet sounds that only I get to hear," he groaned in her ear, "you make me so damn hard I hurt. And you're going to make it better, baby."

She bucked underneath him, clawing his back in heated passion. After several mimicked thrusts, he continued his trek down her body. He caught the G-string in his teeth. She watched him, so desperate and so real that he shook with need.

He yanked, meaning to pull them down her leg, but he heard the fabric tear. Long, deep moans of pleasure spilled from her kiss-swollen lips. Dan refocused as he tossed the panties away. He stroked his tongue over her swollen, fevered mound. "I want to drink you. Don't close your eyes, baby doll." His voice was deep and rough, precisely the way he intended to take her. "You're going to watch me. Every time I look up, I want to see you watching me make you wetter, making you ache."

"Oh god, yes," she whimpered.

He parted her with his fingers and kept his tongue moving slowly up and down the sensitive skin that no one else would ever see. She was his.

She bucked in his face, and he clasped her hips in his hands and pinned her to the couch. "I know what you want. Be a good girl and watch me give it to you." With that, he traced the tip of his tongue in a torturous dance around her clitoris. It was already swollen and throbbing. As she whimpered in desperate need, he took her into his mouth. He lifted her legs over his shoulders and returned to his work. He lifted her up. He stared her down before he began to suck. "Watch me," he commanded.

"Yes," hissed from her lips.

"So sweet, baby, like candy made just for me."

With his fingers now free, he dipped them inside of her. He kept his strokes deep and claiming as he sucked her clit. With his left hand, he caressed her backside and lifted her to gain himself deeper access.

Tender tremors worked through her body. She sank her teeth into her bottom lip. She writhed, and her temperature shot upward. "Do you need to come, baby doll?" he growled.

"Please," she begged.

"You say my name when you let go. Tell me who owns this pussy." He returned to his work, and his words freed her. She gasped as she filled his mouth with her sweet release as his name echoed in her moan. The energy was exquisite. He delved between her lips and sucked her harder. He wanted it all.

Unable to catch her breath, her entire body shuddered and convulsed uncontrollably.

Simply unable to wait any longer, Dan leaned up and grasped her hands. He positioned her on her knees with her stomach to the back of the couch as he crowded behind her. He grasped her hair gently and tugged her head to the side so he could kiss and mark her neck.

"Please, please," fell from her mouth as she arched her back and moved her lush ass against his erection.

"All mine." He grasped her waist and pushed inside of her. He forced himself to start slowly. He stayed shallow by sheer strength of will, but the feeling was heavenly. She leaned forward to urge him on. "Such a greedy, greedy girl," he moaned as he filled her. He slapped her ass, and she groaned out her pleasure.

He let her body envelop him inch by delicious inch. He shuddered as her energy began to consume him. Her muscles quivered and rhythmically pulled him deeper. She milked him, and he thought he'd lose his mind.

He moaned in her ear, "You feel so damn good." She leaned into the couch, pushing back against him. "So hot and wet. I want you to open up for me and take it all. Take it, baby doll. Take it like my good girl." He thrust hard, over and over, listening to her gasp and moan her appreciation.

"You feel that, baby? All mine. You feel how much of you I own?" He grinded into her, pushed her beautiful body against the cushions on the back of the couch, and hit every sweet spot. The angle granted him full access.

He kept his thrusts deep and unrelenting as their energy joined in tantric twists of ecstasy. Her entire body tensed around him as she came again. She writhed between his hard body and the couch.

He gave her ass another firm smack. "You didn't ask if you could come, naughty girl."

She groaned out his name like a prayer he intended to answer.

"Say please, baby."

"Please, please," she whimpered.

"That's my girl. Now I want more."

He moved his hands to her breasts as he leaned her forward and pounded into her. He kneaded the swollen, fevered mounds. He built her again, feeling her body spasm around his throbbing length.

He waited until she was calling out his name and quaking in his arms. He leaned until his mouth was right beside her ear as he grasped her nipples and twisted. "Come for me, honey. Just let it go."

She exploded in his arms as he buried himself deep and gained his own climax, potent and permeating. He struggled for breath as he felt their releases mix inside of her.

While he was brushing sweet, tender kisses on her neck, his body continued to shudder.

He withdrew and sank back onto the couch as he guided her into his lap. She nuzzled her head sweetly into the crook of his neck as he cradled her in his protective embrace.

"You are the most amazing woman in the world, and nothing is more beautiful than when you let me have you like that." She was still trembling and short of breath.

Allowing them a moment to relish their union, he stopped speaking and simply formed his shield around her.

"So, I really, really like couch sex," she whispered a minute later.

"Relax for me, baby," Dan soothed as he casted her and healed the marks he'd left on her chest and neck. Then he pulled her legs up until he was holding her entire body in his arms. She tucked her head under his chin, making him grin in contentment.

"The next time your parents come over and sit down, this is what I'm gonna think about." She giggled at her own joke. She was adorable.

"My mother would pretend you said, 'Dan spilled something on the couch,' and then she'd give you instructions on how to properly clean a leather sofa." He made her laugh harder, that power no less exhilarating than owning her.

"I would say I was sorry about the G-string, but truthfully, I'm not," he teased with a cocky smirk. "I will offer to get you more, but I prefer you without any."

"That was so freaking hot I'm keeping them forever as a memento." Their laughter continued.

"I was thinking maybe you'd keep me forever." He stopped laughing abruptly and watched her reaction.

She lifted her head and kissed his cheek. "That sounds even better," she whispered before tucking back into his embrace. "But I'm still keeping the panties."

"As long as it doesn't go in a box dedicated to lingerie torn off by previous boyfriends."

She giggled again and shook her head. "No, that would go back to how amazing sex is with you and how I know you're perfect for me. No one has ever torn my G-string off for me."

"Any time, baby doll," he assured her with a great deal of confidence.

She glanced down at the panties on the floor. "Aww, and that was a pair I got from the lingerie of the month club." She cracked up again.

As Dan joined in her hysterical laughter, he was overwhelmed by the fact that he could not only have mind-blowing sex with the woman in his lap, but that she was beautiful, funny, sweet, and extremely intelligent. She was everything he'd ever wanted but always refused to believe existed.

"Shall I take you to bed, Miss Styler?"

"Yes, I am suddenly very tired."

Dan stood with an extremely satisfied smirk on his face. He kept her tucked up in his arms as he headed to the stairs. They could retrieve the clothes in the morning.

"Are you up for another round, baby doll?" he asked with no expectation that she'd agree.

"Oh my god, yes!"

CHAPTER 16
TERRORS OF THE NIGHT
LOGAN HAYDENSHIRE

Wednesday morning, Logan awoke gasping for breath and covered in sweat. He threw back the sheets and blankets and tried hard not to scream. It was six fifteen. He swallowed down the bile that had risen violently in his throat as he reached for his cell phone.

Please answer, please answer, my God just answer the damn phone, pulsed through his mind with every harrowing ring.

"Hey," Adeline sang. "What are you doing up already?" Taking a moment to allow breath to fill his lungs once again, Logan willed his voice to engage.

"I was just worried about you. I wanted to make sure you got to work okay."

"What's wrong?"

"Nothing," he lied. "Nothing's wrong. I just wanted to check on you. I think I'm going to go in early today." He decided he was leaving for work right then.

"Oh, okay. I'm fine. I got here at five. I've done a few rounds. We have a salpingo-oophorectomy I'm assisting with in a little while. Do you want to come have lunch with me?" Her explanation rang with concern.

"Yes. Don't go to lunch without me. I'll be there. Just text me when you're ready to eat."

"Are you sure you're all right?"

He couldn't hide anything from her. She knew him too well.

"Yeah, yeah, uh, I just needed to hear your voice."

"Aww, you're so sweet. I need to go break Mrs. Alton's water, but I love you."

"I love you too, baby, more than you know."

"I'll text you after the surgery, and you can come pick me up."

"I'll be there. Don't leave without me."

"I would never do that."

"Right, I know." He tried to remember to breathe. "I love you," he said again.

"I love you too. Bye." She ended the call.

How could I have been so stupid? Logan lambasted himself. He took a shower and pulled on his clothes in mere minutes.

"Hey, you want some coffee?" Rainer held up the pot and reached for another mug from the cabinet.

"No!" Logan's infuriated bellow stunned Rainer and Emily. "I'm going to work."

"Don't you want something to eat?" Emily asked concernedly.

"I'm not hungry." Logan grabbed his jacket and keys. Rainer and Emily stared after him with their mouths hanging open in shock.

He didn't care. He slammed the door on the way out of the house. He needed to talk to Vindico.

CHAPTER 17
SUN RISE, SON SET
DAN VINDICO

Fionna was curled up on her stomach with her arms under her pillow. Dan gazed at her lovingly as sunlight poured into the room. He moved over her, careful to keep his weight on the mattress, as he wrapped his arms around her and brushed her hair off her face. He kissed her cheek and watched it pull into a sweet smile. His morning stubble rubbed against her velvet skin.

"I'm still sleeping," she teased and refused to open her eyes.

"But there's this extremely gorgeous woman in my bed, and she's naked." A broad grin formed on his chiseled features as he watched in awe as her energy swirled in ecstatic waves of happiness.

"Really?" she giggled.

"Mm-hmm, and"—he began dotting kisses from her temple down her cheek and then onto her shoulder—"I really, really want her."

Fionna's eyes flashed excitedly as she rolled but managed to keep her body positioned under his. She gave him an extremely intrigued smile.

"Don't you have to go to work, Chief Vindico?" She waggled her eyebrows as she traced her hand down his abdomen and then up his length. He shook from the attention he craved. She looked very pleased with what she found.

"I'll go to work later, honey. I have something here I really want to take care of first."

She gave him a naughty grin. He brushed his thumb over her lips just before he leaned down and began kissing her slowly. He added to the intensity with each pass, moaning into her mouth, as her heart picked up pace.

∽

Logan Haydenshire

"What the hell is wrong with you?" Rainer demanded as he rushed into the office.

"Why is Vindico not here?" was Logan's furious reply.

Rainer looked deeply concerned. "I don't know. It's barely seven fifteen in the morning. He has a beautiful woman in his bed. Your dad ordered him to stop working so much. It's the day before Christmas Eve, and half of Iodex took today off. Pick one."

Rolling his eyes, Logan continued to pace outside Vindico's office door.

"Would you please tell me what this is all about?" Rainer's tone took on a kinder note. Logan assumed his terror must've been obvious in his tensing shield.

"I can't believe I never thought of this, that *he* never thought of this." Logan gestured to Dan's door in stunned disbelief.

"Thought of what?"

Logan glanced around. No one was in the office yet, and Rainer was right, most of the department had taken the day off to start their holiday celebrations. Terror surged through his shield. He stalked toward Rainer and grasped his shirt. "She's an Australian princess!"

Rainer scowled as he jerked away from Logan. "And?"

"And her mother's drug-dealing pimp works for Wretchkinsides, the guy I am currently on a task force trying to take down!" Logan willed Rainer to understand.

Governor Haydenshire came through the doors from the governors' wing into Iodex. "Son, what is going on?"

"I thought you and Mom were entertaining the *Premier's son*," Logan sneered hatefully.

"I'm not certain what's wrong with you, and I am well aware that you're twenty-one years old and a married man, but I'm going to give you approximately two seconds to change your tone of voice," Governor Haydenshire demanded furiously.

"Sorry." Logan allowed only Rainer to see his eye roll, just as they'd done since they were old enough to roll their eyes.

"Your sister called me and told me you stormed out without eating. I was rightfully concerned. I can't seem to remember you ever turning down food."

"Vindico is late." Logan threw his arm back to the office door. *Tattling*, that was low even for the situation. He scolded himself.

"It's not eight yet, and since I'm the one who told him to cut back on his hours, I don't really think it would be fair for me to reprimand him for doing what I instructed him to do." The governor gave Rainer a quizzical glance. "Did you and Adeline have a fight?"

"No, Dad, we're fine."

"Do you know what's wrong?" Governor Haydenshire demanded of Rainer.

Rainer gave Logan a sympathetic look. "I think so, sir."

CHAPTER 18
OH, WHAT A BEAUTIFUL MORNING
DAN VINDICO

"But I don't want you to go," Fionna fussed adorably. Dan's energy moved over them in pacifying waves from just being in her proximity. He pulled her closer and let the shower water cascade over their bodies.

He picked up Fionna's preferred soap from her grandparents' farm in Kauai and lathered his hands. With smooth, solid caresses from his powerful hands, he tenderly washed her silky skin. "I don't want to go, baby, and believe me, you have no idea the kind of power you must hold for me to be saying that."

She grinned against him as he slid his hands down her sides and then gently washed away all that he'd just done to her in the bed.

Her energy rolled in satiated contentment. "Chloe's picking me up around two. I'm not going to the bakery today. I'm going to finish getting everything unpacked. And then the Angels are buying toys and books, and then we're working at the children's home this afternoon." A sweet sigh hummed against him as he let his hands glide over her luscious curves.

"I'm taking the bike, so I'll leave you the keys to the Ferrari if you need to go anywhere."

"Shouldn't you pay for the car first before you loan it out to me? And the harness seatbelt things kind of freak me out."

"I was going to take a check to Sam at lunch, and since I have no intention of racing it, I'm going to have the custom seatbelts removed. I'll have him put in something you're used to."

"I've never driven anything like a Ferrari. I want you to teach me." Her energy, though still serene, took on a nervous edge.

"Okay," Dan agreed, "but I'll still take my bike and that way if you need to leave, you can. I don't want you stranded here." She smiled against his chest. "Ready to get out, baby doll?"

"If we get out, then you'll leave." She stuck her lip out in an adorable pout.

He chuckled and turned off the water. After grabbing a towel, he heated it with his hand and wrapped her up in its warmth.

"I'll try to come home early." The phrase that had just exited his lips sounded extremely odd in his own voice. "I'll pick up some dinner."

"If I get back from the children's home in time, I'll make dinner."

"You don't have to cook for me." Dan watched her dispense with the towel, rub her body down with some kind of oil that smelled incredible, and then shrug into a short, floral robe that barely covered her backside. He unabashedly admired the curves that peeked out from the hem.

A hot cup of coffee with cream and honey earned him a delighted smile and a kiss on the jaw. She began scrambling eggs and served him some, cooked perfectly, as she added toast to his plate.

"Thank you. You don't have to make me breakfast either. I usually just grab a protein bar from the cafeteria at work."

"But I like making you breakfast. I like eating breakfast with you, and I know you're used to all of your meals being free at the Senate, so I can buy the food with my ginormous paychecks. I love to cook."

Dan leaned and brushed a kiss across her cheek as he tousled her hair. "You spend your ginormous paychecks on stuff you want. You spend my mediocre paychecks on food. I'll leave you my check card."

Perturbed, she rolled her eyes. "You know, if we sold my house, you could use the money to pay for the Ferrari."

"Fi, honey, it could get very complicated if the press got wind that you were selling your house. Please believe me when I tell you that I am not destitute because I invested in the Angels. We are fine. Just give me a little time and then we can really start our lives together." He tested her.

Hope once again overwhelmed him. *Damn it!* he scolded himself. Hope was the most lethal of all emotions. She nodded and gave him the grin that set his entire world ablaze.

"And you are *not* buying me a car."

"We'll see," was her reply. Dan stood and rinsed his plate before grabbing his briefcase and badge and pulling on his holster.

Fionna began smashing up an avocado and a banana. She separated an egg and added the white to the strange concoction. She opened the cabinets and revealed a bottle of olive oil.

As Dan certainly hadn't had any food in the house before she'd moved in, he assumed that most of the ingredients had come from her house.

"Don't ask." She began giggling again.

He kissed the top of her head and headed toward the door. "Not asking."

"I love you." In a sudden move, she flitted to him and wrapped her arms around his chest. He hugged her tightly.

"Careful, baby." He turned his side and the pistol away from her. "And, me too."

CHAPTER 19
THE ACE OF HEARTS
LOGAN HAYDENSHIRE

"Where is he?" Logan demanded furiously as he began pacing again.

"Logan, he's a few minutes late. Geez, give the guy a break," Rainer insisted as Governor Haydenshire nodded his adamant agreement.

Vindico stalked in carrying the mail from his post office box. "Governor Haydenshire, I thought you were taking the day off, sir."

His deeply satisfied smile only provoked Logan's mood. "'Bout damn time!"

"Logan," Governor Haydenshire warned.

Vindico spun and glared furiously. "You have a problem, Haydenshire?"

"Could we talk in your office for a few minutes, Daniel, so that Logan can apologize for his extremely disrespectful tone to his boss?" Governor Haydenshire menaced. Indignation tightened Logan's throat.

Vindico threw open the door and gestured the men inside. He kept an infuriated glare on Logan. He tossed the mail and the keys onto his desk and crossed his arms in abject fury.

Distracted momentarily from his anger, Logan wondered again how he could cross his arms like that, with all of that massive muscle in the way. He could feel the heat in Vindico's temper reverberate in the energy between them, and the weight of his discomfiture seated him.

"Look, I'm sorry. I just freaked out, but when I explain this to you, you'll know why."

"Well, I, for one, would love to hear it," Governor Haydenshire quipped.

Vindico huffed, "I'm waiting."

Logan tried to swallow down his terror. "It's Adeline. Just think about it. Her father, the freaking Prince of the Australian Realm, is going to march into the courtroom in two weeks and announce that she's his daughter and get her mom put away or whatever. As soon as he does that, Wretchkinsides will know where she comes from and what kind of money and power she has at her fingertips. Candy's pimp is employed by the Interfeci. They'll be all over her. And the fact that I'm on the task force will only make them more brutal about it." Impending doom sank heavily in his gut as he stated the reality of the situation.

Shocked understanding etched Vindico's chiseled features.

Governor Haydenshire looked visibly disturbed. "I never thought about that."

"Me, either," Dan agreed, though he seemed to take the news like a failure on his part.

"But you'll keep her safe, right?" Logan was well aware that he sounded like a frightened child.

"I told you and Rainer both that I wouldn't let anyone live what I've lived. So, now I'll tell you the same thing I told him." Vindico gestured to Rainer. "Bring her to the office with you when she's not at work. They're not going to take her from a hospital full of people," he finally stated the first thing all morning that gave Logan some hope. "Make certain she doesn't leave work without you. If that means you're sitting out there to pick her up when she gets off at two in the morning, do it and don't complain."

Logan nodded his understanding.

Vindico began pacing behind his desk. "Believe me, no one is more committed to ending Wretchkinsides than I am. Fitzroy has a guy high up in the Interfeci. He's finally been accepted into the inner circles. Bridgette is still spying for me at The Tantra. We have undercover officers embedded as well, so I am constantly aware of most of what's going on. I will keep her safe. But you're going to have to explain this to Adeline and to her father." He seemed genuinely sorry for Logan. Telling Lucas would certainly be a delicate situation.

"I'll explain it. I'm sorry I freaked out," Logan admitted to everyone seated in the room.

To his shock, Dan chuckled. "Guess I'll give you that one, but don't let it happen again."

Relief and confusion fought for dominance in Logan's shield. He understood that if he continued his lack of respect, he would be reprimanded. He knew his father wouldn't step in on his behalf if he felt Logan deserved the punishment, and Vindico's reprimands were harsh.

He recalled shoveling dirt and gravel at Coriolis for hours in the suffocating heat the last time he and Rainer had gotten into trouble. What he didn't understand was what had softened Dan Vindico. The man before him was not the same guy he'd been working for.

"Rainer, Logan, would you head back to your desks? I'd like to speak to Daniel before I go," Governor Haydenshire requested.

They stood to leave, but Vindico halted them. "Before you go, let me say this. Elite Iodex has taken out several heavy-hitters in the Interfeci. A couple of weeks ago, we confiscated over $480 million dollars. Wretchkinsides is furious, and he's getting desperate. When men like Wretchkinsides get desperate, that's when they're the most dangerous."

Rainer and Logan nodded their understanding as they moved toward the door.

"And Logan," Vindico called, "you have two weeks before anyone will know anything, so try to enjoy your first Christmas together. At this point, Sawyer owes your dad, your best friend, and me quite a bit. I'll make him understand the situation, and see if we can't make her schedule and yours work together."

"Thank you." Logan glanced at his father who was visibly

impressed with Vindico. Rainer pulled the door closed as he made his exit.

~

Dan Vindico

Dan sank down in his chair, overwhelmed with harrowing thoughts and bitter defeat. Governor Haydenshire waited on his attention. Dan wished he'd leave him to his ponderings and misery.

"I am well aware that unsolicited advice most often falls on deaf ears, but you stopped asking me for my advice ten years ago when you stopped listening to anyone's voice besides your own. So, I'm just going to go ahead and say this."

Dan knew what Governor Haydenshire had already said was correct. He had stopped listening to anyone or anything besides the vengeance that had corroded his heart and his mind. This time he decided to really listen.

"How did you always know when I needed advice?" He couldn't quite keep the annoyance from his tone. He recalled asking Governor Haydenshire about numerous things throughout his childhood and early in his career. He'd asked about his arguments with Amelia, and Iodex, and life in general. The governor always seemed to know when something was getting to him. Suddenly awash in defeat and memories, his shield pulsed weakly in an effort to bolster his ego.

Governor Haydenshire gave him a genuine smile. "Let's see here, I've been married for well over thirty years. I've survived fool's hill more times than I care to count. I've been a governor for the last several decades, and I have eleven children of my own and several others I'll claim, you included. Lawson was my best friend. I'm Crown now, so you could say I have a little life experience," the governor rattled off his résumé.

Dan chuckled. He had to agree with his reasoning. "I'm listening." The words tasted bitter.

"If that's really the case, son, I'd say Fionna Styler might not only be a beautiful, sweet, caring, intelligent woman. She's also a miracle."

"She is that."

"Then listen to me." The governor's intonation turned to a soothing tenor. "You can do this. I know perfectly well that you're sitting there beating yourself up because you didn't realize that Adeline might be in danger. You're wondering if you can still beat Wretchkinsides and have a life that exists outside of this office. I'm telling you that you can. It's just going to take a little finesse.

"Everything happens in its own time. You've spent the last ten years killing yourself slowly because you didn't think you deserved to live. And I would never say that I want men like Wretchkinsides to have any additional opportunities to commit the heinous crimes they're so well-known for, but if you let him choke out your life then he's already won. You've already been beaten.

"So, work on it. If anyone can bring him down, it's you, but you have to allow yourself the good things that this life has to offer as well. Otherwise what are you working for? You'll learn to strike a balance. It might take a little time, but you're an extremely intelligent guy. I'm certain the woman you've used your finesse and intelligence to woo not only into your home but into your bed can help you as well."

"What if I'm losing my edge?" Damming up the words hadn't worked.

The governor looked as shocked as Dan felt. He studied Dan intently. "What if you're gaining your life?" The governor stood. "Find the balance. You can do it. I trust that Miss Styler has Christmas presents from you under the tree?"

An automatic smile formed on Dan's features. "They aren't under the tree, but I'm picking up the last one at lunch."

The governor nodded his approval. "I'm going to go ahead and put another demand on you because I'm also aware that guilt has been the driving force in your life for the last decade. This way you can just go ahead and be mad at me if it will make you feel better."

Dan's brow knitted, and the governor gave him a wry grin. "Do not come into this office until the day after New Year's, Chief Vindico. Have a real Christmas with your family and with Fionna. Go to Vegas and keep her safe and, please, for me, keep an eye on Emily. Then come home and spend some time with the woman who has given you so much and who deserves so much of you. And then come back to work, and we'll work on striking that balance."

Dan was aware that he wasn't allowed to disagree. The shock came in the realization that he didn't want to.

"Yes, sir." Somehow, he could still feel Fionna's energy inside of him. It was assuring him that it would be okay, that she would be there no matter what.

"Can I give you one more piece of advice before I leave you to work, and I head home to make certain my twins haven't tied up a foreign dignitary?"

"Sure." Dan laughed.

"I know life hasn't dealt you a fair hand, and I'm truly sorry for all that you've been through. I just think maybe the ace you've turned over this time was the ace of hearts. What I'm trying to say is I think you found your Lillian. And you need to hold on to her with everything that you are and never let her go."

The words of wisdom resonated through Dan's body. The governor was kindly throwing his own advice in his face. He was well-known for his belief that you should never make a move until you held all the aces. "I know, sir." He choked back emotion as it overwhelmed him.

"Merry Christmas, Daniel."

"Merry Christmas, Governor Haydenshire," Dan managed to respond, still trying to draw deep, steadying breaths.

Dan's phone chirped as the governor closed his office door. He extracted it from his pocket.

Are you ok? was Fionna's text. She still had his energy inside of her, as well. He touched her name.

"Hel-wo," Fionna mumbled almost unintelligibly.

"Fi, are you okay?" Dan panicked.

"Yesh," she supplied and then began laughing.

The sound made Dan smile as his world began to settle once again.

"Hang on a shecand."

He heard her set the phone down and then a second later she returned. "Okay, sorry," she spoke clearly now.

"Everything all right?"

An abashed giggle, the songs of angels, rang in his ear. "Yes, sorry. I was bleaching my teeth."

"Ah." Relief flooded through him. "And do you still have guacamole in your hair?"

"You are not allowed to ask that."

"Is this some kind of pre-Christmas beauty treatment day I should get used to?" Dan tried to figure out what had her so concerned about her already gorgeous appearance.

"You're not supposed to know how vain I am. I felt like something was wrong though." He immediately recognized the redirecting of the conversation.

"Yeah, just a few complications I hadn't thought of that I really should have. I'll tell you about it tonight."

"Okay," she agreed but sounded deeply concerned. "I'll call you when we leave the children's home."

"Have a good time today, sweetheart."

"I love you."

"Me too," he replied readily.

Dan climbed back in Rainer's Porsche holding Fionna's Christmas present after thanking Sam profusely for his work. Fionna texted again. *So, I wrapped all of the presents for your parents and sisters, and I baked some more cookies for the kids. If you'll tell me where you hid my gifts, I'll wrap those for you too.*

She ended the text with a smiley face. Dan laughed. *Nice try*, he responded as Rainer gave him a goading grin. "She's been trying to find her Christmas presents since she moved in last weekend."

Rainer joined in his laughter. "Yeah, I have to wrap Emily's and give them to her mom, or she'll have them unwrapped long before Christmas." Rainer shook his head with a grin Dan recognized as one of deep love for the woman he was discussing. "Receivers can feel the energy that went into the gift, so they're a big deal to them. She's probably picking up on the effort and your excitement." He gestured his head to the gift Dan was holding.

"Yeah, I remember you saying that in Sydney."

"I heard Fionna booked one of the suites on the Angels plane for the Vegas trip." Rainer seemed uncertain which role to play, employee or friend.

Quickly deciding to try to guide him into the ways to be both, Dan allowed the question. "That was all Fi. I'm really not into the whole team knowing what's going on in there."

Rainer nodded his understanding. "Yeah, Emily's asked about it. I know she wants to use one. It just seems odd. I told her I'd rather book a flight for just the two of us if she wants to join the mile-high club."

Dan chuckled. "Yeah, because the pilots who fly those aren't complete pervs who just want to watch the show."

Rainer scowled. "Forget I said that."

Dan tried to hide his smirk. Lawson was an odd mix. Thoroughly green yet surprisingly adept at keeping his head when things were tough.

"I've never been to Vegas," Rainer admitted as if that were a failing on his part.

"You haven't missed much."

"I thought it was supposed to be a big party town."

"It is that, twenty-four seven."

"The place we're staying is supposed to be pretty nice."

Dan supposed he agreed. "Most people never see the actual room they're staying in. They just pass out there when they're either shit-faced or broke or both."

Rainer gave him a concerned nod as he pulled onto the Senate parking deck. They hurried to get lunch from the cafeteria and then dove back into work.

CHAPTER 20
AN ANGEL IN ACTION

At four thirty, a knock sounded on Dan's door. "In," he called in his usual response as he pulled himself from the evidence from Wretchkinsides's briefcase. He'd reread the same line four times on a document he'd been over more than a dozen.

"Hey." Logan eased inside. "I was just wondering… Adeline's shift is over at five, and I know no one knows about her dad yet, but…"

Dan debated. His mind went to war with his newly resurrected soul. "Go on, Haydenshire. Have a Merry Christmas."

"Thanks, and I really am sorry about this morning."

"It's forgotten. Go get her. Keep her safe. Believe me, I do understand the desire."

"Yeah," Logan agreed. "I hope you and Fionna have a nice Christmas."

"Thanks. You too."

With a wave, Logan disappeared just as Dan's office phone rang. "This is Vindico." He spoke with the Non-Gifted police chief for a moment and thanked him for working through Christmas. His cell rang as he hung up the office phone.

"Hey, baby doll, I'm sorry. I was just getting ready to leave." He remembered that he'd promised to leave early.

"No, it's fine," Fionna sighed.

"What's wrong?"

"Is there any way you could please come pick me up? I'm at the Children and Family Center on Crofton Ave. It's not far from the Senate. It's a Non-Gifted home. There's no one around here. They have security everywhere because it's an abused children's refuge. No one would see you. Please."

"Honey, I'm leaving now. It's fine. I'll be there in just a minute. I thought Chloe was bringing you home."

"She was," Fionna spat, "but she started chatting up this guy who was here volunteering today, and they've decided to go out and party. I have no ride, and Garrett can't come because he's trying to help his mom. Adeline put her back on bed rest this afternoon at her appointment. Her blood pressure spiked. He's gone to the farm to get the twins."

"Gotcha." Quickly scooping up all of Fionna's presents he'd stowed in his office, he grabbed a set of keys to one of the Expeditions and raced to the parking deck. He loaded the gifts in the back and threw his jacket over them before he raced to the driver's seat.

"I'm on my way, baby."

"I'm okay," she assured him. "I'm in here with the kids. I'm just very unhappy with Chloe." Dan was aware that she was editing her language for the children in her presence.

"Well, I'm pissed the hell off," he supplied for her and made her laugh.

After a few quick turns and several less-than-kind words over DC traffic, Dan spotted the children's home attached to a church. He found a parking space, fed the meter, and raced inside. He flashed his badge repeatedly. She was right. The security was tight. Dan was impressed.

Fionna was sitting on the floor of what appeared to be a small classroom. She had a little boy in her lap and was reading a story. There were several other young children seated near her, listening intently and pointing to things on the pages.

Dan smiled. She was astounding, truly a beautiful person with a beautiful soul. He was overwhelmed as he watched her. He slipped quietly into the room.

"Just let me finish," Fionna whispered.

Nodding, Dan sank down on the floor nearby. She grinned at him before continuing the story.

Suddenly, one of the little girls who'd been standing beside Fionna, clinging to her shoulder, moved and seated herself in Dan's lap. Not certain what to do, Dan smiled and watched the tiny girl's deep-blue eyes. She was scared.

His heart ached. Somehow, he knew that it was a man who had hurt her. There was a reason she was living in the home, but somehow she'd decided to trust him.

Fionna gazed at him adoringly as he gently patted the little girl's back. She tucked into his body and clung to his wrist. Fionna finished the book, and the little boy in her lap requested that she read one more, with an adorable, lisping plea.

She raised her eyebrows to Dan in question. He nodded his agreement that she should continue. Several books later, the women who worked at the home told Fionna they needed to get ready for dinner, so Dan and Fionna waved goodbye and promised to come back soon.

They stepped out into the freezing night air. Fionna wrapped her hair and face in a pashmina. She left only her eyes and nose exposed to the elements. She wasn't recognizable. She clung to Dan as he wrapped his arms around her and hurried her to the car.

"You know, guys who are so sweet with kids are really, really sexy." She unwound the scarf from her face and gave him his smile. He forced the heater to warm the car faster. Dan scoffed. Who wouldn't be kind to kids living in a children's home?

"Meredith's kids will be at my parents' tomorrow night, so you'll get to meet them."

"How old are they?"

"Uh." Dan racked his brain. He remembered going to the hospital when they were born. "I'm not exactly sure. They're walking and everything. I think Olivia started kindergarten this year, and Oliver is little and always sticky."

Fionna laughed at him outright. "So a toddler?"

"Yeah." *You really should know how old your own niece and nephew are, moron.* "Why don't I pick us up some dinner? I'll just run in. No one can see you in here with the tint on the windows," he reminded her and hoped that she wouldn't ask any more questions he didn't know the answers to.

She considered for a minute. "Wanna get takeout and then go home and cuddle on the couch? There's a great Chinese place near the airport."

"That sounds perfect." Dan headed toward Ronald Reagan.

"How old are Fitz's kids?"

Dan chuckled as he thought of his rambunctious godsons. "Alex is eight, and Alfred is seven."

"Aida just turned seven a couple of days ago. That's the little girl from the orphanage in Brazil I told you about."

Dan suddenly remembered. He pulled the mail he'd picked up earlier in the day from his jacket pocket and handed it to Fionna. "I think you got a letter from Aida, sweetheart."

"Really?" Her entire face glowed from the news as she began going through the mail. "This is such a great Christmas present." She landed on the small letter with multiple postage markings written in a childish scrawl.

Dan was overwhelmed once again. She looked truly elated by the letter from Aida. The expression on her face was just as delighted as if he'd given her an expensive piece of jewelry.

"Here." He turned on the light directly over her seat. He was certainly capable of driving with the interior lights on. He'd done it dozens of times when he was after criminals. "I'm fine. Go ahead and read it." She opened the letter with a great deal of care.

"She's thanking me for her birthday presents." Fionna was gazing at the letter with adoration. She told him several things mentioned in the letter and directed him to the restaurant where she wanted to get food.

Dan pulled into the parking lot as Fionna folded the letter delicately and slipped it in her purse.

"Just sit tight. I'll be right back. Shrimp chow mein and fried rice, right?" He was buying time. He'd memorized the order instantly but wanted to scan the surroundings to make certain they were safe.

It appeared to be nothing more than a low-end Chinese takeout restaurant, and no one was lurking in the parking lot. The light from the restaurant glowed harshly against the black night. He was able to study most everyone inside, just families or singles picking up a quick meal.

"And egg drop soup, please," Fionna added to her order.

"You got it. I'll be right back. If you need me, call me." He held up his phone.

"I think I can manage myself in the car all alone." She chuckled at his warning.

Still performing methodic scans of the surrounding area, Dan was assaulted by the hot, thick air permeated with the smell of frying eggs, oil, and an overly sweet flavoring he couldn't quite identify.

Eager to return to Fionna, he stepped up to the counter and placed his order. Assured that it would only be a moment, he moved farther down the cheap, laminate bar to wait.

His mind wandered back to the document he'd been studying when Fionna had called for a ride. Why was Wretchkinsides still sending money to Belgium? He'd been doing that for months. Never large sums, only a few thousand dollars each time, but he didn't even own property in Belgium that Dan knew of. And neither he nor Fitz could ever seem to locate the actual accounts the money was being moved into. Always aware of his surroundings, he noted that a door to his right had opened. He checked his watch and glanced at the health code rating posted near the cash register.

"Dan?" A flirtatious, female drawl reached him, and he panicked. *Oh shit!* He spun and tried not to glance toward the Expedition. He was in plain view of the large windows. Fionna could see everything, but he had no hope of seeing her reaction.

"Bridgette." His head sank in defeat. This was going to be a disaster.

He retreated several steps, but she advanced.

"You look even sexier than the last time I saw you," she flirted.

Dan fought not to vomit. He caught her hand as she reached to run it down his chest. "Don't touch me."

"Playing coy now? I know what you like. Let's get out of here and make up for lost time." She sounded thrilled as she slid her left hand up his bicep and squeezed.

Dan shuddered and jerked away from her roving hands. He'd released her right to escape her left, and she'd continued her progress until he was backed up to a booth by the windows.

"Bridgette, we are done. Turn around and walk away. I don't ever want to see you again."

With a dismissive scoff, as if his disinterest was somehow unfathomable, she managed to press her cleavage against him.

He grasped her shoulders and edged her away. As he pushed her back, she brought her hands back up to his chest and pawed at him.

"Baby, we were good together. I know you miss me."

Dan noted that she was still wearing a Tantra waitressing uniform, such as it was. Clearly her employers hadn't given much thought to her prostitution charge.

"Get the hell away from me."

In the next horrifying second, Dan's world effectively fell apart. A woman behind the counter called, "Order 162," Fionna burst into the restaurant with a white-hot storm of fury burning in her eyes, and in Dan's distraction, Bridgette managed to slip her hand down his zipper line.

Fionna gasped audibly. Panic seared through Dan's veins. With the shrill, echoing howls of loss reverberating against his skull, he knew what had to happen.

Members of the Interfeci occupied seats at The Tantra Gentlemen's Club every single day. Bridgette danced for them, served their drinks, and, for a fee, listened in on their conversations. The fatal flaw in his brilliant plan was that Bridgette wanted him. If she knew what Fionna meant to him, she would turn on him just for revenge.

Repulsed by what he was about to do, Dan spun away from Bridgette. He ignored Fionna completely. "That's mine." He moved to the counter. The words choked on the devastation that obstructed his throat.

He picked up the bags of food and proceeded to abandon the love of his life in a low-end, hole-in-the-wall beside the woman he'd banged without any care at all for several months before he'd met Fionna.

The bitter cold stung his eyes. They already burned with the finality of what he'd just done. It was the coldest winter Virginia had experienced in over a decade. The biting, glacial wind was nothing compared to the numbing cold that took up residence in his soul.

Certain Bridgette had paid no attention to which car Fionna had exited, since she'd only had eyes for his crotch, Dan set the food on the floorboard. His heart shattered as he cranked the car and backed out of the parking space.

Fionna's mouth hung open in shock as she watched him leave.

CHAPTER 21
LOST AND ABANDONED

Certain he had never hated himself more, Dan circled behind the restaurant and hid the car in an employee parking space near the dumpsters. From his vantage point, and he had a profile shot of both women. With a fervent prayer for help, he texted Fionna and tried desperately to explain. Bridgette's order was called, and she made her exit.

Fionna refused to answer his texts, but he could see her holding her phone. He didn't have to guess who she was about to call to rescue her, and he hated himself more.

Bridgette made her exit and climbed into an Audi A3. Dan's brow furrowed. She'd driven an old Ford clunker the last time he'd been around her. His Visium Predilection tried to push his shield away, but he refused it. As soon as Bridgette's car turned onto the highway, he called Fionna.

"This is Fionna. Leave me a message. Aloha!" He heard the message three times before he debated putting his fist through one of the windows.

On the fifth call, she answered.

"Fi, please don't hang up. I'm here. I just…I just couldn't let her know. Please. I know you hate me. Just come outside. Turn left out of the door. You'll see me. I would never have really left you."

She said nothing. Air seized in his lungs. Acid burned his throat. His body rejected the loss. "Please, baby, please. Let me explain. I'll take you to Garrett's, just please, please let me explain. I won't touch you… just please."

His heart managed a few irregular, burdened beats when she stormed out of the restaurant. He saw the plate glass windows that constructed the restaurant shake as she slammed the door behind her. Her rhythms were flooded with red fury that pulsed in horrifying waves. Refusing to meet his terrified eyes, she climbed into the car, folded her arms over her chest, and remained as far away from him as she could manage.

The black asphalt adhered to the dark, moonless night. Dan couldn't see either. His eyes only managed to see the oddly motionless black of his future. The weight in his chest made his breaths staggered and anxious. "I'm sorry," he choked.

She shot him an infuriated glare and moved so close to the door he was afraid she was going to try and leap out of the car.

With a half nod, he accepted his fate. He couldn't have her. He should never have tried. He'd never deserve something so perfect.

"Did you get Garrett when you called? I'll take you to his apartment."

His shield was so weighted with guilt and terrorizing fear that she lost some of her unmitigated wrath when she finally allowed herself to feel his emotions.

"Why did you leave me there?" her voice broke. She turned her face away. She didn't want him to see her cry. He wished she'd just backhand him. That couldn't have hurt as badly as the crippling blow of her refusing him her tears.

"Please, baby, look at me." Dan checked his rearview mirrors and pulled off the road into an old, abandoned gas station parking lot.

Utter devastation ravaged her eyes as she spun around and stared him down.

"Fi, Bridgette works with Wretchkinsides's men every single day. Remember, I told you that's why I dated her in the first place. I only wanted the information she could get me. I also told you I was an asshole, and I apparently just proved that. I swear I did it to try to keep you safe. If she knew about us, and it pissed her off enough, she could go straight to Nic. I'm so sorry. If I'd shown her what you mean to me, he'd never let you live." Any steadying calm eluded him. She shook in her heavy coat. Her tears jolted through her body and became sobs.

Unable to sit there and do nothing, he reached out for her, but she jerked away from him.

Hot tears that refused to obey escaped his eyes. He managed a nod. "I'll, uh…I'll just take you to Garrett's." His own voice sounded fractured and distant. He didn't want her to be alone. He needed to know that she was safe and that someone was taking care of her. He pulled back onto the road and headed back toward downtown DC. Garrett had an apartment near the Pentagon.

"I don't want to go to Garrett's," shrieked from her a few minutes later.

Confusion added itself to the volatile cocktail of desperation and casualty that existed in his gut. "I want to go home." With a great deal of effort, she forced her voice to calm.

Dan nodded and tried not to imagine where she was going to sleep in her old house. There was virtually no furniture left. "Why don't you just stay at my house tonight? Please. I'll go back to the office."

"What? Where else would I stay? Why would you go back to the office? What is wrong with you?"

With his mind in anarchy, from somewhere hope gave another hesitant show in his shield.

"I was trying to give you some space. I'll do anything you want."

"I want to go to our house!" she demanded in a deafening screech.

Dan tried to swallow down that damned hope all over again. *She probably wants to pack.* He slowly drove home, delaying the death that was certain to overtake him when he got her there.

As he shifted into park, she stormed up the walkway, used her own key to open the door, and then slammed it shut.

She didn't lock it. He stood and stared at the door. It was over, and he was going to be sick. The alarms began blaring. She hadn't remembered to turn them off, so he eased inside after her.

What he found once he stepped inside astounded him. There were at least a dozen beautifully wrapped packages under the tree, stockings hung from the mantel, and the entire house glowed from being scrubbed and polished. The smell of freshly baked cookies infused the air. The carpets were vacuumed, and Fionna was lying face down on the couch sobbing onto her folded arms.

The sight was more than he could bear. He quickly turned off the alarms before every Iodex officer on the force was on the front lawn. He set his keys on the antique washstand that had come from her home and moved to the floor beside her.

"Baby, please, please don't cry. I'm so sorry. She meant absolutely nothing to me, and you mean absolutely everything to me. I had to leave you there. I had to. I'm so, so sorry." He brushed her hair away from her face and wiped away the steadily flowing tears. "Please believe me." It was such a stupid and selfish request. How could he sit there and ask her for anything after what he'd just done to her?

"I do." She rubbed her hands over her face and curled up in her ball in the corner of the couch.

"Can I sit beside you?" He would take nothing for granted, and he wasn't certain he would survive her jerking away from him again. That was too much.

She gave a slight nod, and he eased himself beside her, careful to still give her space between them.

"I'm so sorry." He'd say it until the end of time. If she was about to walk out, he hoped the apocalypse came that night.

"I know," she fussed pitifully. Then to spite herself, it seemed, she fell forward on his chest, and his entire being rejoiced as he held her.

"You don't know. You have no idea how hard it was to walk out of there. You have no idea what that did to me. I can't tell you how sorry I am."

Suddenly, she erupted, this time more violent than the last. She shoved him away. "Ugh! I could feel it! I can feel everything! I could feel everything you felt and everything about her! Stop telling me what I already know! How could you have dated someone like that? She is awful! Her energy is horrible!" She raged in his face.

Renewed tears, momentarily burned away by her fury, spilled

from her eyes. Her hands impacted with his chest again. He did nothing to stop her from hitting him.

Dan had no idea what to say. He didn't understand. "Baby, she's not Gifted. She doesn't have energy."

"Everyone has energy. You just can't feel it." This seemed to infuriate her.

"Okay, I know how powerful you are, but what do you mean everyone has energy?"

She wiped away her tears again and managed a convulsive breath.

"Not energy like we have that you can access and do stuff with. It's just that everyone has a spirit. How they act, and think, and the things they do, it all affects their spirit. Hers is just,"—Fionna clenched her jaw and tried to think of a word to describe Bridgette—"yucky!" She glared at him. "She's manipulative, and she's deceptive, and…and mean. She's a mean, mean person and she's doing something awful! I could feel her glee and her guilt. That's how mean people feel."

In absolute shock that he was grinning, Dan nodded his agreement. "I'm sorry. I can't feel that like you can, but please listen to me. I never paid her enough attention to have felt anything from her at all. I used her, and she used me. That was fine with me. That's how far I had fallen from the man I should be. I told you I don't deserve you. I'll never deserve you."

Still furious, though she seemed to have halted the tears falling from her eyes, she shook her head. "I don't hate you. I could never hate you. Stop thinking that. It hurts me." She held out her hand and summoned. The brilliant magenta hues of her Receiver's cast danced in her hand. Dan studied them. The bands were tensing in irritated rhythms. He tried to regulate his emotions by strength of determined will.

"Not all Receivers can feel it, but Emily can, just a little. She has to concentrate. I don't. I feel them all the time from everyone." She clenched her jaw. "All the time!" She repeated the part that she clearly felt was the most unfair.

As he began to understand more, Dan gently moved her closer to him. Her extraordinary gifts left her feeling out of place. He had no idea that anyone could pick up on the energy of a Non-Gifted person, but all he longed to do was help her. Being a Double-Predilect of equal Gift was extremely rare, and though it certainly helped him in his job, he'd often felt that even his closest friends didn't understand how he did some of the things he was able to do.

"Sweetheart, I am so sorry for what I put you through. I'm ashamed. I am ashamed of the man I was before you took me home and gave me the life I've always wanted but was too damn terrified to work toward. I doubt you would like the energy of any of the women I went out with before I met you. And, baby, you are so extraordinary, please don't ever be ashamed of the woman that you are. I'm so proud of you and so thankful for you. I don't think anyone else could ever have saved me from myself—no one but you."

She lifted her tear-stained face, and he stared into the depths of her misty eyes.

"Thank you." She shivered against him. Her chin still trembled, effectively shattering what was left of his heart. "I can even feel other people's emotions when I'm inside shields, which isn't fair at all, and it isn't how it's supposed to work," she huffed. "But I can't feel anything but you inside your shield." She tried to explain what he meant to her, but he didn't deserve the accolades.

"Can I cast you, sweetheart, please?" He wasn't certain she would let him in. He couldn't blame her.

To exist inside his shield, to let him hold her so intimately, might've been more than she could bear considering the course of their night. But if she would let him shield her, she could feel his love, his adoration, his pride, his desperation to keep her safe. He could calm her heart and her mind. Because they'd existed together as one, he could cast her and restore her soul.

With the draw of an uneven breath, she nodded. His shield spilled from his pores. He filled it with tangible heat and ethereal, calming love. A full minute passed before she relaxed against him. The tears his angel had cried finally dried.

She seemed to be able to push the abhorrent reality of what had happened outside of his shield. Without dinner or a bed, she fell asleep in his arms, exhausted from all the work she'd done and all that he'd put her through.

CHAPTER 22
CHRISTMAS EVE

At noon the next day, Dan seated himself on the bed beside her sleeping form. He held a mug of coffee prepared just the way she preferred.

She'd slept on Dan the evening before for only an hour. Terrified to do more than recline them on the couch, Dan watched over her as she slept. Just before he carried her up to their bed for the night, she sat up and rubbed her eyes.

He'd offered to indulge her in a *Sex and the City* marathon, still trying to undo even a modicum of the damage he'd inflicted. They ate cold chow mein, cuddled on the couch, and watched until late in the night.

He wondered if he should let her sleep more, but they were due at his parents' house in a few hours. And truthfully, he just wanted to hear her voice and see her smile.

"I made you coffee, baby doll, and I miss you." That dizzying grin appeared on her face as she forced herself to awaken. Dan had been up for hours. In an effort to gain himself the balance Governor Haydenshire had encouraged him to find, he'd slipped from the bed, careful not to awaken her, and had run several miles. He'd stalked around the house, arranged her Christmas presents under the tree, and tried to keep quiet. He wanted his baby to sleep.

While eyeing several of the gifts under the tree with his name on the tags, he'd ordered himself not to shake them or move them at all. He wasn't a kid anymore, but something about having a real Christmas with her filled those places inside of him that had been dead and gone.

That evening, Dan tied his tie in the bathroom mirror while Fionna flipped through an entire closet full of clothes and declared that she had nothing to wear.

He had no desire to take Fionna back for another round of Vindico family dynamics, the Christmas edition, so he smiled. "If we stay home, you don't have to wear anything at all."

Fionna giggled as she stalked into the bathroom with her hair rolled in large loops and pinned in metal slip clasps.

"Daniel," she drawled sassily.

"Uh-oh."

"Would you please behave?" Her delighted grin thrilled him.

He feigned consideration. "I can't think of a reason why I would."

"Then I will have to punish you." She lifted her eyebrows in challenge.

Dan groaned, reached over, and slapped her backside through her jeans. He'd been thoroughly enjoying the show of her walking around in nothing but a hot pink bra and tight blue jeans.

"Yet another reason we should just stay home."

She giggled but then changed flow. "I know we aren't opening our presents until tomorrow morning, but I have one I want you to open tonight."

Dan smirked. "There is one incredibly beautiful present I plan to open tonight, baby doll." He gestured to her crotch.

"Are you planning on behaving this way at your parents' home this evening, Chief Vindico?"

"Says the girl who didn't wear panties when she took me to meet her folks."

Heat worked up from her abdomen and settled in her cheeks just before she cracked up.

After running a brush through his hair and spritzing on cologne he knew Fionna liked, Dan reclined on the bed and flipped on the TV. He pulled his phone from his pocket.

Fionna finished putting on her makeup and released the pins from her hair. He watched as it fell in rolling waves that dripped down her back. She kicked off her jeans, and he wolf whistled.

She shook her head at him and moved back to the closet. "What are you doing?" She emerged with several hangers full of clothes.

"Looking for restaurants that are open on Christmas Eve."

She changed out of the matching hot pink thong and pulled on a white lace one. His mouth watered. She thoroughly distracted him from his task.

"But we're eating at your parents'."

He'd hoped a cleansing breath might wash away the fantasy taking place in his mind, but it didn't. He tried to focus on what she was saying. "No, baby, we're being served food at my parents', but as you already know, my mother is a terrible cook. I thought you might like to actually eat this evening." With another mischievous smirk, he chuckled. "You know, before I eat you."

"Dan," she drawled his name into four syllables. He watched her blush return. "Your mom isn't a terrible cook." She forced the outright lie from her lips and cringed from the effort.

Dan laughed and recalled his childhood. "My mother has five dishes that she makes in succession, and none of them taste like food. Soupy meatloaf, and spaghetti that is undercooked served with sauce that's somehow ninety percent canned black olives and so thin you could drink it with a straw. That always comes with wheat bread that she cuts into triangles, slathers with margarine and garlic salt, and then burns to a blackened crisp. Pork chops you need a chainsaw to cut alongside mashed potatoes that you could use to waterproof a house. Some kind of chicken shit she drowns in sour cream and then puts corn flakes on top of that she calls a casserole. Then there's Marion Vindico's specialty, rubberized ham with canned peas."

Fionna had begun laughing with the first item on Dan's list and was now doubled over, giggling hysterically.

"Oh, and it's Christmas Eve, so she'll also break out my

grandmother's Jell-O mold from 1982 and make a festive strawberry Jell-O salad, but to spice it up a little she'll pour a can of mixed fruit in." Fionna's laughter kept him going. "I wish she'd just pour the damn bottle of vodka in, then at least we could have Jell-O shots, and not have to suffer through the rest of the meal. I tried my best to either eat at Will and Garrett's or over at Amelia's house every night growing up."

Fionna shook her head at him. "I'll fix you something yummy to eat when we get home, if you don't like the meal, which I'm certain will be delicious."

"First of all, I already have something delicious to eat when I get home." He grabbed her hand and spun her onto the bed beside him. His index finger traveled down her body. He started at her neck and tracked downward over the swells of her exposed breasts. He kissed her heatedly, parting her lips with his tongue and then softening the kiss to a gentle exploration.

A luscious moan filled his mouth along with her tongue. "I have to get ready." Regret colored her tone a moment later. Dan gave a begrudged nod.

"And second,"—Dan continued staring at her nipples, drawn taut from his tender touch—"the meal will not be delicious unless you're cooking it here and bringing it with us."

"I asked your mom if I could bring anything, but she said you only liked *her* Christmas dinner." She tried to hide the confusion and hurt. Her eyes and her rhythms betrayed her.

Fury bubbled in Dan's gut. "She said what?"

"You know how moms are." She slipped into her self-appointed peacekeeper role. "You're her little boy. She wants to make you Christmas dinner just like when you were a kid."

With a great deal of disdain, Dan clenched his jaw. As much as his mother desperately wanted him to marry, settle down, and continue the Vindico family name, Fionna's appetizers at their last meal together had shown up her elastic ham. She'd gotten irritated. He willed away his aggravation that his mother had hurt Fionna's feelings.

"Is this okay?" Fionna's voice shook Dan from his reverie. He stood as he took in Fionna in a pair of cream-colored, silk dress pants and a matching cashmere sweater with a deep cowl neck. She'd added a pair of off-white stiletto heels that strapped around her ankle. Her dark, chestnut hair and the deep glow of her olive skin beautifully accentuated the ensemble. The sweater showed off the curves of her breasts. The pants looked like they'd been custom-made to show off her ass without giving too much away.

"You look like an angel." He couldn't take his eyes off her. Doubt of his compliment was echoed in her scoff.

A thought occurred to Dan as he watched Fionna add pearl earrings to her ears. "So, I get to open a present tonight?" He was still unable to look anywhere but at her.

Fionna nodded as she rubbed lipstick onto her lips.

"Just a second, then." He raced from the room and returned a few seconds later. He handed her one of her presents from under the tree.

"What's this?"

"Open it."

"Are you sure?" She sounded like she was afraid to break a Christmas rule. Dan nodded and chuckled at her bright-eyed excitement. She eased the paper off the long thin box.

Watching closely, Dan prayed she'd like it. She popped open the velvet box. She gasped his name as her hand flew to her mouth. As that was the precise reaction he was hoping for, he was extremely pleased.

"If you want to wear it tonight, I thought it would look nice with your sweater."

"Dan, this is…" She shook her head and blinked back tears. She gently lifted the necklace from the box and caught the single pearl that hung from a diamond pendant.

"I did a little research." He took the necklace from her hands and moved behind her to attach the clasp. "I hope you don't mind, but I do have access to just about any file I want, perks of being Chief of Iodex." She nodded. "I pulled up your mom, and I found her birth and death dates. Since her birthstone was a pearl and yours is a diamond, I sort of thought this was perfect." She began to cry in earnest.

"You're absolutely amazing," she stuttered through her tears.

"Thank you." She spun around and wrapped her arms around him with a squeeze. "I am the luckiest girl in the entire world." Dan knew that was far from true. The luckiest girl in the world wouldn't be stuck with him.

"Are you ready to go?" Dan rubbed his hands up and down the soft sweater.

Fionna gave him his smile. Warmth shot through his veins. She soothed all of the places where he was worn and anxious.

With a nod, she let him lead her down the stairs and out into the freezing cold night.

CHAPTER 23
COLLISIONS

Dan pulled the Ferrari into his parents' driveway. His stomach churned as he recalled the last time he'd exposed Fionna to his family in haunting detail.

He helped Fionna pull the gifts from the trunk and guided her up the walkway. She was nervous as well. He could feel it. She touched the pearl around her neck and smiled every time she felt it in her fingers. Dan kissed her cheek as he stuck his key in the lock.

"Whenever you want to leave, just say the word."

She was visibly appreciative that he was aware of her turbulent nerves and nodded her agreement.

Dan pushed the door open after finding it already unlocked. He guided Fionna into the foyer and started to announce their arrival, but as he stared into the music room, his voice tangled in his throat.

As if he was being choked violently, his body begged for air as he stared at his parents smiling at him, having halted their conversation with Mr. and Mrs. Richmond, their lifelong next-door neighbors—and Amelia's parents.

"Dan, it's so good to see you." Mrs. Richmond moved to the entryway and gave Dan a kind smile.

While trying to force himself to draw breath and to remember how to speak, Dan formed his face into what he hoped was a pleasant expression.

"Faith, uh, how are you?" His body swayed. His shield tried to balance him. Heat filled his head, but he could no longer locate his feet. She embraced him, and he patted her back awkwardly.

Fionna stood quietly beside him. He tried to remember his manners. "Uh…this is my…uh," he stammered stupidly.

"Fionna." She extended her hand with a tender smile.

"Hi, Fionna. Marion's just been telling us all about you," she gushed. "I'm Faith Richmond."

Immediate understanding lit Fionna's eyes. She offered Dan a sweet, understanding smile. "It's so nice to meet you." Fionna discreetly slipped her hand into Dan's and soothed him. Her cast brought air back to his lungs and allowed his brain to begin functioning again.

"Fi, this is Gerald Richmond," Dan supplied as Amelia's father made his way into the entryway, carrying a glass of eggnog. "Gerald, this is my…uh…Fionna." *Motherfucking coward.* He couldn't do it. He couldn't call Fionna his girlfriend, not to Amelia's parents.

Mr. Richmond nodded as he slapped Dan on the back. He seemed to understand his hardship.

"So nice to meet you." Mr. Richmond smiled as Fionna shook his hand. She looked deeply concerned for Dan.

"We didn't mean to stay so long. I was just dropping off some of my wedding cookies. I remembered how much you used to like them." Mrs. Richmond completed Dan's horror with wedding cookies.

At one time in his life, they'd been his favorite. Amelia baked them frequently. Whenever they'd gotten into one of their screaming matches, which was fairly often, she would bake them to try to make amends.

"Faith, you and Richard should stay for dinner. The girls will be here soon," Mrs. Vindico encouraged. Dan prayed to any deity willing to listen that they wouldn't agree.

"We'd love to, but we're having dinner at Isabelle's tonight. We're staying over to see what Santa's bringing the little ones." Mrs.

Richmond sounded excited about their Christmas plans, but she hadn't taken her eyes off Fionna.

"Uh, how is Isabelle?" Dan managed to stammer, with Fionna still supplying him with calming, soothing energies.

"She's good. Brian's a pilot with one of the big airlines, so he's gone a good bit, but they make it work," Mrs. Richmond absently explained Amelia's younger sister. She didn't seem able to concentrate on the conversation. Dan found himself in the same situation.

He nodded and hoped that was an acceptable response.

"Well," Mrs. Richmond choked back emotion suddenly, "we'd best be going. Have a Merry Christmas, and it was so nice to meet you, Fionna."

Dan wondered if what she was saying was actually true. She didn't sound sincere. That was very unlike Faith Richmond.

Dan knew Christmas had to be difficult for them. It was Amelia's favorite holiday. She would start playing Christmas music right after Halloween. Dan would complain about it until New Year's.

"You too." Dan remembered that Fionna could feel whatever Mrs. Richmond was feeling. She looked deeply remorseful, but she smiled kindly at both of Amelia's parents.

Kara and Zach came through the door before the Richmonds could make their way out.

"Kara, I hear we're expecting." Mrs. Richmond hugged Kara to her. Kara looked stunned as she glanced from Fionna, to the Richmonds, and then to Dan's expression.

"Yes, ma'am. We just found out...uh, a few weeks ago...so it'll be a while." The words tripped and stumbled out of Kara's mouth.

"We need to head on. Izzy wants to put the kids to bed early. Clearly, she doesn't recall herself and Amelia on Christmas Eve." Mr. Richmond's broad grin at the recollection pierced through Dan's shield, and deep regret worked through him once again.

"Tell Meredith and Lindley we missed seeing them," Mrs. Richmond requested.

"We will." Governor Vindico held the door for the Richmonds. He waved as they left.

"Are you okay?" Kara whispered as she hugged Dan fiercely.

He nodded though he wasn't certain that was the truth.

"Kara, could you…" Dan choked out the half request. He gestured his head toward the hallway leading to the kitchen.

"Of course." She grasped Zach's hand and pulled him behind her. They followed Dan's parents.

"I'm sorry." He was terrified he'd hurt Fionna's feelings on top of everything else.

"You have nothing to be sorry for." Fionna wrapped her arms around him and forced her healing energy through him. "You aren't okay." She jerked his shirttail out of his trousers and slid her hands to his back. She was able to force more of her energy through him this way.

He let her in, though his shield was fighting to envelop him in a steel-like encasement.

"I'm fine. I love you so much. You didn't do anything wrong." Fionna closed her eyes and turned the full force of her powerful energy on him.

Dan was unable to speak. His body inhaled the peace and the calm and the tranquility she fed him in unending supply.

He clung to her as she worked her magic, and several minutes later, she eased back.

"Better?" She placed a tender kiss on his jawline.

"Thank you." He felt weak and worn. He hated that he needed so much of her, but he knew he could never live without that astounding life force she offered him.

She gave him another of his smiles as she nodded. "Any time."

Governor Vindico made another appearance and politely ignored the fact that Dan looked rather bedraggled.

"Scotch, son? Just opened a bottle of 18-year Glenmorangie."

Dan nodded and quickly tucked his shirt back in.

"Fionna, what can I get you to drink?" he asked her.

"Oh, a glass of wine is fine. Whatever you have." Fionna was keeping a close watch over Dan. His father handed him a glass of Scotch, and he drew a long sip.

Meredith and Tim made their way in with the kids. They helped

Kara arrange the gifts on the hearth since Mrs. Vindico preferred the tree to be in the dining room.

Fionna smiled at Olivia who was studying her intently. Dan smiled and felt a little more himself.

"Olivia, this is my girlfriend, Fionna," he explained to his niece, who twisted her mouth in curiosity.

"Do you like to play dolls?" Olivia gazed at Fionna as if the answer to that single question held everything she would ever need to know.

Fionna beamed. "I love to play dolls."

Olivia grinned. "I'm almost six in two weeks, and my name is Olivia Anne Hutchens, and this is my little brother, Oliver. He's only two, so I'm the oldest by four years." She held up four fingers.

Fionna glanced at Dan. She seemed pleased he was regaining his equilibrium. "That makes you very special, doesn't it? You can teach Oliver all kinds of things." Fionna gave Olivia a smile that clearly made her feel as if they were very close friends. Olivia tittered as she nodded her agreement. Her eyes were alight.

"You're so pretty. I have a dolly that has long hair like yours."

"Oh." Fionna looked astonished as she smiled. "Thank you. I think you're very beautiful. I really like your dress."

Olivia spun, making her hunter-green dress with an intricate lace collar flare out, and then she preened for Fionna.

"Can I tell you a secret?" Olivia moved closer to Fionna.

"Sure." She leaned down and moved her ear close to Olivia's mouth. Olivia cupped her hand and then announced, in a rather loud whisper, that Santa was coming to her house that night and had been instructed to bring her a princess crown, and a new baby doll, and maybe a dollhouse.

Dan chuckled as he tousled his niece's hair.

"Well, I hope you get your crown and your new baby doll and maybe your dollhouse."

"Now, Dan,"—Mrs. Vindico whisked into the living room and placed the white poinsettias on the bookshelves out of Oliver's reach —"I decided to make a turkey this year, but I also made the Jell-O salad you like."

Fionna and Dan both fought hard not to laugh.

"Great, Mom." Dan sighed as he wrapped his arm around Fionna, and she scooted closer to him on the couch. Mrs. Vindico situated herself in one of the stuffy armchairs near the sofa.

"Now, Fionna, I wanted to get your opinion, dear. I'm planning on ordering these next week. What do you think?" She thrust a catalog folded back to the page in question into Fionna's face. It showed a picture of a heavily upholstered, quilted valance box and thick curtains that were navy blue with the outline of large birds in top hats stitched in gold.

Fionna's eyes goggled as she took in the most hideous curtains Dan had ever seen, and that was saying something.

Fionna cleared her throat. "Uh…well…where were you going to hang these?"

"I was thinking for the living room and the bedrooms."

Fionna nodded and swallowed down a long sip of her wine. "I really think you should stick with the ones you have in here. They're very"—Fionna studied the gaudy yellow curtains with blue toile designs—"nice."

"Oh, no, dear." Mrs. Vindico scoffed. "I meant for Dan's house."

Dan gave an audible huff as Fionna's mouth dropped open. "Mother, you are not ordering curtains for OUR home. Fionna is perfectly capable of decorating however she wants it."

"I was trying to be helpful, Daniel."

"Stop!" Dan demanded.

"I just haven't really had a chance to decide exactly what we want to do." Fionna tried to smooth over the irritation. She glanced nervously between Dan and his mother. "I like to take my time with things."

"Marion, I'm hungry. Let's start serving dinner. I'm sure Lindley and her date will be here soon," Governor Vindico redirected his wife's attention.

"We probably should. I want the kids to be able to enjoy their presents before they head home." Mrs. Vindico pulled Oliver up into her arms. She carried him to the dining room while instructing him to use his manners and not make a mess with his dinner.

"Un-fucking-believable," Dan spat as he helped Fionna up.

CHAPTER 24
NOT QUITE CHRISTMAS DINNER

Fionna gave him a sympathetic smile as she shook her head. "At least it's turkey. That wasn't on your list."

Dan kissed the top of her head. "Don't worry, baby, my mother can burn anything." He pulled her seat out for her at the table and then seated himself beside her.

Mrs. Vindico and Meredith were each holding a spoon. One had come from the diaper bag Meredith had carried in. It was blue plastic and had a fat nubby handle suitable for a toddler's inexperienced hands. Mrs. Vindico had supplied a polished silver baby spoon that matched her silver pattern. The handle was long and sleek. Dan wondered momentarily if they were going to have some kind of very awkward spoon-sword duel.

"Mother, he just turned two. He is going to get food everywhere, and he doesn't know any manners yet. He's just now successfully using this." Meredith jabbed the plastic spoon toward her mother.

"*En garde*," Dan drawled under his breath. Fionna and Kara began giggling.

"Meredith, if you don't teach them early, they won't learn."

Dan and Kara shared a sympathetic glance with their little sister.

"Now, I really went all out this year. I even used the Internet," Mrs. Vindico announced proudly.

"Dear God." Dan grimaced as Fionna choked back laughter.

"Arthur, would you get the tuna loaf?"

The governor grimaced and then moved to the refrigerator. He revealed something that looked like it had come from a sub-freshman chemistry lab.

"Fionna, I didn't know if you were watching your weight, so I prepared several options." Mrs. Vindico patted Fionna's right hand. Unadulterated wrath exploded in Dan's shield. The room filled with sizzing green energy. Fionna looked stunned, and Kara scoffed.

"Mom, why on earth would Fionna be watching her weight? Most women would give their right arm to look like that." She gestured to Fionna, only furthering her deep embarrassment.

"I think she's put on a little since she and Dan started dating. I read an article in *Women of the Realm* that said if you want to have children soon, you should maintain your weight in the months before you conceive, so that your uterus will be ripe when the seed is planted."

Dan's mouth dropped open in abhorrent shock as Fionna glowed crimson. "Mother! Fionna can eat whatever the hell she wants to eat. She's perfect. Look at her! And we are not having children any time in the next several years, so would you please pick a new topic!" His roar echoed off the glass china cabinet.

Zach and Tim both offered Dan sympathetic gazes as they joined in his fury. Mrs. Vindico ignored Dan's diatribe. In true Marion Vindico fashion, she simply went on with the explanation of her dishes.

Fionna was thoroughly shaken and seemed to be walking a thin line between breaking down in tears and asking Dan to take her home. He was about to offer to do just that when Governor Vindico appeared carrying a platter containing a semblance of a turkey that looked like it had been in the oven for approximately three weeks.

"Now, I did something a little different this year." His mother clapped her hands together to applaud her own efforts. "I decided to stuff the turkey, so I made a liver and sausage stuffing that your father and I used to like when we first married. I just crammed it full."

Fionna looked horrified, and Dan fought not to gag.

Kara rolled her eyes dramatically. "I can't eat liver. I'm pregnant."

"It's Christmas, Kara, you'll be fine. If you don't want that, then eat the tuna loaf."

"I can't have tuna either. I am pregnant!" Kara shrieked.

"Kara Denise Vindico, stop being overly dramatic right this moment!" Mrs. Vindico scolded Kara as if she were Olivia's age. "I also made a Kris Kringle salad." She gestured to the small salad plates at everyone's places. Dan glanced down at his plate with an angry scowl. There were two slices of apple and one slice of a brown avocado covered in a bright red liquid.

"You just melt those red cinnamon candies in water and pour them over it. Doesn't it look festive? I found it in last year's *Women of the Realm* anniversary cookbook." Mrs. Vindico beamed at her creation as all of her children shuddered. "We still had a bag of those candies from when you kids were little. I finally got to use them up."

Dan and Kara shared a horrified expression.

"And these are mint-glazed carrots and peas." She pulled the lid off a Pyrex dish and proudly exhibited the odd combination for everyone.

"And here's the Jell-O salad that's Daniel's favorite. I made it with sugar-free Jell-O this year. That should save some calories. And I used grapes instead of the can of fruit, less sugar."

Dan's stomach rolled as the green salad with grapes suspended throughout it jiggled ominously. The fat grapes gave the impression of eyes staring up at them.

"Let's start passing and then we'll just make Lindley a plate," Mrs. Vindico ordered.

"Bet Lindley wouldn't mind if we didn't," Meredith huffed to Dan who nodded his adamant agreement.

"Dan, I don't eat organ meats. Ever," Fionna whispered. "I…just don't." She sounded terrified she was going to offend someone.

"Don't eat it, baby. I will find you something if I have to drive to Maine tonight." He kept a cold glare leveled at his mother for her earlier comments about Fionna's weight. He happened to deeply appreciate her curves that had broadened just a little in the last few weeks.

"I'm really sorry you can't drink, Care Bear," Zach whispered in

Kara's ear. He angled his head so that Dan and Fionna could hear him as well. They all chuckled as Kara nodded her agreement.

"Turkey, Fionna?" Governor Vindico cut a slice of the very odd-looking poultry concoction.

"Yes, sir," Fionna managed to choke out.

"Hey, sweet car, man," Zach complimented Dan.

"You and Kara can take it for a spin if you want."

"Thanks." Zach looked shocked.

The bowls and platters went around the table. Everyone seemed to draw steady, bracing breaths before they allowed any of the creations to come in contact with their forks.

Kara's plate contained the carrots and peas, some Jell-O salad, and nothing else. "I am *starving*," she fussed quietly to Fionna.

"I'm so sorry. I'm sure you are." Fionna looked devastated as she glanced around as if something that would be safe for Kara to eat might appear out of thin air.

Dan checked the other end of the table. His parents were engaged in a somewhat heated discussion as to Lindley's whereabouts.

They had to at least make it appear that they'd eaten something, so Dan slid his fork through the carrot and pea mixture. He brought it to his lips with a slight shudder and tried to hide his grimace, as the heavily overcooked peas mushed in his mouth. The carrots were effectively raw. They were so severely undercooked they had to be chewed numerous times.

Kara had decided to try the same dish and stared at Zach in horror as she forced her mouth to keep moving. Kara was an Occamy Predilect and an excellent cook, but her mother tended to downplay her abilities.

"I don't like it," Olivia fussed to Tim. She looked confused by what her grandmother had put on her plate.

"Smart girl," Dan quipped under his breath.

"Olivia, we need to try everything on our plate, okay?" Meredith guided her. Everyone at the table was well aware it pained Meredith to say the words.

While looking thoroughly put out, Olivia lifted her carrots from her plate with her fingers and chomped down on one dejectedly. "May

I have Ranch dressing please?" She turned her pleading green eyes on her Aunt Kara.

Before anyone could object, Kara leapt. "Of course, sweetheart." She bound into the kitchen and returned with the dressing. She poured several helpings onto Olivia's plate.

"Kara, the carrots go with the peas, and they have a mint sauce," Mrs. Vindico corrected her.

"I was aware." Kara left the dressing within Olivia's grasp.

Dan watched Fionna delicately cut the turkey away from the liver stuffing and then place a hesitant bite in her mouth. Dan did the same. He tried to taste what Fionna was tasting. He wanted to know if she was going to lie and tell him it was good.

Truthfully, it was without any flavor at all. It did require a great deal of jaw strength to work through the bone dry meat, however.

Mrs. Vindico was not impressed with the lackluster response to her preparations.

"Fionna, did you get a chance to go through any of the catalogs I left for you?"

Dan reached for her hand. She'd been there when he'd needed her the most, and he would do the same. He concentrated and tried not to let anyone else at the table know what he was doing as he began supplying her with his fierce strength, his love, and his protection.

She drew from him in heavy doses. He fought not to drop his fork and revel in the heady sensation. A hungry groan filled his lungs, but he kept it at bay.

He watched the tense edges around her beautiful face soften. With an extended blink, a timid smile played on her lips. She continued her draws of his energy in the offered, steady supply.

With a sigh, she turned back to Dan's mother. "I've flipped through a few of them. I was a little busy this week." She splayed her hand wider in Dan's to pull more from him.

"I read in the paper that the Angels had this week off," Mrs. Vindico pressed as if she'd caught Fionna in a lie.

"Yes, ma'am, but I worked at my dad's bakery this week because right before Christmas is so busy. Then Emily and I took anything that didn't sell to the homeless shelters. Yesterday, I baked Christmas cookies and took them to the children's home that the Angels volunteer at in DC. The whole team spent the afternoon with the kids."

Everyone at the table was visibly impressed. Fionna shook her head. She wanted no praise for her volunteer work. She smiled. "Dan came by after work yesterday. We read to the kids." Dan appreciated how she left off what had happened after that.

"Yeah, Mom, somehow curtains just didn't seem to be more important than homeless kids at Christmas," Dan sneered.

"I wish you'd called me. I would have loved to help." Kara looked deeply impressed.

"I'm sorry. I didn't know. We work up there all year, so I can call you next time we go."

Kara smiled and nodded. She looked excited by the prospect.

"That really is a lovely thing to do." Mrs. Vindico was sincere in her compliment.

"I think the Angels do almost as much volunteer work as the entire Auxiliary department of the Senate." The governor winked at Fionna, who was still running a steady shade of crimson. That was far from true, but Dan appreciated his father trying to soothe the emotional bruising his mother wielded without thought.

"You're playing in that big exhibition in Vegas, aren't you?" Zach commented as he ate his Jell-O. He didn't look nearly as offended by the dish as Dan felt.

Fionna smiled. Talking about Summation was a topic she was comfortable with, so she seemed to settle in. "Yeah, we leave early Saturday morning. Teams come from all over the Realm. We're excited to try to bring the cup back to Arlington again."

"Stephen told me that Garrett and Rainer are flying out for the exhibition, as well," Governor Vindico tried to keep the Summation conversation going. "He's hoping the press will leave Rainer and Emily alone while they're there."

Fionna nodded. "They've been all over Emily about the wedding."

"That poor kid. Joseph would turn over in his grave if he knew the hell the press puts Rainer through now."

Fionna and Dan both nodded their agreement. "Emily really

wanted to get married on the beach, but Rainer told her there wasn't a good way to secure the oceanfront so they couldn't."

Dan was impressed that Rainer had realized that and had managed to convince his bride of that fact.

"I'm certain Stephen and Lillian will put on quite the show for the Crown's baby girl." Mrs. Vindico tried unsuccessfully to hide her jealousy. The wedding of the decade would have nothing to do with her.

"Fi's going to be one of Emily's bridesmaids," Dan announced while trying to hide the Jell-O and tuna under his turkey.

"Really?" Kara and Meredith's eyes lit. Fionna seemed more comfortable with the attention now. "They've kept everything so hush-hush. I know the papers must be begging for any information they can get." It seemed Kara was looking for a little information herself.

Fionna chuckled. "Yeah, and Emily has such great taste. It's really going to be beautiful." She gave nothing away.

"I hope we get invited." Kara was nearly bouncing in her seat.

"Of course you'll be invited. Your father is one of the governors," Mrs. Vindico declared.

"So what? I don't know Emily or Rainer at all."

Mrs. Vindico scoffed as if the fact that Kara knew neither the bride nor the groom would keep her from the wedding.

"Can you tell us what colors she's using?" Meredith begged.

"I'm sorry. Emily swore me to secrecy." Fionna looked concerned that she was hurting Meredith's feelings, but Dan was impressed with her dedication to her friend.

"Is your father making the cakes, dear?" Mrs. Vindico asked pointedly.

"Mom, she just said she couldn't talk about it," Dan deflected. He knew Mr. Styler was making the cakes and that Fionna would have a difficult time working her way out of that particular question without lying outright.

"Well, speaking of cakes, I decided to try a recipe out of *Women of the Realm*," Mrs. Vindico used her segue quite liberally.

Dessert meant that they were one step closer to leaving, so Dan welcomed the advance. "Great, let's have it."

Fionna giggled when she realized why Dan was eager for dessert and why his mother had asked about the wedding cakes.

Mrs. Vindico moved through the kitchen to the laundry room. Everyone braced for what she might be carrying. She emerged with a three-tier cake that was leaning precariously to one side.

"This way everyone can have whatever kind they like," Mrs. Vindico announced proudly. "The bottom is a pumpkin cheesecake. The middle is a chocolate cake with banana frosting, and the top is a red velvet cake with chocolate frosting." She looked quite pleased with her extremely odd-looking creation.

The cheesecake being on the bottom would explain the leaning. The center layer was decorated with sliced bananas that were quickly turning brown, and the top layer had small candy canes pressed into the sides.

"It looks like it was attacked by some kind of deranged clown," Zach gasped under his breath. Dan and Kara cracked up.

"The magazine said to use artificial sweetener, so every layer is sugar-free, and I used egg substitutes to lower the cholesterol. And I got this lovely silver platter from the magazine for ordering more subscriptions."

"Oh no," Fionna mouthed. She was unable to hamper the words flowing from her lips. Dan smiled at her, certain he could never love anyone more. His mother set the cake on the sideboard and pulled out the engraved silver cake server from her and the governor's wedding.

"Fionna, which kind would you like? I'll just cut you a little piece." She patted her own abdomen as if to indicate why Fionna would only be allowed a small portion.

It was not the first time in his life that Dan's mind had invented images of him choking his mother.

"I'm really full from dinner." She gestured to her plate still brimming with food. "I'll just have a little of the cheesecake."

Mrs. Vindico went around the table, taking requests.

Dan commanded himself to cut into a small piece of the

cheesecake. He brought it to his lips and shuddered. It tasted like artificial, pumpkin-flavored cough syrup.

"It's really hard to cook with artificial sweetener," Fionna whispered in explanation, "and cake doesn't require many eggs, but you need the yolks to bind it."

"Oh." Fionna smiled. "I almost forgot. I brought a tin of the cookies that I made yesterday."

"I'll get them." Dan rushed to the living room. He returned with the cookies just as Oliver's tongue gave protest from his mouth. He pursed his little lips and shook his head. "It's no-no!"

Meredith and Tim tried hard not to laugh.

"Here, buddy." Dan popped open the tin of cookies and supplied Oliver with a snickerdoodle. He beamed up at Dan as he attempted to inhale the cookie and thank his uncle simultaneously.

Dan scrubbed the top of his head. Cookie crumbs spewed from his mouth. Mrs. Vindico rushed for a wet washcloth.

"May I have one too, Uncle Dan?" Olivia begged.

"Sure, sweetheart." Dan leaned down and offered the tin to Olivia for her to choose. She picked up a delicate snowflake cookie that was covered in powdered sugar.

When Mrs. Vindico returned with the rag, she looked highly irritated. Dan ignored her as he passed the tin around.

A fierce knock sounded on the front door. "Oh, there's Lindley." As if there was a spring in her chair, Mrs. Vindico leapt back up.

"Mom, when's the last time Lindley knocked?" Dan pointed out as he moved to the door ahead of his mother. He pulled the sheers away from the windows surrounding the door. "What the hell now?" He flung the door open and glared hatefully at Lindley and what Dan assumed was her new boyfriend. They were both in cuffs, standing between three Iodex officers who were on call that evening.

"Picked them up downtown, sir," Officer Sanders informed Dan.

"What'd she do now?"

Lindley scowled, but her companion seemed to be too high to recognize the verbalization of words.

"That patrol we were working out on Third. It seems they were looking for a little fun before Christmas, I guess. She didn't have enough on her for anything more than a misdemeanor, but he had quite a bit," Sanders informed Dan.

"Pot?" Dan prayed that was it.

"No, sir, angel dust, and she downed something else when she saw us coming. I don't know what it was or how much she had."

Dan shook his head in disgust. "Take her to Felsink. Lock them up. I'll look over the case next week. It's time she realized there are consequences to her actions. She can sober up out there before she heads to rehab."

"Daniel, no!" Mrs. Vindico was outraged as she and the governor joined Dan at the door. Lindley smirked. She was getting her way yet again.

Infuriated, Dan spun to his father. "If you want it swept under the rug again, you sign her out. I'm not doing it anymore." Dan stomped back to the table. He was spurned by the injustice of it all.

"Sign her out, Arthur," Mrs. Vindico demanded.

"Lindley, why do you do this?" The governor's tone was perforated with exhaustion and failure.

"We were just having a little fun, Daddy. It's no big thing." Lindley had perfected her cooing pout years before.

Fionna laced her fingers through Dan's in an effort to calm him down, but he was too angry to let her in. To Dan's shock, he heard his father's voice turn commanding.

"No, Marion. Dan's right. Take her on to Felsink. I'll sign the papers Monday."

Kara and Meredith's mouths hung open in shock.

"Arthur!" Mrs. Vindico gasped.

"Daddy!" Lindley was stunned.

"Now!" The governor wasn't backing down, much to Dan's delight. With that, he closed the front door as everyone stared in shocked silence.

Dan put his arm around Fionna. He wasn't certain how his mother would react, and he knew the emotions would be quite a bit to have to withstand.

Mrs. Vindico began angrily clearing the table. "Well, why don't we have coffee and open presents?" It seemed she'd decided that ignoring the fact that her daughter was being hauled off to prison would keep reality from ruining her holiday meal.

With nervous glances, everyone stood and followed her lead.

"Can I help you with the coffee, Mrs. Vindico?" Fionna asked hesitantly.

"I'll get it." Mrs. Vindico stormed from the room. She returned several minutes later with the silver tea service and handed out teacups full of coffee. She seemed to have regained her composure while she was alone in the kitchen. She pursed her lips and set her face to a stone carving of martyrdom.

The governor looked relieved that she was at least going to make it through the evening with her children without shouting at him for his decision.

"Now, I suppose I'll let Lindley know this Monday." She was not going to let the governor off without several quips and dirty looks, however. "But I got all of my girls,"—she seated herself and patted Fionna's leg to let her know that she'd been included in the group—"a three-year subscription to *Women of the Realm!*" Mrs. Vindico tittered in her excitement. Fionna looked stunned by the inclusion. She grasped Dan's hand.

Kara and Meredith didn't look any more thrilled with the gift than Fionna.

"Thank you," Fionna managed as she tried to hide the horrified expression that broadcast from her features.

Women of the Realm was a bimonthly publication that, as far as Dan was concerned, was only suitable for kindling. It contained recipes, generally quick on time and short on health and taste, remedies for medical problems that either didn't exist or should be handled by a medio, relationship advice that generally preached that sex was immoral, and advertisements for everything from plant watering trays to bladder pads. It was also chock-full of outright lies about Realm celebrities—everyone from Governor Haydenshire to the Angels to Rainer and Emily appeared without their permission with regularity.

"Three years," Fionna whimpered to Dan as Olivia and Oliver began pulling open their packages.

"Twice a month," Dan added morosely.

"All right, Fionna, since you're a guest, why don't you open a gift?" Mrs. Vindico shoved a present into Fionna's hands. Dan wasn't certain which was worse, his mother's attempts to include Fionna in the family or her reminders that she was not yet a Vindico. Oddly enough, the attempts to be inclusive seemed more off-putting.

"Thank you. You really didn't have to get me anything."

Dan studied the present. His left shoulder twitched. His shield shimmered in his hands. His body attempted to shield Fionna without him consciously ordering it to. It was an odd sensation for his shield to move of its own accord onto someone who wasn't him. *Receivers can feel the emotion that went into the gift. They're a big deal to them.* Rainer's words seared through his mind.

Fionna hesitantly pulled the tape on the package. Dan wondered how big of a disaster this was going to be. He sincerely hoped the things he'd gotten for her would somehow make up for the pile of presents gathered at her feet. She smiled sweetly and feigned excitement.

Mrs. Vindico looked quite proud of herself. "I happened to notice that old sewing machine you had in your guest bedroom at your house," she explained. "So, I thought maybe you could learn to sew. That might be a nice hobby when you finally decide to stop all this Angels nonsense."

Dan ground his teeth and narrowed his eyes.

Fionna held a book in her lap called *Let's Sew Something Together*, with pictures of beginner sewing projects straight from the early 1970s on the cover. It must've belonged to Dan's grandmother.

"Once you get through straight lines and picking out material, you can get to patterns and actually making things." Mrs. Vindico patted Fionna's leg again.

In the past month, Dan had not seen Fionna sew much of anything. He assumed that was because her machine wasn't working and because he'd been taking up all of her available time. But he knew that all of the intricate quilts in their home she'd sewn. Not to mention that she often sewed banners for the Angels, all types of clothing, pillows, and all of her extensive apron collection that she used regularly. She certainly didn't need a beginner's sewing book any more than she needed a quip about her career. Dan rubbed his temples and prayed the book would be the worst of it.

"Well, uh, thank you." Fionna glanced at Dan and then back to the book in her lap.

"Didn't you sew all of the Auxiliary Order banners when we were in school?" Kara quizzed.

"Yes, but you can always use a refresher course."

Kara opened gifts for the baby, and Olivia pushed around the doll carriage Governor and Mrs. Vindico had purchased for her with great delight.

Kara and Meredith were elated with the rather expensive cashmere wraps and Diptyque candles Fionna had picked out for them.

"Dan, you open one, son." Governor Vindico handed Dan a box. "This is from me. Your mom wanted to get you socks."

Dan chuckled and pulled the paper off. His father was telling the truth. The wrapping was rather crude. The governor had clearly both wrapped and picked out the gift.

"Wow!" A broad grin spread across his face. Fionna looked excited that Dan was so pleased. "Dad, thank you." Dan lifted the Colt .38 Special from the box.

"It was your grandfather's," Governor Vindico explained though Dan already knew. "It's over fifty years old. Still shoots perfectly. He wanted you to have it when you made chief. I've kept it for a few years."

Though he was truly honored, Dan knew why he hadn't been given the gun when he'd made chief. Grandpa Vindico was the only other Ioses Predilect in the Vindico line. He'd taught Dan to shoot. Amelia had died on the anniversary of his grandfather's death. The date had been crushing. Dan wasn't certain he'd ever recover. His father wasn't going to be the one to hand him the pistol. Instead, Dan had tried to use his own twice, and Garrett had saved him.

"This means a lot to me." More than the cherished memories of the times he'd spent with his grandfather, it meant that his own father could see the changes and the healing taking place in Dan as well.

He flipped open the barrel and spun it quickly before popping it back in.

"Open this one, Fionna. It's for both of you." Mrs. Vindico lobbed a large, rather heavy box onto Dan and Fionna's laps.

Clenching his jaw to keep from shouting at his mother, Dan eased the pistol out from under the new package. His mother's present had driven the barrel into his thigh. He eased the gun into its box and set it out of reach of Olivia and Oliver.

When he returned, he gestured for Fionna to open the package. A moment later she bit her lips together. Dan watched blood pool in her cheeks as she pulled out a baby-blue hand towel from several matching sets. They were all embroidered with a large, yellow letter V.

"Mother!" Dan spat. "*Vindico* is not Fionna's last name. Why would you give this to both of us?"

"I assumed that since she is now living with you, Daniel, that you would be changing her last name."

Infuriated, Dan shoved the hand towel back into the huge box full of towels and dropped it quickly to the floor.

"Now, Fionna, when you want to add the D and F to them, I can tell you where I had them done. You don't want them monogrammed improperly."

Fionna sighed. "Or at all," she breathed. She looked exhausted with the entire evening. Dan could feel the heat of her embarrassment in her tensing rhythms.

A few more rounds of gifts went by, and Dan kept his steely eyes leveled at his mother. She was ignoring the glower.

"Fionna, open your last one." Kara clearly hoped whatever the box contained would help smooth over the towels and the sewing book.

Fionna was now a nervous wreck, and Dan was too angry to calm her as she picked up a relatively small package and began pulling the ribboning off it.

"This was just a sweet little gift I put together for you." Mrs. Vindico moved closer. Dan pulled Fionna tighter to him. Her body gave a timid shudder. Her internal Receiver's shield was setting. She blocked Dan and everyone else out. She didn't want to feel anything else.

She opened the box, and Dan's head dropped in horror. But Fionna relaxed a little and choked back laughter.

Inside was a framed photograph of Dan in his Cub Scout uniform at the age of seven and then a bound ring of notecards.

"Those are all of my recipes of the things that were Daniel's favorite things to eat growing up. See, here's my meatloaf, and pork chops, and my chicken casserole, oh, and the ham you had here a few weeks ago." She showed Fionna the recipe cards as Dan whimpered audibly. "You'll want to learn to make them."

There was a recipe for every single one of the dishes that Dan had whined about just before they'd arrived for their horrific evening. Fionna was unable to keep from laughing, though she tried to hide it from Mrs. Vindico.

"Thank you so much. This is so thoughtful." She pulled out the rather dorky-looking photo of Dan performing the Cub Scout salute, smiling broadly, displaying a gap-toothed smile.

Fionna turned to beam at Dan, who was certain that his face was as red as hers. "You were so cute."

Dan squeezed his eyes shut in defeat.

CHAPTER 25
ECHOES OF HOME

Suddenly, Fionna's cell phone began ringing. Her teasing grin turned into one of heartbreak.

"Please excuse me. That might be my dad."

"Of course, sweetheart." The governor nodded before his wife could respond.

Fionna raced to her purse and extracted her phone. She slipped into the entryway as she answered.

"Daddy, what's wrong?"

Dan stood and set Fionna's gifts where he'd been seated. He rushed to her, pulled his own phone from his pocket, and looked up the enhanced flight schedule to Monterrey, Mexico. There was a flight out in an hour and a half.

"Oh." Her entire body slumped in relief. "Hey Nana." Tears formed in her eyes. She leaned and laid her head tenderly against Dan's chest.

She'd been through quite enough for one evening, and his shield wasn't taking no for an answer anyway. It surrounded her with the fierce double bands of his protection without Dan summoning it at all. It moved of its own accord. He reveled in the satiated peacefulness he brought her.

"I miss you so much." Tears were now flowing down her face. Dan wiped them away and kissed her forehead silently as she spoke. He grinned as she pushed her hand under his jacket, in an attempt to crawl into his chest. He pulled the sports coat open and blanketed her in it, hiding a bit of her face. She nuzzled against him.

"You sound better than when I talked to you a few days ago."

Dan squeezed her tighter and strengthened his shield around her.

"Well, you need to do what the medio says."

Governor Vindico halted abruptly as he took in Dan's shield. He took several steps back. "Son, why don't you take her upstairs?"

Dan took Fionna's hand. His heart pounded out an SOS with every step he ordered his feet to advance. His gut seized as he listened to Fionna talk to her grandmother.

Like he'd been given a cadenced marching order, Dan passed the door to his father's study. One foot in front of the other, he walked past Lindley's door and the bathroom. Kara and Meredith's rooms were to his right, beside his parents' master suite. At the end of the hall, he swallowed down bile as he opened the door to his childhood bedroom.

Not certain what he was supposed to feel, he gave himself a moment to let the memories of the life that the room had once held wash over him.

His mother had taken down the Ioses banners and posters of motorcycles, typically with bikini-clad women splayed across them, when he'd moved in with Amelia. She'd changed the bedspread and curtains, but the room was basically the same. His desk, his chest of drawers, his bed. He cringed as his eyes traveled from one piece of furniture to another. He tried to push the memories outside his shield.

Get it together, you moron. He guided Fionna into the room. She seemed hesitant. She studied him but kept up the conversation with her ailing grandmother. He closed the door behind her.

Fionna had nothing to do with what happened here, and she needs you.

"Did Daddy make you your haupia pie?" Fionna asked her grandmother sweetly and then smiled at her response.

"I loved them. Thank you, but you didn't need to send me anything."

Dan distracted himself by wondering what her grandmother had sent her and when she'd sent it.

"Yes, Daddy gave them to me at the bakery on Monday."

He forced himself to do this by remembering that he'd been a complete coward when it had come to introducing Fionna to Amelia's parents. Dan led her to the bed.

He seated himself with determination and then pulled her onto his lap.

"Nana!" Fionna giggled. The sound eased Dan's breathing. "Yes, he's very cute." Her blush returned. She rolled her eyes, and Dan was shocked to hear the chuckle that spilled from his own lips.

"No," Fionna argued. "He's the most amazing man I've ever met." She held Dan's eyes with her own. He swallowed back the emotion that had him in a chokehold as he shook his head.

"Yes, I'll tell him you want him to come to Monterrey," Fionna agreed in a placating tone, and then she giggled hysterically. "No, I will not tell him that. Nana!" Fionna gasped loudly.

Dan gave her a wry smirk. He was, once again, astounded. She could even make him feel loved and comforted in a room that held memories now harrowing, with too much pain for him to manage alone.

"I think you need to back off on the pain medication."

Dan laughed outright as he rubbed her back and watched her eyes dance from hearing her grandmother's voice.

Her grandmother began talking rapidly, and Fionna grinned again.

"All right. I need to go. I love you, and I miss you so much."

Dan could feel her misery and her longing to be with her own family. He was sick as his mind replayed their evening in gory detail. "I will." Fionna agreed to a request. "I love you. Merry Christmas," were her parting words.

Fionna ended the call and blinked back another round of tears. She needed a minute. She curled herself up in her ball in his lap. He cradled her against him and brushed his thumb over her cheek in a tender caress.

"Baby, I wish you'd told me you wanted to go. I would've taken you down there." He had no idea how he would've made that happen, but he would've come up with something.

"We would've just had to come home tomorrow." She buried her face in his chest. Abruptly, she sat up and glanced around. "I'm sorry. You don't want to be up here. Let's go back downstairs." She tried to stand though the task seemed a heavy burden. Dan held her back.

"No." He prevented her from moving farther. "Just stay right here with me for a few minutes before we go back to all of that insanity." He gestured his head to the hallway outside his door.

"Are you sure?" To test him, she linked their fingers and drew a healthy dose of his energy.

"Did I pass?" He gave her another cocky smirk. She grinned and nodded. "I'm fine, honey. I just want to hold you." He wanted that more than he wanted anything else in the world.

Utter relief washed over her, and she curled herself up inside his embrace.

"What did Nana say?"

Her giggle made him all the more curious. "She seems so much better. They have her on some new medications. Mama took her to see a new medio."

"What did she send you?" He hadn't meant to ask. He hoped she didn't feel like he was intruding.

Fionna didn't seem to mind. "I wanted to make a quilt for Mama with some fabrics from Mexico, so Nana sent me a bunch of fat quarters. Those are what you use for quilting squares. I didn't have the heart to tell her about my sewing machine." She hesitated. "She was so excited that I wanted to make it. She binds all of my quilts for me."

Dan gazed at her, curled up in his lap, as he kissed the top of her head. "What were you not going to tell me?" He curved his fingers and tickled her ribs. She wiggled and laughed hysterically then clamped her arms to her side.

"Do not tickle me!" she shrieked through more laughter. Dan waggled his eyebrows.

"What did she want you to tell me?"

"I'm gonna scream for your dad." Fionna looked delighted with their game.

"Uh-huh, go ahead." Dan knew perfectly well she'd chicken out because she wasn't frightened in any way. Fionna giggled deliciously. "Tell me, baby." Dan wiggled his fingers between her ribs for a split second.

"Okay, okay," she agreed. Dan raised his left eyebrow in expectation. Fionna was the color of a ripe strawberry as she tightened the hold of her arms against her rib cage. "But my Nana is really a spry, old lady, and kind of dirty." Another round of laughter overtook her.

Dan joined in and put away everything that had happened to him in that room. That was a lifetime ago, and right now, everything he could ever want was curled up in his lap.

"And her dirty comment was?" Dan lifted his hand to threaten another assault of her rib cage.

"You know I really like it when you do other things with your hands."

"We'll get to that later."

Fionna rolled her eyes and finally acquiesced. "Nana said to tell you if you think I'm hot in the bedroom, you should see me in the kitchen." Her entire body, hot from her embarrassment, cringed into Dan.

While doubling over with laughter, Dan nodded. "Oh, I like Nana."

She continued to giggle as she went on, "And she said to tell you that she taught me all of my moves."

"Mmm, I need to send Nana a Christmas present," Dan drawled, only making her laugh harder.

Suddenly, he was overcome with the love he felt for her, and the way she'd illuminated everything in his dark and terrifying world.

She soothed every strain and nursed every wound back to health. He stared into her beautiful eyes as she gazed up at him. Their laughter ebbed in light of their love.

He leaned in as she arched her back. Their lips met passionately in the middle. He was soft and tender with her this time. He moved his right hand to her cheek, kissing her slowly and gently. He guided her mouth with his own.

She trembled in his arms. Overwhelmed with the need to tend to her, to ease any emotion she'd had to endure, he reclined her on his bed and moved over her. Slowly he traced her bottom lip with his tongue, until she parted her lips and took him in.

He needed to taste her, to explore her, to pull the energy from her as he supplied her with his own. She was so damn sweet and soft in his arms, small and helpless under his rippling muscles and his towering height.

Their tongues moved in syncopation. Her energy seeped into his mouth and gathered in the emanating heat between her legs.

He was desperate for more of her, so he slipped his hand under her sweater and drew from her now-exposed side. Desire defeated her trepidation. She wanted more of him too, it seemed. Her hand slid down his chest and she worked it into his trousers. A shocked, guttural groan tensed from low in his abdomen.

She gasped as she felt how hard he was hung all for her. Insatiable, she wrapped her hand around him and drew his own hunger and need straight from its source. The responses of his body to hers ignited a blaze through her veins. Aware that he was holding a heavenly fire in his arms, Dan longed to be consumed.

Continuing his ascension up her, Dan removed the barrier. Nothing would ever stand in the way of having her in his hands. He lowered the cup of her bra so he could feel the heavy, fevered flesh.

He worked with gentle care as he felt her nipples begin to beg his palms for the nurturing they craved. They throbbed in a directive he had no choice but to obey. He lowered his mouth to her right breast. Her breath caught, and her body shuddered as he began to suckle.

A luscious moan gasped from her.

"Mother, are you crazy?" Dan heard Kara reprimand.

He jerked away and gasped for breath as he eased Fionna's bra back over her swollen breasts. He was careful not to hurt her as he'd just made her quite tender. He heard his mother's contentious rap on his door.

"Daniel, we'd like to go on with the gifts. Is everything all right?" Fionna released his erection, and he attempted to will it away.

"Be there in a minute, Mom." Dan prayed he didn't sound as turned on as he was. *At least she didn't just barge in this time.* Dan shut that thought down as he recalled what he'd been doing the last time his mother had thrown open the door on him and Amelia.

He forced himself to sit up so that Fionna could regain her composure as well. Her face glowed enticingly. Her lips were kiss-swollen, and her cheeks were flushed just like they were when he brought her. She couldn't seem to steady her breath. Dan knew the expression on his face, dark and ravenous, was doing nothing to help douse her heat.

She seemed unable to help herself as she laced her fingers in the back of Dan's hair and grasped the knot of his tie with her other hand. She lowered his head back to hers. Without need for anymore provoking than that, he began devouring her mouth again.

"God, I want you. I need to be with you. Just let me take you home and make you mine."

Her body gave a rapid shiver, and her breaths gasped in her desire.

"I hurt," she whispered as she fluttered her fingers up his length again. "I ache for you. I need you inside of me. I feel empty, and I'm scared."

All-consuming devotion to protect her surged through his body and his shield. He lay back over her and groaned as she spread her legs for him. They encircled the steel-like pressure against her mound. "I'm not gonna let you hurt, sweetheart. Never be afraid. I'll take it all away. I'm right here, and I'm going to make everything feel better." He rocked his body against her.

"Yes," she panted as he consumed her mouth again.

Another hesitant tap sounded on the door. "Dan, I'm so sorry, but Mom's getting all flustered," Kara pled.

Several key curse words flew from his mouth as Dan moved away.

"We're coming, Care Bear." He swallowed down the desperate need that permeated his entire being.

With her face set in a mix of frustration and sadness, Fionna stood from the bed and eased into the bathroom that the governor had added between Dan and Lindley's room.

She splashed cool water on her cheeks and tried to return them to their original color. She smoothed her hair and drew measured, steadying breaths.

"Come on. Let's just go give my parents their present, and then we're going home." Dan followed her into the bathroom as soon as he was able to walk. He was careful not to touch her. The temptation was far too enticing. Their energy was frantic to be joined. Fionna grinned at him sweetly. "We have to stay until everyone's ready to leave."

Despite the cool water, her face was still flushed, her lips swollen, and her eyes hungry. Damn, but she was too much. He'd never get enough.

He cupped her backside and rubbed his hands over the silky pants.

"Fine, but when I get you home, baby, I hope you're ready, because I'm going to own you."

"Stop. I just got calmed down."

His body jerked from the order.

She gave him a sultry, seductive grin. "Besides, you haven't seen the present I want you to open tonight." She breathed the words in his face, and her eyes turned eager. He panted as he backed her up to the sink and pinned her between it and his hardened body.

"The only thing I want to open tonight, baby doll, is that tight little pussy that already belongs to me." He squeezed a handful of her ass greedily as she moaned. Her pulse raced against him. "So tight, so hot and wet, you feel like heaven." His erection was back as soon as he was within ten feet of her. He pressed himself into the soft, heated skin of her stomach.

"Daniel!" shrieked Mrs. Vindico as she pounded on the door. Dan's eyes bulged in fury as he marched out of his bathroom and flung open the door.

"Damn it, Mother. I am thirty-two years old, and I told you we will be down there in a few minutes! Could you back the hell off?"

"If there is nothing wrong, then there is no need for you and Fionna to be up here alone. Where is Fionna?"

"She's using the bathroom. Is that all right with you?" Dan seethed.

"Well, then there is no reason for you to be up here at all."

Dan bit back all of the hateful comments that clambered in his brain. The most prominent was that he and Fionna lived together, that they shared a bathroom and a bed. He clenched his jaw shut and reminded himself that his diatribe might embarrass Fionna.

After gliding hesitantly from the bathroom, Fionna took Dan's hand and led him back down the stairs.

Dan wrapped his arm around her on the sofa as she explained that her grandmother had been quite sick and that she'd wanted to wish Fionna a Merry Christmas.

"I don't get to talk to her very often. She's been so tired lately."

Dan couldn't help but revel in the guilt-ridden expression on his mother's face.

"Well, Mom, why don't you and Dad open your present? Fi picked it out." Biting fury flowed openly into his tone.

Fionna elbowed him in an effort to get him to be nice. As that was not an option in Dan's book, he ignored the jab.

Governor Vindico gave Dan a look that said he'd better tone it down as he handed the box to his wife. Dan rolled his eyes and then narrowed them at his mother. He was not a child and wouldn't be ordered around by his parents.

Mrs. Vindico pulled the brochures from the small box Fionna had wrapped.

She smiled. "Oh, this is lovely."

Fionna beamed at Dan as the governor began studying the gift.

"You can go whenever you and Mom want. Just call the number there and book your trip. It's all paid for." The defiant anger never left his tone.

"You shouldn't have spent so much." Mrs. Vindico looked truly touched by the weekend getaway to Biltmore Estate. Fionna had suggested it, and as Dan wasn't much with gifts for anyone but her, he'd quickly agreed. His dad could golf to his heart's content, and his mother could visit the spa and shop and relax for several days.

"This is really thoughtful." Governor Vindico offered a pleading gaze to Dan. He seemed to be asking for peace.

They began planning when to take the trip, which thoroughly delighted Fionna.

Oliver was sound asleep on Tim's shoulder. Olivia was cradling her doll and sitting near her stroller, but she was yawning constantly. Her blinks were extending in length.

Meredith scooped her up. "I think we better go home and get in bed before Santa comes."

Olivia nodded her agreement. "With my princess crown?" she begged through a deep yawn.

Dan and Fionna chuckled as they watched Dan's adorable niece.

"With your princess crown," Meredith assured her. Tim stood and kept Oliver cradled closely on his shoulder. He grinned at his wife and little girl.

For all of Tim's annoying hypochondria, he was a good dad.

Lindley's presents stood in a pile on the hearth. Everyone tried not to see them as the wind picked up outside.

"We're leaving as well," Dan informed his parents. He offered Fionna his hand and then helped her with her coat.

Defeat lurked in the governor's eyes, but he saw them to the door.

Fionna gazed out the windows at the Christmas lights in the neighborhood as Dan steered the car through the first few snowflakes.

He drove slowly, being careful of ice. When he noted her blinking rapidly and trying to discreetly wipe her eyes, he panicked.

"What's wrong, sweetheart? I'm sorry about all of that. I don't know why I keep taking you over there."

She managed a smile and shook her head. "It's not your family, and even though they drive you crazy, don't ever take them for granted."

Understanding tightened his chest. She rolled the pearl pendant between her fingers nervously. "I'm sorry, baby. I know how much you miss her."

He sensed that she didn't want to discuss her mother, so Dan offered her his hand. The luminous green glow of his shield pulsed there for her. She smiled and laced her fingers through his. Her immediate draw sped his heart.

"Take everything you need, baby. It's all for you."

She continued her draws for several long minutes. It was astounding. His energy permeated her. He calmed her and restored her. In that moment, he allowed himself to believe that he could be everything she needed him to be.

The heady satisfaction drove away the plague of unease as he watched the snow gather in the medians. If he focused only on Fionna, he could push away the guilt over Lindley being in Felsink under his orders in weather like this.

CHAPTER 26
PERFECTION

"You know, I don't think I've ever made out with a Boy Scout before." Fionna giggled as Dan drove home. The wind howled, and the snow gathered on the windshield out of the wipers' reach.

"Yes, you have." Dan laughed. "Will was in my pack."

She grinned and then gazed up at him in the light of the streetlamps as they reflected off the swirling snow. "I love you."

The whispered vow took Dan's breath away. "Me too, sweetheart, so much."

She was quiet for several minutes, gazing at the snowflakes whipping and whirling in the crisp night air.

"Will you tell me about the gun? You were so excited when you opened it."

Dan chuckled. He was mildly embarrassed that she'd picked up on his joy. "It's a Colt .38 Special. It was one of the only pistols used by police and Iodex for years." He swallowed down the memories. "My grandpa was an Elite officer as well, so it means a lot to me, I guess. He taught me to shoot."

"I saw all of those marksmanship awards in your office. I didn't know you were a sniper. He must've been some teacher."

Dan scoffed. "Never a sniper—just qualified to be one."

Fionna was the one person he didn't want to brag to. Something about the way she accepted him made all of his commendations and accolades unnecessary.

"I've never shot a gun or even held one." Her tone was introspective with a note of concern.

"Ever?"

"They scare me, I guess."

"There's nothing wrong with that. They're a dangerous weapon. But if you want to learn, I'll teach you." Fionna looked pained as she nodded her understanding. "I wasn't finished, baby. Just listen. If you don't ever want to touch one, that's perfectly fine too. I just want you to be the phenomenal woman that you are. I know a lot of people try to change you. They try to make you into who they want you to be. You don't have to change one single thing for me."

A soft smile formed on her lips. Relief flooded her rhythms. He focused on the road ahead of him as the snow began falling in heavier clumps.

"Looks like some storm." A deep pang of regret permeated his heart.

Fionna picked up on his concern. "I'll ride out there with you to go get her."

He shook his head as he summoned and raised the garage door. "No, it's fine," he lied. "Maybe tomorrow. She's got to grow up. She's going to end up dead if she keeps this up, and the drugs she's buying are just getting harder and harder."

"If you change your mind, we can go."

Dan nodded. He didn't want to think about Lindley anymore. He didn't want to think about his mother, or the Richmonds, or anything except Fionna.

The inflicted wounds from the past few days were chafed and raw. Dan longed to hold her in his arms and to erase everything that had come between them. He sought to rectify every insecurity he could feel plaguing her soul.

He met her at the door, pulled her into him, and kissed her. He was strung so tightly he had to force himself to soften the demanding kiss. He needed to work slowly, paying careful attention to every lesion on her soul. She needed thorough attention to heal the anguish that set a storm of worry in her eyes.

She pulled away with a slight shiver. Her need was fractured with heat, desire, and a nervous tension that he'd yet to alleviate.

Dan followed her into the now warm, inviting home, all due to her presence. With a deep breath, he brought her scent into his lungs and clarity into his mind. Tonight, he needed to worship her body, to bring her peace, and make certain she knew she held his heart forever.

He set their gifts on the kitchen counter and watched her slip out of her coat. She turned back to him and swallowed down what appeared to be an insistent case of nerves.

Uncertain if it was his mother, Bridgette, Lindley, desperately missing her own mother, her island, or both of her grandmothers that had made her so uneasy, he reached for her hands and drew her against his chest. He wrapped his massive arms around her and offered her sanctuary from the world.

He was never going anywhere. He would take care of her always, and he would show her with his body what he couldn't seem to vocalize.

Trying to exercise authority over herself, though it seemed to take a great deal of effort, she pulled away and began. "So, the gift that you get to open first…isn't nearly as special or as beautiful as what you gave me." Her hand nervously smoothed a lock of her hair and then stopped at the necklace as a touchstone.

"Stop." He shook his head as he guided her back into his arms. Her mind battled her body, and the war tensed in her rhythms. She'd had a plan, but the desire held more of her fight. The desire to be cradled and worshipped, to be tended to, gently this time, to be shown the endless bounds of his love, tensed in her fluctuating energy streams.

"But I was gonna…" She pointed to the stairs. She didn't have the energy to put on the show she'd planned. The evening's emotions had thoroughly drained her, and what she needed was to be filled with his reassurances, his love, and his energy.

"Yeah, baby, I know." He cradled her face in his powerful right hand. Tenderly, he brushed his thumb along her cheekbone and watched her long eyelashes flutter from his caress. "You were gonna go put on something so damn skimpy and sexy I'd be done before I got in the room. You were gonna put on a show, all for me, make me harder than a fucking railroad spike, where I would lose all sense of control and take you fast and furiously, because I can't ever seem to maintain any self-discipline when it comes to you."

She grinned at that admission, but the fatigue lingered in her eyes.

"You're an amazing woman, but that's not what you need right now, and it's not what I want. I want to take care of you. I want you under me, in my arms, safe and warm. I want to spend hours making certain you know what you mean to me. I want you naked, unadorned. I love you in lingerie, baby, but tonight I just want you. I want us, together, slow and constant. I want to stare into the most beautiful eyes in the entire world. I want to look into your soul. That's what I want to see in you tonight. I want to bring you over and over again, just me and you and nothing else."

Her body shivered from his words. A small nod showed her acceptance to his plans. He lifted her into his arms, and her body relaxed against him.

"That's it, baby doll. Just let me take care of you."

He carried her up the stairs, stood her beside their bed, and kissed her again. Trying to leash his lust for her was no small task. He ordered himself to slow it down. He traced her bottom lip with his tongue as his hands moved to the lower hem of her sweater.

Desperate to touch some piece of her silky skin, he slipped his right hand under her sweater. He hesitated at her bra strap but moved his hand to her left shoulder blade, keeping her in his substantial embrace.

With his left, he allowed himself a few luscious squeezes of that pert, round ass that drove him wild.

His mother had been correct, *damn her for mentioning it*. Fionna had put on just a little weight in the last few weeks, but Dan had never seen anything more intoxicating. He hoped she'd gain a little more. He imagined her round, full hips with another few pounds and her breasts just slightly heavier.

If he'd thought she was gorgeous a month before, now she was absolute perfection. The last thing he wanted her thinking was that she needed to lose weight. Those curves made him drunk with desire every time his eyes feasted on the magnificent landscape that was Fionna.

He wiped his mother from his mind and concentrated on proving to Fionna that she was devastatingly beautiful, a celestial star that danced only for him. Her light was the only guiding force in his life, the only thing that had ever made sense.

Their tongues moved in heated accord. He consumed her slowly, until he paused to lift the sweater from her curves. Quickly, he tossed it away. He wanted her flesh. He dug deeper. Releasing her breasts of their lacy enclosure took but one flick of his wrist.

As if driven by a magnetic force, his hands moved to her large, swollen breasts, heaving in their need. He lifted their weight and groaned from the sensation.

"So beautiful, baby, and all for me." He leaned and tempted her nipples with his tongue until they drew into stiff eager peaks, and he rewarded their effort.

Eager and yearning, he began to suck her right nipple while he caressed her left with his palm. She trembled against him and let her head fall back as she gave herself over to his hunger.

"Yes," echoed from her in a breathless whisper as he drew her into his mouth and sucked with more force. His resolve slipped with her every panted breath.

He pulled her body closer and gave himself a modicum of relief as he pressed his tightened strain against her abdomen. With a groan of need, he throbbed fiercely against her.

She jerked his belt from his pants, pausing to run her hand up and down his zipper line, until she finally worked the trousers apart and revealed him. Her hand sought his cock, and a guttural groan tore from his lungs.

But a moment later, she lost a little of her desperate drive and allowed the worry back in. Dan drew her back to his chest. He dispensed with their pants and then braided his right hand in her hair and kept his left roving her body.

"I'm right here. I've got you."

She shuddered in his arms and began to rock her body against the steel-hard strain pressed against her. He could feel the wet heat that gathered in the cotton thong.

His eyes closed as he ordered himself to take his time. The way she came for him, fevered and rhythmic, drove him wild. He knew if he allowed himself to cup his hand against that beautiful flower, so ripe for him, he could make her bloom. He could coax out the tension with virtually no effort. The way she melted for him was automatic.

He knew how to touch her, where to seek the liquid heat that burned so copiously within her, how to hold her, what to do and say to make her unravel like spools of ribbon in his hands.

Lifting her into his arms, he laid her tenderly in their bed and tracked his fingertips from her shoulders over her collarbone. He spun them around her nipples as they darkened and beaded tightly. Then he moved down her taut abdomen, drawn in anticipation, until he slid the panties down her long legs and stared at her throbbing lips. They were flushed and full, just waiting to drown him completely. He finished stripping before cupping his hand and summoning the erotic energy surging within her. He sealed her closed before moving on.

She pitched and bucked as he allowed his inquisitive fingertips to stroke over her slit and up to the tender rise of nerve endings pulsating under her mound. She watched him intently as he separated her and gathered the dew seeping from her. He gently circled her opening until she began to beg.

He wanted more. He needed more. He brought his fingers to his mouth and tasted the nectar of her. It wasn't enough. He fell to his knees. Her eyes widened in their elation, and her back arched. He lifted her thighs over his shoulders and continued his feast.

"So damn sweet," he grunted as he stabbed his tongue into her, then softened and spun it up to her now distended, pulsing clitoris. Her inner lips were swollen tight. If he'd ever just given her a little time, he could have seen this incredible show before. He'd always been too frantic to own her, too desperate to allow himself to arouse her slowly.

Reading the cues her body offered, he brushed his tongue over that beautiful, throbbing flesh that hid her pearl. His five-o'clock shadow chafed her inner thighs as he allowed himself to devour her. She groaned from the conflicting sensations.

She shook, and her legs tightened against his jaw. *Oh, hell yeah.* Her breaths were short and seemed to elude her body. He pulled her apart gently, granting himself access to the elusive pearl that belonged only to him. He continued to torture her with his tongue. A longing, desperate moan lit through the air from deep within her. Her abdomen trembled. *Perfect.*

"Let me drink you, sweetheart." The verbal coaxing sent her over. He covered her clit with his mouth and sucked until she dissolved. When he'd drunk her dry, he moved up her body to build her again.

Her right hand located the trail of dark hair that would ultimately lead her precisely where he craved her touch. She traced her index finger along the path and then splayed her hand over the patch of coiled fur at the base of his shaft.

A searing growl thundered from him as she flipped her hand and caressed him. He was trying to keep everything soft and gentle that night, trying to care for her and tend to her slowly, but his cock ached harder than granite. He throbbed in her hand, fierce and demanding. Dan's baser nature threatened to slice his resolve to shreds.

His eyes rolled back as her fingers slipped through the pearly liquid that leaked from his head. He tried to channel his patience by clenching his jaw and grunting out his desperation. She lifted her head and proceeded to lick him clean.

Certain he was going to lose it, he grasped her waist and forced her back. "I'm trying to go slow, baby, and you're not helping," he informed her as he plunged two fingers deep within her, simply unable to wait. Her delighted grin over his predicament did nothing to strengthen his discipline.

Closing his eyes seemed to help, if only for a moment, to gather his wits. Watching her hot, writhing, and hungry fragmented him completely.

Her muscles tugged his fingers deeper. She wanted more. She clenched around his hand, and the knowledge of what that felt like against his cock sent fire surging through his veins.

The air was perfumed with her scent and her heat. He filled his lungs on the vanilla and coconut musk of her and of sex. The ragged need only intensified with every breath. She held the only antidote to his exquisite pain.

"I need you, baby. I need to be inside you. Look at me." He gathered her hands, pinned them to the bed above her head, and positioned himself between her legs. He paused to force himself to be gentle, and then he pushed into her.

"Wrap your legs over me." He released one of her hands long enough to secure her legs over his back before he rocked forward and felt her encase him completely.

With every slow, deep thrust, she met him. His body shuddered as he felt that lush ass tease his sac where they joined.

Her eyes closed in the ecstasy between them as he forced his rhythmic pounding to a slow, thorough cadence.

She trembled. Her muscles cinched around him. They taunted rhythmically at his resolve. Her temperature shot upward, and the heat radiated through every ounce of chiseled muscle in his body. He pushed harder.

"When you come, I'm gonna lose it, baby doll. You look at me when I bring you."

Her eyes flashed open as a moan of elation shook from the quivering muscles within her. Her body nursed his cock. He pushed past his hilt, burying himself inside her, and as she unfurled, he lost it all. He lost everything inside the only woman who could ever have made him whole.

She collapsed under him into a pile of soft, sexy skin and weakened, trembling muscle. All signs of tension and stress evaporated into the thick air around them.

"More, please," she begged.

"There's my greedy, greedy girl," he moaned as he continued to rock. His double bands didn't let him down. He pounded into her as she writhed.

Again they came together sated and exhausted. Quite pleased with himself, Dan eased from her and guided her up onto his chest. He tried to hide his pompous smirk. He never left a job unfinished.

"I had a whole outfit to wear for you tonight." She looped her right leg over his.

"Mmm, you can wear it for me when we get back from Vegas, but I just got everything I could ever have wanted."

"It had pasties." Her satisfied tone completed the perfection they'd just shared.

"Pasties are great, baby doll, but they make it hard to suck you, and I think that's way better." Dan gently rolled her right nipple between his fingers. She shivered beside him.

"When you said the only thing you wanted for Christmas was me naked in your bed, I guess you meant that."

He chuckled with her, certain that some kind of egregious mistake had been made, because he could never deserve everything he had lying in the bed beside him. "You are amazing. That was amazing, and I'm overwhelmed. You are perfect with lingerie or without."

CHAPTER 27
WORDS

"Dan?" she whispered solemnly.

"Fi?" he responded, while trying to read her. She smiled against him.

"Can we talk for a little while?"

Though he was exhausted from his all-encompassing releases, there was nothing else he wanted to do.

"Of course. What's wrong?"

"Nothing's wrong. I was just kind of curious…."

Dan cradled her closer. "About what?"

"Your mom, mostly."

Dan couldn't help but laugh. "Baby doll, we can talk as long as you want, but if you want me to make my mother easier to understand, we'll still be lying here next Christmas."

She giggled but then seemed to command herself to calm. "I'm serious," she finally pled.

Dan drew a deep breath and awaited the incoming questions.

"So…your mom is kind of…" She paused to search for a word.

"Infuriating," he supplied for her.

She laughed again but shook her head. "Let's go with relentless," she decided tactfully. "About you getting married, having kids, carrying on the name and all that." Dan nodded with a sigh. "I guess I'm just kind of confused."

She sounded like his mother's insanity was her fault.

"We're all confused, sweetness."

"Be serious!" she demanded as she visibly quelled laugher.

"Sorry." He ordered himself to focus on what she wanted to know.

"At dinner, she was wanting to ripen my uterus for your seed." She shuddered through hysterically abashed laughter. Dan cringed at the very idea and the embarrassment it had caused. "But then, when we were in your room alone, she was furious. Wouldn't that be what she wanted?"

"Ah." Dan understood her confusion. "My mother is a Vis Virres Predilect, so when she wants something done, woe be unto anyone who stands in her way. But there is a way things are done, and there is only one way things are done—the Marion Vindico way. She is very adamant that the Vindico name not end with me. It doesn't matter what the hell I want or that the system is grossly patriarchal. But one of the most important things in the world, to my mother, is what other people in the Realm think of her and of our entire family."

Fionna listened intently.

"Especially since Dad's a governor, so what would make my mother elated is if I proposed to you right now, we let her plan an extremely elaborate ceremony that the entire Senate would be invited to where she would be showcased, and then I knocked you up on our wedding night. But one can't come before the other because that might tarnish her reputation. So, the baby better not show up one day before the nine-month anniversary of our wedding." The longer he spoke, the more furious he became. Who the hell did his mother think she was to make Fionna feel this way or to try to plan their life?

"Gotcha." Fionna carefully considered everything Dan had informed her of. She wanted to ask more. He could feel the curiosity swirl in her energy.

"What, baby? Just ask me."

She bit her lip and studied him closely. "What happens, if way, *way* off in the future, you do decide to get married?"

"Or in the relatively near future." He stared down into her eyes to see what she thought of that idea. She couldn't quite hide the delighted grin that formed on her face. Warmth flooded through him. Love filled him. Determination found its rooting again in his heart. He couldn't have one without ending the other. He had to end Wretchkinsides. He refocused as he heard her next question.

"Well, whenever that happens, if you get married and then decide to have kids, but you only have girls. What will happen then?" She pointed out the one failure in his mother's elaborate plan for his life.

Dan chuckled as he rubbed her back and kissed her forehead. "Since I've spent the majority of my life trying to infuriate my mother, that would be perfect," Dan admitted, making her laugh heartily. "So, I'd say it serves her right, but truthfully, I don't know. I never thought about having kids, even with Amelia." He choked on her name and tensed slightly, but Fionna's energy moved through him again, and she soothed him.

"Can I ask you something else? You really don't have to answer this."

"Ask me."

She shrank into his side as he tightened his arms around her. "Did your mom like Amelia?" She cringed as she asked the question.

Dan considered the question and her insistence that he didn't have to answer it. "Kind of." He wanted her to know everything about him, and as she'd reminded him not so many weeks ago, Amelia was a big part of who he was.

"I can't really figure out if she likes me or not." Fionna tried to explain her question.

"Amelia fit well into my mother's plan for my life. She was there. We were in love, and she wanted to have kids. She always had. She came from a family my mother considers to be her equal socio-economically. She would have vastly preferred it if Amelia had been Gifted." He tried not to feel the fury that always brewed within him whenever he thought about his mother's prejudices.

"You don't have to tell me anymore."

Dan went on, "As for you, my mother loves you, which is a double-edged blade, trust me."

"I don't really think she likes me."

Dan felt her sorrow as she stated this out loud. "Honey, what makes you say that?"

Fionna shrugged. "I don't know. She told me I was fat and then got mad that we were up in your room. I never feel like I answer her questions correctly."

"Hey." Dan rolled to his side. He wanted to look into her eyes. "I don't give a damn what my mother thinks. You are everything to me. You are the first person in ten long years who's made me think life was worth living, so my mother can stuff it, because you're it for me. And you are not fat! I told you she's insane."

"I just love you so much," she confessed as Dan's heart stuttered momentarily. "I want your mom to like me."

Although the relationship between Dan and his mother had always been fraught with dissension, it certainly hadn't improved in the last few years. But he'd never been so furious with the woman who'd given him life as he was in that moment, seeing what her nonsensical drivel had done to the woman he wanted to spend his life with.

"Fionna," Dan whispered, "someday, I swear to you I'm going to be able to say the words, but all I can do is pray that somehow you understand what you mean to me. I don't give a damn what anyone else thinks, especially my mother."

She smiled against his chest. "You don't ever have to say it. I can feel it, and it's the most incredible thing I've ever felt. No one has ever loved me like this."

Though it was shocking to hear her confirm that, he knew what she was saying was true. He could feel it in her as well, and no one had ever loved and accepted him the way that she did. It was truly incredible.

CHAPTER 28
STORMS

Thunder echoed in the distance, and the house shuddered in the howling winds. Dan tried desperately not to think of Lindley as Fionna tensed. Her fingernails bit into his sides.

"Hey, shh," he soothed, "I'm right here." He wrapped her up in his long, overmuscled embrace. She buried her face in his chest as he wrapped the sheets and blankets around them.

"I don't like storms. I know it's stupid. I'm not a little girl."

"Most Receivers don't like storms." He wasn't certain why he remembered that particular bit of information from his Energies of the Earth classes at the academy, but it stuck out in his mind.

"How did you know that?"

"I don't really know." He truthfully couldn't recall why they didn't or anything more than that particular part of the notes he'd taken so many years before.

"There's a lot of energy in a storm. It's all so volatile. Besides all of the electrical energy, there's the atmospheric energy as well. We have a hard time reading through it all. It makes me uneasy. I'm not used to there being energy I can't predict or understand, that I don't have any control over. It makes Emily nervous too."

It seemed Emily, a powerful Receiver herself, had become Fionna's own personal barometer. Fionna had felt alone in the abundance of her abilities. She'd gone for a long time believing no one else understood what she was feeling or seeing, until she'd met and befriended Emily. That was probably the reason they'd become so close despite their age difference.

"Actually, storms are the one thing that Emily feels even more strongly than I do," Fionna explained hesitantly. She looked to Dan for reassurance.

He brushed a tender kiss on her forehead. "Why?"

"Emily has associated storms with all of the worst parts of her life. She's become more attuned to them because of the emotions she ties to them. She freaks out, but don't ever tell her I told you that. It embarrasses her."

"I would never share anything you tell me with anyone, honey." This seemed to soothe Fionna into going on. Dan recalled the last bad storm they'd had, and he did seem to remember Emily calling Rainer numerous times throughout the day. It had irritated Dan at the time.

"They found out about Cal during a really bad storm." Fionna hesitated as Dan nodded. He remembered as well. He'd never forget the look on Garrett's face when that call had come in.

"Emily was only sixteen. She could feel all of the horrible emotions in the house the day they got the call, and she couldn't find Rainer. She couldn't find her Shield. She had to try to process every devastated, lost emotion all by herself. Poor thing—I just can't imagine what she lived that day, feeling all of that from her whole family. Rainer had gone to Norfolk to check on his uncle. She got in her car, convinced she could find him in the storm, and the press chased her down. I think they wanted to be there when she told Rainer. She was in that horrible accident. And then, after she got out of the hospital, Rainer took her home in the rain. Then, it was still storming when he left for London. I'm not sure she'll ever get over that."

Fionna obviously could feel Emily's pain just from hearing the story. It tensed in her rhythms.

"He did it because he loves her," Dan defended Rainer.

Fionna smiled. "I know that. She knows that, but she feels that terror whenever it storms."

As Dan had never seen a couple closer than Rainer and Emily, he knew that if Emily had channeled the energy of her terror into storms, Rainer felt it as well. He felt everything she gave off. That's why he was so patient with her when she called repeatedly during thunderstorms. He blamed himself for making her afraid. Dan knew because he would blame himself in the same situation.

"He'll never leave her again."

Fionna nodded. "You know, you could let Rainer know how much you like him. He really looks up to you."

Scoffing, Dan couldn't fathom why Rainer Lawson or anyone else would look up to him.

"I'm serious."

"Lawson knows I like him," Dan assured her. "We're fairly close, or as close as I ever get with my officers. The fact that I didn't chew his ass when he decided to fly down to Brazil without telling me should be all the assurance he needs."

Fionna giggled. "That was so sweet. I was really worried about her. I wasn't sure she was going to make it two more weeks. She was a disaster. They'd been through so much with the election, and she was so worried about Mrs. Haydenshire and the baby, and Rainer after his uncle and everything. Plus, experiencing the emotions of the orphans was hard, really hard."

"I had no issue with him going, but he's an Elite Iodex officer assigned to the Wretchkinsides task force. We do not just charter ourselves a flight and leave the country without letting me know."

"That's what made it so romantic." Fionna swooned.

Dan rolled his eyes and chuckled at her. "Yeah, well, I'll give you this much, I get it now, and I sure as hell didn't then." He squeezed her tight, letting her know why he understood.

Thunder clapped again, and she curled herself up in his embrace. "Anyway, Receivers don't like storms because we feel all of the violent energy that comes with them, and we can't always read through them. Sometimes people do crazy things in storms, and we can't predict it." She brought the story full circle.

"I'm right here, baby. I'll keep you safe." He kept his arms wrapped around her as he rubbed her back and kissed her head. It took him over an hour to finally soothe her to sleep. The harrowing winds and thunder wouldn't give her peace. Dan locked his shield over her, until she could no longer be bombarded by the forces outside their bedroom.

By three in the morning, the storm had reached them in full force. It was raging in a violent mix of snow and icy rain. It shattered against the windows in sizzling hisses. The thunder was relentless. Lightning lit the bleached white of the falling snow.

Dan was sick. He couldn't do it. He couldn't let his baby sister stay underground without access to her powers in a storm like this.

Fionna was morose. The storm had her reeling. Dan was too consumed with fear and worry over Lindley to be of much help.

"Let's just go get her. She can stay here tonight," Fionna begged yet again.

Unable to stick to his guns any longer, Dan finally agreed. Fionna rushed out of bed and quickly threw on warm clothes.

Dan piled blankets on the couch to take with them, along with water and other provisions, in case they got stuck. He checked out the window. The streets were mostly clear as far as he could tell. The temperature wasn't quite low enough for the ice to stick to the blacktop yet. He backed away from the window as lightning shook the frame, and Fionna trembled.

He pulled her to him and took a moment to calm her and assure her that he was right there, and that she was his top priority even if he was worried about Lindley. He located one of his Iodex jackets designed for extremely low temperatures and swathed Fionna inside of it. He heated the heat syncs sewn in the lining of the jacket to make certain it would keep her warm.

"Wow." She reveled in the warmth which made him smile.

"Now you're warm and bulletproof. I may make you wear this all the time."

"But what are you going to wear?"

"I have several, baby." He shrugged into another jacket. The heat syncs weren't as large in the one he'd put on, but he wasn't going to tell her that.

They moved through the garage. Fionna had added more blankets and coats. She pointed out that it would be hours before Lindley would be able to warm herself.

Dan helped Fionna into the Expedition. The Ferrari wasn't weather-rated for conditions like this. He heated the interior and then backed down the driveway. His cell phone rang, and he glanced at the screen with a knowing grin.

"I'm already on my way," he assured his father.

"I'll meet you there," was the governor's response.

The icy rain gathered fury the farther and farther out into nowhere they drove. Moving by familiarity alone, Dan would occasionally reach over and make certain the syncs in Fionna's coat were fully loaded with heat energy.

"I'm fine. Don't you need to conserve all of your energy if you're going down there?" Unable to take his eyes off the road, Dan could still hear the desperation in her plea.

"I'll be fine, honey. I want you to be warm. I'm going to have to leave you in the car."

Fionna was unusually quiet. Dan assumed she was exhausted since it was after three in the morning. She hadn't slept well, and they'd worn each other out thoroughly a few hours before.

Dan slowed the SUV yet again as he edged over the gravel roads toward the prison. He noted his father's Range Rover just ahead of them. He parked in the closest lot to the prison. It would still be quite a walk through the rain and pelting ice.

Suddenly, Fionna uttered a harrowing, gasping groan. Dan panicked. "What's wrong?"

She was convulsing and shivering. The joule meters on the heated jacket were fully loaded. He couldn't understand what was wrong.

The governor moved slowly toward them. Dan could see him bracing in the headlights of the Expedition.

"Dan, I…" She shook her head and curled her body forward.

"Fionna!" He flipped on the interior lights. She was as white as a ghost. Her energy was weak and erratic.

"...can't be here," she completed her earlier plea.

"Damn it. I'm so sorry. I'm an idiot." He started to crank the car but couldn't reason through his panic. Of course she couldn't be there. He lambasted himself. She was the strongest Receiver of their generation, and he'd brought her to a place saturated with dark energy.

His father had reached the Expedition. Dan flung the door open. "Dad," he shouted, "quick!"

The governor sprinted the last few steps but slipped in the wet gravel. Dan caught his arm before he hit the ground.

"Take her away from here. Just drive until she's better. What was I thinking?"

"What's wrong?" Governor Vindico joined his son's panic.

"Just drive until she doesn't look like that anymore. I'll get Lindley. I'll find you!" Dan shouted through the driving rain.

Governor Vindico handed Dan the keys to the Range Rover and then set to follow Dan's order.

"I'm gonna be sick," Fionna whimpered.

Dan stepped back as she leaned out of the car. He tried not to think about how thoroughly embarrassed she was going to be from vomiting not only in front of him but in front of his dad.

"You poor thing." Governor Vindico's tender, fatherly nature came out in full force.

"It's the prison. Just get her away from here," Dan commanded as he let the cold rain soak through a sweatshirt he'd located in the back of the Expedition. He wiped Fionna's face with it.

"Go get your sister. I'll take care of her."

"I'm so sorry, baby." Dan kissed Fionna's fevered forehead and then sprinted away from the vehicle toward Felsink Prison.

He halted at the Range Rover, opened the passenger door, and extracted the flashlight his father kept in the glove box. He needed all of his own energy if he was going to get Lindley and then help Fionna stabilize when he returned. He couldn't light his own way.

He raced through the bitter night, gasping in the thin air as he forced himself to go on. He was consumed with guilt and angst about Fionna. He doubted his ability to really take care of her.

While battling for breath, Dan fumbled with his badge and finally managed to get the sliding door to allow him in after he'd waved it over the magnetic reader.

Guards met him with menacing glares.

"It's me." Dan flashed his badge and moved into the dimly lit area.

"What're you doing out here so late, Dan?" Capshaw queried in disbelief.

"Get my sister out." He didn't have time for small talk, and he wasn't interested in the typical derisive chuckles that came from the Non-Gifted guards. They rather liked the fact that Dan was so weak from the environment of the prison set up to mute Gifted energies.

"She's right down there. You get her." Capshaw threw Dan the keys to the cell. He wasn't going to help. Dan stumbled as the energy drain set in.

"Are you okay?" Capshaw chuckled. Dan nodded but wasn't able to answer audibly as he held on to the walls and edged toward the first cell.

His heart fissured. He could hear her sobbing. Urging his feet forward, he let his baby sister's pleas drive him on.

"Lindley," he panted as she raised her head from her huddled corner and broke down completely.

She sobbed as he opened the cell door. Not certain where the energy to carry her had come from, he lifted her up into his arms. He assumed it was love, despite all that she'd put them through, that gave him the strength to carry her back to the entrance.

CHAPTER 29
APOLOGIES
GOVERNOR ARTHUR VINDICO

"Any better?" Governor Vindico helped Fionna with the water bottle he'd given her to drink from since she'd stopped shaking so violently and seemed able to draw full breaths.

"I'm so sorry." Her chin trembled again.

"Sweetheart, why do you keep saying that?"

"I've never been out here. I didn't know it would do that. I should have thought of that."

"I'll tell you this, Daniel didn't think of it either, or he would most certainly not have let you come with him."

Fionna wiped away more tears that wounded Arthur's heart just like when one of his own girls cried. "He probably thinks I'm entirely too much trouble."

He knew she was desperate for reassurance. He shook his head as he handed her the water bottle again. "If my son thinks that, he isn't the man I raised or the man you fell in love with."

He gently touched her forehead to see if her fever was any better. It hadn't gone down much, unfortunately. "I know you didn't really know much about Dan before you began dating, but I've seen such wonderful change in him in just the last few weeks." He wished he could make her understand that she'd saved his son's life.

"I cannot believe I puked in front of you and him." She squeezed her eyes shut tightly.

He couldn't refrain from laughing. "I raised four kids. That's not the first time I've seen someone get sick, and we're working on our third grandchild so I doubt it will be the last."

She gave him a sweet grin he was certain she probably reserved for people she cared about.

"I remember when Dan was eighteen or nineteen, he went on one of their regular campouts with Will and Garrett. I think they dragged Levi along too. Wes Willow went and a few other boys from the academy." The governor shook his head at the memory. "I don't know what those boys mixed up out in the Haydenshires' back fields, but I can tell you that both my and Stephen's liquor bottles were much lighter than they'd been before the boys left. And the next time I went to pour myself some brandy, it tasted distinctly like water." He shook his head. "Anyway, when Stephen dropped Daniel off, I'd never seen someone so sick."

Fionna gave him a weak smile. She seemed to enjoy hearing the story.

"He was a disaster. His mother wanted to take him to the medio, but I kind of thought it might be best to let him learn his lesson. And it worked for the most part…until…." He didn't know what Dan had shared with her. He wasn't certain he should bring up Amelia.

"I know." She seemed to understand what he was referring to so he continued.

"I wasn't aware his body could hold that much alcohol, but it all came back violently the next day, trust me. Are you feeling any better?" he asked again as he tried to study her in the dim interior light of the Senate Expedition. The headlights bounced in eerie patterns off the translucent snow outside.

Fionna nodded though the motion seemed to set her back.

"Dan should be along in a minute. I'll take Lindley, and he can get you home and feeling better." He was certain it was Dan who would make her feel safe and secure and could steady her rapidly fluctuating rhythms. He'd become her Shield. Arthur smiled at the realization. "Truthfully, I can't take this place myself." He noted that Fionna seemed to find solace in his voice. Her rhythms eased slightly when he spoke. "I'm not as young as I once was. Every time I have to come out here, it takes me longer and longer to recover."

"I can't imagine being in there," Fionna fussed, before drawing another slow sip of water.

"I can't think of a single Receiver I've ever sent out here. Sometimes, I think it would be better if we could all feel the energy of the people that we're hurting or considering hurting. It would make the world a much better place." Governor Vindico gestured his head toward the headlights edging slowly toward them. The tires were slipping up the graveled hill, but his son knew how to drive in the conditions and was making headway. "He'll be here soon."

"I'm really so sorry, sir."

"You have nothing to be sorry for."

She smiled weakly. "You sound just like Dan." She was still using most of her energy to draw steadying breaths.

"I'll consider that a great compliment," the governor allowed, "because he really is a great man. I'm so thrilled he's letting you see that. We're so thankful that you've somehow made him able to recognize himself through all of the hell he's put himself through. Besides, I'm the one who's sorry. Lindley's the reason you're out here on Christmas Eve, sick and miserable, instead of at home and comfortable, and I imagine tucked up in my son's arms."

That brought on a real smile. She seemed to revel in the thought. She touched the necklace lying against her sweatshirt. She'd played with it ever since she'd been able to sit upright.

"Early Christmas present?" The governor wondered if he could begin to read Fionna the same way he read his girls.

"Yes, sir."

Dan eased the Land Rover beside the Expedition and stumbled to the passenger side. He flung open her door.

"Are you okay?" he gasped, white as a sheet and panting, as he stood in the driving rain. He only had eyes for Fionna.

"She's all right, son. Are you?"

"I'm fine, Dad." Dan never met the governor's gaze. "You need to eat, baby."

"I'm okay." Fionna looked thoroughly exhausted. "Your dad took good care of me." She scooted away from the cold blast of air and let her head fall back against the seat.

"Thank you." Dan raised his eyes, dark from exhaustion and the energy drain, to his father's concerned face.

"My pleasure, son. Are you sure you're all right to drive?" He tried to gauge Dan's reaction time.

"I'm fine. I need to get her home."

Governor Vindico knew better than anyone that arguing with his son was most often fruitless.

"Lindley's in the back. She's freezing. I covered her up, but she was a mess in there. She'll be out for several hours. She downed something hard just before they took her in. I don't know what it was. She may need to go to the hospital."

Helpless defeat settled on Arthur. It was a feeling he knew only too well when it came to dealing with Lindley. "I think it's high time I stop letting your mother pretend this away, and we get her some real help."

He slid out of the SUV and waved goodbye to Dan and Fionna before he leapt back into the Range Rover.

"Daddy," Lindley's weak, timid voice shook from the back seat. His heart shattered and tears burned his eyes as he ran his heated hands over the blankets Dan had swathed her in. He brushed her hair away from her face.

"I'm right here, sweetheart. Let's go home."

"I'm so sorry," Lindley pled in a forsaken whisper. Arthur had to remind himself to breathe. She'd never ever apologized for all of the wild stunts she'd pulled over the last twenty years.

"Good." He eased the car out of the parking lot and back down the gravel road.

CHAPTER 30
NOT SO MERRY CHRISTMAS
DAN VINDICO

"I'm so sorry," Fionna apologized for the fifth time in the distance of a mile.

"Baby, I'm the one who's sorry."

"I didn't know I would do that. That only happens to me when I'm around black energy, and no one in there has used that."

That was true. Felsink didn't house rapists or murderers. It was reserved for lesser crimes, but it was also rather full at the moment. Dan allowed himself to ponder if perhaps someone in the prison had summoned black but hadn't been tried for that crime.

"I think there was enough darker energy there to have gotten to you." Dan leaned forward and narrowed his eyes. He tried to see through the pouring slush. "I should have left you at home. This is all my fault. I'm sorry, sweetheart." Remorse swirled into a maelstrom in his gut.

"I would have been scared if you'd left me there."

Dan's heart swelled as he reached for her hand. "Then I should have let my dad get Lindley, and I should have stayed with you."

"Is she going to be okay?" Fionna shivered convulsively again. Dan swallowed back regret.

He longed to reheat the syncs in her coat, but her fever was raging as her body tried to regulate her energy. Truthfully, he didn't know if

Lindley was going to be okay this time. Whatever she'd taken was much harder than angel dust.

She'd turned a corner, and they would all have to wait and see if she was going to reach back out to life or if she was going to continue to consume her own death. "Maybe," he allowed. "If Dad can get her some real help."

While keeping his eyes locked on the empty road ahead of them, Dan reached and pulled another bottle of water from his pack. "Here, baby, keep drinking." He had to keep her hydrated, or he was going to have to get Garrett out of bed on Christmas morning to take her to Georgetown. Fionna Styler being admitted to the hospital the day before the biggest Summation exposition of the year would be the headline in every paper in the Realm.

Dan tore open a power bar and inhaled it. He had to cast her as soon as he got her inside. She could use his ample stores of energy to regulate her own. He just had to get her home.

After what seemed like an endless drive, Dan pulled the Expedition into the garage beside the Ferrari. He sprinted to help her out of the car and prayed his energy would keep up after being at Felsink.

"Come here, baby." Dan put one of the blankets he'd packed between her and his soaking-wet clothing. He was freezing, but he deserved the biting pain. He carried her up the stairs and laid her tenderly in their bed.

"Let me take a quick shower and get dried off so I can keep you warm. You keep drinking that water. I'll get you some more." He raced to the kitchen and pulled off his coat and sweats on his way.

Quickly easing her into a sitting position, he plied her with more water.

"I'm so tired." Her entire body shook violently.

"I know, baby. Try to relax for me. I'll be right back." In less than two minutes, he'd showered and dried himself as best he could.

He reached and lifted her sweatshirt off. "I'm so sorry, honey." He felt cruel, robbing her of clothes when she was freezing, but he needed access to her skin.

He gave her some medication to lower her fever and hoped against hope that her energy was stable enough for her to keep it down. It would help him heal her faster.

He slid into bed beside her with a fervent prayer that his waning energy would be enough. Cradling her to him, he pushed his shield out over her. He used every ounce of power he could muster.

She stopped convulsing. Her body went lax against his. She certainly didn't have any fight left in her, so he pushed his energy through every available surface without her having to consciously let him in at all.

Her body calmed, and her fever broke an hour later. She was covered in sweat but sleeping soundly. Dan used all of his concentration to regulate her energy until her rhythms became steady on their own. Just after seven, he gave out and fell asleep, with Fionna cradled in his arms.

Dan awoke from his exhaustive sleep and blinked in the blinding sunlight that had followed the storm.

"Merry Christmas." Fionna appeared beside him holding two mugs of coffee.

"Are you okay?" Dan panicked as he pulled himself upright in the bed. She seated herself beside him and handed him the coffee.

"Just a little weak."

"What time is it?" Dan tried to clear his throat by sipping the soothing liquid.

"It's almost eleven."

He watched her take hesitant sips of coffee. Her eyes closed as she allowed her favorite beverage to restore her.

"You really need to eat something, baby." Dan rubbed her back and tried to determine whether her fever was gone. She slid back and appeared wary of him. He couldn't figure out what had happened in the last few hours. The loss settled on him harshly.

"I had a few crackers when I was downstairs making coffee. I was going to make sure those would stay down." Her face colored from embarrassment instead of fever. "I look terrible. I need a shower."

Dan studied her. He was desperate to dissolve the invisible rift between them that seemed to contain nothing more than rumpled sheets.

"I always think you're beautiful." He was completely honest without any exaggeration. She was always astoundingly beautiful. Her soul was beautiful. The rest of her was icing on the cake.

Fionna rolled her eyes and shook her head. She did look rough. She was pale and drawn. Her voice was strained and her eyes were watery, swollen, and red. Her hair was mussed from her fever breaking in the night, but Dan still didn't think he'd ever seen anything more beautiful.

"Come back to bed with me, please." He just needed to hold her until they felt like them again. That was all his mind offered him as a way to heal the space between them. "You need to rest if you're going to challenge tomorrow." Another round of guilt settled harshly in his throat.

"Tomorrow night is just the banquet dance thing. We challenge Sunday." She looked mildly disappointed that he'd had to be told again.

"I know, honey, but I'm not sure how much sleep you're going to get in Vegas."

With a great deal of hesitation, she set her mug on the bedside table and let him hold her on his chest. He could feel the abhorrent absence more intensely. She was blocking him out. She'd retreated back into the shield her body had developed out of necessity. Scalded from the loss, Dan tried to modulate his voice to a calm intonation.

"Fi, what's wrong?"

"Nothing." There it was again. She poured vinegar in the wound. She was unable to look him in the eye and lie to him outright.

"Hey." He lifted her face in his hand and gave her little option but to look into his eyes. "Don't lie to me, please. What's wrong?"

She jerked her head out of his hand defiantly.

"Fionna." Panicked, he clenched his jaw and ordered himself not to demand anything from her. The sting of her combative move angered him.

Her chin trembled as she fought to blink back the tears that darkened the golden flecks in her sienna eyes.

Realization softened his irritation. "How long have you been up?" Her eyes weren't weak and red from her fever or getting sick several hours before. They were red because she'd been crying.

"A while." She tried desperately to choke down her emotion.

"I'm sorry about Lindley, and that I took you out there. I wasn't thinking. I've ruined your Christmas," Dan immediately spewed forth everything he could think of that could possibly have upset her so much. She loved Christmas, and he'd stayed in bed until eleven on top of everything else.

"No, that's not it." She drew a haggard breath.

Dan's heart ached physically not just emotionally.

"Help me out a little then, because you're scaring the hell out of me."

Angry, frustrated, humiliated tears overthrew her tenacious grip on her emotions.

"Baby, please!" Dan continued to beg.

"I'm not too weak to be with you." She broke down completely.

Utter confusion permeated Dan's entire being as he held her. Her tears ran down the chiseled lines of his chest. "What?"

She convulsed against him and held his biceps in a death grip with her hands.

"Baby, what are you talking about?"

She shivered in his arms. "I can handle it. I just have to learn how." He racked his brain and tried to determine what on earth she was telling him. Dan rubbed her back and wiped away her tears.

"What do you have to learn how to do, sweetheart?" Patience had never been his virtue, but he ordered himself to try.

"To go places like that and be around criminals or whatever. I can learn how. I'm not too weak," she fumed. Her tears turned furious. "I'm not too weak to be your girlfriend!"

Dismayed over her take on the night before, Dan tried to formulate the words to express to her that he'd never thought she was weak.

His shook his head in disbelief. "You are one of the strongest people I've ever met."

She shook her head in abject defiance. "I just made everything so much worse last night."

"Honey, you didn't make anything worse. You never could. Just listen to me. It means the world to me that you were willing to go out in a snowstorm with me to get my little sister out of prison. I feel horrible that I took you out there and didn't realize that with your exceptional abilities, it would affect you." He sighed out his deep regret. "And why on earth would I want you to put yourself through hell trying to learn to be around people like that?"

She lifted her head and stared at him. "Because that's your job, and you love your job. I want to be with you forever, so I have to learn to deal with your job even if I hate it." She laid out everything that she'd been crying over downstairs alone. His heart shattered as he watched her cry. "And I can, and I will."

"I don't want you to," he soothed quietly. "But you're right. It is my job to deal with criminals and addicts alike, but that doesn't mean that you can't be the most important thing in the entire world to me. And you know what else? My most important job right now, and I really hope for the rest of our lives, is to make sure that you're safe and healthy and happy. The most important thing to me is being your Shield. So, if at some point me being the Chief of Elite gets in the way of all of that, then I'll quit in a heartbeat." He held her gaze with his own. He wanted no doubt in what he was saying. "You let me finish off Wretchkinsides, and I'll walk away. That's all I want."

"I don't want you to quit because of me."

Dan smiled. "I can't fathom another situation where you would ever have to be near Felsink or any other prison. I sure as hell don't want you near people I arrest and take in, so how about if we let my work stay at work, and you and I exist outside of all of that."

Fionna nodded, and in her relief her internal shield begin to ease away. It brought cleansing breath back to his parched lungs. His own shield eased back inside of him.

Dan scooted down in the bed and kept her tucked to his chest. He hoped he could soothe her back to sleep. They lay there in peaceful silence for a long while. Her breathing steadied, and her tears dissipated, but she remained awake.

"Will you tell me something?" The ease that had engulfed the tension in her voice brought him another round of relief.

Dan kissed the top of her head. "Of course."

She gazed up at him with a sweet grin. "Your dad told me about the time you went camping with Will and Garrett, and you all got drunk and you got sick."

Dan laughed from the memory as he nodded.

"He was trying to make me feel better because I was so embarrassed."

"You are really hard on yourself, you know that?"

She ignored his reminder. "Is that what guys always do when they camp or have a sleepover or whatever?" It seemed she wanted to hear the other side of the story.

"I'll have to thank my dad for sharing some of my finer moments with you."

She giggled but looked extremely curious. Dan caressed the soft features of her beautiful face. Her healthy, olive glow was slowly making a triumphant return.

"In that case, we were all complete morons who got shit-faced drunk and then passed out." He shuddered at the memory. "Wes Willow and Garrett got this brilliant idea that instead of bringing beer, which was the standard fare for our campouts, we would all steal stuff from our dads' liquor cabinets and make our own mixed drinks. Only Wes and Garrett failed to understand that occasionally a mixed drink contains things that are not alcohol, so we just mixed glass after glass of straight liquor like the idiots that we were. I threw up pure alcohol for two days straight. And you think it burns going down? My God!" He could still recall the event down to the clothes he was wearing.

"Oh, you poor thing." Fionna hugged him gently. Her genuine sorrow over his pain touched those places in his heart that she'd brought back to life.

She relaxed completely against him. He allowed himself a moment to revel in the peace and love he could feel from her once again.

"Yeah well, where were you back then? Because I got no sympathy, trust me." He laughed again at his own stupidity. " I got my head out of the toilet about three o'clock Sunday morning, and my dad made me go to school the next day. Then all of our fathers made us come to the Senate and work after our classes. Will, Garrett, Wes, Levi, and I emptied every trash can in the entire freaking Senate. Then we had to scrub the dumpsters."

Fionna gazed at him adoringly and wrinkled her nose. "I take it you didn't do that again?"

"Uh, no, we kept it to beer and Playboys until we graduated."

Fionna giggled again. "Why is it that whenever groups of teenage boys are together, there are pictures of naked women?"

"Because teenage boys are pigs, and at eighteen, are mostly unable to think with the head above their belt line, although we're actually better at eighteen than, say, fifteen."

Fionna gave him a wry grin and narrowed her eyes. "And how are they at thirty-two?"

"If I'm lucky enough to get to see you naked, honey, I sure as hell don't need porn. But,"—he sighed and tucked her closer still—"how about we save all of the other stories of my knuckle-headed adolescence for another time, and I go make you some breakfast and then I hold you and you go back to sleep for a while?"

Her rhythms were still weak, and though they'd steadied in the early morning hours, they were still distressed.

"No. I need a shower, and then I want you to open your presents."

He would never be able to argue with that adorable pout, so he grinned. "You eat something for me, something with protein. I'll give you a shower, and then we'll open presents. But then we'll take a nap." Though he tried to sound as if he were offering a negotiation, he was not.

"We have to pack."

"You have to get better, sweetheart."

She wrinkled her nose in consideration and narrowed her eyes. "A nap on the couch."

"No." He stared her down.

"You have to stay in bed with me the whole time I sleep," was her next try.

"You got it." He winked at her. He was more than happy to give her more ground.

CHAPTER 31
PRESENTS

Dan managed to make scrambled eggs with cheese and several strips of bacon under Fionna's guidance. He made her stay seated at the island as he worked, but she did cut up an avocado from her seated position.

They'd showered, which did greatly improve her mood. They dressed in sweats and moved toward the tree.

Complete contentment washed over him. Dan reveled in the heavenly sense, one he never thought he would feel ever again. Fionna's excitement had him grinning as he moved her gifts toward her.

"You got me way too much," she fussed yet again.

"Would you hush and open one?"

Her eyes sparkled as she beamed at him. Certain that was the precise look she would've given her parents on Christmas morning growing up, Dan began to understand her father's strict hold on her. He was still an ass, but Dan certainly understood the deep desire to protect her.

She was so precious and fragile in her all-encompassing strength. The juxtaposition was both fascinating and exhilarating. It drove him. She needed his ultimate protection, but she needed no help to stand firmly on her own.

"Which one did you say was more for you than me?"

He pointed to a large, square box. When she'd continually fussed about the number of gifts under the tree for her, he'd offered up that cryptic clue, trying to calm her.

He knew she would assume it was lingerie, so he braced and hoped she wasn't going to be disappointed. Her brow furrowed as she lifted it onto her lap.

"This is heavy."

Dan smiled and wished she'd started with a different gift. "You'll like the other ones better."

"I have you, and the most beautiful necklace I've ever seen. I don't need anything else."

"I had fun spoiling you."

She tore the paper to reveal a brown cardboard box. She started laughing as soon as she opened the lid.

"Well played."

"I thought so," Dan agreed as she lifted the motorcycle helmet out of the box.

"Does this mean I finally get to go for a ride?" she sassed flirtatiously. He cocked his right eyebrow up and smirked.

"Depends on what you want to ride, baby doll, but today you're not doing anything more than eating, opening presents, and sleeping."

She gave him a dramatic eye roll. "You open one. I had fun spoiling you too."

Concern plagued Dan as he wondered what she'd purchased him. He reached for the smallest box, but Fionna blushed violently.

"No, not that one!"

"Okay." Dan wondered what difference a few minutes was going to make, but she seemed quite adamant. "Which one?"

"That one." She pointed to a large, rectangular box. Her bottom lip slipped through her teeth. "I hope you like it."

"I'll love it." It didn't matter what it was. It was from her, and that was all that mattered. He slid his fingers under the tape on the paper. As he removed the wrapping, he could feel her nerves move through the space between them. Furrowing his brow, he opened the box, and his mouth fell open.

"Fionna, how much did this cost?" He couldn't stop the words from leaving his mouth, which hung open for several seconds before he formulated the question.

"You don't get to ask that. Now try it on."

Dan swallowed hard as he lifted the black leather, custom Vanson Continental Daytona motorcycle jacket from the box. He knew the custom size needed to fit over his biceps and chest tacked on another heap of cash. He'd lusted after that jacket since he'd gotten the Agusta, but considering the exorbitant price of his bike, he'd denied himself the jacket.

"Baby, this is way too much."

"Stop it. Put it on. I want to see."

Dan shrugged into the butter-smooth, leather jacket. It was a perfect fit. He watched her grin excitedly.

"Totally hot. I may have to borrow that. You know, when I'm not wearing anything else."

Dan growled from the thought as he removed the jacket. His brain held a debate between his love of the coat and his worry over how much she'd spent.

He fervently hoped that his other gifts cost next to nothing, and he urged her to open another one.

"Do you like it?"

"I love it. I've wanted that very jacket for years, but that was a lot of money." He felt badly that his reaction hadn't been what she was looking for.

She grinned sweetly with her eyes still alight. "But you look really hot in it, and I'm the girl who gets to look at you in it so it's kind of a gift for me as well." She giggled at his thorough embarrassment.

He shook his head at her reasoning and gestured to the pile of presents at her feet.

"Which one?"

"You choose, but those two kind of go together." He pointed to two similarly sized rectangular boxes.

She reached for another gift instead. She realized it was a book before she pulled the paper off and grinned. "This isn't a beginner's sewing book, is it?"

"Nah," he assured her, "it's the basics of Summation." They both cracked up as she pulled the paper off the rather large, heavy book.

Her mouth fell open and then pulled into a delighted grin. "Oh, my gosh! I love it!" She hugged the book to her chest and squealed.

"I kind of thought you might." Dan was extremely pleased with her reaction.

She opened the book and slowly began turning pages of *The Complete History of Lingerie*. Dan tried not to chuckle over how adorable she was as he watched her.

"Look, it even has patterns!" She flipped to the back, revealing numerous sewing patterns. As soon as he'd seen the book online, he'd ordered it. How he'd seen it online had brought on guilt that he planned to alleviate now.

"I have a confession to make." He grimaced.

"What did you do?" She giggled, probably at the look on his face.

"I tried to figure out a book that you might like because I know how much you like to read. When I was helping you unpack all of yours, I tried to figure out an author or something you'd love, but I wasn't sure. You know John Ramier?" He paused.

"He's the Elite Technology Specialist guy at Iodex, right? He has that geeky sexy thing going on."

Dan cracked up. "I have no idea, but yeah, he's the computer guru of our ensemble cast. I got him to help me. I would never have let him look at anything at all. I swear. He wouldn't do that, and I watched him to make certain. But I had him hack your Amazon account. I'm really sorry. I just wanted to find something you'd like. I wanted to see the suggested lists. That's all I looked at."

The book contained four hundred full-color pages of everything from bras to panties of every description, bustles, corsets, pasties, negligees, stays, and anything else related to the world of lingerie. It went over in great detail how all of them had come to be and who'd worn them best. It was made to be displayed on a coffee table, and Dan secretly hoped Fionna would leave it out the next time his mother was over, though he'd never admit that out loud.

She giggled at him again and shook her head. "Because I love the book so much and you so much, I will forgive you, but you and your detective skills are going to get you in trouble, Chief Vindico. You swear Ramier didn't see anything else?" Concern replaced her humor.

"I would never have let that happen, and Ramier would never do that. I swear to you."

"Good, because one of my favorite vibes came from there." The flush of her cheeks gave away her embarrassment, but her smile returned.

Still beaming, she lost herself in the book for a moment, but then placed it to the side and leapt into his lap. She wrapped her arms around him tightly. "Thank you!"

He could feel her elated energy, and he was overjoyed. "You're welcome, honey. I'm sorry I had to resort to reconnaissance to come up with it."

She moved off him, crisscrossed her legs up on the couch, and pulled the book back into her lap.

"Will you make me more coffee?" She never took her eyes off the book as she began slowly turning page after page, completely enrapt.

"Of course." Dan chuckled as he headed to the kitchen.

"Best, best, best boyfriend ever," she gushed as he handed her the piping hot mug.

Gazing down at her, Dan knew he could never love anything more than the phenomenal woman seated beside him on the couch, wearing no makeup and old sweats, caught up in a book. He could've stayed there staring at her all day long.

"Oh, I'm sorry." Fionna took the million-mile journey back from her lingerie voyage in a matter of moments. "Open your other presents."

"I like watching you read," he informed her before he lifted another gift off the floor.

"Why?"

"Because it makes you happy. And I can sit and watch every single emotion going on in the book by watching your face and your rhythms. I like the way your energy feels when you read. Your eyes sparkle and you bite your bottom lip just a little when you read a love scene from one of those romance novels you like."

She laughed. "That's so sweet." She hugged him again, still holding the book. "Thank you for loving me like that."

He'd never considered his fascination with every single thing about her to necessarily be love, but he supposed it was.

"Can I take it with me to Vegas?"

"Of course." That seemed an odd question, but he was thrilled she liked the book so much. When her face fell, Dan set the present aside.

She gnawed the side of her mouth, and her energy, which had been swimming with bliss a moment before, dampened dramatically.

"What's wrong?"

"It's stupid, and you'll make fun of me."

"I would never make fun of you. I might tease you, but that's it." Her words stung.

"I know. Sorry."

"Tell me what's wrong."

With a dejected huff, she shrugged and wrinkled her nose. "I don't like Vegas."

"Neither do I."

"Really?" She sounded shocked.

"Really."

"You don't have to go." Her offer only seemed to further her angst.

"I want to go. I want to go anywhere you are, but why would you think I would make fun of you for that?"

She shrugged. "Everyone else loves it. All the other Angels look forward to this every year. They throw this huge banquet, and you get to meet players we don't usually challenge against. We party for several days." Her head drooped and her voice was strained. "Most times, I just go hide up in my room because it's so exhausting. There's a lot of yucky stuff going on, and I have to feel it all. And even the not yucky emotions are so hard to feel all the time because there's so many people." She shrugged. "But there's almost always someone who's considering cheating. I can feel the deceptive energy. When people are drunk, they're very erratic. It's hard to read them. There's sadness and desperation everywhere. Everyone is doing something they think will make them feel better, but it makes them worse, and I can feel it all. It makes me depressed."

Dan nodded. "And you wanted to take the book and stay up in our room." He had no real concept of what being Fionna Styler really meant until that moment. He had no idea how incredibly strong she was. The strength of her soul, her heart, and her mind was more powerful than any amount of muscle or energy he possessed.

"And that's so lame. Chloe always makes fun of me about it every year," she sighed dejectedly. "It's this huge, great party, and I don't like it at all. So, obviously, there's something wrong with me."

"Baby, there is nothing wrong with you, and you're not the only person who feels that way. You're just the only one brave enough to admit it and go up to their suite," Dan said. "If Chloe says anything to you, just blame me."

"Blame you for what?"

"We have to be even more careful in Vegas than we are here. The Sirens are playing in the exhibition, so obviously Marlisa will be there. Hell, Nic may show up. I doubt it, since we had eyes on him in Bucharest an hour ago, but still."

"I thought you were checking your email." She tried not to chastise but missed her mark.

"I'm trying," he offered apologetically. He tried not to check in often, but the desperation to have her only added to his desire to end the monster that was the Interfeci.

"I'm going as a team owner, and Governor Haydenshire floated it that I was going to keep an eye on Emily. I really just want to be able to dance with you once or twice at the banquet, and I want to watch you win that cup, but otherwise we can't be seen anywhere together. I can't act like your boyfriend anywhere in public, and it's not just Marlisa. The Interfeci have several large rings in Vegas. They run drugs, take gambling hits, and launder money. We busted a human trafficking ring linked to them out there a few years ago." Dan shuddered from the memory. Fionna looked petrified.

He shook himself and went on. "I was just gonna hang out with Garrett and Rainer and get some work done. If you and Emily were there, I wouldn't mind that, but I can't act like we have anything more than a professional friendship. I'm so sorry."

A blistering pain moved through him as his warning and his rules brush-stroked disappointment on her features. After a moment, she was able to gaze up at him sweetly. "Will you hold me for a minute?"

"Nothing would make me happier." He lifted her onto his lap and cast his shield over her as soon as she was settled. "Sweetheart, please believe me when I tell you that if I could, I would skywrite the fact that I somehow managed to be lucky enough to get to call you my girlfriend. Nothing means more to me than you. That's why I have to do it this way."

"I know." She shrank farther into his embrace.

"I know I'm disappointing you, and I feel terrible. I'll stay here if you want me to."

"No." The very idea seemed to terrify her. "I wish everyone could know that we're together, and how much I love you, and how much I love being your girlfriend, but that isn't important right now. We don't have to stay at the banquet for long after dinner. It will be fun to sneak away, just me and you."

"You are the most incredible woman in the world." Dan was unable to believe that after he'd told her he would essentially have to ignore her completely at an event designed to recognize her talents, she was willing to leave it all just to be with him.

"So, I don't guess you'll be wearing the *My Girl's An Angel and I keep her tank full,* T-shirt with my number on it to the challenges." She giggled again, righting every wrong that had taken up residence in his mind.

Dan chuckled. "Maybe next season, honey, but I will tell you this, after I make myself sick watching pricks hit on you all night long, and me not able to let them know whose you are, I sure as hell will keep your tank full."

"Dan," she scoffed, "no one is going to hit on me. I'll make Garrett dance with me a couple of times. Then I'll accept a dance from the hottest new Angels owner, and then I'll be really tired and turn in early for the challenge the next day. I just told you I don't like hanging out in the casinos and watching people get drunk and poor. I'd rather be up in our suite curled up in your arms."

"Well, that makes me the luckiest guy on the planet, baby, but I still feel like I'll be ruining your trip. If you want me to stay here, I will."

"I've been partying in Vegas every year for the past seven years, and I tried to like it. I really did. But I don't like it. It's not me, and until now, until I met you, I wouldn't admit that even to myself." Somehow, she thought he'd given her the strength. Dan started to protest but she went on. "I've even done the…" She halted abruptly and grimaced. "Well, you know…the one night stand kind of thing." Dan fought with every fiber of his being not to scowl. "But I still hated it. I just want to be with you whether we're out with everyone or all by ourselves."

"Will I have the privilege of meeting this asshole that I now want to murder?"

She cringed. "He captains the San Antonio Synthesizers."

Dan's stomach churned as he clenched his jaw.

"Dan, you know I love you, and even though I've been with other guys, I've never been in love before you. Plus, he was a ginormous douche-canoe with a leak and no paddles."

He nodded and bit back all of the imbecilic, possessive phrases that pulsed in his mind.

"And I like that I'm yours," she answered his unspoken remarks with a sweet grin.

"I really am sorry. I wish I could tell the world."

"Maybe we will someday. But, right now, it's Christmas and I really want to know what else you got me."

His childish fit of possessiveness abated. "Open them, baby."

"No, it's your turn."

Dan lifted a tall, rectangular box. He knew by the weight what it was. He pulled the paper off and prayed she hadn't spent any more than what a bottle of Talisker Scotch cost. His eyes goggled. "Fionna Kalani Halia Styler," he gasped. "I'm going to have to marry you right now, so I have another name to use because I cannot believe you did this."

She giggled hysterically. "Well, I hope if you decide to pop the question that's not the only reason."

"Honey, how did you get this? They haven't produced any for the public in years." He lifted the 2015 Old Pulteney 21 Scotch from its box, and tried desperately not to think about how much she'd spent on it.

"Daddy has lots of friends in the restaurant industry, so I made a few calls, and I got a good deal."

"When I said not to buy me Talisker because it's too expensive, I did not mean buy me Scotch that's five times the price."

"Stop. You're hurting my feelings."

Chastising himself, Dan drew a deep breath. "I'm sorry. This is incredible. You are incredible, and I will never ever deserve you." He leaned in and brushed a kiss across her lips. "But you still have a nap to take, so get to opening."

"But I want to read my book."

"If you read it all today, what will you do when I keep you holed up in our suite all weekend?" He flirted suggestively.

She gave him the naughty grin that always made him weak. "Other far more dirty and delicious things."

With a shuddering groan, Dan set the Scotch gently on the coffee table and pulled Fionna into him. He wrapped his hands around her waist as she straddled her legs over him. He slid his hands up to her face and guided her lips to his own. He let his hands trail down over her breasts and back to her waist. They kissed heatedly, with her gasping and moaning as he sucked her tongue and nipped her lips.

"Let's go upstairs."

"No," he forced the word from his mouth. "I want you to open your presents, and you need to rest." He knew she wasn't really up for another session when she didn't argue.

"Okay, but tomorrow on the plane."

"I'm all yours, baby doll." He patted her backside.

She crawled out of his lap begrudgingly.

"These require some explanation." He forced his concentration to her last two gifts. Standing, he lifted them onto the couch beside her, since they were rather heavy. "Open them both, and then I'll explain."

She pulled the paper off the plain cardboard box first, and then moved on to the box containing a brand-new, deluxe sewing machine.

"Dan! Oh, my gosh, look at all it does! How much did this cost?"

He laughed outright. "Right, because you get to ask that." He gestured to the eight-hundred-dollar bottle of Scotch on their coffee table.

She continued to gaze at the sewing machine, reading all that it would do. "I don't even know how all of this works. It does heirloom stitches!"

Dan leaned and kissed her forehead. He was simply unable to keep his lips off her.

"Wait, what's in here?" She pulled open the first cardboard box.

"I had Sam fix your mom's." He hesitated, but then watched as tears began flowing from those huge sienna eyes. "I talked to Mrs. Haydenshire, and she said this one was the best and that you would love it." He pointed to the new sewing machine. "But I wanted you to have hers as well." She began to sob again. Dan grinned as he recalled Logan Haydenshire's remark that *Receivers cry all the time.*

Though he hadn't believed him at the time, Fionna was extremely emotional. But how could they not be? How could they bear the emotions of the world, all of the good and all of the bad, and not react?

"Sam knew an old Singer supplier who had some retro parts it needed. He said it should be as good as new now." He tenderly held her as she cried into his shoulder.

"Thank you." She wept in his arms. "You are the most amazing man ever." Before he could adamantly object, she lifted her head. "You are!"

He gazed at her tenderly and whispered, "If I am, it's because of you." He held her while she calmed, and eventually she let him wipe away the last of her tears.

Dan lifted the old sewing machine from the box. "If you don't want the other one, I'll take it back and get you something else."

"I want them both."

Dan was thrilled that she was so happy with her gifts. "Good."

"You have one more." She blushed violently. "And it didn't cost me hardly anything except maybe most of my pride and a lot of my dignity."

Extremely curious now, he lifted the rectangular package and tore the paper away to reveal a small four-by-six photo album, with a heart imprinted in the brown leather cover. She bit her lips together and drew a deep breath.

He opened the cover to reveal a black-and-white photo of Fionna's back. She was seated on her bed wearing nothing but a pair of white lacy thong panties.

"Oh my God," Dan panted. His heart thundered in his chest. He turned the page to find another black-and-white shot of her lying on her back on her bed at her old house. Her legs were crossed. She was wearing the same panties, thigh high stockings, heels, and long strands of pearls spilling between her breasts and over her nipples.

Dan's entire body seized as his pants tightened and his cock tugged at his zipper. "Please tell me Garrett Haydenshire didn't take these for you." He was unable to take his eyes off the provocative photos.

Fionna laughed. "No, I had them done last year. I just didn't have anyone to give them to. I just wanted them. There's a great boudoir photographer in the city. She's amazing."

There were shots of her standing, pulling one side of the thong down, of her in a corset, shots of her shapely legs crossed, wearing sky-high heels, and of her posed on her stomach completely naked, propped up just like the photo she'd taken when she was a toddler on the beach. There were two close-ups of her stunning cleavage, with a single drop pearl tucked seductively between her breasts. A ravishing, artistic shot of her up on the bed on her knees with her legs spread. She was covering her breasts with her arms, but her gorgeous ass was on full display. There was another one of her naked, standing in front of an antique mirror. Yet another of her near a window, wrapped in nothing but a sheet that was draped around her curves. The last was a shot of her in the corset, thong, and heels, staring at the camera and blowing a kiss.

"Can I take this with me to Vegas?" He quoted her, while he flipped to the front of the album and started the erotic picture show over from the beginning. "You are unbelievably gorgeous, and this,"—he held up the photo album—"this is amazing. I will never be able to stop looking at these."

She laughed again and gave him his smile.

"Well, you have to put it down eventually because then you can play with the real thing."

"Thank you," he half grunted and half growled. "This is…"—he shook his head, unable to come up with the correct word—"you are so fucking beautiful."

Eventually he stopped kissing her long enough to remember that she needed a nap. He coaxed her upstairs and tucked her in his arms and then in his shield.

When Dan awoke, a hazy grayness had settled in their room. Time seemed as variable as the light. The bleak skies reflected the ashen snow on the ground. The dismal, monochromatic world offered him nothing that made him want to leave the sanctuary of their bed. He blinked several times and tried to see the clock without disturbing Fionna. She was sound asleep on his chest.

Quickly deciding he didn't give a damn what time it was, he settled back against the pillows and concentrated. Her energy was running in the customary soothing flow against his skin.

At some point, he planned to personally thank Fionna's Tutu for teaching her that the healthiest way for her to sleep was naked. It was an otherworldly gift to be able to feel her intoxicating rhythms move against him each and every night, to be able to ease just a little of the emotional energy she had to take on each day by absorbing it into his shield.

When her guard was lax and she was at peace in his arms, he could feel the overwhelming love she miraculously held in her heart all for him. How could anyone love and accept him like that with all of his hideous flaws?

As he lay there, pondering her rhythms, they began rolling with slightly more heat and stronger arcs. A flutter of sensation moved between her legs. The soft purple energy over her body took on a fuchsia warmth. Dan's heart sped. Her body gave a slight roll and shifted toward his in her slumber.

What are you dreaming about, baby doll? He had to order himself not to awaken her and demand that she recall everything that was happening in her subconscious mind. He wanted to know what fantasies beckoned her and if she dreamed of him.

A moment later, her eyes blinked open hesitantly. The coy grin and shy enjoyment in her eyes let him know he had indeed played a role in her fantasies.

"Hey, baby doll, did you sleep well?" Dan cleared his throat and tried to dislodge the intimacy and yearning that had settled there.

She nodded languidly and stretched out over him like a contented kitten eager to be stroked. He obliged.

As her consciousness awakened fully, she leaned up on her elbow. "How are we going to share a suite this weekend if we have to be even more careful there than we are here?"

Though he was far more interested in discussing her dreams than what the next few days would hold, he knew they needed to plan.

He explained, "As one of the new owners, I graciously volunteered to arrange the suites for everyone." She grinned. "I called in a favor from a buddy of mine who works for the Vegas branch of Iodex. He checked out the hotel for me. Guy by the name of Barron, excellent officer, and I now owe him big. He got a blueprint of the Venetian and made a trip out there to secure everything for me. We're staying in two suites that are next door to one another. They can be combined via a door between them, but they're usually reserved separately. I have them listed as separate rentals, obviously, but I do happen to possess a fair amount of knowledge on how to get through doors that are supposed to stay locked. It shouldn't be a problem. We'll always enter our separate doors. But once we're inside, I'll be all over you."

"You'd better be." Fionna snuggled into his strong embrace.

"Barron took care of casting the security cameras near our rooms, as well. They're running a loop of the empty corridor. None of the Venetian security personnel know that they aren't really recording anymore."

"I would think this was really, really cool if it weren't my life."

"I'm sorry, baby." Apparently, he would never get accustomed to the guilt over the way their relationship had to exist.

"No, I didn't mean it like that. I'm sorry. I don't mind."

He tried to believe what she was saying, but he was far too accustomed to the feeling that he would simply never be good enough for someone as miraculous as the angel lying in his arms.

CHAPTER 32
MILE HIGH

By the next morning, Fionna's energy had completely recovered. They added a few things to the bags for their trip and ate a quick breakfast. They rushed out to the Ferrari, and Dan sped through the gray remnants of snow that had all but melted away.

"Did you bring your photo album?" she teased.

Chuckling, he took her hand. "No, baby, those are for my eyes only. Besides, I'm hoping to get to see a whole lot of the real thing."

A few minutes later, Dan parked and casted the Ferrari in the Angels' parking deck. He grabbed their bags. They joined the crowd waiting to board the Angels jet. It was a large, plush aircraft with everything from bedrooms to a fully stocked kitchen and comfortable seating for everyone.

"Hey, man, did you have a good Christmas?" Garrett shot Dan a knowing grin. Fionna had clearly let Garrett in on the photo album Dan was being given.

"Very nice and you?" Dan ignored Garrett's wry smile.

"Odd." Garrett sighed.

"Odd?" Everyone took another step toward the plane as the pilots and coolant officers boarded.

At that moment, Emily and Rainer joined the waiting line of Angels and their companions.

Garrett turned his attention to Emily. "Is Adeline okay?"

"No, not really."

Fionna and Dan glanced at one another. They weren't certain they should be listening in.

"Logan and Lucas had rather heated words last night before dinner," Rainer, often the diplomat, brought them into the conversation.

Dan grimaced. "How bad?"

"Things have been getting more and more tense every day the Premier's son and his serving staff have been at Mom and Dad's," Garrett elaborated.

"Lucas was kind of upset with the whole Christmas deal at the Haydenshires." Rainer tried to explain what Dan assumed was probably just a rapid escalation of irritation with everyone living in close quarters.

"He kind of thought everyone should have given gifts to everyone else." Emily sighed. "So, when the only gifts for Adeline were from him, his family, and Logan, he kind of got mad."

"He doesn't get Mom and Dad's thing about not living lavishly even if they are the ruling family, and then Logan..." Garrett shook his head and began laughing.

Rainer joined in. "Yeah, probably not his best move, but hey, that's Lo."

"What did he do?" Fionna's intrigue sparkled in her eyes.

Emily and Garrett both guffawed.

"He didn't know Lucas could see him." Rainer immediately came to Logan's defense.

Emily regained her composure, but she was still giggling. "Logan was sitting on the couch helping the twins set up their new train table, and Adeline came into the room. Everyone else was in the kitchen or out playing in the snow." She was overcome by another fit of giggles.

Garrett shook his head at his little sister. "So Lo, genius that he is, didn't realize her dad was watching them from the kitchen. He grabs her and paddles her ass. She tackles him. They start making out on the couch while Logan helps himself to several other things."

Dan joined in Garrett's laughter. "Nice job."

"Yeah, her dad lost his shit, and Dad stepped in. But I'll tell you this, it wasn't what Logan did that got Lucas so riled, it was the big ol' grin on Adeline's face when he did it that pissed her daddy the fuck off," Garrett stated knowingly.

"Poor guy," Dan lamented. Logan was relatively naïve, but he was genuinely a hard-working, honest man who Dan had a tremendous amount of respect for. He was a hell of an officer.

"Yeah, I still think Logan is confused," Emily teased. "You know, just because you married her doesn't mean you can grab and smack all of that whenever you want."

"Wait...what do you mean?" Rainer feigned confusion to keep the laughter going.

They climbed up the stairs of the plane.

"I just don't think it was that Logan smacked her ass or whatever. It was really that Lucas hasn't ever seen anyone act so relaxed in a house full of people," Emily confided in Fionna.

Emily was usually very wise for her years, and Dan thought she'd probably hit the nail on the head.

While trying not to think about the bedrooms on the plane or what he'd promised Fionna they would do on the flight, Dan guided her to a pair of seats, facing Rainer and Emily. Chloe and Garrett took a set of seats across the wide aisle.

He was surprised by the obligatory and somewhat aloof smiles he received from the Angels and their companions as they all stowed their luggage and boarded the plane. They'd all seemed much friendlier the last time he was at the arena.

Fionna giggled in response to his knitted brow. "You're an owner now so they're all on their best behavior until they figure out you aren't a prick."

Dan chuckled. Trying not to be intimidating didn't come easy. He'd spent the last twelve years perfecting his image as a hardass.

Medio Sawyer made an appearance and urged the women to play well and represent Arlington in everything they did all weekend. It was a lecture Dan found rather amusing, considering the fact that his own daughter was likely to be the one causing the most trouble.

The team was then informed that one of the coolant officers' wives had gone into labor Christmas Eve, and that the flight would be slightly longer, as he'd been unable to be replaced the day after Christmas.

Dan was impressed that the women seemed perfectly fine with that, and that they all wanted to make certain the man's wife and baby were doing well. There was talk of what gift the Angels could send for the new baby.

One of the copilots moved from the cockpit to the vast seating quarters. "We'll be taking off in a few minutes, ladies. Buckle up and stow everything. Let the flight attendants know if you need anything. Good luck tomorrow. We'll all be rooting for you."

"I'm gonna run to the restroom." Fionna stood and grabbed Emily's hand.

"Apparently, I'm going to the restroom as well." Emily laughed as she followed Fionna to the bathroom. Rainer and Dan shared a shrug as they watched the ladies disappear.

Garrett spun out of his seat and landed in the seat Fionna had been occupying. He gave Dan a goading grin.

"My girlfriend is sitting there," Dan joked.

Garrett smirked. "I was gonna offer you some sex-on-a-plane tips."

Rainer cracked up.

"I most definitely do not want those, especially from you."

"No man, I'm serious. There's an art to it."

Dan rolled his eyes.

"First, don't try to take her clothes off standing up. Put her in the bed and then strip her."

"Leave now." Dan jerked his thumb back to Garrett's seat.

Ignoring Dan completely, Garrett continued, "I'm serious. Turbulence. Think about it. She could get hurt. You could get hurt."

"I could hurt you," Dan drawled as Rainer continued to laugh.

"Let the plane get leveled off first. Doing it on the climb can mess with your head. And it has to be in the bed or the chair. Up against the wall doesn't work. I've tried," Garrett continued with his informative lecture.

Dan narrowed his eyes in disdain. He had no desire to hear about Garrett's escapades on the Angels' jet. The girls returned just as the engines began to roar.

"Thank God. Now maybe he'll shut it."

Fionna grinned and then promptly crawled in Dan's lap since Garrett was still in her seat.

"Even better." Dan cradled her head on his shoulder.

The pilot made the final walk-through. He chuckled as he took in Fionna curled up in Dan's lap. "Fionna, sweetheart, I have no doubt that Chief Vindico will keep you safe, but I can't take off until you're in your own seat with a seatbelt."

"Sorry, Morgan." Fionna shooed Garrett out of her seat.

The plane began its ascent, and Dan held Fionna's hand. He wanted to be in contact with her constantly for the two and a half hours they would be in the air.

"Are you okay, baby?" Dan whispered in Fionna's ear as she leaned and lifted the armrest between them. She laid her head against his chest.

Fionna nodded as Dan wrapped his arm around her. It seemed she wanted to be in contact with him for the same reasons he'd wanted to hold her hand.

He could tell from the way she curled into him that had they not been on a plane full of her friends and teammates, she would have climbed back in his lap and curled up in her customary ball.

The players all seemed to tuck into the people seated nearest them and began discussing the exposition or what they'd received for Christmas.

Rainer leaned back in his seat. He closed his eyes as Emily reclined in his lap. He reached and pulled a blanket from the seat beside her and covered her in it.

Fionna's eyes darkened as she gazed up at Dan. He could feel the timid hunger swirl in her energy. The need began to surface as she grew more comfortable with the idea of using one of the bedrooms on the plane.

Dan kept her tucked to his chest and brushed her hair away from her face. He kissed her temple and then whispered, "Tell me what you want, baby doll."

Her body gave a slight tremble in his arms. The movement made Dan want to throw her over his shoulder, carry her to one of the bedrooms, and make her scream out his name. She moved her head to his shoulder to carry out his request.

"I want you," she whispered and let her hot breath and her tongue caress his earlobe discreetly. She settled back on his shoulder to make certain that no one was paying them too much attention. She leaned back in and continued, "I want you to make me feel how hard you are. I want you to make me suck you. I want you to lick me until you can taste all of me. I want you to tell me to come for you, and I want you to spank me if I don't obey," she drawled in low breathy whispers of ecstasy that drove Dan wild.

He clenched his jaw and forcibly quelled the thundering growl that built in his chest. He gazed at her with a look that said he'd drink every last drop of her gorgeous body and then devour anything she had left.

"I want to be all alone with you."

Dan shifted to try to hide the effect her pleas were having on his body.

"I want you to take my clothes off, and then I want you to take me, and mark me, because I'm yours. I want you to fuck me until this plane lands." Her eyes were ardent and craving.

Dan tried desperately to draw a deep, steadying breath by reminding himself that he had to walk to the rooms in the back of the plane. Fionna unbuckled and shot him a grin that was somehow wickedly virtuous. He ached. She stood and held out her hand to him with an expectant degree of sass.

Rainer grinned, but he kept his eyes closed as Garrett began to chuckle. The embarrassment made Dan able to stand and take her hand.

"Fiii-oooon-nnnaa," drawled from several of the Angels as they began to laugh and whistle.

Garrett smirked. "Geez, Fi, let him get his clothes off first," he harassed, and everyone else on the plane cracked up. Dan popped the back of Garrett's head as he went by which only served to make him laugh harder.

Dan followed Fionna down the aisle and into the bedroom she'd booked. She was glowing bright crimson as Dan kicked the door shut and promptly locked it.

He chuckled as she moved to him and buried her face in his chest.

"I've got you, baby." He wrapped his arms around her and refrained from pointing out that this had been her request.

She giggled as she nodded against his chest.

"We don't have to do anything, but occasionally I'm gonna need you to scream out my name and moan really loudly, while I either squeak the mattress or bang something against the wall."

She cracked up. "Are you kidding me? I got you in here. That was the worst part. We're doing it." He laughed. She was absolutely adorable.

"Yes, ma'am." Dan began taking in their surroundings. It was a relatively low-key room, containing a mattress on a silver platform mounted to the floor. The bed had fresh sheets and a blanket. There were two cushioned chairs also mounted to the floor. The Angels halo and lightning bolt logo was painted on the wall behind the bed.

Dan gave her a cocky grin as he watched her blush begin to fade. "There were a few things you mentioned that you wanted." He let his hands slip down her back and reach into her jeans. He grabbed her ass greedily and kneaded her flesh with force. She trembled again as her breaths came quicker.

"I need them." Her tone was low and breathy in her desire.

"I've got everything you need, baby doll, and I'm gonna make it feel so damn good. Now, come here to me." He braced her in his arms, leaned in, and began the awe-inspiring ritual of uniting their bodies and their energies, the sanctity of making them one.

Almost an hour later, Dan grabbed the sheets that were now crumpled on the bed and pulled them up over the two of them. He swathed them around her, and set his cast over her as he began healing the deep, purple markings he'd left on her breasts. She grinned at him as she watched him work.

"No." She grabbed his hand as he moved to her hip bone. "Leave that one. I want it there. That's all for me."

"So fucking sexy," he groaned, which thoroughly delighted her. He cradled her close and concentrated on their energy still bonded together as she melded into him. If he had his choice, he'd spend their entire Vegas weekend tucked up with her on the Angels jet.

They talked, cuddled, and even napped until the pilot's voice was projected throughout the plane announcing that they were making their approach into Harry Reid International airport.

Dan stood and pulled his clothes back on and then helped Fionna with hers. She fixed the bed back as close as she could get it to its original state and then gazed at the chair with a very satisfied smile.

Dan chuckled as he pulled her to him. He kissed her hesitantly and then with force. "You know how much you mean to me?" He just needed to make certain she knew before he left the plane and pretended to hardly know her at all. Recollections of leaving her in that Chinese-food dive still haunted his soul.

She nodded, but fear and sadness begin to permeate her rhythms. "I love you so much," she confessed.

"Me too, baby, and I'll spend every possible moment I can with you. You're the only reason I'm here. I'll do anything to make certain you're safe and that you know how much I…" he choked and tried desperately to force the words from his mouth.

She placed her index finger over his lips. "I know."

He leaned and devoured her mouth again.

A knock sounded on the door. "You two gonna come up for air anytime soon? We're landing." Garrett's voice carried through the door.

"That reminds me,"—Dan smirked—"there's something I really need to harass Garrett about, but it has to do with all that we did in here. Is that okay?"

Fionna laughed outright. "If it's to harass Garrett, then definitely."

The plane touched down, and Dan and Fionna made their way back to their seats. They received knowing grins from most of the people on the plane. As they landed, everyone began grabbing their bags.

"You two have fun?" Garrett goaded.

"Hell yeah, and by the way, your whole 'up against the wall won't work' theory is full of crap. Maybe you should work out a little more." Dan popped his hand against Garrett's rather chiseled abs and listened to Fionna laugh.

Dan handed Fionna her designer suitcase and toiletry bags.

"Go on, baby. I'll see you in a little while." The harrowing sense of her absence washed over him as she leaned up on her tiptoes and brushed a kiss along his jawline. Then, she turned and walked away.

Dan was one of the last people to exit the jet. He supposed he appreciated Garrett hanging back with him. He was stunned as he entered the airport. Throngs of press were everywhere.

"Yes, folks, it's those well-known alluring Angels of Arlington, Virginia. Their jet has just touched down. Let's see if any of these talented women will talk with us," one reporter chanted as he sprinted up the rope-lined corridor created for the teams.

"It's Captain Chloe Sawyer! How are we feeling today, Chloe?" the man shouted as he stuck a microphone in Chloe's face.

"We're great! Go, Angels!" Chloe called in a customary response as she picked up her pace.

"And it's the prettiest Receivers in the Realm, Miss Fionna Styler, and the Crown Governor's daughter, Miss Emily Haydenshire. How are we today, ladies? We ready to challenge?" The man angled his way in front of Fionna and Emily and kept them from moving forward.

Rainer bristled but kept his head down. Dan was unable to keep his eyes off Fionna. His fists clenched in a pulsing thirst to take out his aggressions. Anyone preventing Fionna from getting where she wanted to go looked like an excellent target.

"We're ready!" Fionna beamed.

Emily nodded. "Go, Angels!"

"Now, you know, Jim,"—the reporter turned back to the cameraman—"the Crown Governor and the Chief of Iodex, Dan Vindico, have both recently purchased shares in the Angels. Our beloved Crown Governor Lawson's son, Rainer, also purchased major shares recently. It seems the Angels have sent some of the owners out for the exhibition. Chief Vindico, can you tell us what you hope to see the ladies accomplish this weekend?" The reporter put the mic in Dan's face, and Garrett began chuckling.

The Angels were stopping periodically to sign autographs for awaiting fans pleading for their attention. Dan resisted the urge to tell the man to get the mic the hell out of his face. "They're the best team in the Realm. They always make Arlington proud," Dan huffed before moving on.

He watched the Angels climb into awaiting vans that were headed to The Venetian hotel. He headed toward the last van in the line after he watched Fionna climb safely into the one in front.

The exhibition was being held at The Venetian, but only a few teams were staying on the property. The Sirens were staying at the Luxor at the other end of the strip, much to Dan's delight.

"Chief Vindico, there are a couple of places left in the van up there. You and Garrett could go with the other players. I think the last van is full." Katie gave Dan a knowing smile as she gestured to the van in the front of the line.

"Thanks, Katie girl." Garrett tousled her hair and followed Dan to the van she'd suggested. While studying the space around him carefully, Dan made certain he didn't recognize anyone in the crowd exiting the airport. There were hundreds of people rushing about, but no one seemed to have much interest in the Angels now that they'd been escorted out of the airport and their security guards were surrounding the vans.

"You have really nice friends." Dan smiled as he slid into a seat next to Fionna that had been arranged for him. Angels and their companions blocked them from view, but everything appeared very nonchalant from the outside.

"I definitely do." Fionna gave everyone who had played a part in the arrangement broad grins.

"Aww, we love you, Fi. We love that you're happy," Sasha assured her. Her husband chuckled and nodded his agreement.

"Just remember we loved you before he did," Chloe commanded.

Fionna laughed. "I'll always remember that!"

CHAPTER 33
WHAT NEEDS TO BE SAID

Crowds of Summation fans were outside of The Venetian and in the vast lobby area. As there were always conferences of one kind or another going on in Vegas, the Non-Gifted tourists didn't seem to pay them much attention.

Dan exited the van and disappeared. He made certain he could see Fionna, but that no one would be under the impression she'd become the most important thing in his life.

Chloe huffed, "You just be careful, Fi. He seems pretty good at disappearing." Dan watched the pain mar Fionna's features. His heart fissured. Remembering why he couldn't go to her and assure her that he wasn't going anywhere, he made a parallel trek into the hotel, but stayed approximately ten yards away from her.

A prostitute, stationed near the entrance, gave him a flirtatious grin and a wink. She offered him her card. Dan ignored her as he made his way inside.

Immediately recalling one of his least favorite things about Vegas, Dan sighed as the noise of the hotel casino bled throughout the entire grand entrance of The Venetian hotel.

Dancers dressed in leopard-print bikini tops and red skirts were dancing on a side stage and circulating in the entrance. Dan studied the area methodically. He was ever on the prowl for lurking danger.

He noted the moving river that wound throughout the hotel that offered gondola rides.

He heard the money-changing machines blaring loudly with flashing red lights as coins dispensed in rapt accord. Keeping his dark sunglasses on, Dan stepped up to the check-in desk that ran along the back wall.

"Chief Officer Dan Vindico." He flashed his badge as the woman smiled and nodded.

"All of the Angels and the owners are staying in the luxury suites on the thirty-first floor." Dan nodded his agreement. That was where he'd booked them. The woman handed Dan two keycards, a bucket containing ten complimentary hotel chips for the slots, and a map of the hotel.

"The Summation Meet and Greet for all of the teams will be on the Palazzo side of the hotel in the fifth-floor ballroom at three, and the banquet will be in the Galileo ballroom tonight at seven," the woman chirped.

"Thanks." Dan headed toward the elevators while pretending to study the map of the hotel. Fionna received her room keys and chips and then, ignoring him completely, stepped onto an opening elevator. Dan followed in behind her along with a dozen other people.

He moved to the back corner, while Fionna stayed near the front. An angry frown creased her features, but she never looked Dan's way. She rolled her eyes and scooted away from two men standing near her. She'd picked up on something in their energy she didn't like.

Dan bristled and narrowed his eyes at the guy nearest her.

"Yeah, but what about Sandy and the kids?" His friend sounded intoxicated, though it was just after noon.

"Hey, it's Vegas, baby. You know what they say. She'll never find out, and you only live once," was the other man's response. Dan knew immediately what had Fionna so irritated.

By the time the twenty-nine was lit on the elevator, everyone had exited, save Dan and Fionna.

"Cameras," Dan spoke through his teeth while offering her a polite, indifferent grin. She gave him a hesitant smile, the one she saved for people she hardly knew. It wounded him.

He followed Fionna out of the elevator and down the vast corridor, but he kept his distance. She stopped outside of room 3145. Rainer and Emily were unlocking room 3143, just as Dan had arranged. He slid his keycard into the lock of 3147. He decided to call Roy Stegman, the commander of Nevada Iodex, and give Barron his high praises.

Wasting no time to look over his own living quarters, he closed the entry door and rushed to the steel door between their suites. Extracting a lock-pick set from his pocket, he had the lock unbolted in a matter of moments. He moved to the magnetic lock below the key set. Trying the typical range of magnetic pulses first, Dan summoned, and a moment later the door between the rooms slipped open.

She'd been staring at the door hopefully. Relief washed over her as he stepped through it.

"Hey, baby doll," he soothed as she fell into his arms. The stress of their arrival, Chloe's warning, and their elevator ride seemed to have gotten to her. "Are you okay?"

"Now," she whimpered. "But what if I want to get to you? I don't know how to do all of that." She gestured to the still open door. Her voice was riddled with confusion and insecurity. Dan regulated his own emotions to keep her from picking up on his disdain that Chloe had made her feel insecure about him.

"I'm not going anywhere, sweetheart. After they deliver our luggage, I'll unpack in my suite in case someone goes looking for something, but anytime I'm in there we'll leave the door open. If you want me to teach you to pick the locks, I will." He wanted her to have every option that might make her feel more secure.

"Maybe later." She glanced around the room but still clung to his forearm. The matching suites were rather plush. A vast king-sized bed sat in the bedroom area, two steps above the living area, complete with a picture window that displayed the strip. Each bathroom had a massive steam shower. There was a small kitchenette as well.

A knock sounded at the door to Dan's suite. He grimaced. He didn't want to leave her again. "Let me get my luggage and then I'll be right back."

She seemed to will bravery. She gave him a hesitant nod. A louder repetitive knock sounded.

"I'll be right back." Closing the door between their rooms, he answered his own. After tipping the bellman, he waited on him to deliver Fionna's luggage.

She seemed more sure of herself as they explored the identical suites. She ordered lunch and had it delivered to her room. Dan stepped out once again when it was delivered and then cuddled her on his lap on the plush sofa as they ate.

"I have to be at that meet and greet in uniform at three." She set her plate aside and nuzzled her head under Dan's chin. He smiled. The gesture completed him.

"I know, honey, but it's barely one here. The time difference, remember? If you want to go do something with Garrett or Emily, it's fine. I'll hang out up here." He didn't want her to stay holed up in their rooms if she didn't want to.

Fionna shrugged. "Is it bad if we hang out in here? I don't want to hurt their feelings."

"No, baby, they'll just think you're tired because I wore you out on the plane." He gave her a wry grin and watched a reminiscent heat creep up her neck.

"Well, you did."

Dan kissed her cheek and began running his fingers through her hair. She melted into him. "They're probably unpacking, sweetheart. Just stay right here with me."

"I need to hang up my gown." She leapt off the sofa.

"Or don't," he sighed and followed her lead. After unzipping his luggage, he located his suit and the couple of shirts he'd brought and hung them in his room.

She unzipped a garment bag and pulled out a long, white, flowing chiffon gown with a plunging neckline. She removed the plastic dry cleaning bag, and Dan's mouth hung open.

The lace-covered neckline dropped all the way to her waist. Material would cover her breasts, but just barely. There was a revealing slit that would run the length of her leg from her feet to her midthigh. The back was nonexistent. The chiffon was made to drape over that luscious ass and put it on provocative display. A set of cutouts would showcase the skin between the bottom of her rib cage and the top of her waist.

"Fionna!" Dan gasped. Shocked, she turned to him, furrowing her brow. "I'm gonna have to beat men back with a bat." His brain ached in confusion from the ardent desire to see her gorgeous curves shown off in that gown and in a sincere wish that she'd picked something that covered a great deal more skin since she wouldn't be arriving on his arm.

"What, this old thing?" She waggled her eyebrows.

Dan drew a deep breath. She was going to enjoy making him drool all evening long. Torturing him was clearly her goal.

"All of the Angels wear white to the banquet every year. You know…Angels." She lost a little of her flirtatious fire as she moved to hang the dress in the bathroom. After turning on the steaming hot water to release the nonexistent wrinkles, she came back and began unpacking all of her things and arranging them around her suite to order her space.

"I wouldn't want some other girl to turn your head, since I can't be your official date." She tried so hard it cut him like a knife. She tried to pretend she wasn't really worried, that she was confident that she was it for him. But she didn't believe that, not at all.

Dan moved to her. "Have I not made myself or my intentions perfectly clear to you, sweetheart? There aren't any other women who could ever hold my attention for even a split second."

"I know, but I just… I wanted you to think that I'm the prettiest girl there." Her confession weighted her head and her voice.

Dan shook his head and guided her gently into his arms. He brushed a kiss across her forehead. "You could come into the banquet tonight wearing sweat pants and a T-shirt, and I would still know you're the most gorgeous woman on the entire planet. The other night when you were sick and I cleaned you up, you were still the most beautiful woman in the universe. It doesn't matter what you wear or how much makeup you have on because I adore *you*. You have my whole heart and my entire soul that I honestly didn't even think existed anymore until I looked into your eyes. You and no one else."

Her energy soared as she beamed and blinked back a sudden onslaught of emotion. She wrapped her arms around him and let him embrace her fully.

"I just wish I could go with you." She finally choked out the thing that she'd been trying not to confess since they'd talked about the trip on their couch the day before.

"I know, baby, and believe me, I wish I could walk in there with you on my arm tonight and let everyone know I'm the luckiest guy in the entire Realm. And someday I will." The fire that burned in his gut every time he thought about taking down Wretchkinsides ignited in him again.

I'm buying a ring. He hugged her tighter. *And I'm getting down on one knee and begging her to marry me as soon as he draws his last breath.* His fervor and determination was so potent Fionna picked up on it. Her brow knitted as she lifted her head to study him.

He gazed deeply into her eyes. "Don't say anything for a minute, please."

Fionna nodded and watched him closely. Dan's heart hammered. His stomach rolled and then clenched tightly. *You can do it. Just tell her. Don't be a coward,* he ordered himself. *She deserves to hear you say it.* His hands shook as he held her shoulders.

His mind was suddenly awhirl with images both beautiful and horrifying. Sunlit days where nothing could go wrong mingled repugnantly with images of that grave. Amelia's laughter shattered with gunshots. His body twitched and rejected the metallic scent of blood mixed with her favorite floral perfume.

"Dan,"—Fionna shook her head—"don't do this."

He shook his head and laid his index finger gently on her lips. She was scared. He had to do it. He had to say it.

Quickly, he let his eyes close in a fervent prayer that nothing he said would hurt Amelia. He opened them to stare into those soulful, sienna eyes, the ones that brought breath to his lungs, blood to his weary frame, and made life worth living.

Tears were forming on her lashes.

"I...uh." The words snagged on the boulder in his throat. He chastised himself again. She started to shake her head, but he was determined. "Fionna…I…love you," he managed in a choked whisper.

"Oh my gosh." She fell against his chest and clung to him fiercely. "I love you too."

"I know. I don't know why, but I know." He was still stunned by all he had when he held her in his arms.

"Because you're the most amazing man ever. You know you don't ever have to tell me that. I can feel it."

"I know, but I wanted to tell you. I needed you to know."

"I do know." She tried futilely to blink back another round of tears.

"I don't just want you to feel it. You need to hear it often, because I feel it constantly." He wiped away a few tears and then realized that was going to be pointless. She began to sob. He offered her sanctuary in his arms and let her ruin his shirt.

CHAPTER 34
DON'T COUNT YOUR CARDS

They'd ended up reclined on the couch in Fionna's suite. Dan's professing his love had built a stronger intimacy than the one they'd shared with their bodies that morning on the plane.

Garrett called at a quarter to three to ask if Fionna wanted to walk down to the meet and greet with him. She'd agreed, so Dan kissed her heatedly and then watched her walk, in full uniform, out of her suite on Garrett Haydenshire's arm.

With a deep breath, Dan headed to the closet, pulled out a polo shirt complete with the Angels insignia, and shrugged into it. He paced anxiously in his boredom until three fifteen. He grabbed his keycard, made certain the door between his and Fionna's suite was locked, and then headed to the elevators.

When he entered the ballroom, his left shoulder gave its customary twitch. He moved on instinct and scanned the large room methodically. The Sirens' table was situated closest to the entry doors. He and Marlisa shared a hate-fueled glower.

The Angels' table was in the center of the room. Memorabilia hung behind them, and fans who were begging for autographs and photos surrounded them in long lines.

Dan's stomach lurched as his eyes fell on Fionna. She was seated between Emily and Sasha and was being chatted up by a well-built guy in a San Antonio Synthesizers uniform.

Dan's body waged war with both his brain and his brawn. Overcome with desperate need to march over there and introduce himself forcefully, he ordered himself not to move. The order became much easier to heed with one quick glance back at Marlisa. Dan clenched his jaw and shuffled slowly toward the Angels' table.

Fionna looked uncomfortable and reached for a picture of herself that a little girl in front of her held. The girl stared up at her in wide-eyed amazement, but she seemed too shy to speak. Fionna beamed at her and asked her name, which she seemed to have momentarily forgotten. Though Fionna studiously ignored him, the guy kept talking as she signed her name on the photo and spoke with the young fan.

Rainer was stationed directly behind Emily. He was wearing a shirt similar to Dan's and glaring at the Synthesizers player. Whatever he was saying, Rainer didn't care for.

Garrett was behind Chloe but was also glaring at the Synthesizers challenger. He was trying to hang back to let the ladies have their moment. He caught Dan's eye and made his way through the fans. "Keep it cool, man. Marlisa's all over you."

"I'm fine," Dan lied outright.

"Uh-huh, sure you are." Garrett rolled his eyes. Dan joined Rainer who gave him a sympathetic look.

"It was nice seeing you again, but I need to get to all of these," Fionna gestured toward the lengthy line of people awaiting her attention.

"Save me a dance tonight, sweet thing." The guy winked at Fionna, gave her a cocky grin, and then took a small step toward the Synthesizers' table. He didn't seem to care that the Synthesizers had fans of their own awaiting his attention.

Fionna sighed. "I'm seeing someone, Trevor. I've said that four times."

He chuckled pompously. "Yeah, but he's not here and I am. It's Vegas, baby. We had a good time last year."

Dan's blood boiled. Garrett's hand grasped his shoulder, and he realized that he'd tensed and leaned toward Trevor.

Ignoring his comment, Fionna stood and posed for a picture with two teenage boys who seemed woefully unable to get their eyes above her rack.

"It's gonna be a long damn night," Dan huffed to Garrett and Rainer. They both nodded their agreement.

He made certain he didn't spend any time near Fionna. He followed Garrett's lead and stalked around the room, talking to fans, challengers, and other teams' owners.

"Come on, let's hit the casino for a few," Garrett urged.

"I don't want to go to the casino." Dan was still furious at Trevor and his relentless winking and grinning at Fionna while he signed autographs from the Synthesizers' table.

"Yeah, it'd be better to hang out in here and watch other guys she has no interest in make you furious and themselves look like the broken douche-nozzles they are."

Drowned by defeat, Dan glanced nonchalantly at the Angels' table. They were still surrounded by fans, and Fionna seemed to be enjoying talking with the young girls who idolized her. Their line was longer than any other team's.

The Synthesizers' table had picked up as well, and Trevor was bragging about his skills to several admiring fans. Bile burned Dan's throat when he let two girls of approximately sixteen years of age squeeze his bicep.

"Fine." He certainly wasn't doing any good in the ballroom, and he was probably making Fionna nervous. "Text her and tell her where we're going." His infuriated tone was rude, but he didn't care.

Garrett pulled his phone from his pocket and did as he was asked.

They exited the elevators on the ground floor and entered into the obnoxious whir of one of the many gargantuan casinos in the hotel.

More red-skirted, bikini-clad women were moving around the casino taking drink orders. Garrett engaged an attractive brunette until he got a free beer.

Dan shook his head. He stepped back and let Garrett work his charm. All the while, his heart ached. He missed Fionna.

Garrett sipped the beer and scanned the room. "Well, well, well." He gestured toward a blackjack table with a gotcha grin.

Dan had already seen Victor Roslov and Gentry Messnick seated at the table. They ran a low-level money-laundering ring for Wretchkinsides.

"Shall we?" Garrett was eager to play.

Already feeling vile repulsion from seeing Wretchkinsides's men and mutinous from Trevor's advances, Dan decided walking away with a take from Wretchkinsides wouldn't be a bad way to spend an hour or so.

Roslov and Messnick wouldn't likely recognize either Dan or Garrett. They weren't high enough up in the Interfeci to be concerned with national law enforcement. If they recognized Garrett, due to his father's job in the Realm, they'd be excited to try and take the Crown Governor's son's money.

Both Dan and Garrett were extremely good at counting cards, especially when they played together. They sauntered to the table.

"You know how to play blackjack, man?" Dan feigned confusion.

"I think so." Garrett came off as macho and desperate to prove his worth. They'd performed this act many times before.

Dan discreetly pulled a few bills from his wallet. He was careful not to let his license show. He handed them to the dealer.

Roslov and Messnick looked excited. They seemed to have taken Dan and Garrett for newbies in town for the exhibition.

To prove the point, Dan flipped over his first card to reveal a king, and Garrett revealed a jack. They both asked for a hit.

Dan watched Messnick turn over a two and then a seven. Roslov flipped an ace.

"Hit me?" Dan mocked hesitation, and then asked Garrett the rules of the game again. The dealer laid down another card, an eight.

"Again?" Dan asked quizzically. He drew an ace and then asked Garrett what that meant.

Garrett feigned confusion. "I think it's worth ten."

"One or eleven, gentlemen." The dealer grew impatient quickly. "You're at nineteen. Do you want another card?"

Dan nodded and hid his grin when he busted badly.

"Try again. You are just learning," Roslov encouraged.

Dan shrugged. "I guess." Roslov and Messnick both kept up their encouragement, and Dan played along.

"See now, how about a little side bet? Just for fun," Messnick held up three one-hundred-dollar bills.

Dan and Garrett pretended to discuss. The rules were established, and they eventually agreed to the side bet. The dealer discouraged Garrett. They'd play-acted well.

They played several rounds with Garrett lucking out with twenty-one only once, before he and Dan really began to play. Messnick urged them to lay down more money. He looked like he'd just been named Crown.

Dan and Garrett discussed momentarily and then agreed. An hour later, they left the casino with a fifty-eight hundred dollar gain that they split. They laughed heartily all the way back to the ballroom.

"See, the day wasn't a total loss," Garrett encouraged on the elevator.

"No, it's been a great day. I just hate what I'm doing to her," Dan admitted. They were alone on the elevator.

"She's all right. She knows why, and she's crazy about you."

"Yeah, well, the feeling's mutual."

Fionna's entire face lit in a broad, beautiful grin when they entered the ballroom, but she quickly glanced away.

The crowds had dwindled as the clock approached five, the designated time for the end of the meet and greet.

Trevor approached again as the fans began exiting the ballroom, loaded down with photos, T-shirts, and posters from their favorite teams.

"Let me walk you back to your suite, *Angel*." He waggled his eyebrows and gave Fionna a cocky grin as he laughed at his own joke.

"I'm going to kill that guy," Dan growled as he made the last few steps toward the table. Garrett halted him forcefully. He shoved Dan to the side and slid into position.

"Hey, I'm Garrett Haydenshire." He stuck his hand out toward Trevor and narrowed his eyes.

"Oh." Trevor's brow furrowed as he took in Garrett's heavily tattooed, bulging biceps and his scowl.

"Trevor Sanders. I captain the Synthesizers."

Garrett chuckled. "That's rough, man. Gotta be tough to captain the worst team in the Realm." He turned to Fionna and left no room for rebuttal. "Are you ready to go, baby?" Relief and jealously splintered Dan's shield. He wanted her away from Trevor, but dammit, he wanted to be the one to rescue her.

"Yes," she huffed angrily as she took Garrett's hand.

"I'll see you tonight, Fionna." Trevor looked somewhat confused by what had just happened.

Dan let the fury permeate his body as he watched Fionna leave with her head on Garrett's shoulder and his arm wrapped around her back protectively. Dan took his phone from his pocket and slipped into a small closet off the ballroom. He phoned Portwood.

"Hey man, how's Vegas?" Portwood answered on the first ring.

"I need you to run a name for me," Dan demanded.

"No problem." He heard Portwood's keyboard click.

He explained the problem.

Portwood chuckled. "The last time she was in the office she looked like she was head over heels for you. I don't think you have anything to worry about."

"Humor me," Dan ordered. "Find out anything you can. Parking tickets, drunk and disorderlies, hell, jaywalking, I want anything you've got."

"You got it," Portwood agreed. "Sanders, right?"

"Yeah, he challenges for the San Antonio Synthesizers," Dan concluded as he felt a spiteful smile form on his face. "Just text me with whatever you find."

"Will do."

"Thanks, I owe you."

"It's fine. I have one of the laptops here, and Julie's mother is driving me nuts. This way I can hide out for a little while. You know, work and all."

Dan chuckled. "Glad to be of service and, hey, no names in the text."

"Come on, give me a little credit. We'll keep her safe. You know that."

CHAPTER 35
THE MANY MOODS OF A WOMAN IN LOVE

Dan reentered his suite and then moved back through the door between his and Fionna's rooms. He wondered momentarily if he should knock before entering her suite.

She was curled up on the couch sipping something hot that Dan assumed was a mug of her tea. Her uniform was in a crumpled heap on the floor. That was very unlike her. He studied her and tried to discern what had happened.

She'd replaced the uniform with a pair of Angel knit pants and one of his Iodex T-shirts. Her face was drawn in a frown, and she seemed to be trying to take up as little space as she possibly could on the massive sofa.

The sight of her in his shirt had his ego contented once more. "Can I come in?"

Confusion eased her frown but only slightly. "Of course."

"Care if I get something to drink?" he asked politely, while still studying her.

She rolled her eyes. "Dan, we live together. You can get whatever you want."

Quickly grabbing a Dr Pepper from the refrigerator, he lowered the temperature a little more, the way he preferred it, and then moved to sit near her on the couch.

"I'm sorry for all I'm doing to you. I shouldn't have come. I'm just making you miserable." The bitter words scorched his lips.

"No!" She immediately softened, but he wasn't trying to make her feel guilty.

"Honey, yes, I am. You deserve a guy who can at least walk up and introduce himself as your boyfriend to pricks who won't leave you alone."

"Stop." She set her almost-empty mug on the table and crawled into his lap. "It's just a lot to feel in a room with so many people, so many fans. I never ever want to disappoint them, but some of them have me cast as superhuman. I can't live up to their expectations. I'm not the two-dimensional picture on their television screens they want me to be. And it would be great to be able to introduce you to Trevor, and I would love to introduce him to these," she teased as she cupped her hands over his massive biceps, eliciting a smile from Dan. "But I saw the way Marlisa watched you, and I know you're keeping me safe. That means more to me than anything in the world. You're going to all of these lengths to keep me safe and to still be here with me. Thank you for all you do for me. Besides, I'm not upset with you. I'm upset with me," she finally admitted in a dejected humph.

"Why?"

"Because it was such a stupid thing to do. *He* was such a stupid thing to do. I'm an idiot." She buried her face in his neck.

Not entirely certain how to respond and not wanting to add to her self-imposed guilt, Dan sighed. "Believe me, I've done a whole lot of stupid things in the past few years. You met one of them at the Chinese restaurant a few days ago, remember?"

This at least gained him a slight giggle. She allowed her face to surface.

"And, oh my gosh, he was horrible in bed! Awful!"

Dan was both extremely pleased to hear this and simultaneously disgusted by the thought.

"He thinks he's God's gift to women, and trust me, he isn't."

He bit his tongue to keep from ordering her not to tell him about being with other men.

"I just…ugh." She reburied her face in Dan's neck. This time she completed her customary ball form.

Although he hated that she was upset, especially with herself, Dan loved that she would let him hold her when she was feeling low. He loved that she felt safest curled up in his lap and in his arms.

"Please don't beat yourself up about Trevor. If we're going to start punishing ourselves for our pasts, then I should just go ahead and jump off that balcony." He gestured toward the sliding doors of the suite.

She lifted her head to give him a frustrated glare before she returned it under his chin. "I just don't want to go tonight. I'd much rather stay curled up here with you, and then maybe curled up with you in that steam-shower thing, and then maybe that taking-me-up-against-a-wall thing, because wow!"

"You liked that, did ya, baby?" He was unable to help himself.

"Yum," she purred, making him hungry all over again. She drew a deep breath and then pulled her head back to study him. "You really just sort of stepped right out of my fantasies." She always knew how to make him feel like a king.

Dan gazed at her beautiful face and cradled her cheek in his powerful hand. "I could never have even dreamed up something as astonishingly beautiful or as incredibly sweet and smart and wonderful as you are."

Her energy soared. "I love you." He could feel the fervent hope move through her rhythms.

"I love you too, baby." He was extremely impressed with his ability to reply without having to force the words from his mouth.

"I don't want to go. I want to stay here with you."

"Honey, I'm going with you. You don't have to stay long after dinner."

"All of the Angels decided we'd go in together, so you can at least walk down with us."

Dan was immensely appreciative of how much her friends and teammates clearly adored Fionna.

"But I still want to stay here," she huffed in a fitful pout. She nuzzled against him.

Certain she was the most precious thing in the world, Dan kissed her forehead.

"I'm sorry we can't stay up here." He certainly couldn't get her out of the banquet. If she wanted to challenge the next day, she had to make appearances tonight.

Defiance pulsed in her rhythms. Fionna climbed out of his lap and marched around the partial wall that obscured the bed from the entrance to the suite. She returned a moment later carrying her lingerie book.

She laid it on the couch, and Dan watched her head to the refrigerator to get a Dr Pepper for herself. She settled back on the couch and pretended that they had absolutely nothing to get ready for.

Dan shook his head and grinned at her. He knew he could never love anything more as he watched her begin to absorb the book.

"Honey?"

"Shh," she demanded with a sheepish grin. He chuckled.

With a shrug, he scooted closer to her. "If we're going to sit here and pretend we're staying in all night, can I at least look with you?"

He wanted to watch her read and learn. She was so fascinated with it all, and he was endlessly fascinated with her.

He fervently wished he could keep her tucked in their room all night. He'd make her tea, feed her dinner, and listen to her talk, while they laughed together.

He wanted her to share the secrets of her heart. He longed to kiss away the corrosive world. He needed to touch her and knead her curves. He yearned to rock her luscious body to sleep and then cradle her on his chest. He wanted to feel the energy of her dreams.

She giggled adorably. "Because you want to see other women in lingerie?"

"No," Dan assured her, "because sitting here watching you read, and listening to you tell me about what you're reading, and just being beside you means absolutely everything to me."

She gazed at him with all of the love and adoration he felt for her. With a slow nod, she scooted beside him now that she was certain he would let her have her moment of denial.

He would not only let her pretend that they didn't have to leave their rooms and act like they hardly knew one another, but he would help her hide away, even if it was only for a little while. He would be her Shield always. He positioned her between his legs and let her lie back against his chest.

"I'll get ready soon." She sounded like a frightened little girl. It broke Dan's heart.

"Whenever you want to, baby, but I'm going to sit here with my arms wrapped around you for as long as you'll let me."

"I don't want to see him. He makes my skin crawl." She shuddered against him as she slowly turned a page, still distracting herself with the book.

Dan's cell chirped just then. He pulled it from his pocket, eager to hear from Portwood.

Sorry, boss, not even a parking ticket. He does still live with his parents, and he's thirty-four. So he's more of a douche bag than a criminal. An ex of his actually told a San Antonio paper that he was a sexy douche bag in fact. Read another interview where he admitted to owning over a hundred pairs of sneakers and that he gets off by watching himself jack off in a mirror. He has a Synthesizer teeth plate that he wears to challenge in. I'm not thinking you have a lot of competition. Maybe see if you can get him to talk about his shoes. LOL

Feeling much better, Dan chuckled and returned his phone to his pocket.

"Who was that?" Fionna glanced up from a page covered in corsets.

"Portwood. I may have gotten a little irritated with Trevor, and I may have had him look up a few things for me."

"And?" She cracked up.

"I'm very disappointed that his only crime is being a guy other than me who slept with you, which I can't arrest him for. But let's just say I'm much less concerned."

"He's such a jerk." She all but gagged. "He kept telling me how good-looking he was, and then how lucky I was to get to sleep with him. Then, like two and half minutes later, when I made him and his tiny penis, that he calls 'The Stud Junior,' leave my suite, he told me he wouldn't mind me telling all of my friends that he'd just given me the best sex of my life. Seriously, he came before I was even undressed."

Dan choked back hysterical laughter. She shuddered convulsively.

"I cannot believe I have to deal with him all night. I just wish you could do your whole *'she is mine'* thing that gets me all turned on."

Bitter regret surged through him. He longed to intimidate the hell out of Trevor. He could make Fionna feel safe, and adored, and incredibly turned on, apparently.

"Me too, baby. But you are mine. All mine." Her pulse sped in her rhythms. "And after we sit through dinner and I make myself sick watching Trevor and a hundred other assholes make a play for you, I'm gonna bring you back up here, and I'm gonna show you that every single part of your gorgeous body belongs to me and only me."

A moan escaped her lips as she turned and stared up at him. She angled her head for a kiss. She wanted to be claimed. "All mine."

Her lips were soft and hungry. Her mouth, the energy it held, was delicious and craving. He wanted to get drunk on her.

"You're making me wet." She let her hand travel down his chest and then to his erection now prodding against her hip.

He groaned from the thought of her dripping hot and wet for him as he kept her locked to his body with one arm and let the other hand grope her ass. He groaned. She wasn't wearing a bra. Her nipples pleaded against his shirt. Her energy spun in tantric pulses, needing to be soothed.

Dan slid his right hand from her ass to the waistband of her pants. He dipped his hand down them and under the innocent cotton panties she was wearing.

"I want to feel it, honey. I want to feel how wet you get for me. Always such a good girl."

"Yes," she panted and shuddered against him. She let her legs fall open for him. *Wet indeed*, slick and fevered and needing to be coaxed to fruition.

Unable to make himself wait, Dan pushed his fingers inside of her, listening to her moan and pant her approval. "This sweet pussy is mine, baby doll. All of you. All of the places only I get to touch, and the places I get to lick, and suck, and bite. No one else's. Only mine."

She clenched against his demanding fingers, and then a loud knock sounded at her door. She whimpered as Dan gasped for breath. He begrudgingly eased his hand away.

"Fi! I need to borrow your hair straightener!" Chloe shouted.

A long string of expletives spewed from Fionna. The effect of his sweet baby running through an impressive list of curse words made Dan laugh. She stomped to the door, carrying her hair straightener, and Dan ducked out of sight.

"Here!"

"What is wrong with you? Why aren't you getting ready? We have to leave soon."

"Go away!" Fionna demanded.

Chloe's eyes narrowed, and it didn't take long for her to size up the situation.

"Oh for crying out loud, just get ready."

"Just go." Fionna slammed the door, and Dan slipped back in the room. She was mutinous.

She marched back to the seating area and crossed her arms over her chest. "Fine," she seethed. "We're getting ready. And then we're going down to the stupid banquet! And having stupid *dinner*!" She shrieked the word like they were being served something his mother had created. "And then I'll dance with whatever! And then we're leaving and coming back up here and you're doing that and a whole lot more to me until I don't remember any of the rest of this stupid, stupid, stupid evening!" She erupted violently.

Dan bit his lips together. He tried not to guffaw as she stomped her feet.

"Ugh!" She bound into the bathroom and began flinging curling irons and cosmetics about fitfully.

Dan followed her. He was unable to hide his grin.

"Okay." He yanked the curling iron out of her hand and then laid it gently on the counter.

He didn't have time to give her what he knew she needed. Wrapping his arms around her instead, he held her until she stopped struggling. It took virtually no effort on his part. When she stopped wriggling, he kissed the top of her head.

"First of all, you are the cutest thing I have ever seen. And second, I will make it my entire goal to make up for whatever annoys you or makes you mad this evening."

"You better!" she huffed. "Now go get ready. We have to go."

"Yes, ma'am." Dan gave her a wry grin as her fit began to wane.

CHAPTER 36
LET'S HAVE A BALL

Dan shrugged into his new suit jacket. He'd dispensed with the Armani coat he'd purchased a year ago since it had been covered in Cascavel's blood. He straightened his tie and spritzed on Fionna's favorite cologne before moving to sit on the couch in her suite to wait on her to emerge from the bathroom.

"Oh, yum," she enthused as she made her appearance.

Dan stood as soon as he'd heard the bathroom door slide open.

"Damn." His eyes goggled as he took in the revealing dress, which put her cleavage and ass on display in ravishing perfection. She looked absolutely stunning. "You are devastatingly gorgeous, baby doll." Her face turned up in delighted grin.

"You look pretty studly yourself, Chief Vindico. You make me want to do dirty, dirty things in hopes that you'll take me prisoner."

Dan's groin tightened and tugged as he gave her looks that said he wanted to consume her slowly and thoroughly.

Fionna had pulled her long chestnut locks up into a sophisticated twist that showed off the beautiful curvature of her neckline. She was wearing stiletto heels that were nothing more than a sparse, double row of rhinestones across her toes, then another that strapped around her ankles.

"Absolutely stunning. I can't believe I can't walk in there with you on my arm."

She gave him his smile and brushed a light kiss across his jawline. "Just because you can't escort me into the room doesn't mean I'm not yours."

"And I'm the luckiest guy in the world."

Fionna's phone chirped. "They're ready to go."

Certain he was being rent in two, Dan drew her into his arms. "I'm so sorry, honey. Someday..." Remorse held him in a chokehold.

"Stop. You're keeping me safe, remember?"

Cradling her face in his right hand, he guided her lips to his, lavishing her mouth with a deep, drawing kiss.

A knock sounded on Dan's door this time.

"I'll see you in just a minute," he assured her. She seemed to will resolve to make herself leave his arms.

His heart pounded. Anger and lust swirled in a volatile cocktail in his gut. He closed the door between their suites and relocked it, then opened the entry door to his suite.

Garrett chuckled as he stepped inside. He was dressed similarly to Dan in a full suit but was wearing quite a smirk.

"Uh, you might wanna..." He rubbed his thumb over his own jaw. Dan moved to the mirror near the door. He was covered in Fionna's burgundy lipstick.

"Thanks." Dan rubbed the lipstick away, both embarrassed and panicked to think of what might have happened if he'd walked to the party like that.

"No problem." Garrett laughed outright. They exited and met most of the Angels and their dates at the elevators.

Dan saw it immediately. The way the light in the hallway illuminated her almost made it glow, but he couldn't do anything about it in front of all of her friends. He couldn't even move to her and block the top of the deep purple marking he'd left on Fionna's hipbone that showed through the side cutout of her dress.

Fionna was admiring Emily's dress, which was a long, flowing white gown, with a tight bodice that clung to her abundant cleavage. Rainer couldn't quite keep his eyes off what she'd put on display.

Racking his brain as to how to let Fionna know she needed to return to the room and let him heal her, Dan began to panic.

Numerous security cameras were placed strategically throughout the hallway. He'd only had Barron change the feed on the ones near their suites. There were half a dozen near the elevators still running a live feed.

Garrett's eyes narrowed as a broad grin spread across his face. He noticed it as well. "Seriously?" He shook his head at Dan and laughed. "Hey, Fi, come here a minute." He grasped Fionna's hand and dragged her down the hallway.

"Garrett!" Fionna stumbled from the force of Garrett's tug.

While choking back hysterical laughter, Garrett continued to drag her away until he'd turned the corner to get her out of the active cameras' sights and away from her teammates.

Dan forced himself to politely ignore them though he was both seething and thoroughly embarrassed.

"Garrett, no!" Dan heard Fionna argue. "Just leave me alone."

All of the Angels and their dates glanced curiously at Dan but tried to ignore whatever was going on.

"Fi," Garrett huffed, "just stand still a second."

"No, it's fine. I want it there," Fionna insisted as Dan's face burned hot. He clenched his jaw tightly.

Highly amused, Garrett was still laughing. "My God, I will never let you live this down. Now come here to me. I'll leave part of it."

Several minutes later, Fionna returned. She was glowing crimson. She blinked back embarrassed tears.

Dan discreetly glanced down to where the hickey had been and noted that Garrett had only healed the very top of it. He'd left the rest at her request.

A person would have to be extremely close to her and staring directly down her dress to see what was left.

Several elevators had come and gone, but upon Fionna's return, the Angels all crowded into the next arrival.

Garrett was still laughing and shaking his head as he joined Dan as the last person on the elevator. They exited on the floor where the Galileo ballroom was located and meandered down the corridor.

"So damn sweet and then wild in the bed, that's the way it goes. That's what I've always said. Clearly, I should have tapped that when I had a chance," Garrett teased with a goading grin. Dan glared at him. "I'm kidding. I'm kidding."

Rolling his eyes, Dan bit back the phrases that formed on his tongue. *"She asked me to do it and then asked me to leave it,"* being the most prominent.

As they moved into the ballroom, Garrett continued, "Didn't even want me to heal it up. Wanted to wear it. Did you hear her? My God, how the hell did you get a woman like that?"

"Thank you for doing that." Dan finally forced the acknowledgment from his mouth.

"No problem. I'm sure you can re-damage my repair work when you get her back to the room." Garrett stuck his tongue between his teeth and cracked up again.

"Please don't embarrass her," Dan pled humbly.

Garrett stopped laughing. Dan's plea visibly threw him.

"Hey, I love Fi, and she loves you. I don't give a damn what you do as long as you keep making her smile. She's been lit up like a fucking Christmas tree for a month now. I'll never say anything else *to her*." Then with another wry grin, he chuckled. "Now, you, on the other hand. You, I will harass mercilessly, but not in front of anyone else because like I said, I love her," Garrett explained the rules of his new game.

"Fine." Dan was willing to do anything to save her embarrassment over the things she liked. Teams were appearing in the ballroom and walking around the opulently decorated space.

The tables were dressed in linen tablecloths with the teams' logos on runners situated down the length of their assigned tables. While keeping a keen eye on Fionna, Dan saw her glance around discreetly. She gave him a quick, nonchalant smile as she discreetly switched two of the place cards.

As the Sirens hadn't yet arrived, Dan chuckled. He winked at her and then looked away. Each team's banner was displayed on the walls with the players' names and numbers.

"So, let's have it. Just how dirty does my sweet girl like it?" Garrett chided under his breath.

Dan leveled a cold glare at him.

"Oh, come on, I just healed up your bite." He lifted a chill-casted glass of beer he'd just removed from a tray as it went by to block his mouth to keep anyone else from hearing him.

Dan drew a sip of his own beer with a huff. "Not a chance in hell," he quipped with disdain.

"She's told me about every other guy, and I hear about how amazing you are all the time." He smirked and then promptly began laughing again.

A broad, cocky grin spread across Dan's face. "All right, since she tells you everything, tell me what happened with her and Captain Cumbucket." Dan gestured his head toward Trevor. He'd just entered the ballroom with the rest of the Synthesizers.

He was wearing a gray tuxedo jacket, jeans, and had completed his ensemble with white leather tennis shoes that had *Synthesizers* spelled out on the sides in emerald-green rhinestones.

Garrett nearly choked on his beer. "What the fuck was she thinking?" He shook his head. "It was bad. He pretty much told her he was the greatest thing ever and then jizzed his pants before she got in the room. She must've been hard up is all I can figure. We've had a strict rule since the academy. We're best friends, and we do not ever, ever want to fuck that up because we can't make it without each other. But I would've obliged her to keep her away from him if I'd known she was that bad off."

The thought had Dan reeling. She'd clearly needed something, and he'd been who knows where, doing God knows what with some unknown woman who meant nothing to him or with his head buried in work. Disgusted with himself and disgusted with Trevor Sanders, Dan drained his beer.

Fionna seated herself, which brought about another round of regret. Garrett gestured toward the table.

"Come on, let's go. I may have to mop Rainer's drool off my sister's rack." He rolled his eyes and elicited a genuine chuckle from Dan.

The Sirens made their entrance at that moment. Four of them had dates that Dan, Garrett, and Rainer immediately recognized. Apparently, Wretchkinsides had dispensed members of the Interfeci to escort his daughter and her teammates to the banquet. That was enough to cure Dan of any desire to act like he'd ever even met Fionna before.

He pretended to search the table for his name. She'd been quite smart in her rearrangement of the cards. He was sitting between Rainer and Chloe, and diagonally from her.

Governor Sapman, who governed all of the American Summation teams, took the podium and welcomed the teams, coaches, and owners along with their dates. He was given courteous applause as the first course was served.

Rainer kept Dan engaged in conversation, and Dan never even looked Fionna's way, though the task nearly killed him. Throughout the meal, he considered leaving numerous times and simply waiting for her in their combined suites. The one time he allowed himself to glance her way, she looked morose from the dark energy that had entered the room in the form of four members of the Interfeci.

Rainer held Emily's hand throughout dinner and occasionally went slightly slack-jawed as she drew from him. The dark energy had her weak and uncertain as well.

The night wore on with one laborious course after another until Governor Sapman returned to the stage to thank everyone for coming and to tell them to please enjoy the bar and dance floor after dessert.

To Dan's relief, Shane Zacharian and his date left the party soon after they'd consumed their dessert.

"That leaves three," Garrett huffed with his teeth clenched. Dan was sick as he watched Fionna visibly deflate. "I'm gonna go take care of our girl. Just relax. I've got her." Garrett slid from the table and asked Fionna to dance.

Bile left Dan's mouth ashen. He'd never wanted to be Garrett Haydenshire as much as he did in that moment. Fionna fell into his arms weakly, and Garrett supplied her with energy through her hand. He cradled her in his arms and forced his soothing protective energy through her exposed back while he swayed her gently. She visibly reveled in the relief he gave her.

Clenching his jaw and ordering himself not to march over and jerk her out of Garrett's arms, he watched as she buried her face in his neck. No one but Dan seemed to notice how Garrett was able to make her feel safe and healthy immediately. She whispered something in his ear that made him laugh.

He kept her cradled in his arms for the next several songs as well. They laughed and talked almost the entire time. Fury threatened to overtake Dan when Garrett kissed her cheek, and she hugged him tighter. Dan ordered himself to stop being such an asshole.

They were laughing hysterically as she explained something to him by the time the fourth song ended. Dan made his way to the bar. The bartender raised his eyebrows.

"Scotch, strong, expensive, and don't fuck with it."

The bartender looked mildly offended. "S'posed to be a party, man." He slid the drink to Dan. "Go ask one of those Angels to dance with you. They say they are heav-en-ly."

Only one of them, Dan thought. To further Dan's ire, Marco Ferratus, a cousin of Conrad, who Dan had taken out in Paris several months before, sidled up to the bar and seated himself beside Dan. He'd been moved up the Interfeci chain when Dan and Fitz had landed Conrad in Coriolis with a life sentence.

"What's the matter Vin-di-co?" he drawled hatefully. "You missing your girl back home?"

Dan glared hatefully at Ferratus. "Go to hell."

Although he was certain it was a shot in the dark, Dan was delighted that no one in the Interfeci believed he had a girl and that she was there in Vegas with him. His resolve strengthened as Ferratus chuckled and ordered a Cosmo. Dan laughed at him outright.

"What's the matter? Uncle Nic not teach you how to drink like a big boy?"

"It's for my date." He was clearly attempting to rub it in Dan's face that he didn't have a date.

"Right," he sneered. "Go ahead and add an umbrella and an orange slice for him," Dan instructed the bartender.

The bartender didn't seem to like Ferratus any more than Dan. He popped a toothpick umbrella and an orange slice into the hot pink drink and gave a hearty chuckle.

Ferratus flipped Dan off and slithered back to the Sirens' table. As he scanned the room again, Dan spotted Fionna standing with Emily, Rainer, Sasha, and Katie. She met his gaze for a split second but then glanced away.

Dan drew a long sip of the Scotch. He reveled in the burn all the way down. The scorching pain somehow felt better than the hollow numbness. The absence of any feeling at all when he was without her threatened to pull him under.

The lights lowered more, and the DJ began playing the music a little louder. To Dan's horror, Chloe made her way to the DJ and made a request. She instructed all of the Angels to take to the dance floor.

The rap song that encouraged the ladies to shake what they had, the one that Dan had been enthralled by when he'd seen it performed at Anglington's a little over a month before, began blaring. Dan watched the routine the ladies had come up with as they performed it to raucous cheers and applause.

Fionna looked slightly embarrassed but played her part well. She shook her cleavage and then her luscious ass as the song instructed. Before the song even ended, Trevor was all over her. Dan's stomach clenched and churned violently.

Rainer stepped in and asked Fionna to dance, but Rainer wasn't as comfortable with her as Garrett. They danced awkwardly with enough space between them for Dan to have stood. *Good God, Lawson, this isn't middle school,* he scorned. He didn't care that Rainer was trying to do him a favor. He wanted to be angry, and Lawson's prepubescent moves certainly weren't enough to fend off Trevor.

Dan took another careful scan of the ballroom. Ferratus and his date had taken to the dance floor. The woman he was with appeared to have her entire tongue down his throat. He was feeling her up in clear view of everyone.

Emily appeared beside Dan and ordered a glass of wine.

"I was thinking." She raised the wine glass she'd been supplied to her lips and made certain no one else could hear her. "If you'd like to dance, maybe you and Rainer could switch at some point."

Dan took back his vengeful thoughts on Rainer's dancing and decided that Lawson had outdone himself when he'd picked Emily Haydenshire as his one and only as a toddler.

"Care to dance, Miss Haydenshire?" he drawled loudly enough for Marlisa to hear him.

"Oh, sure," Emily feigned surprise. She set her wine glass on the bar and then let Dan lead her to the dance floor.

As Marlisa despised Emily Haydenshire above all others, she narrowed her eyes hatefully and demanded that her date dance with her as well.

Dan wrapped his arms around Emily. She was quite short. Dan grinned down at her. Rainer was several inches shorter than Dan, so he supposed it worked well for him.

He let his eyes glance toward Marlisa. Her date, Quentin Vitrio, a mid-level thug in the Interfeci, seemed about as interested in her as he was in watching paint dry. Fionna and Rainer had relaxed some. He'd pulled her closer, and they were chatting as they danced.

Marlisa buried her face in Vitrio's neck and attempted to force him to cuddle her closer.

Emily rolled her eyes and shook her head. Dan chuckled. "Did you have a nice Christmas?" He swayed her back and forth, unable to think of a topic to discuss with her that didn't involve Fionna or Adeline and the upcoming trial.

She smiled. "It was great. Rainer got me this." She lifted her wrist and showed Dan the delicate tennis bracelet dripping with diamonds. It must've cost Lawson a fortune. "My uncle made it, but the press found out about it when he shipped it to Rainer. They published pictures of it two days before Christmas. I love it, but he was really disappointed he didn't get to surprise me."

"I'm sure." The press had gotten woefully out of hand when it came to Rainer and Emily.

"Every time he's gone in a store for the last month, the press has hounded them to tell them what he bought. They tried to pay some clerk five hundred dollars for a copy of his receipt from that lingerie shop near the Pentagon, but thankfully the store refused." She glanced wistfully toward Rainer and Fionna.

Dan wondered what could be done about the press's interference. They technically hadn't broken any laws.

"I'm sorry," he offered sincerely.

"It's okay. He's worth it."

Dan could feel the depth of her adoration for her fiancé swell in her energy.

Marlisa stepped hard on Vitrio's foot. He jerked away from her and scowled but was clearly afraid to piss off his boss's daughter.

The song reached the last few notes of the chorus. Rainer gave Dan a quick, discreet glance and then thanked Fionna for the dance. He cut in on Dan and Emily with a very sleek move.

Dan nodded to Emily and then glanced around as Fionna feigned disappointment but didn't leave the dance floor. Trevor moved back in, but he was a step behind Dan.

"Care to dance, Miss Styler?" Dan asked politely. He pretended that they were no more than professional acquaintances.

"Sure." Fionna feigned mild disinterest.

Very, very carefully, Dan wrapped her up in his arms and tried to make it appear that it wasn't the place that she belonged. He attempted to hide his love and all-encompassing desire for the woman who fit in his hands like she was made for him alone, but she melted into him.

Relief soothed her fraying rhythms. She drew a deep breath, inhaling his cologne and his musk. Discreetly, she touched his wrist and pulled his energy into her own. Dan fought not to groan from the sensation. He embraced her and let his energy work through the bare skin. "I've got you, baby." The words disappeared in the blaring music. Only she had heard them.

Marlisa seemed to pay no attention to Dan now that he was no longer dancing with Emily.

Rainer, however, had leaned in and was sweeping his tongue through Emily's mouth. She was responding heatedly to his advances. Marlisa glared at them and then attempted to make Vitrio kiss her.

Xavier Metrione, one of Wretchkinsides's underbosses, was Jessica Salamond's date. She was one of the only Sirens with any real talent. He had her in his lap at the table with his hands all over her, which she didn't seem to mind. A moment later, Metrione stood and pulled Jessica out of the ballroom.

"I love you," Dan whispered in a tone barely audible to even Fionna as he swayed her and made certain to keep his space.

"Me too," she quoted his line for her for all of the past weeks. She then laughed politely, like Dan had made a funny comment, and she'd felt she had to respond. She was a good actress.

Trevor had been skulking about the dance floor like a jackal stalking his prey. "I'm cutting in," he demanded.

Fury burned through Dan's veins as he turned to glare at Trevor. "Try it, Sanders."

"You know this guy or something, Fionna? You need me to get rid of him, baby?" Trevor offered in an epically stupid move.

Panic flashed in Garrett's eyes as he danced Chloe near Dan and Fionna. Dan's entire body tensed violently. Utter revulsion and rage throbbed in his shield.

With a huff, Fionna rolled her eyes. "This is Dan Vindico. He's the Chief of Iodex, and he's one of the new Angels owners. We went to school together, not that it's any of your business."

"Well, the next dance is mine."

Dan tried to quell his hate. "We were dancing, Sanders. Why don't you go find someone else to annoy the fuck out of?"

"You know, I think I'll just hang here." Trevor looked delighted with the challenge at hand, and Dan could do nothing at all to stop him. He felt the fear, the hate, and the hopeless apathy permeate Fionna. It made him sick.

"If I dance with you, Trevor, will you go away?"

Trevor laughed at her as if she only had two brain cells that were both confused. "You don't want me to go away, honey. Not without your keycard." He waggled his eyebrows and gave Fionna his customary cocky grin.

Acid burned every organ in Dan's body.

"You are not getting my keycard, but if it'll get you to leave me the hell alone, then fine." Fionna jerked away from Dan angrily and turned to Trevor.

He gave her a pompous grin. "Come on, baby. You know you need another round. I'm sure just one night of me is never enough."

From the corner of his eye, Dan noted Marlisa growing furious with Vitrio's lack of interest. She shot another hate-filled glare at Dan.

He backed away from Fionna though he was certain the few steps he took were the hardest he'd ever made.

Fionna was scowling at Trevor, who continued to sway with her and try to talk her into coming to his suite. Dan fell into the chair where he'd eaten dinner.

Garrett rushed to him carrying two beers. He handed one to Dan and seated himself beside him. "Don't get stupid. She can't stand that prick."

He didn't respond as he watched Trevor's hands slide lower and lower down Fionna's back. He was caressing the skin he felt there. With every inch he gained, venom-filled rage seared like consuming fire through Dan.

His muscles vibrated of their own accord as he narrowed his eyes. The thought of Fionna being in his arms, of his hands being on her, made Dan want to vomit. Trevor pulled her closer, but Fionna jerked backward. Her eyes flashed in a menacing dare for him to try anything.

The entire room was distracted momentarily by Vitrio as he abandoned Marlisa on the dance floor. "I'm leaving. Your dad's not paying me enough to make out with you," he announced with a disgusted glower.

Marlisa was furious, and Dan shuddered as he heard, "I'm telling Daddy," fly from her mouth just before she raced out of the ballroom.

"He'll be dead by tomorrow." Garrett looked extremely concerned. Dan nodded, but he wasn't certain he cared.

He turned his attention back to Fionna and Trevor. The look in Trevor's eyes made Dan want to sink his fists forcefully into his smug face. He traced his hands back up Fionna's back and then caressed her face.

Dan stood, but Garrett used every ounce of power to pull him back into the chair. "Marlisa's gone, but there are too many people here for you to go letting everyone know who she belongs to!"

Fionna bristled and turned her face away from his roving hands. Dan couldn't stand it. He couldn't watch some other guy who'd held her, who'd seen all of her, have her back in his arms even only for a dance.

She was his, his baby, his life, the only person who meant anything to him. The way her sweet smile formed on her face, those deep sienna eyes that grew dark and hungry from his touch, her adorable nose, her beautiful lips, swollen and ripe when she wanted his kiss. The thin skin of her delicate neck that always held her heady scent.

The graceful curvature of her spine, the way her breasts swelled from her desire, the way her nipples darkened and puckered just for him. The way her hands felt when she clung to him. Her voice soft and raspy as she begged to be taken. The silky perfection of her satin skin. The perfect indentation of her stomach and the beautiful swelling curve of her backside. The dimples that she hated, and he adored, where her back met her luscious ass.

The way she smelled like vanilla and coconut and heady musk. Her lush lower lips, the way they swelled and glistened for him. The sweet, intoxicating flavors of her. He would eat his way through fire just to taste that tight, wet space between her legs that formed around him like she was made for him alone.

The way she moaned when he filled her. That perfect gasp on his first ragged thrust when he staked his claim. The way she screamed out his name as he brought her to climax. The way her long hair flowed around him when she pulled him deep into her mouth.

Her long shapely legs and her adorable feet that she thought were unattractive, but Dan thought completed her perfection. It was all his and his alone, along with her heart, her tenderness, her vulnerability, her fears, and her dreams. Her very soul, all his. And some pompous asshole was trying to make a claim. Dan couldn't sit there and watch him offer her his keycard yet again as the song ended.

She is mine. The thought pulsed with every beat of his heart. It reverberated in his shield and solidified his muscles for a fight.

He stood and moved to her before Garrett could halt him again.

"Since our last dance was interrupted, would you care to try again?" Dan gave Trevor a look that said if given half a chance, he'd snap him in half with his bare hands without even breaking a sweat.

But it seemed Fionna wanted nothing else to do with dancing. She glared hatefully at Trevor. "I'm sorry, Chief Vindico, but I'm a little tired. I have to challenge tomorrow. I'm going to turn in."

Garrett had rushed toward them when Dan had begun his march toward Fionna.

Trevor looked hopeful but was disappointed when Fionna turned her pleading eyes on Garrett. "Will you walk me up, please?"

"Of course." He looked deeply concerned.

Dan's heart ached from not knowing exactly how Fionna was feeling and if she was mad at him for the entire situation.

Before she was even off the dance floor, Trevor had located another woman and was trying to sweet-talk her into his room.

With a spiteful gleam in her eye, Fionna stopped Garrett and moved to Trevor and the woman, who played for the Los Angeles Links. She leaned in, and Dan watched closely. He saw her head snap in defiance as she held up her hand, with her thumb and her index finger approximately an inch apart. She then gestured to Trevor's crotch before whirling around and marching out on Garrett's arm.

Strung too tightly to laugh, Dan did feel a rush of air return to his lungs. *Yep, that's my girl.*

As soon as Garrett returned, Dan thanked him and made certain no one was paying him any attention before he disappeared to the elevators.

CHAPTER 37
REQUISITION

H is heart was thrumming. Heat and impatient greed surged through his shield. He was hot-wired and aching for the sweet pulse of her release around him. Savage claims of ownership filled his mind.

Dan summoned and casted the elevator. While watching as buttons lit up from guests calling the elevator to their floor, he kept it going at a fevered climb. Everyone else could wait.

Excessive desire consumed him. He let his mind reel with lurid fantasies. Dan halted the elevator on their floor. He shoved his way past two businessmen who looked offended as they started to get on. He didn't care enough to apologize. Dan forced himself not to sprint to his room.

He wanted her, wanted to own her, to possess her, to brand her, to fill her, and fit her to him and no other. He wanted to feel her hot breath on his neck, see her body splayed under his, feel her fevered flesh meld into his as he took her hard just the way she preferred.

He flung open the door to his suite and frantically threw his jacket and tie off as he knocked on the door between the suites. He had it unlocked before she could respond.

She glided toward him. Her eyes were dark and covetous. They were locked on his with abandon lit in their depths. She'd released her hair from the pins holding it, so that it fell down her back in waves. Her heels had been kicked off when she entered.

He wrapped his hands around her hips and jerked her forward. He stared greedily into her voracious eyes for the length of one heartbeat, and then at her lips, begging and daring him to own her. He'd casted her on the plane. She was still closed off, so carnal desire was his only concern.

She panted. Her rhythms were jagged and wild. She needed to be tamed.

"Mine," he growled as a gasping moan escaped her while he devoured her mouth. He wasn't soft. The kiss was demanding and urgent. His tongue stroked hers, commanding consent. A low, rapacious groan spilled from his mouth into hers.

Releasing her hips, he slid his hands up the chiffon of the dress and over her breasts. She trembled as he caught her nipples between his thumb and index finger. He was too far gone, too raw in his need to be gentle.

His hands continued their climb to her neck as he continued to consume her mouth. He pulled away and spun her around. He edged her against the wall in front of her.

Dan released the chiffon bow tied at her neck. The bodice of the dress cascaded down, but the dress caught on the curve of her ass. With one push, he watched the gown fall in a puddle of satin and lace at her feet. He groaned as he took her in. She was exquisite.

He grabbed her wrists and held her hands to the wall over her head. She cried out for him in fervent need and ecstasy. While huffing hot breath on her neck, he kissed and licked up her right shoulder and then returned to suck her earlobe from behind her. With a hungry nip, he listened to her groan in pleasure.

"I'm gonna fuck you so hard you never forget who you belong to. You understand me? Mine," he growled in her ear.

"Yes," hissed from her deliciously as she quaked and shook from his promises.

He liberated her hands and spun her back around with force. "These are mine," he declared hotly as he grasped her waist and jerked her forward. Her back arched from his pull. He drew her right breast into his mouth and sucked. She let her head fall back, and he dragged his teeth over the swells and then nipped at her nipples.

Her moans were loud and eager. She laced her fingers through his hair, pulling him closer. Dan sucked her voraciously. His hands gripped her backside, squeezing and pulling her apart as he consumed her. His touch was rough and ragged. There was no time for finesse. There was no time between them at all. There was only need for deep, desperate requisition.

With his right hand, he took a firm hold of that sexy ass and jerked her forward, pressing her mound to his strain. He was hard and unrelenting, fierce in his demands, and she was the only thing that could bring him relief.

With his left, he grasped her breasts and lifted one to his mouth. He bathed them with fiery heat from his tongue and tested her again with his teeth, until she was begging to be set free.

He sank his bite into the sensitive spot between her neck and shoulder, and his name gasped from her swollen lips.

"That's right, baby, all mine. Now, I want you to go get in my bed and take these off on your way while I watch." He slipped two fingers under the slight crotch of her G-string.

He stabbed his fingers between her folds. He had no intention of asking permission for anything. He was rough and quick, pulling away almost as fast as he'd entered her. Her body quivered. It tried to trap his fingers there, but she was too slick to hold him captive, already dripping wet, hot, and restless.

"And then you lie there, and you wait until I come and pound that sweet pussy, because it is all mine. No one else's, not ever again."

Her eyes flashed in ecstasy as she panted and moaned. She stared at him for a moment too long.

He rubbed a spot on her plump ass and then smacked it with force. "Now," he demanded.

"Oh my God." She fought off imminent climax from his demands as she turned from him. Parading a few steps away, she slowly dragged the G-string down her legs. He watched, unable to take his eyes from the provocative display.

She turned and stared him down. She flung the panties in his face defiantly, driving him wild, as he caught them and inhaled deeply of her musk.

She turned back and let her hips sway as she traipsed slowly to the bed. Trying desperately to rein in the wild animal instincts that had taken over his body proved futile.

Removing all of his clothing, Dan followed the trail she'd blazed. She was already writhing, splayed out, and waiting on him. She stared him down and dragged her fingers through the wet heat between her lower lips.

"Christ," hissed from him as he took her all in. He grabbed her hand and sucked her honey from her fingers.

Her eyes were voracious. Her lips were swollen from his bite. They tempted him. Her hair splayed over the white sheets. Her body was fevered with an aching need to be penetrated, to be full of him. Lust and desire surged heavily through his veins. His body could barely contain the craving heat.

Dan pulled her legs apart and began kissing his way up her inner thighs. That simply wasn't enough. Nothing made sense but to consume her. She was his.

He sank his teeth into her thigh and then sucked the sensitive skin beside her pulsing lips until he'd left his brand. He continued torturing her with his teeth and then pacifying her with his tongue. She bucked, and he clamped his hands around her waist. He knew he was being too rough, but damn it, he couldn't stop himself. "Be still and let me enjoy you. You're mine."

She cried out for him as he lapped up the nectar spilling from her. He circled her clit with his tongue to force more of her honey into his mouth. He flicked his tongue in slow syncopation over her, then pushed his fingers back inside her, owning her thoroughly.

Never gentle, only demanding, he let his hand fuck her before he granted his cock the pleasure. With another torturous prod of his tongue, she broke free. He forced himself to pull away to make his next command.

"Good girl. Now, don't come again until I tell you to. Do you understand me?"

Her mound pulsated in a heated mass of tender nerves. She writhed and pleaded for more as she managed to nod her understanding. A shuddered cry echoed from her as she reached and used two fingers to spread her lips apart. "Please."

Dan went wild. He took in her hands on her lips, showing him the deep pink, swollen entrance to her perfection. A low, wounded growl echoed from him as he returned to her and licked what she was showing him, drinking in the liquid heat her body made in preparation for him. The very embodiment of her energy filled his mouth, and nothing would ever feel as good or taste as sweet as that.

Giving her no warning, he pulled his mouth away and plunged his fingers deep inside of her again. He listened to her scream out her approval and his name. Her eyes closed in ecstasy as his fingers pounded into her.

This time he sussed out the spot deep inside of her that made her drip and ache as the nerve endings coiled and vied for his attention.

He moved up her body, bringing his mouth to her ear as his fingers pounded inside her with no relent. "This is mine. Only for me. When you ache, when you drip, it's for me. Say yes, sir," he demanded.

"Mmm, yes, sir," she complied.

Her breath caught as her body tensed. He continued to caress the perfect spot, feeling her muscles clench tightly around his fingers as her body devoured him. He ripened her until she could hardly draw breath, and her energy peaked high on the brink of climax.

"You are mine," he growled again. "Say it!"

"Yours," panted from her lips.

"Good girl." He pulled his hand away, leaving her desperate and tender. Her body flushed frantically as her back arched, and she shuddered below him. "Watch me." He brought his index finger to his mouth, sucking the ecstasy of her. "All mine."

She went wild. Her energy was frantic and urgent. Her body rolled in rhythmic waves against his.

"Spread your legs for me. I'm going to own you."

Her legs fell open wide, and she clawed the sheets beside her. Grabbing her wrists, he pinned her arms over her head, and with one ragged, piercing thrust, he filled her completely. He was thick, solid, and heavy. She trembled from the force. He pressed harder for relief.

"All mine," he gasped in her ear as he began to grind against her, listening to her moans of pleasure.

He filled her to overflowing and knew he was too much, but he had no control. "Feel it," Dan commanded as she met his every thrust and begged for more. She lifted her hips against his but could barely manage him. "Every inch of you is for me and only me."

"Oh, god, yes, yes," she panted.

He was overwhelmed by the heavenly sensation of her energy consuming him. He groaned and growled as her body nursed away his pain, his agitation, and his need.

"So fucking tight, baby doll," he grunted in deep appreciation. "Open up and take me. Take it all like my good girl." He pushed harder, driving her to the brink of climax but then holding her back.

"Not yet, baby, not yet. Not until I tell you." He kept his tone soothing, but in control, as she spun frantically. Her body was desperate for release. He backed off and stayed shallow for a few rhythmic thrusts before he plunged into her fully again.

"Be a good girl. Let it build for me." He could feel her trying to do as he told her. She trembled against him. Her body pleaded as she tried to fight the orgasm. Her head shook back and forth.

Dan pumped her full, filled her completely, and then pulled away, coated in her perfection. The sensation was heavenly. He could never claim enough of her, never delve deeply enough, to satisfy himself.

She couldn't do it. She couldn't fight it. She wasn't strong enough to deny the ecstasy she craved from him. He released her hands, and her fingernails immediately dug into his biceps, leaving marks of ownership all her own. The pain was unadulterated perfection.

"Do you need me to let you come, baby doll?"

"Yes, sir, please," she whimpered. Another hungry groan thundered from his lungs.

"Come for me, baby. Make me wet, because I'm not finished with you," he ordered, and she let it go with an echoing scream. The hot, heavenly pulses of her climax licked like consuming fire around his strain, nearly ending him. She soaked him down. He fought the release as it gathered in his groin. He pumped her harder and faster, riding the waves of her orgasm with no reprieve, and then building her again.

He lowered his mouth to her right breast, sucking and dragging his teeth over the fevered flesh. "I want another one, honey. Give it to me. They're all mine, all for me. When you come, you come for me." He listened to her gasp his name in bliss-filled awe.

He slipped his right hand down her abdomen. He kept his thrusts deep and unyielding, making every hidden space of her all his own, while he brushed his fingers over her clit.

He coaxed it gently and then with more coercion, until he held it between his fingers as he pounded inside of her.

Her body convulsed. The exquisite, incessant pain drove her mad.

"Tell me again who owns this pussy. Say it loud."

"Oh god, you," she groaned out her ecstasy.

His heart pounded. His climax threatened to detonate at any moment. He wasn't going to last much longer. He buried himself deeper. "Say my name when I let you come," he commanded, and she lost it all screaming out his name.

His climax shattered through his determined resolve. She was too much. He buried himself inside of the perfection of her and her love. He lost more than his own release. He lost all of himself inside the woman who healed his every wound, the woman who made him whole.

When he regained the ability to see and breathe normally, he begrudgingly withdrew and fell beside her on the bed. She languidly slipped to his chest, still quaking and shuddering from the last orgasm, more powerful than the ones before. She gave a replete sigh, making him grin as he wrapped her up in his arms.

"Have I mentioned that I really, really like your possessive side?"

Dan chuckled. "Have I mentioned that I really, really hate it when you dance with other guys?"

"Aww, poor baby, but if making you jealous is what I have to do to get that, it might just be worth it." She gave him a wicked grin.

"Behave, Ms. Styler. It was all I could do not to turn you over my knee."

She smirked. "Mmm, jealous is definitely the way to go."

"Hey baby doll," he whispered as she settled back down on his chest. She angled her head up to look into his eyes. "I love you." He could feel her heart stutter out of rhythm against him.

"I love you too." She leaned up on her elbow and kissed his cheek.

CHAPTER 38
VITRIO

A jarring rap rang in Dan's head as he slept. He squeezed his eyes shut tighter and tried not to hear it. *Damn it.* Its alarm shook through the room again. While forcing his head to raise off his pillow, he kept Fionna cradled on his chest with one arm and rubbed his eyes with the other.

He heard it again but couldn't understand what it was. He studied the clock on the bedside table, trying to make the numbers compute. It was three forty-eight.

"Vindico!" The plea was frantic.

Fionna whimpered, "Make it go away."

"Shh, baby, it's okay," Dan soothed as he tried to determine what to do.

"You gotta help me, man! Please, I'm begging you. I'll help you out!"

"Honey, stay right here. I'll text you when I want you to open either door. Do not open them until you get my text."

Fionna sprang up in bed. Terror riddled her features.

"Get dressed for me," Dan instructed as he began his calculations. She yawned and rubbed her eyes..

He noticed a slight twinge of pain when she walked. She was raw from his force a few hours before. He'd expected that, but he'd also been certain she would be able to sleep soundly in his arms all night and that he could cast away any residual pain that morning. She slipped on a sweatshirt and yoga pants.

Whoever was at his door took precedence at the moment, but he swore to himself that he would make sure she was in no pain as soon as he dealt with whatever had come their way.

Dan grabbed his Glock from his holster and pulled a pair of sweatpants from his luggage. He locked the door between the suites. His heart stormed against his rib cage.

"Please, man! I'll help you, but you gotta keep me safe. Please, he's gonna kill me!" Dan finally recognized Quentin Vitrio's pleading voice.

"Shut the fuck up, Vitrio!" Dan ordered through the door as he called Garrett's cell. "Get out here with a gun. I can't see him. He's outside my door. The cameras are running an infinite loop. He might be armed, and no one from security is going to come," he demanded through his teeth.

"On my way."

Dan repeated the same order to Rainer who assured him he was also on his way.

"You armed, Vitrio?" Dan demanded through the door.

"I brought you two guns, big take, illegal, whatever. You can arrest me for them. I'll tell you where we took the stash. It's a bunch of stuff. Some women. Just arrest me. He's gonna kill me. He sent Adderand!"

Dan tried to process the information. He glanced back at the door to Fionna's room, and his mind scrambled. With a quick breath, his instincts ran the show for him. He raced to the bed in his suite, unfurled the sheets and blankets, and drove his fist into one of the pillows to make it appear he'd slept there.

"I've got him, Dan," Garrett called.

Dan flung open the door to his suite. Vitrio was on his knees. His fingers were laced together on his head. Garrett's personal Beretta was aimed at his face, and Rainer's service pistol was at his heart.

There were two large, striker semi-automatic rifles at his feet. Garrett grasped Vitrio's hands and cuffed him as Rainer raised his Glock a few inches and took aim at Vitrio's head.

"Look, man, I'll help you. I'll tell you everything I know. Just take me in. Just keep me alive," Vitrio begged again.

"If Nic's got women anywhere they don't want to be, you better start talking now. When's Adderand arriving?" Dan demanded.

"I just got word from a guy I know. Nic sent Adderand out from Moscow as soon as that bitch called him. He's on a flight due in at ten. Commercial," Vitrio couldn't seem to get the words from his mouth fast enough. "There are four guards and about a dozen women. We took them from Baja. They're going to Guadalajara tomorrow. They're with the guns, a bunch of them, in a storage facility warehouse thing, about forty miles out of town, in the desert. Pravus's doing, not Nic's. Nic got the guns. He don't know anything about the girls."

He was telling the truth. Dan had no doubt. That was a hell of a confession. "All right, Vitrio. I'll scratch your back, you scratch mine. If I get Adderand, you get to keep breathing."

"He'll be in at ten, I swear."

"Where's Marlisa?"

"She's at the Tropicana, in the, uh, casino," he tripped over the words in desperation to get them out of his mouth rapidly. He was scared, possibly to death.

"Aren't you supposed to be with her?" Dan was certain that keeping up with Marlisa and doing whatever she wanted to do was Vitrio's assignment from Wretchkinsides.

"She got mad and told me to leave. I had to do what she said."

"Anybody else know you're here?" Garrett huffed.

"No, nobody. I swear."

Excitement and hope rolled in Dan's gut. Adderand, the asshole, in the flesh. He was Wretchkinsides's newest hit man since Dan had taken out Cascavel. He was just as brutal. Adderand was just under Pendergrath and Pravus on the Interfeci chain, and arresting him would be an extremely crippling blow to the entire organization.

"Keep that on him." Dan gestured to Rainer's gun.

Rainer nodded his agreement though he looked quite exhausted.

Dan returned to his suite and closed the door. He texted Fionna that he was going to unlock the door between their rooms and instructed her to keep quiet.

He worked through the locks and made certain the door never made a sound. Fionna looked terrified. She fell into his arms..

"I'm so sorry, honey." Dan rubbed her back and kissed the top of her head.

"For what?"

"He wants to work a plea. Nic put out a hit on him," he explained in pained whispers.

"Oh my gosh. He kills his own guys?" She was still clinging to Dan and talking into his chest.

"Yeah." He needed to get back to Vitrio. "I'm gonna call Nevada Iodex to take him in. Then I'm going to take several of their teams along with Garrett and Rainer to the airport to meet the assassin's plane. The Interfeci rule is that if you don't make the contracted hit, you kill two other people in the place of the one you missed. I have to stop Adderand before he realizes I have Vitrio."

Abject disgust washed through both of them. He refused to say anything about the women. He'd take care of them, but he wouldn't terrify her further.

She shivered against him. He set his shield over her and filled it with soothing heat. "Listen to me, baby. I need to go back out there." He laced her fingers through his. She drew from him, and he supplied her with love and courage in heavy doses. She knew what he was going to say.

"I won't be back in time to see the beginning of the challenge, but as soon as I get Adderand in custody, I'll be there. I swear." Guilt barbed his veins.

"I don't care about the challenge. I don't want you to get hurt. Please, please be okay. Just make someone else do it."

"Fi, baby, look at me." Dan cradled her face in both of his hands as she blinked back tears. "I will be fine. I promise you. I'm going to be there to see the Angels win that cup. This is what I do, and I'm pretty good at it." He hoped for a smile that he didn't receive.

Dan drew a steadying breath and tried a different tactic. "Adderand doesn't have any idea Vitrio turned himself in. He has no idea we're coming for him. He won't have been able to get on a plane with a gun. He's looking to pick up one while he's here, but I'll have him long before that."

She stepped back and stared up at him with a terrified look in those eyes that cut him to the quick. "You…you promise me! Promise me you'll be okay. I can't make it without you."

"I will be fine. I promise you."

Her chin trembled, and his heart fractured.

"How about this?" Dan willed his heart to continue beating in rhythm as tears obscured the golden flecks in her eyes. "Let me go get Vitrio locked up and then meet Adderand's plane. As soon as I have them both, I'll be back here to cheer you on. Tonight, after the Angels crush all of the competition, we'll spend the whole night celebrating." Dan prayed that he could somehow soothe her fears and ease her heartache.

"Promise me." Her right hand shook as she lifted it up with her pinky extended. It took him a split second to realize what she was doing. He grinned and linked his pinky with hers.

"I promise, sweetheart." She managed a nod just before she gave in to the frightened tears. Dan pulled her to his chest and felt her hot tears drip down his abs. "I promise you," he vowed again.

She nodded and tried desperately to regain her composure.

Dan retrieved his phone from his pocket. A second later, he rang Emily's cell. "Rainer and I are going to take Vitrio in, and we have a few things we're going to have to do before we can come to the exhibition. Rainer's going to text you when we've got him on the elevator. Once we're gone, would you come hang out with Fi for me, please?"

"Uh, sure," Emily's voice shook. She sounded just as terrified as Fionna. Dan ended the call.

"I'll call you before you start the challenges, okay?"

Fionna nodded. She was waging war against additional tears. "I love you," she choked out in a terrified stutter.

"I love you too, baby, so much." He grasped her shoulders and brushed a tender kiss on her forehead. "Let me heal you before I go." He gestured his head toward her crotch.

"I'm okay." She blocked his hand.

"Are you sure? I don't want you to hurt."

"I'm not. Please just be okay, and I'll be fine."

"I promise," he vowed once more before he ducked back into his own suite.

CHAPTER 39
WAR

Dan dressed and then returned to the corridor.

"Where'd you go, man? What the hell?" Vitrio stammered. Dan ordered himself not to feel sorry for him. He clearly only trusted Dan to keep him alive, but he was still a rat bastard who'd committed unspeakable crimes all for his beloved boss.

"Shut it, Vitrio. I'll ask the questions, and if I don't like your answers, I'll drop you off at the fucking airport and save Adderand the trip." He pulled his own pistol, and Vitrio's eyes goggled. "Go get dressed and get back out here," he ordered Garrett and Rainer as he kept aim at Vitrio. They returned two minutes later, both fully dressed and wearing badges. They looked far more official.

"To the lobby," Dan ordered. Garrett hoisted Vitrio up, and they marched him to the elevators. "Text Emily, and tell her we've left." Rainer followed orders with only a quick tensing of his brow.

Dan phoned Roy Stegman. It rang numerous times before his rasping growl answered, "What?"

"Stegman, it's Vindico." The man may have been almost forty years his senior, but Dan was the Chief of Elite and would be treated thusly.

"Sorry, Dan. What's wrong?"

Dan explained what he needed and was assured that Vegas Iodex would be there in minutes.

"We're going to the precinct. We've got to get officers out to that warehouse, and I'm hand-selecting the teams for this mission. We're meeting that plane."

Garrett and Rainer nodded their understanding.

A few hours later, Dan was pacing in Stegman's office as they checked in the illegal weapons Vitrio had turned over.

"You know, most boys your age prefer to have women crawling out of the walls looking for 'em in the middle of the night, but you probably like it this way," Stegman drawled with a hearty laugh before taking a long drag of the fourth cigarette he'd had in the last hour.

Dan chuckled and shook his head. He was hardly able to believe what had happened himself. "Nobody's more surprised he showed up than I am, trust me, but I suppose that would depend on the woman, wouldn't it?"

Stegman gave another laugh. They were waiting on word from the teams that had been dispatched to the rental storage facility that Vitrio had described.

Dan had ordered in a specialized rescue team from Carson City, complete with sexual assault counselors, medios, and Auxiliary Department trauma treatment units to the area, but Iodex had to take out the guards without getting anyone killed first.

"Uh-oh, now don't tell me Dan Vindico, the love 'em and leave 'em king of DC, finally landed on one he's trying to keep." Roy Stegman had been the Commander of Nevada Iodex for nearly thirty years. He'd been offered appointment in DC numerous times and had always turned it down with the signature line, 'If I have to take off my cowboy hat or give up my spit can, then there ain't no need me coming to DC, 'cause I'm happy as a stud in the pasture of horny heifers.'"

He was an outstanding officer and kept Vegas and the surrounding desert relatively safe. He'd shut down money-laundering setups, drug rings, and gun-running operations of Wretchkinsides with outstanding precision.

Dan shook his head, still terrified to discuss Fionna with anyone at all. Stegman slapped Dan on the back.

"I knew it," he coughed uproariously. "I can always tell. Gotta smile looks like a pig just been slopped. Always tell." Stegman seated himself at his desk, leaned back in his chair, and propped his feet up.

"Let's see here." Stegman grabbed two Cokes from his desk. He hand chilled them and handed one to Dan. "Just bought yourself a hunk of them Angels, took off work to come see the exhibition, had Barron out checkin' the rooms of the Venetian." Stegman chuckled. "Don't sound like Dan Vindico to me. Don't tell me you gone and clipped the wings of one of those heavenly bodies of Summation?"

Dan's muscles twitched. He downed some of the Coke. His mouth was suddenly drier than the Mojave where he currently stood. He fought not to cringe. He didn't like how quickly Roy had put all of that together, even if he was an outstanding detective and one of the strongest Visium Predilects Dan had ever seen. He was the only commander of a state Iodex branch who wasn't an Ioses Predilect.

"Aww, now, come on. You know I'll take it to the grave. Which one of those fillies keepin' your sheets warm, Danny Boy?" Stegman half laughed and half choked.

Dan shook his head. "Think I'll just keep her between me and my sheets."

Stegman guffawed over the double entendre. Just then the phone buzzed.

"Let's see if Mr. Vitrio's gonna sleep with the fishes tonight," Stegman growled.

Dan edged closer. He was eager to hear if Vitrio had come through for them. Vitrio had all of the markings and reactions of a dead man walking. Dan knew he wasn't sending officers into an ambush.

"Yeah, I knew there was somethin' goin' on out in Swensen, but damn!" Dan's eyebrows shot up in intrigue. "You need more help for the recovery, or you got it?" Stegman nodded to whatever the response had been. "Well, I s'pose we better get ready. We're about to have us a showdown at the airport. Thanks, McCoy," he offered sincerely before hanging up the phone. "I knew it. I just couldn't find it." Stegman sounded disgusted with himself. "I've had guys out there for a week now."

"Vitrio said they just stored them there a few days ago," Dan reminded him.

"It's my job to snatch 'em up when they make the delivery. Don't let nothing get a foothold."

"What'd they find?"

"'Bout two hundred those strikers, dozens and dozens of MAC 10s, M-16s army grade, 10 cases of grenades, several hundred kilos of cocaine, and twelve women, one dead."

Dan's mouth fell open in shock.

"Yeah, I hope you're keeping that sweet thing safe, 'cause it sounds to me like Nic Wretchkinsides is going to war."

Dan's blood ran ice-cold, and his heart stuttered as it tried to push the ice through his veins. The air burned through his lungs. His feet moved of their own accord. He marched out of Stegman's office and slammed the door behind him.

Picking up pace, he rushed by Garrett and Rainer, who were directing the teams as to how Adderand would be taken in without any bystanders getting hurt.

With every strike of his boot on the tiled floor, Dan fought back bile and revulsion.

"Dan!" Stegman shouted after him.

Dan gasped for air that wouldn't singe his lungs. He waved his badge in front of the holding cells in the Vegas precinct. A deadly combination of love and hate swirled violently in his gut as he raced down aisles of cold, gray bars.

He halted in front of Vitrio's cell and watched terror swirl in the man's eyes. "What the hell is he planning with all of that?" he demanded furiously. "Tell me right now!"

"I don't know. I swear. He's been selling some of 'em. You drained him dry, but he's been stocking up too." Vitrio stood, but he stayed near the back of the cell. "Probably got a big sell or something. He's after money."

"That's it? Just money?"

"Yeah, he's got several buyers in town. He's got runners out in Cali.

He's mad as hell, though. Wants to know how the fuck you found all those accounts, so watch your back."

"Is there anything else I need to know?"

Vitrio seemed to genuinely consider the question. He shook his head. "Nic's staying in Bucharest. Left Marlisa here with Lucinda's sister, I think. Cindy's out in Kyzyl. Nic's got several of his mistresses out there with him licking his wounds. Soap's in Miami, but he goes back and forth. Nic's got Pravus in Costa Rica, running the drugs and guns. Pravus side lines the women, but Nic don't get a take on that," Vitrio spewed forth everything Dan already knew.

"What about me? What does he know about me?" Dan seethed.

Vitrio looked confused. "That you want him dead, but everybody knows that. Couple months ago he had Soap trying to find your house, back in the spring. Thinks you bought something way out, bunch of property up in Maryland. Pravus told him you wouldn't live that far out, but he told him you would. He's got guys stalking around there. So, if you live there, you may wanna move, but that's all I know."

Usually, hearing Pendergrath's ridiculous, self-assigned nickname of Soap made Dan laugh, but he was too angry and too terrified.

"You better be telling me everything you know, or so help me when I finish him off, I'll come back for you."

"I am! I swear!" Vitrio willed Dan to believe him. He was still terrified that Dan would let him walk, quite literally, into his own death.

CHAPTER 40
THE MAN

Dan drew several deep breaths and paced back into the main precinct.

"Are you okay?" Garrett studied him closely. Rainer shifted on his feet and stared at Dan. The conversation they'd been having with Stegman stopped short.

Dan ignored the question and checked his watch. It was a quarter after seven. The exhibition started at nine.

"Can I use your office?" Dan asked Stegman. The tone let him know that it wasn't really a request.

"Of course." Stegman gestured to the door. Still trying to draw steadying breaths, Dan touched Fionna's name on the screen of his phone. He wished desperately that he could touch her soft skin instead.

"What's wrong?" her sweet voice answered on the first ring.

"Hey, baby doll," Dan choked. He swallowed the terror that had cinched his throat. He tried not to sound panicked. He didn't want to scare her. While pinching the bridge of his nose with his thumb and index finger, he started to pace. "My girl okay?"

"I'm fine. But you're not," she said. "What happened?"

"I'll be all right. We're just getting ready to set up the teams at the airport. I miss you." He could almost hear her smile.

"I miss you too. Emily and I are cuddling." She giggled in an effort to make him laugh.

He offered her a forced chuckle. "Then I wish I was Emily."

"We're going to order breakfast here and then head down to start the challenge, but my first heat isn't until ten-thirty. Maybe you'll be back by then." Her voice held notes of both hope and fear.

Dan was certain he was being stabbed brutally. "I'll try, honey. I swear I'll try. But you'll do great even if I'm a little late." He willed her to believe in herself.

"I hope."

"I'm going to end him. I swear to you," erupted from Dan's mouth without him making the conscious decision to say the words. "So that I can be there, always, and you don't have to be alone ever again." He choked back raw emotion. Her beautiful face swam before his eyes. It was obscured by M-16s and grenades, and kidnapped women, terrified and hungry. He swallowed back vomit.

She was silent for a few seconds. Dan heard the bathroom door in the suite slip closed. "Dan, I know you will. I'll be fine as long as I know you're all right. I know I'm never alone. Everything's going to be okay."

The words were like a healing balm, the same salve that he felt when he was in her presence or lucky enough to be receiving her intoxicating energy.

"I love you so much." Dan begged her to really feel the depth of his love through the telephone.

"I know you do, and I love you too. Just please be careful."

"I will. I promise. Good luck today, sweetheart."

"Thank you."

"Tell Emily I said to take care of you." He was rewarded with another one of her sweet giggles.

"She will."

As soon as Dan finished talking to Fionna, he phoned his father.

"Daniel, is everything all right?" was his father's greeting.

"Been better, Dad. Listen, Wretchkinsides found Uncle Gus's old hunting property, so make sure no one goes up there and uses it."

Governor Vindico sighed. "No one's been up there in years, not since Gus passed. Let 'em look. There used to be some pretty big mountain lions up there, maybe the cats'll get lucky." Dan chuckled at his father's optimism. "Is Fionna all right?" Governor Vindico made no effort to conceal the concern in his voice.

"Yeah, she's okay. This trip has been something, but as soon as I take care of a few things, I'll be back with her. How's Lindley doing?"

"I had her put into an Auxiliary Rehab unit until her trial. She's detoxing and probably hates me right about now, but it is what it is."

"Don't hate yourself for doing right by her, Dad," Dan instructed.

"Dan, let me come out there. I'll be on the next flight. I'll call Stephen."

"No, I'm fine. I need to go." Dan tried to be thankful for his father's willingness to help, but he had to focus.

"Whatever you're about to go do, son, please be careful."

"I will." Dan ended the call and exited the office. He began going through all of the things that needed to happen before Adderand's plane landed.

"See here, now, Danny. Believe you got yourself a real officer right here." Stegman cupped his hand and pounded on Rainer's shoulder.

"Only kind I hire," Dan challenged. He felt like arguing anyway.

"Asked Haydenshire who the lucky lady pulling your chain was. He said, 'Hey, if Dan didn't tell you, don't ask me.' But Lawson here said, 'I didn't know he was dating anybody.'" Stegman guffawed.

Garrett and Rainer laughed, and Dan had to smile at Rainer's quick thinking.

"Your grandpa know?" Stegman asked Garrett.

Garrett shook his head. "Don't think so, old man." Roy Stegman and Bill Haydenshire, Garrett's grandfather, had gone through basic training and the Gifted Army together. As far as Dan knew, Roy was the only person in the Realm Grandpa Haydenshire actually liked.

"I'll figure it out. Just give me time." Stegman was driven by the challenge.

"I wish you wouldn't," Dan half ordered and half suggested.

. . .

At nine thirty, Dan stood in a baseball cap and dark sunglasses, pretending to read a newspaper. He was stationed by the exit door that would have the loading bridge attached to it as soon as Adderand's plane was in sight.

Garrett and Stegman were positioned on the other side of the door. Rainer, working with Chase Barron and Trenton McCoy, was seated to the side of the door in the seat for passengers boarding the next flight. Twelve high-ranking, undercover Iodex officers were positioned in the gate area. They were all dressed to look like passengers waiting to board, but they were heavily armed and well-trained.

Dan had been through every scenario. If they had the pilot try to hold Adderand on the plane, the pilots and coolant officers were not likely to live to see lunch.

If Iodex attempted to board the plane, there was enough fuel on board for Adderand to blow the plane sky-high, killing hundreds of people.

They had to take Adderand by surprise when he exited the Jetway.

"Get him restrained and then drain him instantly," had been Dan's order to every Iodex officer situated throughout the entire airport and the parking lots. They'd shut down five gates. The only people in the area were officers. He'd ordered in the closest high-security jet from LA. It was waiting to take Adderand back to DC, and then seven teams were to escort him to Coriolis where he'd wait until his trial.

While pushing all thoughts of life outside of the Interfeci from his mind, Dan tapped into the hell-bound desire to end each and every person who had ever had anything to do with Dominic Wretchkinsides.

His steely nerves fed his demons. They swam just under the surface. His body was poised to strike. He had enough DNA evidence to keep Adderand in Coriolis for the rest of his life. He just needed the man.

His left shoulder twitched. His blood pulsed rhythmically in his ears. He let his instincts drown out the noise around him. He was going to get the man. He was going to be one step closer to ending the Interfeci for good.

Dan reached and touched the pistol he'd shoved in the back of his jeans. He kept his back pressed to the wall, so no one else could see him.

There were no officers in uniform anywhere in the area. Adderand would get no warning, but he would get what was coming to him. Dan watched the minute hand move on his watch.

Dan, Garrett, and Rainer had checked and rechecked the passenger log of the flight to make certain that Wretchkinsides had flown no one other than Adderand out to Vegas. He'd booked a return flight for two hours later. He wasn't expecting it to take him long to end Vitrio.

Marlisa was already in uniform and playing in the exhibition. According to The Venetian's security teams for the Summation Exhibition, she seemed unconcerned about Vitrio's whereabouts.

The minute hand moved past the eleven, and Dan's heart pounded as he watched the plane touch down.

"Watch the passengers. Remember, Adderand is wearing a black sleeveless tank, a Gifted Army jacket, black pants, and combat boots. He's trying to pass as a serviceman. Got a camo duffle bag with him. We don't know what's in that bag," Dan reminded them as nervous energy permeated the air.

"Keep it together, ladies and gentlemen. This guy kills people for a living," Dan warned as the engines of the plane droned to silence.

Everyone braced. They kept their heads down but their eyes up. Dan pulled the pistol from his waistband and chambered a round. He kept the gun low and tucked himself against the wall.

The pilots and coolant officers exited first. They all looked extremely nervous. Dan prayed that they hadn't tipped Adderand off when Dan had called for a description.

A flight attendant helped an elderly couple exit next. The woman was shuffling along slowly behind a walker. Dan tried not to think of what might happen if Adderand exited in the next few seconds.

Several other tourists bustled down the Jetway. They talked excitedly about their plans in Vegas.

His mind sharpened its focus. His blood rushed through his veins. He forced his heart to a cadenced tempo as he waited.

Barron glanced down the Jetway and then slid his eyes to Dan with a slight nod. He was coming.

Dan shifted into position, along with Rainer, Garrett, and McCoy. They were all ready to jump as soon as their target was within reach. The clock slowed. The silence deafened him.

Stegman stood, turned, and kept his back to Adderand. The signal.

Dan spun and stared into Vincent Adderand's hate-filled, black eyes. "You're under arrest."

Adderand threw a cast, but Dan deflected it instantly. Rainer and McCoy leapt and came from behind Adderand as he attempted to throw a shield. They began siphoning the energy out of the shield.

Garrett joined in, and as soon as the shield was weakened, Dan shoved his own cast through it and had Adderand on the ground. He reached for the duffle bag. Dan heard metal cans clink menacingly.

Rainer kicked the bag back down the Jetway. Something popped, and an ominous black gas filled the air. Everyone gasped for breath.

"Keep the passengers back!" Dan shouted as Garrett's knee came down on Adderand's chest. Dan cuffed him as Barron and McCoy drained the energy from his body. Rainer threw a shield around the gas.

"Help him," Dan demanded of the other Iodex officers. Shields surrounded the poisonous gas, and Stegman called in a Gifted Toxic Disposal Unit. There was one stationed at the airport, and they arrived almost instantly. Quickly pulling the toxic substance from the air, they sealed the remaining passengers back in the safety of the plane.

Still coughing, Dan pointed to the plane waiting to fly Adderand back to DC. He helped Rainer and Garrett hoist Adderand's almost lifeless body to the next gate and onto a gurney.

"Keep him drained all the way there," Dan coughed out his command. His lungs struggled like he'd inhaled a solid mass. His throat was charred.

"We always do, Dan. We've never let you down," Jerry Gallahand assured him.

Dan nodded and watched Garrett and Rainer both gasp for breath and tighten the straps on the gurney. Four guards stepped up to keep

Adderand's body from creating any more energy than what he needed to keep his vital organs functioning.

Dan signed dozens of papers on what was to be done with Adderand should he fight, what kind of cell he was to be given at Coriolis, and who was allowed to see him should anyone visit the prison.

They moved off of the Jetway and fell into chairs. Dan winced as a medio darted a steroid shot into his left triceps. "Damn it, a little warning would be nice." He scowled as the cool liquid moved through his muscles. With another sigh, he allowed the medio to strap on an oxygen mask as she pulled the poison from his lungs and bloodstream.

"I'm sorry," Rainer continued to apologize.

"Lawson, if he'd gotten his hands on that canister and it had blown in my face, I wouldn't be sitting here. Stop apologizing. You did exactly as you should've." Dan regretted that it had come that close.

He'd almost broken the promise to Fionna that he would be there to see her challenge and all of the promises he'd made to himself that he would be with her for a lifetime.

CHAPTER 41
A DEMON'S CHALLENGE

It was almost noon when Dan, Garrett, and Rainer stepped into the exhibition arena. They were exhausted but pleased with their work.

Stegman had taken Vitrio to Latimer Prison out in the depths of the Mojave. Dan had no idea what the state governing board would decide about Vitrio's crimes since he'd given a full confession.

Dan fell into a seat in the Angels box and tried to figure out what was going on.

The scoreboards showed each team's scores and then each player's individual scores. The Angels were doing well, but Fionna's scores were lower than her typical exhibition performances. She glanced up at the box, and relief flooded her features. She smiled, but Dan pretended not to notice.

The Receivers from ten teams were lining up to compete in the next round of Receiver Relays. They would compete against each other in a difficult series of transformations. The bottom five would be disqualified in each heat. The top five would go on to compete against additional teams, until the top three were named.

Dan watched intently as the buzzer sounded, the aegis was set, and they began. She had heat from the fire and lit ten light bulbs before Dan could draw a breath.

"Damn," he whispered. Rainer and Garrett looked equally impressed. She moved on to a windmill, spinning it with little trouble and then drawing the energy out into a rubber belt, which she stretched and moved to a series of drivetrains.

"I'm not certain what just happened, folks, but it seems Miss Fionna Styler, number two of the Arlington Angels, has come alive. We'd seen less than her best performance so far today, but she's certainly making up for it now. Look at her go!"

Dan watched the drivetrains pick up pace, and Fionna's joule meter continue to decline. A moment later, the pistons on the engine were firing, and she was sprinting to the next obstacle.

The Receivers from the Sirens, the New Orleans Noethers, and the Boston Bombers struggled with the elastic energy needed to shape the belt and pull it over the drivetrains.

The Angels box went wild as Fionna began pulling chemical energy, in the form of carbon, from the engine. She filled a diode with the carbon, and then, beaming and bouncing up and down, she was the first person through the heat. She was several minutes ahead of her closest competition. Dan couldn't help but stare. Her sports bra couldn't quite contain the jostle of her breasts as she jumped up and down. He salivated and fought not to drool.

He applauded and whistled with the rest of the box. The Sirens' Receivers, along with four other teams, were eliminated, and Emily joined Fionna for the next heat.

The courses were reset and the top five took their places. The five other winning teams were added in and joule meters were refilled by the teams' Valeduto Predilects.

"Come on, Em!" Rainer chanted, giving a loud wolf whistle from behind Dan which Garrett joined in on.

There was a series of decent-sized drums of water that would have to be tipped and poured over dams. Then they were to pull the electricity out of the dam and fill three fuel cells. After that, they were to harness the gravitational energy and use it to pull ten helium-filled balloons to the ground.

"This is gonna be tough." Garrett grimaced. Everyone seated

around them nodded adamantly. Fionna had finished the last relay two and a half minutes before the second-place Receiver from the Powerhouses of Portland. She beamed as two hundred fifty points were added to her personal score, and fifty points were added to the Angels' overall score. She'd just set them firmly in third place. She was on fire.

"Not sure what you're doing, but she hasn't played this well all season," Garrett goaded in a tone barely audible even to Dan.

"She's incredible. It has nothing to do with me."

The buzzer sounded, and Fionna tipped the water, aimed it perfectly, and then moved it to the dams. Dan clenched his jaw as he watched her meter dip. His mouth fell open as Fionna tittered excitedly.

She'd been able to pull the electricity and begin to fill the cells, and she was already harnessing the gravitational pull of the water.

The Angels box was on their feet chanting her name and screaming their approval. The fuel cells were full. She harnessed the balloons.

Dan's heart sank as one popped, but she didn't let it slow her down. In under three minutes' time, she'd completed the course and was visibly thrilled. She received a thirty-second penalty for popping the balloon, but was still in first place.

Emily was trying hard to finish the balloons, but she looked like she'd much rather be celebrating with Fionna. When Emily managed to lower the ninth balloon, Rainer, along with every Angels fan in the area, was roaring with delight. She lowered the tenth and moved into second place.

Emily and Fionna tackled one another, hugging and jumping up and down. The Angels were in second place, only twenty points behind the New York Neutrons.

Boos and gasps sounded from the crowd, and Dan's jaw clenched as the Sirens' Receivers made extremely rude hand gestures at Fionna and Emily.

To his delight, they were both disqualified for unsportsmanlike conduct a moment later.

The entire arena, constructed inside the vast multipurpose room of The Venetian, applauded as they were led from the field.

The last heat lined up. After this, the top five would compete for first, second, and third. Pride and love swelled in Dan's heart. He ached to be able to hold her, kiss her, and wish her good luck. He wanted to celebrate with her, but he could do nothing more than cheer her on.

Fionna blew a kiss and waved to the roaring Angel fans, not to anyone in particular, but Garrett slapped Dan's back. He smirked but said nothing.

The Receivers who'd already competed had their meters refilled, and they returned to the starting line.

The course consisted of piezoelectric discs, which Fionna disliked working with. She grimaced, but determination set in her eyes. The four discs would have to be altered until they produced voltage. The electricity was to be converted to steam heat and forced through a steam-powered whistle, to make it vibrate and produce sound. Then the sound energy would have to be re-harnessed and pushed through a microphone until it produced feedback.

The buzzer rang, and they were off. Dan saw Fionna study the discs. A broad grin spread across his face as she started with the smallest disc. She only needed enough voltage to make the steam. All four discs didn't have to be altered, and the smaller the disc, the easier it would be to contort.

"That's my girl!" Garrett cheered, and Dan fought back the fervent desire to correct him. His molars ached as he locked his jaw, while he continued to applaud her. She started pulling the voltage from the first disc, and then moved to the next smallest.

The Receiver from the Neutrons had contorted the largest disc, but was having a difficult time pulling the voltage and moved on to the next.

Emily was attempting to contort two at a time, but shook her head in defeat and started over with the smallest.

Fionna had two altered and decided to gamble on the amount of voltage she'd gotten them to produce. Dan watched her intently as she continued to harness the electricity. She'd done it! Almost a minute later, her whistle sounded loudly. She immediately pulled the sound energy and pushed it hard through the microphone until it readily squealed. Her entire body lit from her excitement. Dan whistled loudly and got a warning chuckle from Garrett.

The Neutrons' Receiver finished next, and then a Receiver from the Links. Emily fell into fourth place. A full minute and a half behind Emily was a massive male Receiver from the Powerhouses.

The ladies cheered wildly as they were told to sit on the side of the field, while the final relay was arranged. They were supplied protein bars, water, and energy refills.

"Come on." Garrett slapped Dan's chest.

"What?" Dan certainly wasn't going anywhere. The love of his life was about to be named best Receiver in the entire Realm, and Dan had every intention of watching her do it.

"We're getting you a better seat."

There was a twenty-minute intermission before Fionna would challenge for first place. Dan stomped after Garrett. He assumed he could fend off Garrett and make it back to his seat in plenty of time.

"What the hell? Where are we going?" Dan glanced around the empty corridor he'd been dragged to. "I want to see them do this." He gave nothing away.

"Have I ever steered you wrong?"

Dan laughed outright. "How long do you have? We could start with your inability to make mixed drinks," Dan chided as he followed him down the steps.

Garrett cracked up. "Oh my God, that was horrible!" They continued to laugh as he guided Dan toward the doors that led to the field. Garrett pulled his phone from his pocket, switched off the ringer, and held it to his ear.

They halted at the doors to the field where numerous security guards were stationed.

"Yeah, Dad. I'm on my way. I'm checking it now. I'll call you right back," Garrett assured the phone since there was no one on the line. "I'll take care of it."

While drawing an irritated breath, he marched up to the head of Summation security. "Got a call that there was a breach in the Angels' locker room? Some moron called my dad. What the hell's going on down here? He's pissed." Garrett held up his phone, indicating his father.

Dan tried not to smirk.

"What? There wasn't a breach. Who called the Crown Governor?" the guards began quizzing one another.

"I think we'd better have a look, gentlemen. Crown Governor Haydenshire is extremely protective of his baby girl." Dan's orders were rarely ignored.

"Oh, yes, sir, Chief Vindico, of course." The head of security opened the field doors for Dan and Garrett.

Fionna noticed them stalking toward the locker rooms on the end of the field, but Dan was careful not to glance her way.

They moved into the long hallway that contained dozens of doors. After locating the one labeled Arlington Angels, they ducked inside.

"Now you can see her do this, and when she comes flying through that door, you can congratulate her the way you should," Garrett explained.

"Thanks," Dan immediately offered. "Really, thank you for everything." A lifetime of memories washed through his mind. He thought of how much he owed Garrett Haydenshire and not just on Fionna's account.

Garrett smiled. "You deserve for this to work, man. You've been through hell, and she's head over heels. I'm not giving up until she meets you at the end of an aisle somewhere."

Dan was overwhelmed by the thought. His heart flew but then slowed abruptly. His palms began to sweat. He could almost see it, but the picture was distorted, like the lens was out of focus.

He had to end Wretchkinsides before he could really have her, before he could really have a life or love that could exist in the daylight instead of inside a tomb. The demons, previously quieted by taking in Adderand, became restless again.

Dan and Garrett stayed in the locker room with nothing to do for a few minutes, when Dan had an idea. "Hey, will you help me with something else for her?"

"Of course. What?"

Dan pulled his cell phone from his pocket and began working. Garrett seemed eager to help. Several minutes later, Dan popped the lock on Fionna's locker and extracted her phone from her purse. He felt guilty for doing it.

"She won't care," Garrett assured him.

While forcing himself to only find the information he was searching for, Dan couldn't help but note that she had an interesting looking app for different daily sex positions to try out. He decided to ask Fionna if he could peruse the phone with her later that night.

"Three minutes," Garrett chanted as he came back into the locker room after checking the play clock. "And she's looking for you."

Dan had everything he needed. He pushed her phone back into her purse and closed the lock. They moved discreetly back onto the field and leaned against the wall like that was precisely where they were supposed to be. Confidence would get you everywhere. Iodex officers knew this better than anyone.

The head of security rushed toward them.

"Is everything okay?" He looked panicked.

"One of the lockers looked like it might've been tampered with." Dan did his best to sound concerned, and Garrett tried not to laugh. "We're gonna stay here to make sure no one comes or goes who isn't supposed to."

"Yes, sir." The security guard looked genuinely relieved that Dan was staying since that meant the buck stopped somewhere that wasn't on his back.

"Are they okay to start the next challenge?"

Dan nodded. "Yeah, it's probably just some overzealous fans. We'll stay here. Make sure everyone's safe."

The guard moved back to the clustered hive of security by the door.

"Awesome," Garrett complimented. "Overzealous fans."

"Hey, I'm a huge fan," Dan scoffed.

Fionna was thrilled with their location. She seemed to have figured out that if Dan was in the locker room when she finished, he could at least tell her how proud he was of her.

The Receivers began lining up, and Dan couldn't stop smiling. "So, how'd you know that would be on her phone?" Garrett interrupted Dan's fantasizing.

"I knew because she's mine. Plus, they all have playlists like that on their phones." Dan was shocked Garrett wasn't aware of that.

"Yeah, see, I don't really do the whole *romantic night* thing. I'm more about the *why don't you and your best friend come over to my place and we'll see how much fun we can have* thing."

Dan shook his head. He appreciated all that Garrett had done for him his entire life, but he was growing weary of the stories of his conquests.

"If they score in the top three, that'll put Chloe at a fifty-point advantage for the Captains' Challenge." Garrett beamed.

Dan managed a nod. He was trying not to stare at Fionna. Her face was flushed from her excitement, and pride danced in her eyes.

The announcers were discussing the upcoming challenge. "She got off to a slow start this morning, folks, but Fionna Styler of the Arlington Angels has certainly roared to life. If she continues her streak, she'll place the Angels' Captain, Chloe Sawyer, with a fifty-point lead for the final Captains' Challenge."

Dan reminded himself that he might have the best seat in the house and be able to celebrate with Fionna once she was back in the locker room, but every person in the entire arena could now see him as well. He had to play it cool.

The course was revealed. Everyone studied the requirements. A concrete brick containing a gas lantern was on the ground, and the Receivers would have to use a corrosive particle to create friction energy on the brick until they could access the lantern. They had to shatter the lantern and draw both the heat and light from the fire, separate them, and feed them into a thermal box, until they'd raised the temperature by five degrees. They would have to conserve enough energy to also fill a battery, that would be used to lift a door concealing the first, second, and third place cups.

Fionna's entire face was pulled in deep concentration.

Garrett laughed heartily. "It's a friction challenge. She might need your help with that." He swatted Dan's stomach.

"It's like you're still sixteen." Dan tried not to laugh but failed miserably. Fionna shot a sly glance back at him and waited on the buzzer.

"You know you're thinking, *I've got your friction right here, baby*, and if you aren't, then you are not the man Will and I raised you to be."

"Would you shut it?" Dan shook his head. The thought had certainly crossed his mind.

Fionna leaned forward at the starting line. *Come on, sweetheart. You've got this.*

The buzzer sounded, and Fionna added her own heat energy to a large block of corrosive sand paper. She began chiseling the brick.

The muscle-bound Receiver from Portland was through the brick in a matter of minutes. He shattered the lantern.

He's got you in strength, but that's it. Dan kept a commentary running in his head.

Fionna broke through the brick next, just seconds ahead of Emily. Fionna shattered the lantern and immediately separated the heat and light.

The Powerhouse player was having trouble capturing and converting both kinds of energy at once. Fionna clenched her jaw and threw both of her hands out.

She started the battery with one and forced heat into the thermal box with the other.

Dan panicked. Thick, red blood tracked down her forearm. His heart stuttered helplessly. His shield lit in terror. It tried to move toward her, but he was able to draw it back with a great deal of force. She'd cut her wrist on the glass from the lantern. The blood separated into multiple streams and gathered in her sleeve.

The battery rose slowly, but the thermometer shot upward. Emily filled the thermal box first but still needed another degree.

As soon as the thermometer hit 95 degrees, Fionna turned all of her power to the battery. She trembled and tried not to cry from the deep gash.

Dan started to race onto the field. Garrett caught his shoulder.

"No!" he ordered. "You can heal her in the locker room. She's all right. It's just a cut."

Her arm trembled. Her face contorted from the pain as she continued to push heat through her hand that was now gushing blood. The sleeve of her uniform was drenched in crimson.

"She doesn't have to do this. She's hurt," Dan demanded.

"She's fine. Just chill. People are watching you."

His entire body tensed in pain. His shield pulsed in fury, but then he saw the battery charge the door containing the first place cup.

Fionna's eyes closed and tears fell down her face. She grasped her hand to try to stop the blood as she raced toward the cup.

"Go to the locker room," Garrett ordered.

"No!" Dan shouted as the crowds cheered loudly.

"Damn it, Dan. Go in the locker room. I'll bring her back there."

The Receiver from the Powerhouses rushed for second place, and Emily came in third, a half second later.

The Angels flooded the field. Dan gave her one last longing gaze before he slipped away from the frenzy and back into the locker room.

Panicked and pacing, his heart splintered and ached as he waited. His shield whirred disconcertingly. It constantly tried to leave his body to cast Fionna. Several minutes later, Garrett had pulled her from the onslaught. She'd waved off the medios trying to heal her and let Garrett lead her to the locker room.

She was sobbing, both from pain and the emotion of winning. Her uniform shirt dripped blood down her thighs.

"Baby." Dan rushed to her. His shield sizzled around him. Nothing in him could allow her to be hurt. He contented himself with the knowledge that he was about to heal her. "I'm so proud of you." He carefully lifted her hand. She handed Garrett the cup and fell onto Dan's shoulder and gave in to the powerful tears.

"Shh, sweetheart. It's okay. You did it." Dan tried to cast her, but she blocked him out.

"Fi, calm down, baby. Let him in," Garrett eased.

She shuddered against Dan. Her emotions swirled in a confused mass. The pain made her rhythms shudder and tense.

"I'm right here. Just let me heal it for you." Dan kept his tone soothing. She gasped for breath and tried desperately to locate calm. He could heal her faster than any medio. She trusted him, and her body accepted his energy readily.

Dan sat down on one of the benches and cradled her in his lap. "You were amazing. I'm so proud of you. Are you ready?" He braced her. She nodded. Exhaustion was beginning to show on her features. Her joule meter was flashing on empty. The injury had depleted her. "Okay." Dan closed his eyes and held her hand in his. It was a deep, jagged cut. It would've required dozens of stitches had she not been Gifted. Broken skin took a great deal more finesse to heal than a harmless surface mark like a hickey.

Dan continued to tell her what an amazing woman and Receiver she was and how proud he was of her as he worked. She calmed to the sound of his voice. He watched the bloody gash slowly disappear into an angry red mark.

"Deep breath," he soothed. "I'm almost done. Try to relax. It's almost over. Let me get rid of the scar." He pushed soothing energy into her as he healed her. She nodded against him, still shuddering from her tears.

"There," Dan whispered several minutes later, when the puckered red mark gave way to her customary, healthy olive glow.

"Thank you." She shook from the exhaustion and her erratic emotions. Her joule meter gave a shrill warning alarm. Her energy supplies were gone. Dan surrounded her with his shield.

She was the sweetest thing he'd ever seen. It killed him that she'd gotten hurt. He cradled her tenderly.

The adrenaline she'd used to keep going had exhausted her, and she slumped against him.

"Did you get the bad guy?" Her voice was weak and her eyes heavy. Dan and Garrett chuckled as they gazed down at her.

"Yeah, baby, we did." He wasn't certain his body could contain the sheer amount of loving adoration he had for her. She nodded and drew from him in heavy doses.

"She's gotta go back out there for the Captains' Challenge. The press is about to beat down the door," Garrett reminded them gently.

"How does your hand feel?" Dan whispered.

"It hurts a little." She was afraid she might hurt his feelings.

"You cut it pretty badly." Dan weakened his shield to push soothing energy back into her hand.

"Dan, the press is right outside. They want to talk to her." Garrett's tone was panicked.

"Well, they can wait."

"Yeah, well, they aren't gonna wait long."

Fionna eased herself upright. Exhaustion haunted her eyes.

"Let me go talk to them, and then I'll come back after they go cover the Captains' Challenge."

Dan helped her out of his lap, and Garrett offered her a hand so she could continue to draw from him. Dan hid in the bathroom as Garrett eased the door open, and the press swarmed.

"You got off to a shaky start in the first two challenges of the day. What was the turnaround, Fionna?" An overenthusiastic reporter leapt into Fionna's face. Dan watched intently from his hideaway.

"I'm not sure. I just felt really focused and driven today. It paid off, I guess." Dan chuckled at her complete lack of an answer.

"Your scores today are higher than we've seen from you in the past two seasons' exhibitions. What's your secret?" called another reporter.

"You know, I just kind of feel like my life is starting to pan out the way I'd always hoped it would. I'm taking better care of myself. I'm able to focus more now than I've been able to for a while."

Dan smiled. He knew precisely what she meant.

"Ms. Styler, Officer Haydenshire was at your home on the night of the break-in. He took you off the field and obviously healed your hand. You're clinging to him now. You're not really hiding your relationship all that well." The reporter was nearly breathless in her profound declaration. "Perhaps *he* is what is going so right in your life?"

Dan's heart and his brain were immediately at odds. What he needed to hear was only going to infuriate him.

"He's definitely a huge part of it." Fionna chuckled.

"Our relationship is no one's business but ours." Garrett feigned irritation.

They'd very effectively confirmed that they were dating to the majority of the major national news organizations in the Gifted Realm. Garrett had, once again, protected Fionna from Wretchkinsides better than Dan would ever be able to. Bitter gall lorded over his relief.

Silence fell as reporters scribbled furiously what Dan was certain would be the highest-read story from the exhibition. Because she was a female athlete, the news wouldn't be that Fionna Styler was the greatest Receiver in the Realm, or that the Angels would most definitely be bringing the cup home to Arlington, after Chloe gave it her all in the Captains' competition. No, the story that would have the Realm chatting was the fact that Crown Governor Haydenshire's son Garrett was romantically involved with Fionna Styler.

Uncertain what to feel in that moment, Dan didn't hear the next few questions. His cell phone chirped. He read the words, *We've got him, boss. Just leaving Coriolis now. He's done for.* The message came from Tuttle.

Good work, thanks. Dan felt a modicum of relief settle on him as he replied.

Several minutes later, Fionna rushed back into the locker room. She looked terrified. Garrett entered a full minute later. Though this was the agreed upon plan from the beginning, he was clearly trying to decide how Dan was going to react now that the rubber had met the proverbial road on a national level.

Fear and sorrow had replaced Fionna's fatigue.

Dan forced a slight smile. "That's precisely what you both should have said. You were great." The words burned like acid on his tongue.

"Hey, man, you know I'm just trying to keep her safe," Garrett pled as Fionna moved toward Dan.

He pulled her into his embrace. He needed to feel her as much as he wanted to reassure her that he wasn't upset with either of them. He was sickened by the situation that had caused all of the lies and furtive actions.

"I know, and thank you again," Dan choked.

Garrett nodded and then jerked his thumb back toward the field. "I'm gonna go see….something."

Dan drew a deep breath. "Thank you for everything…really."

Garrett looked relieved that Dan was finally allowing his own personal angel to restrain his vicious demons if only for the moment.

"My pleasure…really."

CHAPTER 42
CONTENTMENT

Dan awoke at five thirty that afternoon. He let one eye open hesitantly and made certain Fionna was still tucked into the safety of his embrace.

She'd been exhausted after the awards ceremony where the Angels had indeed taken the first-place cup after Chloe had effectively crushed Trevor Sanders and every other captain in a battle of wits and wills for the final iode.

Fionna had lost a fair amount of blood, had been challenging with little reprieve for hours, and she'd been up since four that morning. She'd yawned endlessly and had lain in his lap while insisting that she wasn't tired.

Unable to stop telling her how proud he was, Dan had finally lifted her off the couch in her suite and tucked her into bed beside him. He'd snuggled her against him and slipped his fingers gently through her hair, until she'd given in and had drifted off to sleep. She'd been out for several hours.

Dan slid from the bed. He tucked the soft sheets and comforter around her, and ran a heat cast through his hand to warm the coverings. He thought of his plans for that evening with a smile.

In her exhaustive sleep, she didn't seem to notice much of anything. Dan brushed a tender kiss across her cheek.

He texted Garrett to see if everything was ready and to thank him again for all of his help. His demons weren't certain what to make of his acceptance of help or his relative calm.

He glanced back to the bed. They may not appreciate being tamed, but they sure as hell loved the woman who was able to silence their shrill howl.

He thought of their time together the night before. Saliva flooded his mouth from the memories alone. She knew precisely which demons to damn and which ones to dance with. His miraculous, conquering angel, his everything.

Food will be here at seven. I'll bring it when they deliver it, and the flowers are here now. Garrett's reply shook Dan from his reverie.

He eased the door open and then stepped out into the hallway. The corridor was empty. Everyone was either abusing their livers in one of the bars or abusing their bank accounts in one of the casinos or both. There were several shows at The Venetian that night, so the rooms would remain relatively empty.

Dan cupped his hand and summoned. He looped the current feed on the cameras from his room all the way to the elevator. They would display an empty hallway on all the security feeds. He would take no chances.

Quickly, he took the few steps to Garrett and Chloe's room. Garrett answered shirtless but wearing sweatpants. He looked irritated.

"Sorry, I guess I should have texted that I would come pick up the flowers."

"S'ok. Chloe's getting in the shower. A bunch of us are going to play the slots and then see a show later. You and Fi could come with."

Dan shook his head. "We're gonna hang out up here. She was pretty excited about me surprising her."

Garrett laughed and nodded his understanding. "Is she okay after all that?"

"Yeah, she's still asleep. I'm sure she'll be out for a while. She was pretty worn out."

Garrett glanced back into the suite. Shower water began to fall. He handed Dan the massive bouquet of Hawaiian violet hibiscus and pink plumeria blooms that he'd paid a small fortune for. "Have fun tonight." Understanding that he was being dismissed, Dan nodded.

"Yeah, we will. Thanks." Dan gestured to the bouquet as he backed away.

"You're not going cheap, I take it?" Garrett's extensive tattoo work tensed as he crossed his arms over his chest.

Dan shook his head. "She's worth every penny and more."

"Agreed. I'll bring the food when it gets here." Garrett offered a half wave before he shut the door.

Dan lifted his cast from all of the cameras in the corridor except those nearest their rooms. He slipped back inside his own room and then accessed Fionna's. He set the large bouquet of her favorite Hawaiian flowers on the coffee table in the seating area. He began to contemplate where exactly they should eat for their date.

"Dan?" Fionna stirred. He kicked off his shoes and slid back into bed beside her. "Where did you go? I missed you."

Dan kissed her forehead. "I was trying to get everything ready for our date since I am now extremely involved with the reigning Greatest Receiver in the American Realm."

Her eyes blinked open though the task seemed to take a great deal of effort. A broad grin spread across her face.

"We're going on a date? I thought we were celebrating here. Is the date my surprise?"

Ignoring the pang of regret, Dan kissed her again.

"We're sort of staying in on a date, and yes, the date is part of your surprise."

She giggled and rolled toward him. She entwined her legs with his.

"Unless you want to go out with Chloe and Garrett tonight. I'm fine hanging here and watching TV or getting some work done." He was rather impressed with his ability to lie outright and sound nonchalant.

She rolled her eyes incredulously. "Greatest Receiver in the Realm, remember?" She lifted her hand, and he was relieved to see her Receiver's cast pulse in a healthy cadence once again. He nodded his defeat. "I want to stay in with you, and I think it would work better if I stayed with the guy I'm crazy in love with who no one knows I'm dating, and if Chloe stayed with the guy she wishes she was in love with but that the whole Realm now thinks is dating me." She sighed. "My life is kind of confusing sometimes."

He knew she was kidding, but his stomach clenched uncomfortably. "I'm sorry, honey. I swear to you I will end him, and then we'll tell the whole Realm who I belong to." He changed his typical vernacular. He wanted her to know that he considered himself entirely hers as well.

She giggled. "I like it better when I'm all yours."

Delighted, Dan cradled her body and slid her just slightly under him. He was careful of her hand. "You are most definitely all mine, Miss Styler," he growled for her as he leaned and held her eyes with his own. He brushed a kiss across her lips, and then a moan escaped him as she laced her hand through his hair and pulled him to her with hunger.

They laid there lip-locked for several long minutes, neither really wanting to pull away or force the other to go back to the confusing and occasionally cruel world that existed outside of their embrace. A moment later, she grinned against his lips. He chuckled and lifted his head. "And what are you smiling about, baby doll?"

"I really like being all yours."

Dan brushed another tender kiss over her lush lips before he settled back beside her.

"Nothing in the world makes me happier than being with you. It doesn't even matter what we're doing."

She tucked her head under his chin and nuzzled his chest. "I guess I better go get ready. Apparently, I have a hot date tonight."

"Someday, I swear to you I'm going to take you on real dates, with nice restaurants, expensive drinks, dancing, whatever you want. Hell, pizza, movies, the stuff we should be doing now."

She considered his promises and slid languidly upward to prop herself on her elbow. Her bottom lip slipped through her teeth as she studied him. "I don't think anything about this relationship is normal or typical, but it's the best relationship I've ever been in, and I love you. I only want to be with you. Actually, I want to be with you…" she choked.

Unable to watch her equivocate, Dan brushed a kiss across her forehead. "Forever?"

"Yes." Relief flooded her energy.

"I still want to take you on dates."

"You took me to Sydney. You brought me here. You somehow manage to take me wherever I want to get food. You make it work, no matter what I ask for. You're amazing. You take such good care of me. I don't need to be picked up from my parents' house and taken out for pizza and then to kiss you on the front porch before I try to sneak you in my bedroom." She giggled at the thought.

Dan considered all that had happened since the night she'd glided into Anglington's Bar and right into his heart. "That's good because I'm not sure your dad would let you date me."

"He never wanted me to date anyone. That's why I became proficient at sneaking out by the age of sixteen."

Dan shook his head as he leaned and kissed her cheek.

"We don't have to sneak out, but at some point, I'm gonna take you out to nice dinners, and to movies, and to get ice cream. I'm gonna hold your hand while we walk, and put my arm around you, and I'm gonna lean you up against my new Ferrari, and make out with you and not care who sees us," Dan promised.

"I can't wait." Fionna gave him his smile. Both his heart and his groin stirred from the sight. "But, until then, I'm gonna make our house our home, and I'm gonna cook you yummy dinners, and then I'm gonna do yummy things to you in our bed after we watch movies and snuggle on the couch. And I will also point out that if we go to movie theaters, I can't sit in your lap and make out with you and then go down on you if the movie's boring."

Dan cracked up and hugged her tightly. "I'll scratch taking you to movies from the list then." They laughed together. The sound was almost as intoxicating as hearing the sweet moans he elicited from her.

"Dan?"

"Yeah, baby?" He smoothed a lock of her hair and brushed it behind her ear.

"You know all I really want is what I already have." She stared deeply into his eyes, into his soul. "I want to hold your hand." She reached and laced her fingers through his. He brought their combined hands to his mouth and brushed a kiss across her knuckles.

"I want to laugh at your jokes, and I want you to tell me I'm beautiful and to snuggle with you on the couch. I want to eat with you and to wake up in your arms every single day. I want to have coffee with you, and for you to text me when you're at work so I know that you thought about me. I want to watch you lose some of that practiced control when I've turned you on, and I want to listen to you tell me you love me. I don't need nice dinners at pretentious restaurants, or ice cream, or to walk around town holding your hand, because I already have everything I've ever hoped for and so much more." She blinked back tears as he swallowed down the rock-like enclosure in his throat.

He nodded his understanding. "I love you so much. You are the most incredible woman in the world, and I will never, ever deserve you, honey, but I swear to you I will never stop trying."

"Will you kiss me again?"

"Anytime, baby doll. You don't even have to ask." He cradled her face in his hands and brushed her cheekbone with his thumb. He gazed at her, certain nothing could ever be more beautiful.

She let her eyes close as he hesitated for a moment, centimeters from her lips, kindling the passion and watching it ignite. He could feel her breath on his lips as he gave up the futile fight and kissed her slowly.

She moaned. The reverberation lit through his soul as he traced her bottom lip with his tongue as she let it fall open.

Unable to stop himself, he slid his hand down her body, pausing to feel her nipples begin to strain against the cotton of his T-shirt that she'd pulled on.

He kept his kisses deep and drawing, intimate, never moving more than an inch from her face as he turned his head and devoured her mouth.

His hand moved of its own accord, however. He slid it up the hem of the shirt until he reached the dip of her stomach and felt her tense.

She pulled away after several long minutes, panting. Her lips were swollen and her eyes begged for more.

"Another good thing about living together before we date,"—she giggled at the odd complexity of her statement—"is that we could shower together before our date."

"I love the way you think."

She beamed as he brushed her long chestnut tresses behind her shoulder.

"Is that what you need, baby? You want me to get you hot and wet before I make you hot and wet for me?"

CHAPTER 43
THE TAMING

Fionna scrambled from the bed and stood waiting on Dan to follow her. The mattress creaked, and his demons stirred anew as he watched her hair swing as she turned and walked to the bathroom. The way her hips swayed, the way the low V-neck of his undershirt almost revealed her nipples but obscured them slightly, made him ache to see what was covered.

He loved the way the hem pulled up as she walked. She was perfect, and she was his, though he still couldn't quite figure out how he'd managed to make that so. Certain a higher power must've been involved, Dan gave a silent prayer of overwhelming gratitude as he followed her into the vast hotel bathroom.

She spun with an extremely naughty grin that had him chuckling.

"That look usually means trouble." He winked at her, and she giggled excitedly.

"Take your shirt off," she commanded.

Dan laughed and pulled the T-shirt over his head. "So, you think just because I fell madly in love with you that now I'll strip for you on command?"

She cracked up. Her beautiful smile lit her entire face. "Yes." She sounded quite certain as he joined in her laughter.

"Sounds fair." He reveled in her glee.

Still sporting a sassy grin, Fionna reached into one of her many makeup bags and pulled out a tube of lipstick. Dan wondered just what she was up to.

She turned to the mirror, puckered her lips, and smeared on a dark burgundy lipstick she'd worn the night before. She rubbed her lips together to coat them. She turned back to him, waggled her eyebrows, and moved closer. The leash frayed as the demons rattled the cage.

She stopped to consider for a moment, then she traced her index finger over his pecs and planted a kiss just below his collarbone, leaving an imprint of her lips on his chest just above the speared snake tattoo. She popped another one onto his jaw line.

Dan chuckled and gave her a cocky smirk. "Are you marking your territory, baby doll?"

"Mm-hmm, and I'm not finished so just stand there and be studly."

While laughing and shaking his head, Dan watched her as she worked. Fionna moved to his left arm. She pulled it up and formed it into a lifted flex, then put another lip print on his bicep as he blushed.

After going back to the counter, she reapplied and then came back for more. She placed kisses on both of his nipples but then spun her tongue around one, making him moan. She continued to let her tongue tease the sensitive skin, while she traced her hands up his groin.

"As long as I get to play too." He watched her eyes flash with heated desire. "Only I'm not using lipstick." He felt her teeth lightly move over his left nipple, and he clasped his hands around her waist. He shuddered from the sensation. The demons rejoiced. "Careful, honey, you're making me hungry, and there are other things that are all yours I want your mouth on."

She pulled away from his grasp. He begrudgingly allowed this as she slid to his side, leaned up on her tiptoes, huffed hot air on his neck, and placed another quick kiss there as she whispered, "Yum."

She left kisses on his back, at his shoulder blades, and then at the top of his jeans. She reached her arms around his waist, and he stared at her hands as she popped the snap of his jeans. She slowly lowered his zipper, and he growled as she shoved them down, along with his boxers. She wrapped her hands around his cock.

After letting her hands trail up him in exploration that drove him mad, she moved back in front of him with that luscious grin. She spun and leaned across the counter, pushing her backside out dramatically, and lifted the hem of his T-shirt. She gave him a quick flash of what he wanted desperately to see as she applied more lipstick.

He grabbed her ass, squeezing her tightly, as she gave him a heady moan.

"There are just a few other things I want to mark all for me," she purred seductively. The demons roared.

"It's all yours, baby. You do whatever the hell you want, but when I get you in that shower, I'm gonna fill up my territory, bury myself inside it, take what's mine, come deep inside of you, and watch my work drip down your thighs when I'm finally finished. So, be ready."

Fire burned in her eyes. She kissed his abs, right behind his cock. She kissed each of his hipbones, then in a quick move she spun behind him, planting a kiss on the top of his ass cheek, making him chuckle.

To his delight, a moment later she fell to her knees and very gently brushed a kiss across his sac as he groaned in anticipation.

"This is all for me," she sassed defiantly as he watched her begin to slowly kiss her way up his length, leaving a burgundy trail of ownership in her wake.

His head fell back as he gasped for breath. He throbbed in her face, hung so fierce he burned. She licked the fiery trail she'd just kissed.

In a move that had him reeling, Fionna put her lips on the side of his shaft and sucked. Dan's breath caught in a sharp inhale. His eyes rolled back in his head as a thundering, guttural groan escaped his lungs.

She planted one last kiss on his head, and then cupped his sac and drew him deeply in her mouth.

Dan's growling moan echoed against the marble covering the surfaces of the bathroom as she worked. He laced her hair around his fist and guided her head to him. "That's it, baby doll. Suck me hard. Take it all for me," he ordered as she moaned against him.

The reverberation incited the demons into a frenzy. Her mouth was soft and wet, drawing and full. He watched her cheeks hollow as she sucked.

She spun her tongue around his head and then went back for more. It was exquisite and overwhelming. He shuddered from the deep, drowning pleasure. The demons shattered their chains.

"Are you gonna drink it like my good girl, baby, or do you want me to put you in that shower and pound into you, because I want it inside of you, now."

With one last fiery lick of exquisite pleasure, she stood. Dan's eyes, dark and covetous, flashed in need acute to the point of pain.

Her hair was tangled from his hands. Her cheeks were flushed. Her nipples stood in strained points. Her mouth was covered in smeared burgundy lipstick, the rest on his cock, and he'd never seen anything so erotic in all his life.

"Take me," she beckoned the demons and began the dance. He turned on the water in the vast steaming shower.

"Come here to me." He reached for her. "I want you to take it all for me. I'm gonna fill up that tight, wet hole, baby, until you can't walk and you can't remember anything except my name," he growled in warning.

"Yes," she gasped. She flew to him and closed the glass door behind her. She let the water cascade over the T-shirt, making it see-through as it clung to her luscious curves.

"You are so fucking sexy. You drive me wild," Dan groaned. A shuddering moan burst from deep within her.

He forced himself to slow down, lest he lose it all before he even began. Dan pealed the soaking-wet T-shirt off her.

"I want to feel you against me while I make you mine, honey." He watched the water cascade down over her curves, beading and then separating over her nipples, puckered dark brown from need. The demons howled.

He pulled her body into his, melding them together as he caressed her left breast and slipped his thumb around her nipple.

He dropped his right hand to her backside. He pulled and groped her, kneaded her flesh with force, and listened to her urge him on.

With adept agility, he edged her legs apart with his right knee and then reached lower, until he was dipping his fingers inside her, and she was moaning in ecstasy.

Her muscles clenched tightly. She pulled his fingers deeper. Her body begged for more.

He panted and forced himself to think with the head above his waist for a split second. "Are you casted, honey?"

She nodded, and Dan grabbed one of the many removable showerheads and set it to a low constant pulse. "Lean back against the wall for me. Keep your legs spread."

She fell back. He coaxed her clitoris softly with his fingers and then held the water spray, so that it kept her slick and wet while he taunted her. He kept up his teasing, torturous caresses over the delicate pearl, timid and yet so hungry. She swelled for him. Her entire body shook.

Her eyes flashed open as she cried out for him. Wrapping her hand around his length, she began to plead for relief. "Now, please, please," she whimpered and writhed. He kept her legs apart with his thigh.

"I'm gonna take good care of my girl. Just relax for me." He dropped the sprayer as she clawed at him in desperation. The demons sang. "My good girl deserves a reward." Dan lifted Fionna up, and she wrapped her legs around his waist. "Seems like she really liked this."

"Yes!"

He positioned her over him and leaned her back against the tiled wall. While guiding her down his shaft, Dan braced her as she gasped her approval.

Overwhelmed suddenly, he groaned from the heavenly sensation. "You feel so fucking good." His eyes rolled back in his head as he groaned from the way she tightened around him.

She arched her back. She wanted more, and he had exactly what she needed.

With a ragged thrust, he drove himself deep into the slick, wet heat that enveloped him fully. "Hold on tight, baby doll. I'm gonna take you for a ride," he commanded as his name spilled from her lips in heated passion.

She clung to his neck as he began sliding her slowly up and down, hitting all the right spots with each pass. She shuddered and convulsed. Her muscles tugged rhythmically as she accepted every pounding thrust.

"That's my good girl. Takes it so deep for me. That feels good, doesn't it?" Dan guided her. Her muscles spasmed against him as her energy unfurled around him.

Dan's heart raced as he continued to thrust into the pulsing, liquid silk. "Tell me you want more. Beg me," he demanded. He longed to bury himself to his hilt, but didn't want to push her too far too fast.

"Oh, god, more!"

Dan braced as he slowly spread her legs farther and then pounded harder. "Take all you want."

She moaned in ecstasy, so he continued pushing and guiding her up and down as she writhed and bounced against him. She was perfection.

He fought the impending climax. He wasn't leaving her until he was forced to. She linked her feet behind his waist and pushed harder, nearly ending him.

Her fingernails dug into his shoulders as it built fiercely inside of her, threatening imminent explosion. The demons exulted in the exquisite pain. "That's it, baby. Tear me up."

"Oh, god," she groaned in abject ecstasy.

"Be a good girl and come with me. I'm going to fill you full." He buried himself in the paradise between her legs and lost it all with a satisfied groan. Her body trembled and shook. She clung to him and milked him dry.

A moment later, she went lax and laid her head on his shoulder. She let him carry all of her weight. He helped her down, still cradling her closely as he withdrew.

He kissed her through the warm falling water, and began to gently wash away everything he'd done to her. He let her hide in his embrace. The demons, now satiated and tamed, were quiet and content. They returned readily to their chains.

"My legs are all wobbly," she confessed as he continued to support most of her weight against him.

"I'll carry you, baby doll." He sat her gently on the teakwood bench that ran the length of the back wall of the shower. He moved behind her and guided her back against him.

"You know when we were in Sydney?" she quizzed, with an extremely satisfied smile on her face.

"I do seem to recall that," Dan teased her.

She smirked and laid the side of her head against his chest. "And you asked me what my top three favorite positions were?"

"Yeah."

"That is now definitely in the top three."

"Is that so?" She nodded against him. "I'll have to remember that, but there are still several others we need to try out before you decide on the top three."

They lay there in the serenity the steaming hot shower afforded them, with Dan cradling her against him. She didn't seem to want to leave, and he wanted to be wherever she was.

"What should I wear on our date?"

Dan slid his hands up and down her arms. "I guess, as long as we're talking optimistically, only being able to date at home means you can wear anything you want."

"What's the likelihood we would actually eat if I wear nothing but a corset, garter, stockings, a thong, and heels?" she asked with a great deal of sass.

The demons were intrigued once again. "Not a chance in hell, baby doll."

CHAPTER 44
THE LIST

She stood, still wearing her replete smile. "I'm gonna go get ready."

He grabbed her hand and pulled her back in for a kiss. He whispered how much he loved her and then watched her climb out of the shower.

Dan attempted to scrub off the many lipstick marks she'd left all over him, while letting his mind replay how they'd gotten there in great detail.

The lipstick blurred but wouldn't seem to do more than turn into a burgundy smudge on his skin. Assuming Fionna had some kind of magic potion in one of her bags that would get lipstick off skin, Dan shut the water off and climbed out of the shower.

He toweled off and dried his hair, before wrapping the towel loosely around his waist and stepping out the bathroom door.

"Fi, baby, I can't get this lipstick off my chest or my package," he called as he stepped onto the carpet searching for Fionna. He found her dissolving into a pile of hysterical giggles. She was standing beside the door to her suite in her short, purple, terry cloth robe with green polka dots. She was right beside Garrett who was delivering the elaborate dinner Dan had ordered to be delivered to Chloe's room.

Garrett cracked up as Dan sincerely wished he could suck the words back into his mouth.

"Wow." Garrett shook his head. "I know way too much about your relationship, but since I'm the guy pretending to be your boyfriend, maybe that's appropriate."

"I'm so sorry!" Fionna cringed. Dan noted that she still had lipstick smears around her lips and on her chin, but it blended in with her heated skin from the shower. "I accidentally used the lip stain stuff that lasts for several hours. I grabbed the wrong tube, but I have something that will take it off. I'll show you." She wrinkled her nose adorably. Dan managed a nod and prayed that the heat from the shower covered his extreme embarrassment.

A minute later, he'd cracked up as well when Garrett complimented the shade on Dan's nipples and asked if he could borrow it sometime.

"The worst part is I can't even tell anybody about this. Well, I mean, other than *all* of Iodex." Garrett couldn't seem to stop laughing. "Oh, and my dad would get a huge kick out of this," he teased as Dan started to threaten his very life.

"Oh, nice," Garrett pointed to the half-moon shaped imprints on Dan's shoulders that had very obviously come from Fionna's fingernails. "Damn, girl, retract the claws." He stuck the tip of his tongue between his teeth and continued laughing.

Dan determined the quickest way to get Garrett to leave so that Fionna could remove the lipstick and they could continue on with their date. He winked discreetly at Fionna and then edged toward Garrett.

"Fi, baby, do you mind Garrett telling people that you give head like nobody's business, and that you're the hottest damn thing I have ever had the pleasure of having my hands on?" Dan knew perfectly well that Garrett wouldn't really tell anyone any of that. He just wanted to harass them.

Garrett shuddered. "All right, all right, I'm going. Have fun, you two."

As soon as Garrett closed the door, she apologized. "I'm so sorry about the lipstick."

"You're serious when you mark your territory, aren't you, baby doll?" The knowledge that there was some way to remove the marks made him able to tease her and laugh with her again.

"Come here." She took his hand. Dan followed her back to the bathroom. He didn't want to ask what he had to know. He enjoyed just being with her, laughing and joking. He didn't want anything to stress her after their day.

With a sigh, he caught her hand as she began digging through the largest of her toiletry bags. "Fi, how did Garrett get in here? You cannot open the door for anyone." His skin was still warm from the extended shower, but his blood ran ice-cold.

"I didn't. I heard him knock when I went to pick out my clothes. I didn't make a single sound, and I started to come back to get you. Garrett did his *'Hey, Fi. It's me. Let me in, baby,'* he always does at my house. I knew it was him. All of that food was kind of heavy, I think."

Dan let the humid air permeate his lungs again. His heart steadied. "'K, I just have to keep you safe," he tried to explain once again.

"I know. It's okay." She continued digging in the bag but didn't seem to want to dwell on the complications of their relationship any more than Dan did.

"What all did you order? And oh my gosh, those flowers! I almost cried when I saw them."

She extracted a small, brown glass bottle of oil. "I'm really sorry about this." She apologized again. Her face was still glowing red. She tipped the bottle over a cotton ball, and Dan recognized the coconut scent.

He smiled as she began rubbing it over the lipstick on Dan's chest. He watched the lipstick begin to disappear.

"What is that?" Dan untied her robe and slid his hands to her soft skin. She shivered slightly and gave him his smile.

"It's Hawaiian kukui oil, coconut oil, and rosehip oil. My Tutu makes it. My Papa grows the candlewood trees and the rosa canina shrubs, and then my grandmother turns it into this." She lifted the bottle. "She adds a little coconut and vanilla scent because I like the way it smells. She sends it to me every month. It's really good for your skin. I use it all the time. I rub it all over."

"I might have to see if I can get in on that." He gave her a cocky grin. She looked thrilled with the idea as she moved to his back and rubbed away the lipstick there.

"My mom used it all the time. She taught me to put it on every day, so the smell always makes me think of her. It'll make you smell like coconut and vanilla," she warned hesitantly.

"I love the smell of you on my skin after I've been with you." His proclamation seemed to delight her.

After most all of the lipstick had been removed from both of them, Dan shrugged into a button-down shirt and slacks. If she was going to have to date him only at their house, or in their hotel suite, he could at least dress for the occasion. She was certainly worth the effort.

Fionna had disappeared behind the divider into the bedroom. Dan could see the provocative outline of her dressing through the fogged glass. His heart raced as he watched her pull on stockings and attach them to a garter.

He reminded himself that they were celebrating her victory, but he drew a deep breath and let his mind fill in the details of what she would look like when he took off the dress she'd picked out.

He summoned a heat cast and lit the candles he'd placed on the glass-topped dining table between the living room and kitchenette.

He set the sushi trays he'd ordered on the table. After retrieving his phone, he flipped to the playlist he'd stolen from her phone in the locker room that morning. He'd copied over all of her playlists.

She'd given them all Hawaiian names, so it took Dan and Garrett a few minutes to Google what all of them meant. After glancing back through the fogged glass, he saw that she was still working on her outfit, so he scrolled to the one he'd roughly translated as *Take me deeply*.

Several of the songs were most definitely written for people to make love to. He intended to ask if she wanted music the next time he had the pleasure of being with her. He was perfectly happy with her gasping moans and her calling out his name.

He touched the first song on the lengthy playlist, listening to the beginning notes of Elvis as he belted out "Can't Help Falling in Love." He casted the phone and raised the speaker volume until it was loud enough to be heard but low enough for them to be able to talk over.

Fionna stepped out of the bedroom wearing a low-cut sweater dress that clung to her curves. She grinned at the music selection.

"You look beautiful. Absolutely gorgeous."

"I can't believe you went to all of this trouble. You are so sweet." She looked truly touched as she took in the flowers, candles, and wine.

"You're worth it." He took her hand and led her to the table. He pulled her chair out for her. She giggled at the formality.

Her eyes lit as she spied the array of sushi. "Oh my gosh. You didn't have to do all of this."

Dan rolled his eyes and ignored that. "I don't know what any of this is, so you have to teach me."

She looked excited to begin, but she raced back to the kitchenette and returned with small bowls for the sauces that Dan had missed on the trays.

"Sorry," he apologized.

"For being the sweetest, greatest guy ever?" she scoffed. "I didn't know you liked Elvis." She gestured to his phone on the counter.

Dan decided to come clean. "I do like Elvis, but I might've snuck into the Angels locker room, and I might've also stolen all of the music off your phone. I kind of figured you had a romantic playlist or two on there."

Though she feigned shock, she giggled at him. "You know, as the Chief of Elite, you really have very sticky fingers, Chief Vindico."

He cocked his jaw to the side, biting his tongue to keep from saying what he was thinking. She cracked up as she read his facial expression.

"You didn't have to steal them. You can use my phone whenever you want. I don't care that you copied them."

Dan laughed at himself. "I didn't want to invade your privacy any more than say, breaking into your locker, taking your phone from your purse, copying all of your music, going through drawers in your room, and having my guys hack your Amazon accounts." He very effectively had her guffawing. "It did all seem logical at the time."

"I should be mad at you," she declared, but she was still laughing. Dan nodded his agreement as she pointed out a sushi roll. She explained that it was a tuna roll, her favorite, and offered him some soy sauce and wasabi.

"But you won't be mad at me because there is still lipstick on my dick."

She covered her mouth to keep from spitting out the sushi she'd just eaten as she cracked up again.

"Deal," she agreed after she managed to swallow. They ate and talked, laughed, and sipped wine for several hours. Dan put away the leftover sushi, and they cuddled up on the couch.

As the lights and noise of Las Vegas tilted into full swing, Dan cradled her on his chest in their bed. She clung to him after they'd engaged in slow passionate love-making. This time, Dan had kept his eyes locked on hers as he'd made their hearts, their souls, and their bodies one. He reveled in her exposed body wound around his in the candlelit afterglow.

"I love you," he whispered as he ran his fingers through her soft, silky hair as it splayed across his chest.

"I will never get tired of hearing you say that." His declaration seemed to have taken her breath away.

"Go to sleep, baby doll. I'm right here." Dan watched her closely as her energy soothed, and her rhythms calmed into low rolling waves, like the tides easing out to sea.

It was an entirely different set of demons that summoned him from the bed in the middle of the night. He quietly slipped to his briefcase and pulled out a blank notepad from one of his dossiers.

He began listing the names. Each mark of his pen fed the demons and chafed the scars on his soul. He wrote every name of every member of the Interfeci in order of importance, all of the big players, every single one by name and their job description within the organization. The demons rejoiced as he sliced his pen through Ferratus, Vitrio, Cascavel, and then Adderand. He stared at the list and let the hate set its icy chill through him once again.

Fionna shifted in the bed, seeking his warmth. He moved back to her quickly, the demons be damned. He tenderly held her on his chest and stared at her in the lights of the Strip.

In that endless moment of calm serenity, Dan knew that *all* he wanted was to give her all of him. She was the only thing in the entire vast universe that he needed, and yet he couldn't really have her.

The consuming fire churned low in his gut again. The demons swam faster and pulled fiercely at the weakened manacles. He formulated his plan.

ABOUT THE AUTHOR

J.E. Neal (aka Jillian) vastly prefers coffee to tea, guac to salsa, the beach over anywhere else, and the world inside her head over the one outside her front door. She also loves not having to choose.

Driven by the question 'what if,' J.E. Neal's world began to manifest. What if there were people with powers the rest of us couldn't see? What if the energy of our world could be summoned and used at their will? Characters with these amazing abilities took shape in her mind. She created—and continues to create—an endless number of stories full of delicious escape from our reality where emotions are visible, desire is palpable, and danger is universal.

Learn more about J.E. Neal at JillianNeal.com

facebook.com/jilliannealauthor
twitter.com/JillianNeal_
instagram.com/jilliannealauthor

ALSO BY J.E. NEAL

ENERGY OF MAGIC

Shield and Shattered Cages (Book 1)

Shield and Faltered Steps (Book 2)

Shield and Splintered Oaths (Book 3)

Shield and Humbled Crown (Book 4)

Shield and Vile Serpents (Book 5)

Shield and Coveted Splendor (Book 6)

Shield and Guarded Shadow (Book 7)

Shield and Worthy Sinner (Book 8)

Shield and Sacrificial Heirs (Book 9)

Made in the USA
Columbia, SC
30 August 2023